COLD
SECRETS

COLD
SECRETS

Toni Anderson

For Deb,
From Broseley to Tokyo,
Tokyo to "The Broseley."
Thanks for a lifetime of friendship.

CHAPTER ONE

IF ANYONE RECOGNIZED Lucas Randall, he was a dead man. He knocked on the plain black door and shifted his weight from one foot to the other. The start of a beard sprouted from his grimy cheeks. Motor oil rimmed his fingernails, and the smell of it radiated from his clothes in subtle waves. Even his old scuffed trainers were smeared with grease. He hunched his shoulders and stuffed his hands deep into the pockets of a stained nylon jacket, shivering from the cold.

The woman who opened the door looked him up and down with eyes as pitiless as a great white's.

"What you want?" she asked.

"Poodle." He repeated the password he'd been given, feeling like a damned fool.

She hastened him inside with a short, jerky motion of her hand, and quickly closed the door behind him. She kept her fingers on the latch as if she wasn't sure whether or not he was staying.

The door behind her was open and gave him a limited view of an office.

"ID?" she demanded.

He pulled out a fake driver's license and she took a picture of it with her cell and handed it back. No way in hell was he leaving this building without that cell phone. "How much?"

"Twenty minutes. One hundred dollars." Her voice was high-pitched, and sharp as a razor-blade. She held out her hand.

The old crone might not be armed, but the look in her eyes was definitely dangerous. He hesitated. "I want an hour, and I want someone young. As young as possible," he muttered gruffly.

"Five hundred dollars." The expression in her eyes didn't flicker. Her hand remained extended.

He dug out some bills. Palmed off five notes and slid the rest back into his pocket. Now she knew he was carrying plenty of cash.

She led him down the featureless corridor, past four doors on the left and two on the right. A white-painted banister led up a honey-colored wooden staircase to the second floor, but they walked past it and hooked a right. The place was nicer than most. A kitchen lay off to one side where two men with Asian features sat at a wide oak table drinking tea. A reinforced steel door with badass locks secured the rear exit. The extra locks wouldn't keep the cops out indefinitely, but they would hold them off for a few extra seconds.

One guy stood at their approach—big, with a face that looked like he'd been dropped on it as a baby. The way his jacket hung lopsided from his burly shoulders signaled a weapon in his right pocket. He gave Lucas a hard stare, then shut the door in his face.

Anger slow-burned in Lucas's gut, but he couldn't afford to show it. The madam approached a door with the number "eleven" screwed into the varnished wood. She pulled a set of keys from her pocket and slid one into the deadbolt, unlocked it, and stepped inside the room. His heart pounded in anticipation. A girl of around thirteen sat on a twin bed that was made up with plain white bedding. A big teddy bear was propped up against the pillows. The girl had long blonde hair and blue eyes, and wore a simple cotton camisole that hugged the small buds of her breasts. As he entered, the girl drew her knees up to her chin. The whites of her knuckles shone through her skin as she wrapped her arms tight around thin legs. There was a bruise on her throat and another on her upper arm.

The madam spoke to her sharply and the girl jumped off the bed, and stood awkwardly in her underwear.

Lucas scanned the kid from top to bottom, and narrowed his eyes. "Too tall. Too blonde."

"She's young. Very pretty. Very good at pleasing men, yes?" The madam's teeth flashed as she aimed a glare at the child. The teen dropped her arms from where they covered her breasts and put them on her hips instead. A sickly smile formed on her naked pink lips.

Lucas backed away, feeling as if his lungs were coated in filth.

"You like." The old bitch was implacable.

He made himself glance at the girl's pubescent breasts and take another half-step back. He hadn't expected it to be easy, but this felt like the fast-track to hell.

"Not her. Not for five hundred bucks." He shook his head. "She looks too much like my wife. What else do you have?" Like he was trading cars, not people.

The madam's lip twitched in annoyance and the girl's eyes widened in both fear and relief. On a normal day he bet he'd just earned the kid a punishment. Considering what was "normal" around here he couldn't imagine what might

3

constitute punishment.

The woman hesitated, probably remembering the thick roll of Benjamins stuffed in his back pocket. "There is one more," she conceded with a calculating gleam in her eyes. She motioned him outside with a nod of her head, carefully locking the door behind her. They continued along the corridor.

Footsteps echoed behind them, making him glance over his shoulder, but the sound moved away and disappeared. The house was a warren of rooms and narrow corridors, which probably made it easier to operate without clients bumping into one another.

Lucas came to a door at the northeast corner of the house, and his brain buzzed with excitement.

The madam paused near the entrance and hesitated. "This one new. Virgin." Her lips vacillated between a smile and a frown, as if physically torn between the need for caution and the promise of cold, hard cash.

He held her gaze. Nodded.

God, he hoped she was still a virgin.

The madam held out her hand. "A thousand dollars. Thirty minute only. If you mark her, I will cut off your balls. If you tell anyone about her, I will slit your throat."

Lucas forced out an incredulous laugh. "Tell anyone? Who the hell am I gonna tell?" He looked at the woman like she was stupid and jerked his chin. "Let me see her first."

The madam harrumphed and opened the door. Inside the gloomy chamber, a small figure was curled up on the bed. The room didn't have a window, just a bucket in the corner and a simple twin bed covered in thin sheets.

He cautiously walked over to the frightened little girl who

lay shivering under the top sheet, sucking her thumb. A scrape ran across her cheek, and her bottom lip was swollen and split. Long brown hair curled at the tips in a natural wave. He smiled. Huge eyes met his, scared and defiant.

"I'm not going to hurt you." He sat on the bed and pushed her hair behind her ear. She hunched tighter into a ball, obviously smart enough to know that whatever came out of his mouth was probably a lie. Relief that she was alive was pushed aside by rage that these animals had stolen her innocence and were willing to sell her body to the first pervert who walked in the door. Luckily for her this particular pervert happened to be an undercover FBI agent.

"A thousand dollars to touch. You pay now." The witch near the doorway snapped the words with all the compassion of a dental drill.

Lucas got slowly to his feet and started digging in his back pocket as he approached the madam. The expression on her face was pure avarice, the thought of the money keeping her off guard. Without breaking his stride, he slapped his hand over her mouth. Her eyes went wide and she struggled, muffled grunts and cries reverberating against his palm. Clamping her jaw shut over her sounds of protest, he forced her backward into the wall. He nudged the door closed with his foot.

The shifting of bedsprings told him the girl was moving. Dancing footsteps crossed the bare wooden floor.

"Have you come to rescue me?" she asked in a piping, too-loud voice.

Mia Stromberg.

The offer of a large reward in return for information on Mia's whereabouts had led to a tipoff from someone who wanted to remain anonymous. That someone had spotted a man carrying a sleeping child into this building, a child who matched the description of an eight-year-old girl who'd been kidnapped off the street yesterday morning.

"Yeah," he told her. "But we have to be real quiet, princess, or the bad guys will hear."

The madam's eyes bugged as he wrapped his arm around her throat and gently squeezed, compressing her jugular, then her carotids, reducing the blood flow to her brain. Her face reddened as he purposely restricted the venous return to the heart and she lost consciousness. He felt no remorse. For a thousand dollars the woman had been more than happy to leave a pedophile in a room with an eight-year-old for the express purpose of having sex. There wasn't a punishment harsh enough in his book.

As soon as the woman's body sagged, he caught her under the arms and dragged her to the bed. He pulled off the leather belt she wore and used it as a gag, uncaring that it would hurt when she woke. Tightly he cuffed her wrists and ankles with plastic zip-ties he'd attached to his own belt.

He dug into her pocket and found keys along with a small plastic vial of drugs, probably roofies, and the cell phone.

A quick and dirty stakeout had revealed that not only were there a lot of male visitors to the property at all hours of the day and night, but had also identified the owner as being the woman Lucas had come to Boston to interview. Mae Kwon—now tied to the bed—was connected to a sex trafficking case he was working in North Carolina. That salient fact had made everyone sit up and reassess the situation. Authorities had assumed Mia Stromberg had been snatched for ransom, since her parents were dot com millionaires, but the sex trafficking aspect meant it was possible she'd been taken purely as a commodity to sell.

The FBI had picked up one of the guys leaving—a high profile lawyer with a wife and kids—and, in exchange for immunity and complete anonymity, he'd fed them a password he'd sworn would get Lucas in the door.

Ideally in a sex trafficking operation they'd take time to build the case. To photograph all the people coming and going from the property and figure out who the key players were. But with this little girl's wellbeing in jeopardy, they'd decided not to wait. Forensics would have to give them the evidence they needed to convict, and hopefully one of the players would roll on the others, sealing the deal.

Lucas tried the madam's cell but couldn't get a line. No surprise—the bad guys were using a signal jammer inside the building. He and his colleagues had speculated it was to stop the women who'd been forced into prostitution from being able to call for help.

He pocketed Mae Kwon's cell and squatted down beside the child. "We're going to walk very calmly and quietly out of here, okay, Mia?"

She stuck her thumb in her mouth.

"Don't be scared and do exactly what I tell you. No questions, 'kay?" he whispered.

She held his gaze and nodded solemnly. Then she grabbed his hand and squeezed his fingers, making his heart clench in response.

They closed the door behind them, locking the evil woman inside. An image of scared blue eyes flashed through his mind, and his fingers tightened on Mia's.

The average age of a teen entering the sex trade in the US

was between twelve and fourteen. A lot of the kids had been sexually abused and ran away from whatever home they had. Often, no one knew or cared what became of them. Many were coerced into prostitution and then felt trapped. Escaping the downward spiral became more and more difficult for children with few options when they already believed they were on the wrong side of the law.

Heat signatures of the three adjoining properties along this backstreet suggested there were upwards of thirty individuals trapped inside. But, having seen the young blonde girl with the big blue eyes, he couldn't abandon her any more than he could have left little Mia Stromberg behind.

They reached the door with the number eleven on it. It was hard to curb his impatience as he methodically tried each key on the madam's keychain. Finally the lock turned, and he and Mia slipped inside.

The blonde girl's pupils went huge, and she scooted backwards on the bed. "What do you want?"

"He's come to rescue us." Mia whispered dramatically to the other girl. "Come on, let's get out of here."

Lucas hid his grin. The kid was like a real-life Disney princess.

He looked around for anything he could use as a weapon, but there was nothing, not even a window to break. He checked the drawer of the bedside table. Condoms and lube. The older girl's cheeks reddened and inside he stumbled a little. She looked the same age as one of his nieces—older than Payton Rooney had been when she'd been taken from her home in that first defining moment of his life, but far too young for this exploitation.

"What's your name?" he asked, quickly closing the drawer.

The girl looked at them like it was a trick. "They call me Rosie."

"What's your *real* name?" Lucas gestured her urgently to his side.

"Becca." The girl relented and scrambled off the bed to join them. "Are you really going to get us out of here?"

"Yes." Or die trying. He listened intently at the door but silence pressed hard against his ears. Quietly he eased it open and let them out, then closed it softly behind them. He moved to the front of their little procession. Mia's hand curled over his as if she was afraid he might leave her behind.

Not a chance.

They reached the main corridor with the front door in sight, and he felt a moment of lightness that they'd made it. Then the doorbell rang and they all froze. Footsteps echoed from the kitchen. He was about to make a dash for the front door when a third man came out of the office. This guy was younger than Lucas, well-dressed, slim build, Asian features. The man's eyes widened as he took in the girls at Lucas's back.

"Up. Quickly," Lucas ordered, and the girls dashed up the staircase.

His heart ricocheted in his chest as the guy reached under his jacket, but no shots rang out as Lucas herded Mia and Becca upstairs. The traffickers were probably reluctant to risk hurting the girls—not because they cared about them, but because they were valuable. The guys who ran this place probably figured they had him cornered. Lucas heard the men conferring downstairs, barking instructions to one another in a foreign language.

Shit.

He started knocking on doors. "FBI. This is a raid. Put

your hands up and exit the room immediately." He banged on six doors and finally heard noises behind one of them. Business must be slow on a Wednesday morning.

A door opened, and Lucas dragged out a terrified looking middle-aged guy doing up his pants, along with two young ladies wearing nothing except satin teddies. The sound of pounding feet on the stairs had him pushing the kids inside the room and slamming the door, making sure it was locked.

This room was vastly different from the plain accommodations he'd seen downstairs. There was a four-poster bed on a raised platform, a mirror on the ceiling and the wall. Plush red velvet drapes. Sex toys on the bedside table, the funky scent of semen and latex in the air.

He tried not to gag.

And if the real thing wasn't enough, the huge TV screen was turned to a porn channel. Mia's eyes doubled in size. Lucas stepped in front of it and urged her toward the window that overlooked the front street. He tried to unlock the catch, but it was screwed shut. "Christ knows what would happen if there was a fire," he muttered.

"Mommy says it's wrong to curse," Mia scolded him.

Despite the mounting tension, he and Becca shared an amused glance. The doorknob rattled. The sound of metal scraping metal as someone tried a key in the lock. The smile on the older girl's lips wobbled.

Lucas grabbed a wooden chair from beside a vanity.

"Stand back." Time to signal his need of assistance. He slammed the chair into the old sash window, and glass exploded into a million different pieces.

That should do it.

The men on the other side of the door went silent as they

reevaluated the situation. Six agonizing seconds later, he heard the sound of a truck pulling up outside and a series of shouted instructions. Then the unmistakable sound of a breacher busting the front door out of its frame.

The troops had arrived.

"I'm an FBI agent. Help is on the way," he told the two girls. They held onto one another as he went to the bedroom door and listened. He couldn't hear anything on the other side, so he unlocked it and eased out, just in time to catch sight of one of the men he'd seen in the kitchen, fleeing into a bedroom at the rear of the building.

Dammit. There had to be another way out. He looked at Mia and Becca. He couldn't leave them behind—but he shouldn't take them with him, either.

No choice. He wasn't letting them out of his sight, and he wasn't letting these assholes get away.

"Follow me. We need to move fast, but quietly. Understood?"

Mia and Becca nodded, both desperate to get out of this hellhole.

He sprinted down the corridor and slid the last ten yards to the room where he'd seen the men disappear. For once his luck was holding, and the door had caught on the latch rather than closing completely. He peeked inside but the room was empty except for a couple of unmade beds. Where the hell did they go? He wedged the door ajar with a chair so his colleagues would know which direction he'd taken. A silk robe swung back and forth on a metal hanger inside the walk-in closet. He shoved the robe aside and ran his hand over the wood. A hidden door sprang open when he pushed against the panel. Bingo.

The opening on the other side was as black as Hades.

"It's like Narnia," Mia whispered.

"Only scarier," Becca agreed.

"Keep close. Hold hands," he instructed quietly. Lucas turned on the light of his cell and felt his way along. He found a handrail, his foot searching out the first riser of the stairs as they began their descent. They crept down the twisting staircase. Suddenly the thundering sound of footsteps got closer and closer. Then he realized it was the cops pounding up the stairs on the other side of the wall.

Becca tripped and he turned to steady her. "Easy."

"Where are we going?" she asked, as if starting to doubt the wisdom of blindly following a strange man down a lightless tunnel.

Smart girl.

"I want to see which direction the fu—" He caught himself. "Which direction the *men* who held you go in, so the cops can catch them."

They kept moving downwards. The staircase became so narrow his shoulders barely fit. It smelled old and musty, like the attic in his parents' West Virginian summer home.

He had no idea how deep they'd gone but the coolness of the air and quietness made him think they'd reached basement level, maybe even lower. The tunnel started to level out and headed horizontally northwest. They sped up to a jog, following the indistinct sounds of the men ahead of them.

The loud noise of a rusty hinge grinding had him moving faster, but it was difficult to sprint when he was virtually blind and leading two children.

A sudden volley of voices up ahead had him slamming on the brakes. The girls crashed into his back with barely a sound.

Survival instincts were out in full force. This wasn't a game. He moved cautiously forward and edged around another corner. Three men stood beneath an open trapdoor near a short wooden ladder. They were arguing over a cell phone, saying something like "char yo" a lot.

Lucas frowned. What the hell was "char yo"?

Suddenly the madam's phone in his pocket buzzed to life and all three of the men looked in his direction. *Shit*—they must have gone beyond the range of the signal blocker. He ducked back around the corner as bullets ripped into the exposed wall beside him. The clatter of footsteps told him they were heading up the ladder, but the bullets kept coming.

"FBI. You're under arrest," Lucas yelled. Now would be a great time to have a weapon, but they'd decided not to risk it for this particular op.

"Fuck you, motherfucker," came the reply. They'd obviously learned their English from Bruce Willis movies.

Mia clasped her hands over her mouth, eyes as big as golf balls. Lucas held back a grin even as tension mounted. He pulled out his cell and jabbed the number for the leader of the task force before passing it to Becca. "When someone answers, tell her to stay on the line."

The shooting stopped, and the trapdoor banged shut. The loss of light had him poking his head out from behind cover. The men had gone. He clambered up the steps and shoved at the hatch, but something blocked it. The sound of a car's doors slamming told him they'd got into a vehicle. He rammed his shoulder into the wood above his head, over and over again. He needed the make and model and maybe the plate of the vehicle.

"Tell them the perps are escaping by car," he told Becca,

who repeated everything he said into his cell.

The weight shifted above his head and he managed to open the door an inch. He got a flash of a sedan driving sedately out of the garage. "Silver Beemer." He reeled off the tag number.

He gave the hatch another shove, and whatever was weighing it down shifted enough for him to force the entrance clear.

He climbed out and turned to help first Mia and then Becca up the ladder. Both girls looked around with dazed expressions. They'd been through hell, but they were alive. He gave them a reassuring nod. "You're safe now."

Mia's brave expression immediately crumbled, and she started to sob. In the same instant, Lucas felt a shudder run beneath the soles of his sneakers. Army training kicked in, and he opened his mouth while simultaneously pushing both girls to the ground.

The force of the explosion threw him up in the air. He hit the ground like a paratrooper who'd pulled his ripcord a thousand feet too late.

Goddamn it.

He lay on his back in a world of hurt, ears ringing and vision blurred.

What the hell just happened?

After a few seconds of staring up at the corrugated roof of the garage, sirens started screaming in the distance. It was hard to breathe because of the smoke and dust and ring of fire encircling his ribs. He coughed and swore, coughed and swore again.

The bastards had blown up the tunnels.

Sonofabitch.

He rolled onto all fours and crawled to where Becca lay unmoving on the garage's dirty flagstones.

Mia hacked noisily a few feet away, but at least she was conscious. Internal injuries were a real possibility—the most lethal aspect of any explosion was blast overpressure. Air waves traveling at supersonic velocities that could rupture lungs, kidneys and bowels. He needed to get them all to the hospital ASAP, but in the meantime Becca's face was bloodless. He checked her pulse and airway and started CPR. Mia staggered to her feet.

"Grab my cell phone," he told her and pointed to where it lay.

Tears made streaks in the dust on her face.

"Call SSA Sloan." He didn't explain how to do it. Kids seemed hardwired into technology. "Put it on speaker."

She did as he asked and held the phone toward him as it rang. Becca wasn't breathing.

"Is she okay?" Mia asked.

"Randall?" Sloan answered.

"Yes, ma'am." He didn't pause the CPR.

"What's your sitrep?"

Supervisory Special Agent Carly Sloan was a former military operator and solid team leader, but she sounded fraught.

"We followed three perps through underground tunnels to a nearby garage but they set off an explosion that prevented us from giving chase." He repeated the details of the car they'd escaped in as he continued to pump blood through Becca's veins and force oxygen into her young lungs. So much for promising they were safe. He heard Sloan give orders for an APB. "We need a bus for a teenage girl caught in the blast. She's not breathing. Also an eight-year-old female needs to be checked for internal injuries." As did he.

"Mia Stromberg?" Sloan asked urgently.

"Yes, ma'am. She's safe. Tell the team I locked up the female perp in a ground floor bedroom in the northeast sector of the house. I saw at least two other females and a male client on the first floor. Not sure where they went."

"Where are you?" There was an odd catch in Sloan's voice.

Finally Becca's chest started moving on its own, and she drew in a rasping breath. Randall heard more sirens and struggled to his feet. He needed an idea of where they were in relation to the command post to direct the ambulance. Outside the garage, he whirled in a circle. His mouth fell open when he spotted the column of dust rising into the air where the houses had been standing.

"Holy crap."

"Yeah." SSA Sloan's voice was hoarse with emotion. "No kidding."

The bastards had dropped the entire row, along with everyone inside—including cops, federal agents, trafficked women, and one of their own. The chance of surviving that devastation was slim to zero, but they had to try to rescue whoever might be alive.

"How many of our guys were inside?"

"Four agents. Eight Boston PD cops." Sloan's voice cracked.

And Christ knew how many others locked in those rooms, including Mae Kwon, who could have been a gold mine of information if they'd gotten her to talk.

Grief fused with anger and settled into his blood like a virulent cocktail. Those dirtbags had killed indiscriminately to save their own asses. It would take months to sort through the debris. Months to piece together the evidence. Months to identify the dead.

As forensic countermeasures went, this was a doozy.

He gave Sloan directions for the medics and noticed Becca's eyes had closed again. "Shit. I think the girl's stopped breathing. Get the paramedics here ASAP."

"I'm on my way."

"Just send a bus." He ran to Becca's side and gave her a series of quick breaths. He put his phone on the ground beside him. "Supervise the rescue. I've got this."

"Negative, Agent Randall," Sloan bit out, obviously in motion. "It's possible you have the only witnesses left alive. We need them safe. Understood?"

He put his finger to Becca's carotid, but the thrum of life was eerily silent. Goddammit.

"I want to go home." Mia started crying. "I want my mommy and daddy." She wiped her face on her T-shirt.

"You've been very brave, sweetheart. Just hold on a little longer while I try to help Becca."

"Is she gonna die?"

The teen's lips were an austere shade of blue, her skin paler than his mother's finest porcelain. His own heart thrashed so hard he could feel it hammering against his sore ribs. Hers lay inert in her chest.

"Come on, Becca. Come on!" Desperation made him pound her sternum more forcefully. The sound of a siren grew closer, but not close enough.

"They're here!" Mia shouted excitedly, looking outside the door.

Finally.

But Lucas had the terrible feeling they were too late to save the kid who lay lifeless at his side. And it didn't seem fair that right on the cusp of freedom, Becca had once again had her life stolen away from her as if she didn't matter. As if she was worthless.

CHAPTER TWO

"WHY ARE YOU calling me on this line?" His inside man, Rabbit, asked in a strangled whisper.

He got his nickname from his online handle "Tinyrabbit." He didn't like hopping around or have big ears; he just liked burrowing into small holes.

Rabbit was useful. Otherwise he'd be dead.

"I need to know what's going on."

"What if they trace this call?" Rabbit sounded frantic enough to hang up. He couldn't be that stupid, could he?

"The bumbling feds? Do you really think I'd use a phone they could trace?" Andrew Britton asked silkily.

"No."

Good. "Do they suspect you?"

"No." Rabbit's voice trembled. "No one knows." He sucked in an audible breath then finally settled. "What do you want to know?"

"Everything."

"They don't have much." A breathless laugh escaped. "Blowing the joint was a stroke of genius."

No remorse for lives lost. No realization that he'd have been as dead as the others if he'd been there today. Just the need for self-preservation.

"Have they identified who they're looking for yet?" Andrew asked.

"No. Just that the three men who escaped had Asian features."

Excellent. Criminal activity was much more satisfying when the feds weren't chasing your tail.

"Witnesses?"

Rabbit cleared his throat. "An FBI agent called Lucas Randall—he posed as a client to get inside the brothel. Says Madam Kwon took him to Mia when he offered her enough cash." Rabbit's tone was bitter, but he was shrewd enough not to pursue it. "He grabbed the kid and made a run for it. He claims to have seen the guys' faces."

That was not good news, but most white Americans were not skilled at telling Asians apart. "The only other survivor was Mia Stromberg?"

"Yes." Rabbit's voice was laced with sweat and trepidation. "Apart from some lucky cops who followed them into the tunnels. They didn't see anything."

Andrew didn't bother to tell Rabbit that none of this would have happened if it wasn't for him. Others might argue it was a risk they both took in their business association. But the fact Rabbit had wanted that particular child, that he'd goaded Andrew's cousin Brandon until his pride had become involved in proving he could carry out such a high profile abduction in broad daylight...that was on him. Rabbit would pay for his appetites, just as soon as he was dispensable.

"According to the reports, Mia didn't see anyone's face except for Madam Kwon," Rabbit added hastily.

Mae Kwon had sealed her own fate by being a stupid, greedy bitch. "And you're *sure* no one else survived?"

"Positive." Rabbit sounded cocky now. Back in control.

"How long were the cops watching the place before they raided?"

"Not long. Twelve hours max."

Not as long as Andrew had feared. They'd have photographs of some of the clients, but not of members of the Devils. Nothing to trace them to the source of their operation. Nothing to bring a SEAL team to his door.

Not yet.

"Twelve whole hours? So why didn't we hear about it?" His tone was deceptively calm.

"I didn't know—"

"Then why do we need you?" he snarled.

Rabbit cautiously kept his silence.

As soon as Andrew had heard about the explosion, he'd pulled the website and disentangled the half-assed attempts to trace his location. It wouldn't take long to relocate the businesses and set up shop again under a different guise. Even without the darknet, the sheer volume of these operations in the US made them virtually untraceable.

"How did they find us?" he asked. "And who gave them the password to get inside?"

The verbal password was only issued to people who applied online. People he personally vetted. It was changed weekly.

They ran an exclusive setup for repeat customers. Clean girls. Nice decor and surroundings. Not some stained mattress in a roach-ridden dive.

"I don't know how they got the password. I'll find out. They found the brothel after an anonymous tipoff claimed to have seen the girl being carried inside on Tuesday." Rabbit was trying to sound useful. It was a good survival strategy.

Andrew narrowed his eyes as he absently watched code scroll down his screen. No one snitched on this organization and lived. No one. And if someone had been watching the business that closely, what else had they seen? "How anonymous?"

"Strictly confidential—about eight people know and I'm not one of them."

"Find out," Andrew snapped.

"I don't think I can." Rabbit's whisper was pitched high enough to raise the hair on Andrew's nape. "The tipster already got a hundred thousand dollar reward from the family but the name isn't in any of the reports. I looked." He swallowed. "I can keep digging if you like."

"No," Andrew said slowly. "Don't draw attention to yourself." He had other means of tracking down the snitch and making them wish they'd kept their foolish mouth shut.

"I have to go," Rabbit said anxiously.

"Keep me apprised of any developments." Andrew didn't raise his voice to threaten or coerce. Rabbit knew the consequences of crossing his family. Death was for the lucky ones.

FBI AGENT ASHLEY Chen followed her colleague Mallory Rooney into the Boston Field Office, hiding her nerves beneath a cool exterior. Tension permeated the atmosphere like acrid smoke and made her chest tighten in much the same way. They passed through security, showed their credentials at the reception desk, grabbed visitor badges, and rode the elevator a few floors. Her pulse ratcheted up a notch as it did every time she entered a new federal facility—a familiar tingle of dread icing her back. The doors opened onto a frenzied hive of activity.

Less than twenty-four hours ago, a bomb blast had killed four local field agents, three Boston PD SWAT officers, and an as yet undetermined number of victims believed to have been forced into the sex trade. Rescue teams were still searching the rubble, working in tandem with forensic techs. There'd been one miracle—they'd pulled five cops alive from tunnels beneath the buildings. It was more than anyone had dared hope for.

What had been a routine shakedown of an illegal brothel and a human trafficking operation had turned into one of the deadliest loss of life incidents in US law enforcement history—the deadliest being 9/11. It equaled Waco in terms of the number of FBI agents lost, and it had come from a direction no one had expected.

The fact that her boss, Lincoln Frazer, had sent two members of BAU-4 to assist spoke volumes as to the importance of this investigation. Murdering federal agents and cops was a sure-fire way to get yourself to the top of the FBI's Most Wanted list. Right now they were still in the process of trying to identify the three perpetrators who'd escaped.

She and Mallory approached the bullpen.

"Where's the task force leader?" Ashley asked a grim-faced agent who was passing.

A blonde woman of about fifty raised her head from where she'd been talking to a handful of people crowded around a table.

"That would be me. SSA Sloan." Her eyes assessed them rapid-fire as she came to meet them. When she shook hands her grip was warm and firm. "Who you with?"

"BAU-4," Mallory answered quickly. "Crimes against adults."

As part of the National Center for the Analysis of Violent Crime—NCAVC—their primary mission was to provide behavioral-based investigative support to various law enforcement agencies around the world. Unit-3 dealt with crimes against children and had also sent an advisor. Unit-1 dealt with bomb related matters—they'd sent an entire team. This was the biggest operation since the Boston marathon bombing in 2013. Everyone wanted to catch these bastards.

Excitement worked its way along Ashley's spine. This was her chance to prove herself.

Mallory indicated Ashley with her right hand. "Agent Chen recently came off a rotation in BAU-2. She's also a specialist with cybercrime and technology if that's what you need."

"Anything I can do to help," Ashley offered.

"You speak Chinese?"

She'd known there was an Asian element to the crime. She hadn't known they'd narrowed it down to China.

"A little Cantonese," she conceded. "But I'm better with computers."

Sloan gave her a measured look and nodded. Ashley saw the doubt in the woman's eyes and tried not to resent it. She knew she looked younger than the thirty years stated on her birth certificate, but age was irrelevant. It was experience and skill that mattered. Give her a piece of electronic equipment and enough time, and she could not only read the program, she could probably figure out who wrote it. It was one of the advantages of having a father in the tech world who'd taught her C++ along with her ABCs.

SSA Sloan squinted at Mal. "One of your agents wrote the profile for the Agata Maroulis investigation, correct?"

Agata Maroulis was a twenty-year-old female from Greece who had answered a job advertisement for the hotel industry two years ago. The girl had flown to the States and had never been heard from again—until she'd walked into a Boston PD precinct just after Christmas and claimed to have escaped from a brothel where she'd been held against her will. Unfortunately, the officer she'd spoken to hadn't taken her seriously. There'd been a language barrier, and the girl had shown signs of living on the streets and being an addict. The officer had sent her away before detectives could question her. Next time the cops had seen her, she'd been floating face down in the Charles River with a 9-mm slug in the back of her skull.

"Agent Darsh Singh wrote that profile," Ashley confirmed. "He's in the middle of an investigation in Portland or he would have been here, too."

"Highly sophisticated people trafficking operation, probably linked to a large organized crime gang. Probably Asian or Russian. Violent. Approach with caution." Sloan had memorized that basic part of the profile. "He was spot-on with his assessment."

"Yes, ma'am. But we don't actually know the two cases are related," Ashley reminded the woman.

Sloan's lips thinned.

Darsh was a smart guy in an arena populated by uber capable people. Ashley knew exactly what he'd be thinking if he was here now—*it didn't matter anymore*. The profile hadn't helped catch the perpetrators before they'd killed a lot of people.

Of all her colleagues, Ashley liked Darsh best. Maybe it was because they were both minorities, and he made off-color jokes about the fact. But she suspected it was more his moral compass that she found so appealing. Darsh was a trained killer, but he was also a good man. And truly *good* men were hard to find.

Mallory Rooney was nice, and they could have been friends—if Ashley was ever foolish enough to allow herself such a thing. But Mallory's fiancé, Alex Parker, bothered Ashley on so many levels she tried to keep her female colleague at a safe distance.

"Agent Singh mentioned an Agent Sumner was in charge of the Agata Maroulis investigation. Could we talk to him about the case?" Ashley asked.

"Sumner transferred to headquarters—you can call him but he isn't at this field office anymore. We have the files, but that investigation stalled for lack of leads." The SSA's eyelids were heavy, the skin beneath them puffy and lined. The grimness around her mouth revealed the full weight of responsibility over the deaths of her colleagues, and it wasn't pretty. She checked her watch. "My SAC wants an update for the mayor in an hour so I don't have much time."

"Where can we set up?" Mallory asked.

"Follow me." Sloan led them down a corridor.

A dark-haired agent stepped out of a side room and closed the door. He wore an expensive navy suit and a blood-red tie. Ashley found her eyes drawn to his broad shoulders and rumpled hair and experienced an unwanted flare of attraction. Must be her penchant for designer clothes and a well-dressed man.

"Lucas?" Mallory called out.

The man turned.

"Mal?" The smile was genuine, but there was an air of exhausted desolation around his eyes.

"I didn't know you were on this task force." Mallory introduced him to Ashley. "Agent Randall is an old friend of mine." She poked his shoulder. "You've been reassigned without telling me?"

"Nah." The guy was the epitome of East Coast handsome with dark hair and a clean-shaven jaw. There was even a dimple in his chin. But a raw scrape along his cheek spoke of more recent adventures. "I came to Boston a few days ago to follow up on an investigation I'm conducting in Raleigh. I barely got started when Mia Stromberg was abducted and they needed someone to go undercover at short notice." He shrugged, as if taking on a whole new identity was no big deal. "It made sense to use me."

"You were caught up in the explosion? You okay?" Mallory's eyes busily reassessed him.

"I survived." *Unlike other people* was the subtext. "Where's Alex?" He scanned the corridor as if Parker was going to pop out of the woodwork. Ashley wouldn't put it past the guy.

"Agent Randall, walk with us and help me get these agents settled." Sloan continued the update as she headed down the corridor. "The task force has expanded to include members of the Boston Intelligence Branch, the Northeast Innocence Lost Task Force, the Boston Violent Crimes Task Force and North Shore HIDTA—that's the east coast drug and gang task force, but we have no solid leads on who runs this organization, or even which organization is involved."

Ashley was forced to move at a brisk pace that made her glad she'd left her high heels at home.

They entered a small empty conference room. Ashley set up her laptop while Sloan talked them through the facts so far. "We found the BMW burned out near the railway yard. It was registered to the brothel's madam, Mae Kwon, who died in the explosion. We are trying to dig up more information on her connections."

Agent Randall caught Ashley watching him—and didn't look away. His eyes were a rich brown ringed with thick black lashes. Intelligence shone from the depths.

Unnerved, she looked away.

"The properties were owned by Mae Kwon and a corporation out in the Cayman Islands, probably a shell company, but we have a forensic accountant trying to find out everything he can about whoever set up those accounts and about Mae Kwon herself."

"Did the madam report income?" Mallory asked.

Sloan nodded. "Filed taxes as a rooming house."

A wave of repulsion rushed through Ashley at the thought of what really went on there.

Mallory cleared her throat. "The little girl who was abducted, she survived?"

"We got her back, Mal." Agent Randall's expression softened. "And they hadn't touched her."

Mallory nodded, and they all pretended she didn't have the sheen of tears in her eyes. Ashley wasn't sure if it was pregnancy hormones or the subject matter that made the other agent weepy—Mallory's twin sister had been abducted when she was a little girl. Any crimes involving kids were challenging no matter how you tried to remove yourself emotionally, but they were especially difficult for people like Mallory who'd lived through the nightmare.

Ashley had her own nightmares to deal with.

"Did anyone besides the cops survive the explosion? Any of the people forced into prostitution?" she asked. A living witness could tell them a lot about these people and how they operated—which was probably why they'd all been murdered in cold blood.

"Only Mia Stromberg survived," Randall told her firmly. "We apprehended one of the johns who gave us the password *du jour* which got me in the door. His deal included immunity from more questioning and prosecution if the code worked."

"You agreed to that?" Ashley asked with disbelief.

Randall shrugged. "We were trying to get a little girl back before she was violated. We felt it was worth it."

"He's a lawyer," Sloan cut in. "Slick sonofabitch. We didn't expect them to blow the place and kill every other goddamned witness."

"Did he tell you anything about how he found out about the brothel in the first place, or how he knew the password, or how he paid?" Ashley asked.

"He gave us a website on the darknet."

"Send me the link," she said excitedly. "I should be able to figure out—"

"Site's gone." Randall's expression mirrored her frustration.

She held back a curse. They could have learned so much from that site.

"From what we've ascertained so far," Sloan continued, "when the women weren't working, most were kept in several communal dorms in the buildings on either side of the brothel itself. Prelim autopsy reports suggest many were heavily sedated when they died. Many had track lines."

"Easier to control workers strung out on drugs," Ashley said.

"Whoever rigged the explosives placed them on the ceiling of the rooms directly below where the women slept." Randall's tone was one of restrained violence.

Ashley flinched. That was cold. Minds destroyed, bodies rented for sex, lives eliminated at the first hint of trouble. Treated worse than Old Testament slaves, just a piece of warm flesh to abuse. So much for progress.

Sloan took over. "From heat signatures before the explosion, we guesstimated about thirty to forty women were kept there."

"Can the girl who survived tell us anything useful?" Ashley pushed.

Sloan shook her head. "She was kept isolated and alone, and was only there for one day."

"What about the explosives themselves?" asked Mallory. "What did they give us?"

"We have bomb squad specialists and BAU-1 examining the explosives. We'll also send evidence to TEDAC for evaluation."

TEDAC was the Terrorist Explosive Device Analytical Center, which examined IEDs from around the world following terrorist attacks.

"They used C4 and standard demolition blasting caps that we're trying to trace. They turned off the jammer they used to block cell signals and triggered the bomb with a cell phone as soon as they'd made their escape," said Sloan. "Agent Randall was lucky to get out alive."

"I learned my first Chinese word." His smile was full of self-deprecating humor. "If someone says '*char yo*' over and over, it means 'run.'"

Ashley eyed the graze on his cheek with renewed interest. The word "*zhàyào*" meant explosives. "Run" worked as a quick and dirty translation.

That the bad guys had planned for all eventualities unsettled her. The use of explosives showed extreme ruthlessness and war-like strategy for dealing with law enforcement. Had they done this before? Did they have military experience, or terrorist links? Or had they been caught previously and learned all the things the law could use to convict them?

"Any priors on the madam?" Ashley tapped her fingers on the tabletop.

"She was wanted on a visa violation in Canada. We have a request in to the Chinese and Canadian authorities asking for any information they can provide."

"She was definitely Chinese?" asked Ashley. Because sometimes people, even smart people, made assumptions about where people came from based on their looks.

"Correct. The males are of unknown nationality, but had Asian features," Sloan confirmed. "But we're looking at all Asian gangs at this point."

A flicker of apprehension snaked between heartbeats—but there were 1.4 billion people in China, and roughly thirty-six thousand Chinese or American Chinese in Boston, if you included the ever-growing student population.

Randall turned to Mallory. "We could use Alex's expertise on this."

Mallory shook her head. "There was a major cyberattack on one of his clients last night. He's busy trying to identify the attacker and what they got away with."

"This is more important than any cyberattack."

"How do you know?" Ashley interrupted. "If you don't know what the hackers were after, how do you know which incident is more important?"

"Maybe the one that just butchered fifty people including seven law enforcement officials?" Randall's tone crackled with condemnation, which made her resent the fact she'd found him attractive earlier. "I'm not saying whatever Alex is working on isn't important, but cyber criminals can wait. These can't."

It pissed her off. Cops often saw cybercrime as a benign act that didn't really hurt anyone. There was nothing benign in stealing someone's identity or destroying their credit rating. There was nothing benign in controlling the world's power grids, banking systems, or economies. Control cyber-technology and you controlled the flow of information for most of the world's population. And cyber-warfare had already begun. Just ask the Iranians about Stuxnet, or Estonia, Ukraine and Georgia about pissing off the Russians.

They glared at one another.

"What evidence do you have that might help us identify these guys?" Mallory asked, cutting through the sudden tension between Ashley and Randall.

Sloan answered. "Mia Stromberg *might* be able to ID some of the bad guys—but she's only eight and in reality didn't see much. They grabbed her from behind, stuck a hood over her head and knocked her out with a tranq. Her family has been placed in temporary protective custody. Agent Randall got a good look at two of the perps and a glance at the third. Boston PD is processing the BMW for prints and DNA. The victims are awaiting autopsy, but that's a lot of work for an under-staffed unit. A request for assistance has been put out. The bomb site is being scoured thoroughly for any material that might yield DNA or fingerprints. We're also looking at traffic cams trying to find any good shots of the men's faces when they were in the BMW. In addition, we have surveillance footage for twelve hours prior to the raid, which we are sifting through. We're trying to ID some of the johns we got on camera and hope they might provide clues as to how the traffickers found their clientele."

"I was hoping to get Alex to look at nearby cell tower data," Randall added. "See if we can figure out the cell phone numbers for these guys and ID them that way."

"Agent Chen is pretty good with technology," Mallory told the formerly attractive federal agent. "She might be able to help."

Randall's brows pulled together. "No offense, but Alex is the best."

He sent her an apologetic look, which she returned with stone. The fact he was right, burned. Alex Parker had an uncanny knack of looking at cellular information and figuring out a perp's shoe size. She had other skills.

"We also have the madam's cell phone," Sloan admitted.

"What is it?"

"An iPhone."

Ashley's head jerked up. "You got into it?"

Sloan shook her head. "Techs can't break the pin. We have a warrant in with the phone company for her records. They're being unusually slow about delivering them."

The cell phone couldn't be the same type used by the San Bernardino terrorists, or it was running an updated version of the iOS software. Rumor was the FBI paid over a million dollars on the gray market for the vulnerability that had allowed them to crack the password on that phone without wiping all the information stored on it.

Zero-day vulnerabilities were big business. The "gray hat" hackers made a lot of money selling software flaws to government agencies, security firms and sometimes even the companies who made the software. But not everyone approved of how governments chose to use those software vulnerabilities. Not everyone agreed with governments spying on their own people. Some manufacturers would rather take the feds to court than appear to cooperate. Personally, Ashley sided with not creating back doors for anyone. Any potential weakness could and would be ferreted out and exploited by some innovative hacker.

Law enforcement needed to be better than the bad guys when it came to navigating cyberspace and technology—that's one of the reasons she'd joined the FBI. They needed agents and behavioral analysts who understood the deeper, murkier layers of the web.

"I can try and get in," she offered.

Randall and Sloan exchanged a look.

"We'll get back to you," Sloan said.

"I graduated *summa cum laude* in computer science from Cornell." In two years, at age nineteen, but she didn't tell them that.

"We'll bear that in mind if the geek squad who came up specially from headquarters get stuck. They have done this before." The sight of Randall's suppressed amusement increased her desire to punch him.

She was better than anyone at HQ and cheaper than the gray market, but drawing attention to herself wasn't part of her plan. Fading into the background and milking the aloof, dedicated, American Asian stereotype was how she operated.

Randall's eyes drifted over her features, as if he'd moved on from assessing her capability as an agent—which he obviously found lacking—to assessing her as a woman. The flicker of attraction that licked over her skin irritated her. She flushed as she looked away and wished it was with annoyance.

Right now, she just wanted to impress her bosses and help solve this case. That meant no men. No sex. Hardly a hardship as most men turned out to be big disappointments in bed anyway.

"So what do you want us to do?" Mallory asked, bringing Ashley's brain back on point.

"See if you can find any similarities with known criminal gangs, give us offender motivation analysis and an insight into what kind of personalities we're dealing with, and what they might do next," said Sloan. "Take another look at the evidence, see if you can link Agata Maroulis to this brothel or find out if there's another one in town we aren't aware of. If so, I want them closed down."

"We'll need access to all files." Mallory drew her laptop from its case.

Sloan nodded, and checked her watch. "I'll arrange it. Now you'll have to excuse me. I need to head to that meeting."

After she left to update the Special Agent in Charge of the Boston Field Office, Randall walked over to stand beside Mallory. Ashley found herself sneaking glances at them.

"At least SSA Sloan seems easier to deal with than Danbridge," Mallory observed with a wry smile.

"Sloan's a good agent and excellent leader," Randall agreed.

Mallory gave a bitter laugh. "Whereas Danbridge is a

sadistic bully with a persecution complex."

Randall grunted as he folded his arms over his chest. To her chagrin Ashley found herself once again admiring the way his suit jacket clung to those broad shoulders. Obviously she had terrible taste in men.

"She's even more bitter since you got the job in Quantico. I think even the SAC is starting to have serious doubts about her professionalism."

"Lucas was my mentor in Charlotte," Mallory explained, catching Ashley's gaze on them.

"Not to mention we grew up together in West Virginia." Randall's smile faded, and Ashley made the final connection. They'd been childhood friends when Mallory's twin sister had been abducted. It probably explained why they were so close and why they'd both gone into the FBI.

He cleared his throat and climbed to his full height. "I need to get back to work." He paused. "Ask Alex if he can look into the cell tower data when he gets a chance, will you? If we can ID these guys we might be able to stop them leaving the country."

"He's your friend, too, Lucas," Mallory said with exasperation.

"But he listens to you."

"Assuming they haven't already fled," Ashley muttered. If only she'd had the chance to check out the website before they'd pulled it down.

Randall's expression darkened.

A grimace touched Mallory's lips. "She's right."

"I know she's right." Randall's expression morphed from pissed to rueful, and his gaze flicked over her again with reluctant interest. "Doesn't mean I have to like it."

CHAPTER THREE

APPARENTLY THEY WERE letting teenagers into the Bureau nowadays. Ashley Chen looked barely legal to drink, never mind anything else. The fact Lucas was thinking about "anything else" one day after the worst day in his FBI career, pissed him off.

She looked vaguely familiar, though he didn't think they'd met before. He scrubbed his face and forced the prickly agent out of his mind. He had more important things to think about.

Someone had put a bunch of fresh flowers on the desk of one of the agents who'd died yesterday morning. A young guy with a family from all accounts. The smell of those flowers caught him unexpectedly, the sweetness tying a knot in his stomach and making him want to retch.

He turned away. God, he felt old. Decades older than when he'd started this op. All that death and destruction, and the knowledge he'd fucked up. If he hadn't stopped to pick up Becca he might have gotten Mia away without the bad guys knowing the cops were onto them.

And the bad guys would still have blown the place when the police stormed the doors.

Intellectually he knew that not one agent on the job would have left Becca behind—but he also knew the locals blamed him for everything that had gone wrong. Hell, he blamed himself.

He was in Boston thanks to the keen eyes of a uniform officer who'd suspected a sex trafficking organization was being run out of a Raleigh location. The feds had subpoenaed the phone records for the people inside the building and discovered one of them was calling a Boston number on a weekly basis. That cell had belonged to Mae Kwon.

After the Chinatown explosion, FBI Charlotte had raided the Raleigh location. They'd blocked every cell phone tower in a five-mile radius and sent the bomb squad in first. No explosives had been found, which suggested the Boston brothel was the hub of the operation and contained a lot of potentially valuable evidence.

Or it had, until it had been obliterated.

As of this moment they didn't know the identity of the players, and the madam in Raleigh wasn't talking. Neither were the women they'd rescued—they were too damaged and traumatized.

He headed to Sloan's office, where she stood in the doorway, checking her watch and talking to another agent—Brianna Mayfield. Mayfield had brought the kidnapping case to the FBI thanks to a personal connection to the family. And she'd been bristling with attitude since the moment he'd been chosen over her to go in undercover, courtesy of the fact he had a penis and she didn't. The agent flashed him a dirty look and strode away.

God save him from pissy women.

Sloan gave him a rueful half smile. They'd spent most of the last twenty-four hours joined at the hip, figuring out how to make Becca disappear as well as coordinating this massive investigation. The fact Becca had survived the ride to the hospital was a secret only a select few knew.

Sloan indicated he come inside and closed the door. "Our little friend is asking for you. She refuses to talk to anyone else."

Lucas's mood dropped. "She needs a woman to question her. Someone from the Office for Victim Assistance with a degree in child psychology."

Sloan shook her head. "Right now our priority is her continued survival and that means complete secrecy. She's the only advantage we have and we need to use it, fast."

Reluctance was like an anchor, pulling him down. He didn't want to "use" Becca for anything.

But Sloan considered it a done deal. "Go see her this morning." She opened her door and said loudly, "Boston PD just brought in some of the local Chinese fire gang. They want you to run your eyes over them, see if they're the men you saw yesterday." She sounded resigned to jumping through a few hoops for a fellow law enforcement agency. Considering Boston PD had lost three officers it was the least they could do.

"Fuentes," she shouted at another agent who was working at his desk nearby. "Go with Randall. I'm already late for my meeting with Salinger."

Agent Diego Fuentes grabbed his jacket off the back of his chair and the two of them strode to the elevator without speaking. Fuentes was shorter than Lucas, built like a Humvee. Before the bomb had gone off they'd laughed and joked around. Not now. Neither spoke. They got to the parking garage and climbed into Fuentes's Bucar, and twenty minutes later they stood on the other side of a one way mirror, looking at three individuals in separate interview rooms.

"Any of them our guys?" Fuentes asked, shifting his feet

impatiently.

Lucas looked at each man carefully then shook his head. "Too short for the one guy, not stocky enough for the other. I didn't get a good look at the third guy, but I think he had a rounder face. Balding, thin straggly mustache." Which might be long gone.

"They all look the same to me," the Boston PD cop at the door muttered angrily. His flat Boston vowels made Lucas's slight southern drawl seem more pronounced.

Arguing with the uniform about political correctness would get him nowhere in a precinct that had just lost three brothers. The cops were pissed and the men being interviewed were known criminals who probably knew or suspected the identity of the people involved in the organization, if only by reputation. But they weren't talking. No one was talking.

Asian gangs were notoriously secretive and uncooperative—they didn't even call themselves "gangs," they called themselves "secret societies"—and didn't that say it all.

"My nephew died in that explosion yesterday. Got out of the Army and followed me onto the force." The cop's expression warred between anger and grief. "Got a place with SWAT just a few months ago. He was thrilled to get in. Now he's dead."

"That's too bad, man," Fuentes said, slapping the guy's back. "Sorry for your loss."

Lucas gritted his teeth against the lump of failure that swelled inside his throat. Yesterday had been a disaster and guilt made him want to find the nearest bar and order a bottle of Jack. But that wouldn't help anyone except the fugitives on the run. He could wallow when this was over.

"Let me talk to them." Fuentes indicated the men in the

interview rooms.

"You speak Chinese?" Lucas said archly.

"Don't tell me these guys don't speak English. That's bull," Fuentes retorted.

The door to their viewing room opened and Lucas looked up expectantly. Kurt Stromberg walked in, holding his daughter's hand, followed by his PA who was also Agent Brianna Mayfield's fiancé. Mia pulled away and ran to Lucas with her arms held high. He scooped her up, squeezed her tight.

"How you doing, princess?" He ruffled her hair and she held on even tighter.

Mia's father strode up to him and shook his hand. "Agent Randall, thank you, again."

They'd met yesterday, but the guy had been crying so much Lucas was surprised Kurt Stromberg recognized him. He held the man's gaze and nodded, reading the genuine relief and gratitude written there. The PA stood in the corner, clutching an iPad and trying to stay out of the way. Fuentes acknowledged the guy with a nod.

Mia was reluctant to let Lucas go. He adjusted her so she was secure in his arms, but he could still reach his weapon. She eyed Fuentes and the uniform officer with suspicion. The kidnappers had given her that. Lucas didn't think it was necessarily a bad thing. In today's world it paid to hold on to a little wariness.

He murmured in her ear so only she could hear. "Don't forget our secret, little one—lives depend on it." She leaned back in his arms, met his gaze, and nodded solemnly.

Lucas gave her a hard squeeze and passed her back to her daddy because the man looked like he needed to have his daughter safe in his arms again.

He and Fuentes were about to leave when the door opened again and a small group of men and one woman walked inside. Lucas recognized Mayor Jeremy Everett and the Boston Police Commissioner, Pete Goodman, from news conferences on TV.

"Hey, Kurt. Good to see you. Glad we had a positive outcome, yesterday." Mayor Everett clasped Stromberg on the top of the arm. "How's little Mia doing?" He reached out to stroke the little girl on the back.

Mia clung to her daddy and buried her face against his neck.

"She's a little shy right now, Jeremy," Stromberg said, angling her away from the other man's touch.

"Understandable. Understandable." The mayor nodded vigorously and backed off a step.

Lucas refrained from commenting. He'd always found society's need for children to be polite to strangers at odds with keeping them safe. He didn't like ill-mannered brats any more than the next person, but he figured kids should be allowed to hone their instincts without being berated.

Mayor Everett's lively blue gaze swung to face him. "And you are?"

"Special Agent Randall, sir." He introduced Fuentes beside him.

"You met my PR man?" the mayor asked with a grin.

Fuentes chuckled. "Sure have."

"No, sir." Lucas reached out and shook hands with a stocky man with a silver buzz cut.

"Brian Templeton," the man introduced himself. "I believe you know my wife, Carly Sloan?"

Lucas nodded:

"The mayor thinks I know everything that goes on in the FBI, but that I simply refuse to tell him." His lips firmed. "Unfortunately my wife is way too circumspect to tell me anything she doesn't want the mayor to hear. Not to mention I barely see her since she was promoted."

"You need to work on your techniques." The mayor nudged Brian with his elbow and gave a sly grin, not exactly appropriate under the circumstances.

"I bet he keeps you on your toes," Lucas murmured when the mayor turned away.

Templeton shot him a glance. "Like a goddamn ballerina."

Lucas changed the subject. "SSA Sloan is a great person to work for."

"Yeah." But the guy didn't look like he was feeling lucky. "She's wonderful."

The mayor's other aides stared at Lucas the way a zebra eyed at a lion. The third, a woman, watched him with feminine appreciation. Unfortunately a pair of tilted black eyes and warm, honey skin chose that moment to invade his mind.

Masochist.

His gaze went to the commissioner who'd remained silent since entering the room.

Goodman was a big guy with winter white hair, snowy brows, and brown skin. His reputation was one of intelligence and toughness, which was a nice counterbalance to the fact the mayor was an idiot.

Lucas wasn't sure what he was reading on the commissioner's face though—anger and grief and maybe something else.

Mayor Everett's mustache bristled as he turned to the viewing window. "So, are these the guys?"

"No, sir," said Lucas.

"Mia?" The mayor prompted.

Mia shook her head—but she hadn't seen anyone. Lucas frowned. Why the hell had they brought her down here when they knew she hadn't seen the faces of the men who'd abducted her? To scare her half to death? To terrify her parents so they never let her out of their sight again?

Back in the interview room a nervous-looking woman in her mid-forties and a detective wearing a cheap suit with a gold shield dangling from a lanyard around his neck were now asking questions. Another man sat in. A lawyer. The man being questioned refused to say a word. The detective showed him a photograph of Mae Kwon.

Had she been awake when the bomb went off?

Had she known she was about to die?

Lucas tried to drum up some sympathy, but failed.

The lawyer told the detective his client had nothing to say and provided an alibi for the time of the explosion. Then he accused the cops of racial profiling and they moved on to the second person detained.

The temperature inside the viewing room was stifling. It was as packed as a subway carriage on the Tokyo subway at rush hour. Mayor Everett pulled out a handkerchief and wiped sweat off his brow.

"I want to go home, Daddy," Mia cried plaintively.

Me, too.

"Okay." Stromberg nodded to Lucas, then pushed his way through the other observers. The commissioner touched Mia's hair and shook her father's hand when they got to the door. Thanked them for coming down.

Once they'd left, Lucas said impatiently, "These aren't the

guys you are looking for and they're not going to tell us anything unless you have some sort of leverage to use against them. You should let them go."

"Scared of a little bad publicity, Agent Randall?" Commissioner Goodman asked.

Lucas straightened his shoulders. "I don't see the point in wasting valuable time or losing the support of the Asian community when we have *no* leads."

"These people know exactly who killed my men yesterday." The glint in the commissioner's eyes was murderous. "If we can't charge them with being part of that criminal organization maybe we can get them for obstruction of justice."

"Which still leaves the bad guys in the wind." Lucas pointed to the slick lawyer who was moving to the third room with the detective and interpreter in tow. "There's no way they're going to give anything up with that piranha hovering over them."

The mayor surprised him. "He's right, Pete. You should let them go. Monitor them. See if you can get someone on the inside."

No chance. But they might be able to set up a surveillance unit, or turn someone using the right amount of pressure.

"Fine, let them go." The commissioner pressed his lips together. "But I want these people caught." He met Lucas's gaze over the heads of the others. "Before anyone else dies."

The entourage trailed out as Fuentes checked his cell. The man grunted. "Sloan wants us back at the field office." He looked up. "Hey, who was the hottie from the BAU?"

Lucas shook his head in exasperation. "Ashley Chen."

"Not the Asian chick. The pretty one with the short hair."

"Asian chick?" The anger that shot through him took him by surprise.

Fuentes grunted. "Don't tell me you're one of those politically correct idiots."

Lucas tamped down his annoyance because he had to work with this guy when all he really wanted was to smack him in the face. "The other FBI agent was Mallory Rooney."

"The senator's kid?" Fuentes looked intrigued.

"I'd advise against hitting on that particular agent," Lucas told him. "She's like a sister to me." He gave the guy a hard look. "Plus, she's engaged." Not to mention pregnant, but that was her business.

Fuentes lip curled. "It's still up to her, right?"

Lucas snorted. "Sure is." Mallory didn't need his protection. Guys had constantly asked her out in Charlotte, and she always brushed them off. The woman could look after herself—not to mention Alex Parker was a hell of a mood killer.

Lucas smiled. "You know what, you're right. Do what you gotta do, but don't say I didn't warn you."

"You ready to head back?" The other agent looked disappointed he hadn't managed to rile him further.

Lucas examined the faces of the men in the interview room one last time, second-guessing himself. Damn, he was tired. He hadn't slept last night nor the night before. He checked his watch. "Not yet. I want to talk to the traffic division here. I'll hitch a ride back when I'm done. Thanks."

He watched Fuentes walk away and pulled out his cell. It rang three times before Alex picked up.

"Lucas? Can I call you back?" Alex said tersely.

"I'm in Boston working the Chinatown brothel bombing."

"You seen Mal? Is she okay?"

Lucas heard the panic underlining the words. He knew it cost Alex to give Mallory the freedom she needed to do her job.

"She's fine. I have a favor to ask." There were voices and shouts in the background, then it went quiet as if Alex had gone into a different room.

"What is it?"

"We're struggling to ID these goons," Lucas admitted. "We have the madam's cell phone, but the geeks from HQ can't crack it. Agent Chen offered to try and help get in—"

Alex muttered something unintelligible.

"I was wondering if you could work your magic with the cell data and figure out the phone numbers for the three men who escaped. They used a signal jammer within the brothel itself. You might be able to use that information to ID them."

There was silence for a few seconds, then a groan of frustration. "I'm neck-deep in a situation here. We have it under control but we're trying to find the source of the intrusion."

Lucas kept silent. He knew his friend could never refuse a cry for help. If Alex had a flaw, that was it.

"Fine. Send me the information and I'll see what I can do in the few seconds I have free while running this case. I want you to do something for me in return."

"Anything," Lucas offered.

"Keep an eye on Ashley Chen."

Lucas blinked in surprise. "You don't trust her?"

Alex didn't answer.

"Is it because she's Asian?" Lucas pushed. If she had family in China she'd be vulnerable to manipulation if the gang threatened them.

"It isn't the Asian thing."

But Lucas knew from their work together Alex was deeply suspicious of state-sponsored spying by the Chinese and North Korean governments—not to mention the Russians.

"You found something suspect in her background?" he asked.

"I didn't find anything suspect in her background—*that's* what bothers me."

"You're not making sense, buddy."

Alex exhaled a long breath. "Every detail of her life is accounted for and it all fits together perfectly. It's like the whole thing has been choreographed."

Lucas grunted. "You don't think the FBI checks this stuff when they hire people?"

"Of course they do. I checked it, too, couldn't find a damn thing wrong, but..." Frustration and exhaustion were rampant in Alex's tone. Lucas knew how the guy felt.

"It's because she's working with your true love."

Seconds ticked by before Alex spoke again, his voice low and vehement. "Everything I care about is up in Boston, Lucas. The fact I'm not there protecting her and our baby makes me crazy, but I know I have to let Mal do her job. There's something about Ashley Chen I don't trust. It might be paranoia on my part." A stint in a Moroccan jail would do that to a guy. "It might be that she's damn good with computers. But whatever it is, I'm grateful you're up there watching Mal's back." He sounded more like the Alex Parker Lucas used to know.

"I'll keep an eye on her." He wasn't sure which agent he was referring to as they hung up.

He had a case to solve, the lives of three ruthless bastards to fuck up, and a sex trafficking network to shut down. Everything else paled into insignificance. But the fact he was still glad of an excuse to spend time "keeping an eye on" Agent Ashley Chen told him more than he needed to know about his own flaws and weaknesses.

CHAPTER FOUR

A FEW HOURS later, Lucas knocked and entered the private hospital room. It was late enough in the afternoon that the sun had gone down and the room was dimly lit, revealing a slight figure covered in blankets, lying still on the bed.

He and Sloan had decided the secret of Becca's survival was too vital to trust with anyone except those who absolutely needed to know. With the FBI stretched as thin as Saran wrap, and Boston PD known to be less than reliable at keeping secrets within their ranks, Lucas had offered to hire private security from Alex Parker's firm. He'd even offered to pay for their services out of his own pocket. Sloan vetoed any plan that involved civilians. Instead, she'd spoken to a friend at ATF and two of their agents were guarding the girl around the clock. Becca had been switched to a smaller facility to prevent anyone from connecting her to the bombing. The doctors and nurses treating her were sworn to secrecy.

The scrape of a chair told him ATF agent Teresa Curtis was still at her post. Lucas gave the woman a nod and murmured, "If you wanna take a break for half an hour, I'll be here."

"Sure," she agreed, stretching as she stood. "I'm going to go grab a Starbucks and check in with my husband. The coffee here might be free, but it sucks. Can I get you anything?"

Lucas shook his head.

He walked Curtis to the door, spoke quietly so as not to disturb the sleeping girl. "How's she doing?"

"Refuses to talk to anyone about what happened or where she came from, but said she'd talk to you." The agent's eyes met his. "But she's doing a damn sight better than I would be if the roles were reversed."

"She's a tough kid."

"She's had to be. Look"—she touched his arm—"I know you've been getting flak from some of your G-man buddies, but you did the right thing." Her eyes were earnest. "She'd be dead without you. Remember that when your fellow idiots give you shit."

He grimaced. "A lot of people died—friends of theirs—not to mention the cops and the other captives. I get their position."

"You've got a dose of survivor's guilt. It's understandable. But no one expected they'd blow that joint." She snorted softly. "You going in there saved two young girls' lives and let us know the perps got away. Now we know they're on the run and we have people who can ID them. That's on you."

Okay. Maybe she was right. The Boston Field Office and local cops had dropped the ball on certain aspects of this case, but the knowledge he'd failed to save all those people ate at his gut.

After Curtis left, he walked over to the bed where Becca lay tucked beneath the sheets. Both of her lungs had been damaged in the blast, and she was being fed oxygen through tubes in her nose. Her other organs appeared healthy, which was good news. The doctor had put her on IV antibiotics for a uterine infection and had ordered blood tests for various diseases and STDs.

If Lucas never discovered the results of those tests, he'd be just fine.

Becca's eyes opened slowly, and her face lit up with a smile. "Hey." Her voice was croaky.

Her hair shone like polished wheat in the lamplight and if she ever saw the sun he figured her face would turn into a mass of freckles. She was lovely, but even if she hadn't been, someone, somewhere should be missing the hell out of this kid.

"Hey, yourself. Feeling better?" He was careful not to get too close. He didn't know if he might do something to trigger a flashback of the abuse she'd suffered. So far she'd proven remarkably resilient.

One day, everything that had happened to her would probably hit her and she'd have to deal with it. But the only thing that mattered right now was surviving.

"I'm still a bit sore." The gash at her temple had been stitched and was starting to heal. She rubbed her chest. One of the nurses had donated a pair of Iron Man pajamas that were slightly too big. They weren't very girly, but Becca seemed to love them. "How's Mia?"

"She's good. With her mom and dad." Inwardly he winced. Mia barely had a scratch on her. He'd been almost as lucky, just a few bruises from getting up close and personal with the unyielding stone of the garage floor.

Becca had been less fortunate, and it didn't seem fair on top of everything else she'd suffered. Her fingers clutched nervously at the sheet. Lucas didn't think she was scared he'd take advantage of her, but it would be a long time before she trusted anyone again—especially men.

Sloan was right. Until they caught these perps her life was in danger. He needed to get as much information out of her as possible to help make that happen. Although he was trained in interview techniques, he wasn't sure how to question a young girl about being part of the sex slave industry. He cleared his throat. "I was thinking it might be a good idea to get a professional in here to talk to you. The FBI has—"

Her knees pulled up to her chin and her expression turned mutinous. "I don't wanna talk to no one."

"You're safe now, Becca, but to keep you that way we have to catch these guys and get all their friends off the streets and into prison where they belong."

Her eyes grew wide and scared, but her lips remained tightly sealed.

"You need to talk to someone," he insisted. "We need to know what happened. We need every scrap of information to help us find these guys. A psychologist could—"

"I'm not talking to no shrink."

"What about your family?"

The grip on her knees grew tighter.

"Or Agent Curtis?"

"You. I'll talk to you." Her blue eyes held such trust he couldn't look away.

"Okay," he said slowly, "but these are difficult questions I have to ask. Questions I'd struggle to answer. Let me call Agent Curtis to be here in case you get scared."

She grabbed his sleeve. "No. Just you. I don't want anyone else to hear this. Just you." She blushed so hard her ears turned red. Then she realized she was touching him and shrank away. His heart broke a little.

"Okay. We can do it your way but I *have* to record the

interview." He took out his cell phone and turned on the voice recorder, setting it on the bedside table out of her line of sight. "It's important that people know I don't coerce or coach you on what to say. We just want the truth, okay? Only the truth matters."

She nodded. Unclenched her fingers. "What do you want to know?" Those eyes of hers looked about a thousand years old.

There were so many things he wanted to know and all of it was ugly. He figured he'd start off easy.

"Any idea why they kept some girls locked up in the rooms downstairs, and others in dorms?"

She shifted nervously and bit her lip.

"Hey," he said softly. "They can't hurt you now, Becca."

Her frown told him she wasn't convinced. And no wonder, since last time he'd said those words they'd almost been blasted out of existence.

"Were the girls who were kept locked up in rooms special in some way?" He was guessing, but he didn't want to lead her too much.

Her lips were bloodless as she pressed them together. "They kept certain girls separate for certain men. Those were the people locked up on the ground floor."

He leaned a little closer. "So there were specific men who came to see you?"

She nodded. "I was told that I had to do exactly what they wanted, and I had to smile and use my manners and say 'thank you.'"

He wanted to gag.

"Madam told me that the more the men said I was a good girl, the more things I'd get for my room—like a blanket and a

TV." Her face flamed with embarrassment.

Lucas felt like someone was holding a blowtorch to his temper. They needed more people trying to trace the johns who'd visited the brothel. He wanted every one of them locked up and made to face public scrutiny of their behavior.

"You think that maybe when you feel a bit better you can work with a police sketch artist? Make pictures of the men who came to your room?" he asked gruffly.

She shrugged and her eyes drifted away. "Sure."

"How many were there?"

Her eyes fixed on her toes, which wiggled under the covers. "For a long time there was just one."

Interesting. "Did he have a name?"

She drew back a little. "He told me to call him 'Daddy.'"

Oh, man. If he ever found the guy he'd beat him until the sonofabitch was unrecognizable.

"Six months ago others started coming."

"How many?"

"Four different men including the first one." She gnawed on her knuckles and wouldn't meet his eyes. Her voice climbed higher. "Some of them hurt me."

He gritted his teeth so hard he heard them crack.

Her lip wobbled but she held it together. "Sometimes they wanted to sleep in the bed with me and stay all night. I hated that. Over the last few weeks there were more men. People like you who I'd never seen before." She swallowed tightly, but then emotion spilled out. "I think that's why they took Mia, because I wasn't good enough anymore...I think it was my fault." She sobbed, hiding her face in the sheets covering her knees.

Lucas couldn't speak. If he did, he'd probably howl. He

turned and fetched a glass of water from the bathroom and avoided his reflection in the mirror, reminding himself he was an experienced law enforcement officer and former soldier. He'd seen plenty of death and destruction, but this prolonged violation of a child who should have been protected...

Dear Jesus.

What sort of people did this? Deviants who passed themselves off as normal but inside were wretched excuses for human beings. He splashed water on his face, wiped himself dry on a paper towel and went back into the room.

"I need to say something, okay?" His gaze held hers. She pressed her lips together nervously. "You *never* did anything wrong. Ever."

"You don't understand." Shame crossed her features.

"Tell me."

She eyed him nervously, like he'd be angry with her. "I hated what they did, but...some of them made it feel *okay*." Her cheeks remained bright pink as she tried to hide her face. "I didn't want to like it, but they did something to me, or maybe there's something wrong with me..."

His heart broke for her. He was so unqualified for this job, but she wasn't talking to anyone else. She needed a child advocate, a lawyer, a goddamned parent.

He cleared the knot in his throat. "Becca, you have nothing to be ashamed of. Sex is supposed to feel good, but it isn't for kids. It's for consenting adults. It's about trust and intimacy and grown-up physical acts and emotions a kid shouldn't have to deal with. You endured a terrible situation and did what you had to do to survive. These men knew it was wrong to touch you, but they did it anyway. They're the worst kind of predators."

How the hell did anyone counsel a thirteen-year-old *on sex*?

"You never have to let anyone touch you like that again. You *own* your body." Fury raced through his veins and made his voice shake. "When you grow up, you get to decide if you want to have sex with another consenting adult or not. And sex can be a good thing. A wonderful thing. Especially if it's part of a loving and healthy relationship. But it *isn't* for kids. And no one should be forced or coerced into having sex. That's rape. Everything that happened to you was rape. Don't ever let anyone convince you otherwise."

Judging from her wide eyes he might have been a little too vehement.

She pulled in a shuddering breath and some of the tension went out of her. He decided to shift the conversation back to the men they were looking for, rather than those who'd used her. He wanted to strangle those bastards with his bare hands, but he wanted the traffickers more.

"How many men helped Mae Kwon? The madam who ran the place."

"Is she really dead?" Becca asked in a small voice.

"Oh, yeah." He nodded. He'd been to the morgue and seen her corpse.

A look of relief washed over the blue irises. "Two men lived in the house, but another turned up a few weeks ago." She looked at the other side of the room as her fingers clenched the sheet.

"Did they ever come to your room, Becca?" he asked gently.

Her fragile shoulders hunched together. "One did. He told me not to tell the others or I'd be sorry."

"The tall, younger one?"

She shook her head.

"The older stocky one?"

She nodded. "His name was Cho."

It was the first lead they had on the men's identities. He made a mental note to put a bullet through the guy's dick should they ever cross paths.

Becca looked wrung out, and he didn't want to exhaust her further. Or maybe he was protecting himself from hearing more of what she'd been through.

"We should probably get in touch with your parents so we can tell them you're okay," he said gently.

This suggestion was met with her knees once again being drawn up to her chest and her face pressed against them.

So far she refused to tell them her parents' names or her family name. There were a surprising number of "Rebeccas" in the missing person database, and none of them matched this kid.

"They won't blame you for what happened."

She remained stubbornly silent. She wasn't giving anything away.

"Did you run away from home?" Part of him wanted to tell her he was sure that her parents missed her and wanted her back, but he'd seen too many cases where that simply wasn't true.

Why even have kids if you couldn't be bothered to take care of them?

She shook her head and looked toward where the light from the streetlamps slanted through the window.

"Don't you want to go back home?" he asked quietly.

She nailed him with eyes that had seen too much. "Can't I

just go home with you?"

"It doesn't work like that, Becca." His voice came out harsher than he meant it to, and her bottom lip wobbled. He forced himself to gentle his tone. "I'm not allowed to take you home. You need someone who's going to be with you all the time and knows how to take care of you properly." Forget the fact he was a single guy and she needed healing and help and schooling. "But I'm going to make sure you get somewhere safe and are looked after properly from now on."

He checked out their sterile surroundings as he turned off his recorder. "And I'm gonna treat you to a day out doing anything you want to do. A water park, Disney. The movies? You name it, as soon as you get out of here, we'll do it."

Her eyes lit up, and he hoped he wasn't making a promise he couldn't keep. Agent Curtis knocked on the door and slipped inside the room.

"See you later, kiddo." He forced himself to ignore Becca's pleading expression. He couldn't afford for her to become dependent on him. He nodded to Curtis as he left the room and wished he didn't feel like he was about to throw up whenever he thought about what these people had done to that little girl.

The full might of the Federal Bureau of Investigation was being leveled against this organization. They wouldn't evade justice for long. Lucas intended to make sure they never operated on these shores again. Maybe then it would be safe enough for Becca to go home.

"Offender motivation seems obvious," Ashley stated,

looking at photographs of the crumbled ruins. "Kill as many witnesses and destroy as much potential evidence as possible."

"They did a hell of a job," agreed Mallory.

"And if they didn't destroy it," Ashley added, "they slowed down collection and analysis by about a year."

Mallory ran her hand through her short hair and made it stick up. "By which time they'll be so far underground we'll have no hope of finding them."

"Hey, did Lucas Randall ever say what his related case was down in North Carolina?" Ashley was itching to explore an angle someone hadn't thought of yet.

"No, I'll ask him for more details. Right now we have lots of possible leads but nothing much to go on." Mallory twisted her lips. "Typically, Asian organized crime families are harder to penetrate than the others. First off, there's the language thing. You said you speak some Chinese?"

"A little Cantonese," Ashley admitted, squashing the sense of guilt she felt.

"Which will be advantageous because my language skills suck." Mallory tapped her pen on a pad of paper. "Human trafficking has been on the rise over the last few years. It's more lucrative while being perceived as less dangerous to the criminals than dealing drugs. This setup feels a little sophisticated for most groups currently known to be established in the US." She yawned widely, and Ashley gave her the side-eye.

Mallory had nearly miscarried on New Year's Eve and since then their boss, Assistant Special Agent in Charge Lincoln Frazer, had taken on an almost tyrannical role in making sure she didn't overexert herself. Ashley had her orders and didn't want to think about the repercussions for her FBI career if anything happened to Rooney, or the baby, on her watch.

"I've set up ViCAP searches for similar operations in the US—underground brothels, prostitution rings, people smuggling, Asian perpetrators, explosives." Ashley glanced at her watch. "Wanna head back to the hotel and grab some dinner?"

"Sure." Mallory stretched out her back showing off her slightly rounded stomach.

No one could really tell she was pregnant unless they already knew.

"I think Lucas might be hiding something," Mallory stated as she swung her coat around her shoulders.

"What makes you say that?"

"I've known him since we were kids and he's got a good poker face, but that's how I know he's holding something back. The effort to look like he's revealing nothing is a huge red flag to me." Mallory's eyes narrowed thoughtfully. "Maybe they have a witness. Maybe someone else survived that explosion?"

"If that's true," Ashley said, packing up her laptop, "it's probably better if everyone thinks he or she is dead."

Mallory shook her head in annoyance. "You're right. My brain is fried. I shouldn't have said anything."

"You and Randall were close?"

Mallory nodded slowly. "We didn't date if that's what you're asking. Our parents are friends so we virtually grew up together. At the Charlotte Field Office he was my mentor and taught me the ropes, but I haven't seen him much since I transferred to Quantico."

Ashley felt a sudden pang of loneliness. She didn't have any close friends. It was easier to keep your distance when you didn't know what you were missing.

"He's single." Mallory glanced at her from under her lashes. "If you're interested."

"He thinks I'm an idiot," Ashley said crossly as they walked out the door.

Mallory snorted. "He thinks you're hot."

The bullpen was eerily quiet.

"Where is everyone?" Ashley was glad to change the subject. This was the sort of case she'd been dying to work on. She didn't want to get distracted by a handsome face.

A lone agent was slumped over her computer. When they walked over to introduce themselves the woman squeezed her temples as if she had a raging headache. Her diamond engagement ring flashed even in the dimmed lights.

"What's going on?" Mallory asked as they introduced themselves.

Agent Brianna Mayfield looked harried and resentful of the intrusion. "An anonymous call came in an hour ago that the three fugitives were seen heading into Conley Terminal—that's the container port. They sent a photograph that looked like it might be our guys. The harbormaster suspended all shipping activity until each boat is cleared. We have teams from this office, Massachusetts State Police, Boston PD, ICE, and the Marine Unit, searching the area." The woman leaned back in her chair. "It's a huge operation and a security frickin' nightmare."

"They need more people?" The soles of Ashley's feet were practically vibrating with the desire to get down there.

"Negative. Sloan's got personnel on rotation so everyone stays fresh. No one wants any accidents. And she wants anyone following evidence or analyzing data to keep at it, in case this lead doesn't pan out."

"But—"

"Look," Mayfield cut her off. "You don't think I'd rather be out there hunting these lowlifes instead of sitting here running facial recognition programs?" The raw grief etched on her features told Ashley she'd known one or more of the FBI agents who'd died.

"Of course, you're right. I'm sorry." Ashley backed away. "I'm available if anything changes."

Mayfield nodded and went back to work.

Outside the building they turned right on Cambridge Street, their breath forming clouds of frozen vapor as the damp, frigid air enveloped them. Ashley huddled deeper into her jacket, wishing she didn't smell the tang of the ocean on the breeze.

"A lot of anonymous tipsters in this case." Ice made the sidewalk slippery, and they were both careful not to fall.

"I know who called the hotline about Mia Stromberg," Mallory admitted.

"I thought that was confidential?" They crossed the street at a light. People hurried along with their heads down, unsmiling, mood grim. Bostonians were furious about what had been going on in their town.

"Yeah, it is confidential. A disabled woman who lives in an apartment block overlooking the back of the building called it in."

"There was a reward offered, right?"

Mallory nodded. "A hundred thousand dollars if it led to Mia's safe recovery."

"That's quite the incentive to be a good citizen," Ashley noted.

"Something tells me the caller knew exactly what was going on in that building but was probably too scared to report it."

"That money could change her life."

Mallory agreed. "In my experience nosey neighbors have better intel than the NSA. She might even have snapped photos."

A shiver of excitement moved through Ashley's bones. "Have the locals questioned her?"

Mallory shook her head. "Part of the terms of the reward was no questions asked and complete anonymity—just like the lawyer who gave them the password." Mallory pursed her lips. "Their hands are tied unless she volunteers more information."

"Or we tie her to a crime." But the DA might balk at that suggestion. "How'd you find her?"

"I could tell you but then I'd have to kill you." Mallory sent her a smile.

Ashley's mouth tightened and she looked away. Everyone turned a blind eye to Alex Parker's hacking. His firm was often hired to test the security of companies and businesses, so he cloaked his more dubious activities behind pen tests and vulnerability probes. He might be the white-hat version of the breed, but she knew he bent the rules—a lot.

Mallory eyed her uncertainly. "I know you don't like him—"

"He doesn't like me," Ashley bit out. "And that's his problem, not mine." Dammit, she sounded like a first grader. She forced herself to chill. She wasn't a teenager trying to fit into the zoo of high school, she was a federal employee with an exemplary record.

Mallory's lips tightened. "He's overprotective—"

"Hey, look." Ashley held up her hand, trying to diffuse the situation. "It's okay. I'm a professional. It's really not important whether or not your boyfriend likes me."

Mallory looked like she wanted to argue but there was nothing left to say.

The air seemed to turn colder as they walked the rest of the way back to the hotel in silence. Sadness and a familiar sense of isolation settled over Ashley's shoulders. Just when she was getting comfortable with her coworkers, she was reminded of all the reasons she shouldn't be.

CHAPTER FIVE

T HE SILENCE CONTINUED until they entered the hotel lobby. The place was midrange, with tall plants growing in ginormous pots and a small waterfall in the atrium that fueled Ashley with the need to pee. Love hearts were everywhere in a slightly nauseating reminder that Valentine's Day was right around the corner.

Most important were the decent security and absence of bed bugs. Anything else, she could deal.

"Want to grab something before we head back to our room?" Mallory asked.

Ashley nodded, grateful her co-worker didn't hold a grudge. No matter the situation with Alex Parker, they still had to work together.

They went straight to the lounge and looked for somewhere to sit. The place was crowded. According to the waitress, a heavy equipment dealer's convention was in town.

"There's Lucas." Mallory pointed to where he sat alone in a booth at the back of the bar.

Reluctantly Ashley followed. She wanted to eat and spend the rest of the evening working, not sit around chatting, especially as the other two agents would probably want to catch up on old times. She trailed behind as Mallory snaked between a group of middle-aged white guys. The heavy slide of

66

a big hand over her ass shocked her for a millisecond. Then the hand squeezed and pinched, and fury rushed through her. She had the guy's arm up behind his back and was shoving his face into a table full of beers before he could blink.

"What the hell!" he exclaimed, squeaking like a pig as she tightened her grip.

"Next time you decide it's okay to help yourself to someone else's body"—she juggled her laptop case as she pulled her gold shield from her pocket and held it up to his nose—"you might want to consider the consequences of assaulting a federal officer."

"Let me go! I didn't mean no harm."

"No harm? How would you feel if someone molested your wife or daughter?"

"It was an accident," he sputtered. "I thought you were a hooker."

Her stomach lurched. *And that made it all right?*

"What's going on here?" a stern male voice asked from just over her shoulder. Lucas Randall.

"You in charge?" A mustachioed man in a sports jacket took a step back as a beer glass rolled onto the thick carpet.

"From where I'm standing, it looks like Agent Chen's in charge. You need any assistance, Agent Chen?" Randall asked, ignoring the audience.

She slid him a glance, grateful he didn't try to take over or tell her what to do. "Just deciding whether or not to charge this sleazeball."

The whole table held its breath. Randall didn't offer an opinion, which was a good thing. Finally she released her hold on the man's clammy skin and took a step back. "I think I'd rather eat."

Randall eyed the guy. "Your lucky day. Make sure it doesn't happen again."

She pushed her creds into her case and started to walk away. The insults didn't take long to start flying, though they were muttered quietly.

A warm hand touched the center of her back, calmed her. "You need a drink, Agent Chen. Come on, I'm buying."

She pulled in a deep breath, strode over to the booth and found herself shepherded into the corner between Mallory and Lucas.

"What happened?" asked Mallory.

"Some asshole played grab-ass with the wrong person," Lucas answered for her. The look he sent her was amused and speculative.

"Jerk." Mallory sent the group a glare.

Ashley let out a long breath. "I should be used to it—"

"What?" Lucas growled. "Why?"

She blinked. And now she was thinking of him as *Lucas*, like he was her lifelong friend.

"Where I'm from, Agent Chen, men don't grope women they don't know, and they don't compound their shitty behavior by calling women names."

"Gotta love a southern man." Mallory winked and fluttered her hand over her heart.

Lucas shot her a glare.

Some of the tension eased out of Ashley's jaw. "I'm normally better at handling that sort of attention."

"Hey, you handled it perfectly." His eyes were reassuring as they settled on hers. "I'd have kicked his ass, but watching you do it was more fun."

She shifted, uncomfortable with praise. She picked up the

menu and flipped through it, hiding her face. "Any idea what's good here?"

"Steak. The beef pie. The salmon and the ribs," Randall told her without looking at the list.

"You've been here a while?" she asked.

The smile changed his features from handsome to smoking hot. "Long enough to be working my way through the entrees, though I generally eat alone."

The waitress came and took their order. Pasta and beer for Ashley. Steak and water for Mallory. Lucas had already finished his meal.

His hands curled around a bottle of Old Thumper. Nice hands. Strong hands. She could feel the pulse at the base of her throat fluttering like a trapped butterfly against the delicate skin there. This heightened sense of awareness she was feeling regarding Lucas Randall threw her. She wasn't used to being affected by her colleagues. She was too good at pushing them away.

"Can you tell us about the related case you were working on in North Carolina?" she asked. Safer to stick to business.

He picked at the label on his beer. "A local cop noticed what he suspected was an illegal brothel operating in Raleigh. He contacted us and we started surveillance. We had enough circumstantial evidence to get a warrant for the phone records for a woman we saw coming and going from the place. Turned out she was making regular calls up here to Mae Kwon."

"The madam who died?" Mallory said.

He nodded. "I came up to interview her."

"It's her cell in evidence, correct?" Ashley wished she could get her hands on the phone although cracking it would be a full-time job.

Lucas nodded and his fingers tightened their grip on the bottle. "As soon as I walked in the door of the brothel, yesterday, she used it to take a photo of my driver's license."

"You think she stored all her johns' IDs there?" Ashley asked sharply.

He shrugged. "I'd bet on it."

That cell phone could hold the mother lode of information about this organization's business dealings. She took a big swig of cold beer. "If you traced Mae Kwon's number from Raleigh, and you suspect the Chinatown brothel was a hub of operations, then there's a good chance there are other contact numbers for other brothels on that cell phone."

"I spoke to Alex Parker about looking into the phone company data." His glance bounced off her.

Did Alex tell him not to trust her? She could see from his guarded expression that Alex had.

Anger had her teeth grinding. "Tell him to search for a secondary location. It's possible that's where they're holed up now." Ashley pushed the irritation away. She might not be too fond of Parker but it didn't mean she wouldn't use his resources.

"Secondary location?" Lucas and Mallory asked together.

Ashley frowned at them. "You said the woman took phone calls on a weekly basis?"

The lines between Lucas's brows added a nice dose of maturity. "Yeah. So?"

"So they either turned off the signal blocker at a specific time every week, or Mae Kwon went somewhere else to conduct business, maybe another property in the city?"

His expression changed. "Because she couldn't have answered the phone in the brothel with the signal jammer in place. Why didn't I think of that?" He looked pissed with himself and impressed with her. It wasn't exactly rocket science, but details could get lost in the scope of a large investigation.

"Did they have a specific time when they spoke?"

"The madam in Raleigh always called Mae Kwon on a Sunday at eleven AM sharp," Lucas told them.

"No rest for the wicked," Mallory said wryly.

"The cell company is being slow providing her phone records, but if we traced any other numbers that called her we really might be able to untangle the whole network." He fired off a text, presumably to Parker.

Their food arrived and Ashley's stomach growled. She waited for the server to mill pepper and Parmesan and then dove in, savoring the first bite which melted on her tongue and reminded her she'd skipped lunch in favor of work.

When she looked up Lucas was watching again. For some reason it made her edgy.

"Those explosives make me think they'd go somewhere else to make their phone calls," she said, as much as a distraction as anything else. "Who'd risk some random signal setting off the C4? And I'd have several signal jammers in place for backup."

"No kidding," Mallory muttered around her steak.

Ashley focused on the case as she ate. "If Parker can locate which cell tower Mae Kwon used at that time on a Sunday, he might be able to find the other gang members' cells by running a comparison with those active close to the brothel. We might be able to triangulate these to give us a more defined hunting ground. We need the phone company to come through on that warrant ASAP. These people will be slipping away as we speak."

Lucas gave her a look she couldn't read then raised a brow at Mallory. They all knew Alex could get a head start on what they needed without the warrant even though it wasn't strictly legal.

Mallory eyed them both. "Fine," she muttered after she'd swallowed a mouthful of steak. "I'll ask him again. But the intrusion he's working on isn't your average private company."

Which meant one of the federal agencies.

"Some of the other phone numbers might belong to some of the johns. We don't know how they communicated or paid. If I can get a list of names we can start working through them." His eyes narrowed. "I want to nail those bastards."

"Oh, yeah. Me, too," Ashley agreed.

"Me, three." Mallory tapped her water glass against their beers. She was making healthy inroads into her steak.

"When you get the phone records, send me that data as well," Ashley said. "If I have time I'll start culling names and numbers to investigate."

His eyes were unreadable as they rose to meet hers. "Okay. Thanks."

Mallory's mouth stretched in a yawn. "Sorry. I'm going to be lucky to last through dinner."

"You okay?" Concern sharpened Lucas's tone. "The baby?"

"We just had a checkup and we're both doing great." Mallory's smile looked a little worn at the edges. "But we seem to have developed narcolepsy." She grimaced. "Nothing eight hours solid sleep won't cure. The bad guys are going to have to wait until morning."

Lucas shook his head. "You always worked harder than anyone I know."

"That was personal." Mallory stated quietly.

"They're all personal." His gaze moved to Ashley. "Did you hear there was a sighting of the three fugitives down at the port?"

"We heard." She noticed the slight increase in tension around his eyes. "You don't think they're there, do you?"

"I think they're smart enough to know the port is a huge warren that will tie up hundreds of law enforcement officers for days, giving them the chance to slip away via private jet or over the border to Canada. In the meantime there are fewer agents following other leads. The assholes have probably already moved most of their operations. Wait another few days and the only thing left will be the roaches."

Mallory pushed back her plate with a grimace. "On that note, I'm done. I'm going to call Alex and go to bed." She gave Lucas a knowing look. "And, yes, I'll tell him how urgent it is to get as much information as possible from Mae Kwon's cell phone records."

"I'll be up shortly," Ashley told her, trying to eat faster. They were sharing a room.

"No rush." The speculative gleam in Mallory's eyes as she glanced between Ashley and Lucas suggested she was playing matchmaker. The woman had more chance of learning to speak Latin in her sleep than finding Ashley a boyfriend.

"I'll try not to wake you," she said wryly. They said good-night and Ashley watched Mallory walk through the bar full of men without a single guy trying to grope her.

Maybe they'd learned their lesson.

Or maybe Ashley really did look like a hooker.

She glanced down at her silk blouse with its low "v" neckline, which she'd teamed with a fitted black skirt. It wasn't how she'd imagined a call girl would dress but maybe these guys had secretary fetishes.

"Stop it."

She looked up in surprise. "What?"

"Trying to find fault with yourself because some guy thinks he can get away with being inappropriate just because of the way you look." Lucas took a pull on his beer.

"You think I look like an easy target?"

"I didn't mean it like that." His expression turned cynical. "He saw Asian features and figured meek and submissive. You just gave him a crash course in reasons not to believe in stereotypes."

She snorted. "I just reinforced the Ninja myth."

One of those intriguing half smiles touched his mouth. "You scared the shit out of him."

"Good."

He leaned back against the seat, contemplating his beer. "It was sexy as hell."

"Ugh." She frowned. "Not good."

His eyes darkened as he turned the bottle with his long fingers. "Finding a woman sexy isn't a sin as long as people keep their hands and thoughts to themselves. At least, until they know whether or not the thoughts are reciprocated." His gaze lifted.

Her heart squeezed. The air went thick and Ashley's pulse raced. *Oh, they were reciprocated, all right.*

There was no doubt from the look that passed between them that they were attracted to one another. It had been a long time since she'd been with anyone and part of her craved that connection. But now wasn't the time. She wanted to prove herself on this case. Not prove how stupid she was. Time to go. She pushed her plate aside and pulled out her wallet.

Lucas waved her money aside. "I'll get it."

"But it's work."

His smile widened. "This is the closest I've had to a date in months."

Even though he was joking, a flush heated her skin.

His lips tightened. "I probably shouldn't have said that, especially after what that dick pulled." Raucous laughter split the air and the moment faded. He put some bills on the table.

"Thanks." She didn't know what else to say so kept her mouth shut.

"Let me walk you out."

She slid out of the booth and gathered her things. "You think I can't handle myself?"

"I know you can handle yourself. I'm just protecting those idiots."

She smiled, then lifted her chin and led the way past the men at the table. They grew silent as they watched her pass. She didn't give them the satisfaction of looking their way.

Thankfully no-one muttered obscenities, but that probably had something to do with her protective shadow. She and Lucas headed toward the same bank of elevators.

"Which floor?" he asked.

"Eight." She watched him.

He nodded. "Me, too."

The doors opened, and they stepped inside the empty car. Her skin suddenly felt hot, and it got harder to breathe as she watched each floor's number light up. They exited the elevator and both headed left. She got to Room 815, but there was no light shining beneath the door. Damn. It looked like Mallory had already fallen asleep. Ashley hesitated. Maybe she should go work in the lounge…but those damn tractor guys were everywhere.

"Problem?" asked Lucas.

"Nothing," she said quietly. Then she relented when he stood there staring at her. "I wanted to review some surveillance footage before I went to bed, but I don't want to wake Mallory. She needs her rest."

"You can use the sitting area in my room if you want."

"You have a suite?"

"I knew I'd be here a while." He shrugged. "I'm going to have a drink and do some work anyway. You're welcome to join me."

She hesitated.

"No ass-grabbing." His lips curved in rueful acknowledgement. "I promise."

LUCAS SHOULD HAVE been exhausted after a sleepless night, but he was wired. So maybe inviting a beautiful woman back to his hotel room wasn't the smartest idea he'd ever had. But he was a gentleman and a professional and he wasn't about to hit on a fellow agent when they had a case to solve. Especially not this case. Especially not this agent.

He removed the "Do Not Disturb" sign off his door and waved her inside. "Excuse the mess. I don't let Housekeeping inside unless I'm here."

The bedroom door was open and the bed was unmade from the last time he'd slept in it. He went over and closed the door. This was business. Not pleasure.

"Have a seat. There's a power outlet in that lamp." He pointed to an easy chair near the fireplace, away from the temptation of the sofa. "Want a drink?"

"I think I've earned a bourbon if you've got it. What's this?" Ashley Chen walked across the room and stared at a board he'd constructed with pictures of the people he knew to be involved. He liked to see everything laid out visually. Three big question marks denoted the men who'd escaped the brothel.

She pointed to one of the pictures. "That's Mia Stromberg and her parents?"

He nodded. "They've been placed in protective custody. So far they're cooperating."

She eyed him sharply. "You think that's going to change?"

He pulled out a bottle of Jack and two glasses. "They want to go home, and they're wealthy enough to afford decent security."

"So, what's the problem?"

"Maybe nothing." He pointed to the picture of the demolished buildings that had once formed part of downtown. "Maybe everything." He hesitated. "I can't help wondering if Mia was specifically targeted. I mean, how much easier would it have been to abduct a kid who lived on the streets? Instead, they take the child whose parents are multimillionaires?"

"The parents let her walk to school alone?"

He shook his head. "Normally the nanny walked her, but she admitted after the kidnapping that Mia often ran ahead without her. The nanny said she always walked all the way to the school but when she didn't see Mia, she assumed the kid was already safe inside."

"You think they stalked Mia. Figured out when she'd be most vulnerable?"

"Maybe it was just bad luck. Or maybe they intended to ransom her, but decided to earn a little extra cash selling her body in the meantime." Lucas's stomach turned as he remembered Mae Kwon holding out her hand for his money while a little girl shivered under the covers.

He wasn't sorry that woman was dead. But he did regret they'd lost a valuable source of information.

"It is suspicious," she agreed. "It's also possible they opportunistically grabbed her off the street when they saw she was alone." Ashley pressed her lips together.

Lucas looked away from her mouth. Earlier she'd worn red lipstick but most of that had worn off. Right now she looked younger than she should, considering she was in the BAU.

Thanks to television shows like *Criminal Minds*, many people applied to the FBI hoping to get into the Behavioral Analysis Unit, but only a select few succeeded. Those who did were rapier sharp, fiercely dedicated and driven by the need to stop evil people from doing bad things. He preferred being a field agent for the variety of jobs he got to work on. Plus, he didn't like being surrounded by a constant string of corpses. He liked helping ordinary people get justice, and he liked putting the bad guys away.

He handed her a tumbler of liquor and took a drink from his own glass. The burn in his throat eased some of the tension that had been stuck there slowly strangling him. It had been an intense few days. If not for the fact he'd pursued the perps down those tunnels he'd be dead, too. So would Mia and Becca. He hadn't even begun processing his own close call with death, but after going to war he'd learned to take every day as a gift. He knocked back the whole glass and poured himself another.

"What did the parents say about the nanny?"

He screwed the cap back on the bottle. "They spent a lot of time assuring the woman it wasn't her fault."

Her brows skipped up. "You ran background checks on her?"

"On all the staff." He nodded. "As soon as the kid was reported missing we monitored the woman's communications and financials. Nothing out of the ordinary."

"They might have been threatening a loved one." Ashley ran her eyes over the picture he had of the housekeeper. "Where's she from?"

"Ohio."

Her grin lit up her face, and he found himself smiling back. She had softly tilted eyes, and hair that looked like raw silk. He wanted to run his fingers through it and find out if it felt as good as it looked. She was tall and slender, didn't look tough enough to survive self-defense training in the academy, but obviously she had.

He wasn't surprised she'd attracted attention in the bar, he was just pissed it had been the wrong kind of attention. But she'd handled it.

He hadn't lied earlier. He'd been so busy with work he hadn't dated in months. Ever since they'd discovered the serial killer Edward Meacher operating in Lucas's backyard, he'd been working non-stop. That investigation was stalled—there were no clues as to who'd killed the sadist and no one was sorry the man was dead. Over New Year's, Lucas had worked a homicide on the Outer Banks and then a bank heist where the teller had been shot dead after she'd tripped the silent alarm.

Now this. It was only February but he'd already had a busy year.

"Who are these three?" Agent Chen pointed to three head shots he'd nabbed from Boston PD's mug shot files that afternoon.

"Members of the fire gang they brought in for me to look at today."

"Safe to assume they're not our guys?" She swirled her drink and took a sip.

He forced himself to put more space between them. The fact Alex Parker had asked him to keep an eye on the woman made him feel uncomfortable. But he'd known Alex for a lot of years and the guy had good instincts.

"They weren't the right guys." He pointed at the lawyer. "This guy turned up to represent them. He's a real shark."

Ashley gestured at another photograph. "Who's that?"

"The interpreter."

Ashley stared at him strangely for a moment. "Doesn't she work for the cops?"

He nodded.

Her head tilted to one side. "You don't trust anyone, do you?"

That was a little too close to the truth. "It's not my job to trust people. It's my job to catch criminals."

A line appeared between her brows. "Did you sit with a police sketch artist to get likenesses of the three men you saw?"

"Sure, but the results weren't great. Apparently I'm not good with faces."

Her shoulders stiffened. "Because all Asians look alike?"

"To an untrained eye? Maybe. Yeah." He watched her chin go up. "Personally I don't know the difference between

Korean, Japanese or Chinese faces. I didn't even know there were different types of eyelids until the police artist asked me about it earlier. And the differences between individuals are more subtle." He shrugged, trying to rein in his frustration. "I had trouble getting what's in my head across to the artist. That's on me."

"Are you sure you'd recognize them again if you saw them?"

He eyed her sharply. "I'd recognize them anywhere."

The lamplight highlighted the blue-black hue of her hair. The satin blouse she wore was conservative but it dipped low and drifted over her breasts and slender waist in a way that left little to the imagination. He dragged his eyes back to hers and that spark of awareness flashed between them again. Invisible energy that only the two of them could sense.

"I should probably go," she said suddenly.

He didn't trust his voice, so he didn't answer.

She walked toward him and he forced himself not to move. She was only a few inches shorter than he was which was a change from the women he usually dated. Her hands rested on his chest as she eased up to kiss him. Her mouth was soft and sweet, and tasted like bourbon.

He wanted to unwrap that shirt from her body and drag her off to bed. But it didn't matter how long it had been, this was a really bad idea.

As she was about to pull away, he cupped her face and took the kiss deeper, feeling the surprise, followed by the searing heat of her response. Her breathing hitched as her tongue met his. He fitted her more closely against him, his calloused fingers rough against the slippery satin of her blouse. Her arms wound around his neck and her hands sank into the hair at his nape. She was hot—body, face, mouth. His body begged him not to pull away, not to stop, but he did it anyway, and stared down into her pretty eyes.

"What was that for?" he asked gruffly.

"Curiosity." Her lips were reddened from their kiss. Her honey skin held a flush of scarlet. "I wanted to see if you tasted as good as you looked."

His throat grew tight. "What's the verdict?"

She pulled away and walked over to where she'd dumped her laptop and coat. Picked them up.

He made himself stand very still as she walked away. Made himself accept that the kiss had been enough.

She opened the door and looked over her shoulder. "Better."

Then she closed the door, severing the connection. And he knew a kiss was never going to be enough.

CHAPTER SIX

A SHLEY HADN'T EXPECTED Lucas to taste that good. She hadn't expected molten heat to be lurking just beneath the surface of his very conservative suit and tie, either.

The kiss had been a rare act of whimsy on her part, a way of satisfying her curiosity. A way of exorcising her interest in the man and putting out the flames that had started to burn between them. Reality never lived up to fantasy. Disappointment was comforting in its familiarity.

But nothing about Lucas Randall's kiss had been disappointing or comforting.

Instead, it had ramped up her desire until she'd forgotten her good intentions. If there was one thing she appreciated, it was a man who knew how to give a woman pleasure, and that kiss had told her all she needed to know about just how good Lucas Randall would be in the bedroom.

Thankfully one of them was sensible enough to stop things before they got out of hand. It was annoying he'd been the one to do it. But her sensual nature had got her into trouble on more than one occasion—another reason to hold people at arm's length.

She headed back to her room and snuck silently inside. Mallory was fast asleep. Ashley crept into the bathroom and booted up her computer. Her email dinged with an incoming message and she muted the volume. Her heart raced a little when she saw the email was from Lucas.

Agent Chen, thanks for your assistance earlier. Any follow up questions regarding that last issue we discussed, feel free to take them up with me at your convenience. Agent Randall.

She laughed, then caught sight of her face in the mirror. Dammit. She looked *happy*. Her smile fizzled. While he might be hot and handsome, Lucas Randall was exactly the sort of guy she needed to avoid. He was too nice. Too tenacious. Too principled. Alternatively she could just fuck his brains out and get it out of both their systems.

No doubt about it, the guy turned her on. Her arousal was obvious in the way her hard nipples pressed against the thin material of her blouse, and was reflected in the huge pupils that stared back at her from the bathroom mirror.

She ached.

Ached to be touched.

Ached to belong.

She ran her hand over her breasts and matching pleasure thrummed hard between her legs. But she didn't try to find her own release. Tonight, rather than freeing and liberating, the idea felt small and lonely.

Tonight, lust wasn't the problem.

Loneliness was.

She pulled her thoughts away from her selfish wants and needs. Lovers were temporary. Reputation was forever. She exited out of her email without replying to Lucas. She had one goal today, and it wasn't to get laid. She wanted to know whether the Agata Maroulis case was connected to the Chinatown brothel.

She checked her watch. Ten-thirty PM. Like most computer nerds she was a bit of a night owl, though she curbed her natural tendencies to be more effective at her job. Her lips twisted. It seemed she curbed a lot of natural tendencies.

She opened a link to the surveillance footage from one of the cameras inside Terminal E of Logan International Airport on the day Agata arrived from Greece. Ashley found the appropriate time frame and watched the girl pick up her luggage in Arrivals, and then navigate Immigration. The woman hadn't mentioned a job to the border guard. Agata's desire for adventure and travel had overridden good sense. Ashley didn't judge her. She'd done far worse during her journey to freedom.

Agata walked out of Terminal E and took the MBTA bus #33. According to the files, the next time anyone reported seeing her was two years later on the day she'd walk into that downtown police station.

The cops should have saved her. It burned that they hadn't.

Ashley should probably wait until tomorrow and put in a request to the transit authority for surveillance tapes—which she would do—but there was nothing to stop her getting a head start and taking a quick look herself.

First, she used the light of her cell to return to the bedroom and find her roll-on luggage, which she carried back into the bathroom. She put on her pjs, brushed her teeth and removed what little was left of her makeup. Then, careful to be as quiet as possible, she took out a second laptop from the bottom of the case and booted it up.

This was an unregistered machine that contained a lot of her hacking tools. The password was encrypted beyond military standards, virtually impossible to crack. It would be easier to torture the code out of her or plant a key logger to pick up everything she typed.

She took the machine back into the bedroom and propped herself up in bed. Mallory's breathing was deep and even.

Getting into the MBTA server wasn't hard at all. She exploited a known backdoor vulnerability in the operating system. Finding the right camera, not to mention the right time and date, took longer. It was midnight by the time she found the place where Agata got off the bus and entered the subway. Her heart ached a little for the Greek woman. Young and vibrant, by all accounts Agata had been bursting with the need for adventure. How it must have devastated her to be tricked into a life of prostitution. Raped and abused on a daily basis, strung out on drugs so other people could make money off her flesh, her pain, her humiliation.

Anger churned like sulfuric acid in Ashley's stomach. She could taste the horror of it, the fierce desire to fight, the pain of defeat, the death of hope.

The fact the cops had let the girl down incensed her, but it was too late now. Agata had died desperate and alone on the streets of the country she'd wanted to explore. All Ashley could do was find those responsible and make them pay for what they'd done to her, so others escaped that same bleak existence.

After carefully searching the footage, she found Agata again as she took the blue line and exited at Government Center. Ashley felt a burst of exhilaration when she spotted the Greek girl getting on the green line toward downtown. A wide yawn told her it was time to quit. She could barely keep her eyes open. She wrote a note to herself about the time and cameras she'd tracked so far.

Using her official laptop, she fired off an email asking for access to the MBTA database. Any evidence needed to be accessed through legal channels in order to be admissible in court. She yawned again and logged off the other servers, making sure there weren't any unexpected communications from their IT department about a breach in security. It looked good so she shut it down and buried the second laptop under her clothes in her case.

She looked at the hotel room door and thought about all the things she could have been doing with Lucas Randall. Crawling under the duvet, she decided this was better. Denying herself a man like Lucas Randall was the sort of penance she did on a daily basis. Anyway, the Bureau was full of hot alpha males. Even as she thought it, she knew she was lying to herself—it was one of the ways she stayed sane.

Honesty wasn't all it was cracked up to be.

———

LUCAS SLEPT LIKE a dead man.

From now on he should include beer, Jack Daniels and searing kisses from beautiful women as part of his nightly routine. He grinned. Fat chance.

He left the hotel and resisted the urge to head a few blocks north to check on Becca. Easier to keep a secret if he didn't draw attention to it.

It was early, but there were plenty of people around during his fifteen-minute walk to the field office. Boston was a city in mourning but facing its troubles with its usual bullish pride. Those emotions were written clearly in the expressions of people he passed on the street.

He grabbed a coffee and headed inside, waited in line to go through security.

Upstairs the bullpen was quiet. Most of the task force was still searching the port. Those who weren't were probably catching a few hours' sleep. Out of the corner of his eye he caught sight of a tall, raven-haired figure walking away from him down the hallway.

Special Agent Ashley Chen.

He should have picked up more coffees, but he didn't want her to think he was reading anything into last night's kiss. They'd both been tired, had a few drinks, and he'd been punch-drunk from exhaustion.

And if those were the only reasons they'd locked lips, they'd have ended up naked in each other's arms.

In the conference room Mal and Agent Chen were both hunched over their laptops. Today Ashley wore a gray pantsuit with a crimson blouse. There were small silver hoops in her ears, and her hair shone like polished ebony. Everything about her appearance screamed dedicated federal employee and he half wondered if he'd imagined that she'd kissed him last night.

"Hey." Mallory looked up and smiled. "Any news from the port?"

Lucas shook his head. Ashley didn't glance up, but the stiffening of her shoulders told him she was plenty aware of him.

He didn't want this to be awkward. They'd only kissed. That's why he'd sent the email last night, but maybe she had read more into it… He'd been trying to keep things light, but this attraction complicated things and he didn't like complicated. He liked simple. He liked honest and no bullshit.

"Agent Chen." He addressed her directly, determined to knock the weirdness right out of the air. "I have those cell records we discussed last night from Mae Kwon's phone company—"

She held up her hand. "Not right now."

He jerked as if she'd bitten him. Yesterday she'd been dogged in her determination to help. Had she changed her mind because of a simple kiss?

Not that the kiss had been even close to simple.

She looked up. "I'm tracking the Greek girl's arrival in Boston, and I think I'm getting somewhere."

Intrigued, he went over to look at Ashley's laptop, pointed at the blonde figure on the screen. "That's Agata Maroulis?"

She nodded, intent on the images.

He pulled up a chair and she jumped as their knees accidentally brushed. So much for the indifference she wore like one of her expensive suits.

"I tracked her from the airport all the way to downtown. This should be her going into the parking lot."

She clicked a different camera and on screen the girl walked out of the station carrying a large backpack and wearing a sunny smile as she looked around. She had a runner's physique and short, curly blonde hair. She wore tight jeans and a green-checkered short-sleeved blouse. She looked like freshness and innocence personified.

Victims like Agata were the reason he'd joined the FBI—to stop people from exploiting others. To rescue those who were in trouble. Unfortunately it rarely ended like the fairy tales.

People died. Bad guys got away with it. But not this time. This time they were going to find these men and make them face the consequences.

When Agata's body had first been identified the FBI had put out an appeal for information. No one had come forward. Not a single person admitted ever seeing her. Someone had known something, though. The people running this gig. The men who'd used her body. The johns had to have known these women weren't willing participants. Lucas wanted to know who those deviants were. He wanted to know how they found out about the underground brothel. And he wanted them to pay for the misery they'd helped perpetuate.

On screen Agata stood on the curbstone, bouncing on her tiptoes. A minivan pulled up.

"Can you stop it there?" he asked Ashley.

She did as he requested and he peered closer. "Run it forward slowly." Lucas felt his pulse kick up as he recognized Mae Kwon getting out of the passenger side of the vehicle. She was wearing an ill-fitting navy business suit that could have passed for a hotel chain uniform. "That's the madam from the Boston brothel."

"So we have a solid connection between the Agata Maroulis murder and the Chinatown brothel that was destroyed." She nodded with satisfaction. "We'll have more leads to follow."

"That's good work." It showed solid investigative skills despite her youthful appearance. He didn't know what Alex's issues were with Ashley, but she'd just proved she was damn good at her job.

Mallory came over and looked over their shoulders. She was wearing her rock of an engagement ring, and the baby bump was enhanced by a form-fitting T-shirt under her suit jacket. She looked healthy and content and Lucas was happy for her. If anyone deserved a chance at a good life, it was Mallory Rooney and Alex Parker.

On screen, Mae Kwon shook Agata's hand and motioned for her to stow her luggage in the rear compartment of the van. Then she reached for Agata's passport, indicating she wanted to check it against a clipboard she was wielding. She waved the victim into the vehicle with a smile.

Agata seemed excited as she got in the van. Her lips were moving animatedly as if she was having a lively conversation. There was no suspicion yet that she'd been duped.

Mae Kwon got in and the minivan pulled away from the curb. How long had it been before Agata had realized her dreams were ashes?

He forced the thoughts away from the young woman. Agata was gone and he needed a clear mind to rescue others still caught up in the nightmare, and to capture those who'd been responsible for her death.

"The methods adopted with Agata were more typical of the Russian Mafia than Asian gangs." Mallory spoke up. "Asian gangs tend to transport illegal immigrants through seaports and hold the documents hostage until the aliens have paid off their debts with forced labor or prostitution. The victims are trapped because of their illegal status and isolated because of the language barriers and the fact they don't know how the system works. Plus, family members back home are threatened with violence if their debts aren't paid off. The job abroad ruse is normally a Russian or Eastern European trick." She touched his shoulder. "Alex said they were getting things under control with this latest intrusion. He might have time to get us some names and addresses from the data you sent him this morning. These scumbags have been getting away with this for far too long."

He nodded and Mallory went back to work. Ashley was replaying the tape.

"Any chance we can get an image of the driver or the plate on the minivan?" he asked.

Ashley's lips twisted. "Let me see if the station has any other cameras, but don't hold your breath." He met her gaze, and suddenly the memory of the kiss they'd shared flared between them. She might portray cool aloofness but her eyes betrayed her.

And there wasn't a damned thing either of them could do about it.

He dialed Sloan on his cell. "Agent Chen found surveillance video of Agata Maroulis getting into a minivan with Mae Kwon on the day the girl arrived in the city. The cases are definitely connected."

Sloan swore. Her people should have found this already and she knew it. It hadn't been a priority before the explosion, but it was a priority now.

"Good work," she told him. "See if Chen can dig up anything else from the Maroulis case that might give us a lead."

"Any sightings?" Lucas asked.

"Not a goddamned thing. Keep me informed." Sloan hung up.

Ashley's fingers flew over the keyboard until she found another camera. The rear of the van came clearly into view but the plate was too muddy to read.

"Let's see if we can get a better angle of the front or the driver when they leave the lot," she told him. But the van drove away without them getting a clear shot.

"Damn." Her lips compressed as if she was angry with herself. "Sorry."

"It's not your fault," he said quietly.

Her eyes were as inky as the night sky when they met his. "It's just there's so much information that's been missed. And although they say once something's online it's online for good, that's not true. Tracks can be wiped. Digital evidence is as ephemeral as a fingerprint if someone knows what they're doing." She stared at the screen and then leaned forward, and then began to rewind the footage.

"What are you doing?" he asked.

"It's a pick-up drop-off zone, right? It's possible they drove past more than once." She kept rewinding at high speed, then slowed. She pointed to the screen; there was the van again but approaching from the other direction. The driver had his window down, elbow on the ledge, face in profile.

Then something drew the driver's attention and, for a single moment, he looked straight toward the camera. Ashley froze the image and enlarged it on the screen. Then she pressed a key, and the sound of a nearby printer burst into action.

"That's what they call in the business the money shot." Randall held up his hand, and she gave him a high-five. "He isn't one of the three men I saw in the brothel." His eyes narrowed because the fact they had another suspect suggested this was a well-organized, well established group who'd been operating in complete secrecy.

He went over to the printer and picked up the piece of paper. "Now let's see if we can ID this sonofabitch."

THIRTY MINUTES LATER, Lucas slipped quietly into Becca's hospital room. He exchanged a nod with Agent Curtis who stood and stretched her arms high above her head. The news was on TV, showing the manhunt down at the port.

Becca's eyes were wide when they swung to him. "They still haven't caught them?"

"Not yet, but we will find them." He injected a confidence he didn't feel into his voice. Ashley was running the image of the driver through facial recognition programs. Then she and Mallory were going to determine what other surveillance cameras were in the vicinity of the brothel and see if they could find any additional footage. The cops had canvassed the area already, but there was no harm in doing it again.

If he could find a clean image of the fugitives the FBI could send it to Interpol and expand the search internationally.

"In the meantime, we need to be careful. They don't know you survived the explosion so they're not even thinking about looking for you."

Her fingers gripped the covers. "I don't want them to find me. I don't want them to hurt me again."

"That's why I'm here, sweetheart," Curtis interrupted, holding back one side of her jacket so her weapon was visible. "No one's getting past me or Agent Bueller."

Bueller was the other ATF agent taking turns to protect Becca.

"And as soon as you're well enough to leave here we'll get you to a safe house." At some point the Trafficking Victims Protection Act would enable them to safeguard Becca, but for that they'd have to reveal she survived. So far Sloan had managed to keep it between the two of them, her SAC and the ATF team. If this thing went to trial there was a good chance Becca would need to go into WITSEC. It would be nice if she could be reunited with her family before she had to disappear forever. They might want to go with her.

"Did you decide what you want to do when this is all over?" He turned to Curtis. "I promised her a day out." They exchanged a glance. They both knew it would be a while until this was finished.

Curtis grinned. "I like that idea."

Becca shook her head mutely and looked away.

"There are no strings attached, Becs."

She looked up and his heart shattered at the uncertainty he saw there.

"You never have to worry about doing any of that stuff again," he said firmly, wondering if he'd said the wrong thing. "If I offer you a treat, it's because I want to give a strong kid something good after how brave she's been. It's not because I want something from you in return. No one's gonna hurt you like that again, got it?" Christ, he hoped he wasn't making promises he couldn't keep.

She picked at a knot of cotton in the sheets, then nodded.

It would be a while before she'd trust him completely. He knew that, but right now he just wanted her to feel secure. "Come on, there's got to be something on your bucket list."

"I wouldn't mind going to the mall," she mumbled.

His heart gave a hard twist. "The mall? Shopping?" Normally he'd make a joke about that being his idea of hell, but she knew that reality better than anyone.

"I don't have any of my own clothes." She pressed her lips

together as if embarrassed.

His throat constricted. "I can take you shopping."

He had no idea how to outfit a young girl. Maybe he could persuade Mallory or Ashley to come with him. Agent Chen looked like she knew her way around clothes shops.

"You can take me shopping anytime, Agent Randall." Curtis winked at him and picked up her bag. "I'm going to grab breakfast. Want anything?"

They both shook their heads and watched the woman leave.

He walked over to the windows and opened the shades just enough to let in more light, but not enough for anyone to see inside. He turned back to the bed, dug in his pocket, and unfolded the printout of the image of the minivan driver Ashley had tracked down. He held it out to Becca. "Do you recognize this person?"

Her blue gaze dropped to the image. Her mouth opened, and her pale skin blanched. Slowly she swallowed.

"Is he the man who took you?"

She nodded again, and his heart sped up.

"How long ago?"

She looked down at the covers. "I don't know."

"A few weeks ago? A month?"

Her gaze went inward as she concentrated. "Longer."

"How much longer? Can you take a guess?" he asked. There was no record of this kid anywhere in the system.

"I don't remember, but..." The sheets rustled as she knelt in the bed. "They made me take a pill every day and at first I counted them."

Roofies? No, they didn't need narcotics to control a kid like Becca. Birth control? A way to stop periods and pregnancy should the child hit puberty? Heaven forbid something as basic as biology got in the way of sexual slavery.

It was a lead they might be able to trace.

"How many pills did they make you take, Becca?"

She wouldn't meet his gaze. "I lost count after I got to five hundred."

Bile hit his throat. He forced himself to unclench his jaw and swallow. She'd been in that hellhole for at least eighteen months? Jesus, she'd have barely been in double digits when she'd been taken. "So the man in the photograph…did he, er, live in the same building?"

"No. But I saw him in the kitchen a few times."

"They let you into the kitchen?" he asked in surprise.

"Yeah. Sometimes I'd help out with cooking and clearing up after meals."

"You like cooking?"

"Better than staying in my room."

The honesty of those words slayed him. A lump formed in his throat. He needed as much information as he could get, but he was scared he'd say the wrong thing and she'd clam up. Or get upset. Or he would.

"Did you see any of the other girls?"

She nodded like it was a stupid question.

He pulled out the photograph of Agata Maroulis. "You ever see this girl?" Why hadn't he thought to ask her this yesterday? Probably because she'd been terrified. Not to mention injured by a bomb blast.

Her pupils dilated, and she gave a rapid nod. "Yeah, but not for a long time." The bed rustled as she shifted position. "I remember she talked funny, but I don't think she was very well. Her hands shook when she ladled soup into bowls.

Madam hit her and wouldn't let her carry the tray because she spilled some." She looked away again. "She was punished."

He wondered what that entailed when you lived in torment. "You meet any other girls?"

She worried at the cuticle on her thumb. "Yes, but we only knew each other by the names they gave us." She nodded toward the photo of Agata. "They called her Greta. I met Mary, Sam, Diana. Julia."

"You never found out their real names?"

"No. They never left us alone and didn't let us ask questions. Some of them must have talked to one another in the dorms, but not those of us they kept in the rooms downstairs." Her brows scrunched. "One of the girls told me there were cameras up there in the dorms too, and anyone who didn't behave was punished. One girl used to cry for her mother, until Cho made her stop."

Her eyes went far away for a moment. Had she cried for her mother? Or was she remembering some other terrible thing Cho had done to her?

"Tell me who your parents are, Becs, so we can tell them you're safe. And if you don't want to live with your mom and dad, maybe we can find another relative—"

"Mom. There's just my mom." She stared off into space.

Okay.

That was something.

He eased into a chair beside the bed. "You didn't know your dad?"

She shook her head.

"Grandparents?"

A frown, then another shake of her head.

"Siblings?"

She flinched.

"Brother?"

She nodded slowly.

"Older?" Was that why she'd run away? Had her older brother abused her?

Her teeth caught her lower lip. "He was just a baby when I left."

That was a relief. "What was his name?"

"Jackson. I called him Baby Jax." Her eyes held his with an imploring look. Unfortunately, he couldn't back off from this now she'd started to talk. He turned on the recorder on his phone and set it on the bedside table.

"Can you tell me where you lived? Somewhere hot? Cold?"

Her eyes darted from him to his phone. "If I tell you you'll send me back to her." Her voice gained a hostile edge. Bitterness and experience and the living breathing knowledge of what it felt like to have no control over her life.

"I won't send you back into danger, Becca," he said, holding her gaze. "I promise you that."

"Yes, you will. You want to know my momma's name so you can send me back to her!"

"I just want you to be safe—"

"It's not safe!" she cried. "She's the one who gave me away—" She slapped her hands over her mouth, but it was too late.

He kept his voice calm. He reached out and took her hand in his and squeezed her thin fingers. "Are you telling me your mother sold you to the people in the brothel?"

She flinched at the word "brothel" but he didn't know what else to call it.

Tears shimmered in her blue eyes. "She owed them money. Lots of money." She seemed to implore him for understanding. "We'd already lost our home and we didn't always have food to eat, but she couldn't stop gambling." Becca's voice rose into a sob, and he sat on the side of the bed and pulled her into his arms, careful of the tubes still connected to her. He rocked her against his chest.

"She said she'd stop going to the casino when Baby Jax was born, but she never did. And then the man came for his money and he hurt her."

"The man in the photo?"

She nodded.

So he was some sort of enforcer. "You know his name?"

"No," she whispered. "But he had the scariest eyes I've ever seen. He beat her, and I thought he was going to kill her. Then she screamed at him that he could take me instead of the money she owed. That I was worth more." Becca hiccupped. "He hit her again until she lay bleeding in a corner and Baby Jax was crying in his crib. Then he turned around, picked me up and took me with him." Those blue eyes rose to meet his again as she curled in a ball in his lap. "Part of me thought living with him might be better than being with her, but I didn't want to leave Baby Jax. I wasn't sure Momma would remember to look after him." Tears filled her eyes and she sobbed. "Momma knew what they'd do to me when he took me away and she just let him."

He closed his eyes and rocked her until she stopped crying. Half an hour later Agent Curtis came quietly into the room and Lucas was still holding Becca in his arms. She'd fallen asleep and he didn't have the heart to wake her to ask her more questions. He gave the agent a nod, then eased Becca onto the bed but she still didn't awaken.

Curtis must have seen the anguish on his face. He shook his head and walked away when she asked if everything was okay. It wasn't okay. He wasn't sure it would ever be okay again.

CHAPTER SEVEN

A SHLEY EYED THE street where the brothel had once taken up valuable real estate in Boston's busy Chinatown. The smell of charred rubble lingered in the cold February air. Members of Boston PD's Crime Scene Unit and agents from the Bureau's Evidence Response Teams continued to scour the ruins, but this was strictly a recovery operation now. There had been no signs of life since the bomb went off.

There was surprisingly little structural damage to the surrounding area. Whoever laid the explosive charges had known what they were doing. The brothel had imploded, blowing out windows in some of the neighboring buildings, but leaving most of them intact. Whoever had planted them had military training, or were demolition experts.

"They haven't found anything useful except for a stash of condoms, contraceptive pills and a couple more bodies." Mallory walked quickly toward Ashley. The blast area was largely hidden from public view by massive tarps, cordoned off by crime scene tape and guarded by patrol officers. Air traffic was banned, but that hadn't stopped the media begging or buying their way into various viewpoints from nearby highrises. Two media vans lingered nearby, but most of the press were currently camped out down at the container port, covering the search for the fugitives. "ERT agents sent the pills to the lab for analysis. Maybe we can get a lead on the manufacturer."

Ashley nodded.

Strictly speaking, she and Mallory weren't field agents, but this situation called for an all-hands-on-deck approach. Their boss, ASAC Lincoln Frazer, had given his permission for them to see if there were any surveillance cameras that hadn't already been accessed for evidence. His was the only authority she needed.

Ashley looked across the street. A corner shop, a tobacconist, and a takeaway pizzeria had clear lines of sight to where the front door of the brothel had been. Their plate glass windows had shattered and were boarded up, but all three businesses were open and glaziers were busy installing a new shop front in the pizza place.

Mallory followed her gaze. "Spot anything?"

She shook her head.

"Pity we don't have a bank or gas station," Mallory muttered. "Then we'd definitely have surveillance."

"Maybe that's one of the reasons they chose this location," Ashley said quietly.

How careful were these people? How experienced?

It bothered her.

They entered the shop on the corner to the innocent tinkle of a bell. It was one of those places where a person could barely fit down the aisle, shelves running floor to ceiling, crammed with everything from wine to mouse traps. Cheap cards and crimson hearts proclaimed Valentine's Day was fast approaching.

Ashley loathed Valentine's Day. It was fake and artificial, and about as close to true love as she'd ever get. It was also her birthday. A double whammy of reminders as to her loneliness and isolation.

She looked around. There were no obvious cameras, but there was a sign on the door warning people they were being monitored.

The man behind the counter saw her coming and eyed her warily. He looked about forty with Mediterranean coloring and thick black hair. She flashed her badge. The eyebrows rose.

She pointed to the sign on the door. "Do you have any surveillance cameras on the property?"

He shook his head. "It's just for show. Stops kids from being stupid."

"You don't have any genuine antitheft devices?" Ashley didn't hide her skepticism.

He puffed out his meaty chest and crossed his arms somewhere in the middle. "I got a baseball bat under the counter, but we don't get no real trouble around here."

"Except for child abduction, sex trafficking, rape, and mass murder?" Ashley flashed him a plastic smile.

"Hey, I had no idea what was going on over there."

"How long they been there?"

He shrugged.

"You're telling me a man like you doesn't keep an eye on what's happening in his own neighborhood?"

He pulled a face, but clearly wasn't going to answer.

"You never wondered about the endless stream of male visitors going down there?"

"In case you didn't notice, the view ain't great out my window." He eyed her stonily, about as friendly as an injured bear.

Right now the view was blocked entirely by the plywood

covering up the empty frames so it was hard to judge what the guy could normally see. An aisle had been cleared to remove the broken glass, and undamaged goods were stacked against the opposite shelf making the narrow space positively serpentine.

"The men from the brothel never approached or threatened you?" Mallory came up beside Ashley, threw a couple of candy bars on the counter and handed over a twenty.

"Threatened me?" He looked insulted. "Those little sli—" He shot a look at Ashley and reined in whatever he'd been going to say. Because she needed a reminder her skin wasn't the same soft peach as Mallory's. He pursed his lips and dropped Mallory's change into her palm one coin at a time. "Nope."

"You seriously didn't know what was going on over there?" Ashley was bad cop for this interview, but that didn't bother her. It didn't take an expert in human behavior to know the guy wasn't telling them everything. After four years in the FBI she was used to people lying to her. It seemed to be an occupational hazard.

His mouth tightened, and some of the bluster went out of him. He leaned forward, and she figured he was about to come as clean as a used tissue. "Look, I practice the three wise monkey approach to doing business. I don't ask questions. I don't rat. Maybe I figured it wasn't your average rooming house, but I never dreamed they'd have kids locked up like that. I mean, I got kids—*girls*. They ever touched my girls I'd have ripped them apart with my bare hands." His nostrils flared.

But not other people's daughters.

"Think you could identify the people who ran the place if

you saw them again?"

There was a malevolent glint in his eyes when he answered her this time. "Not sure I could tell one chink from another. They all look the same to me."

The edge of Ashley's smile grew sharp at the deliberate use of the derogatory term. "Hmm, I've heard that people with small brains often struggle with visual perception."

His expression soured further.

How to make friends and influence people, Ashley.

Mallory handed him her card. "If you remember anything that could help us catch these guys and help keep the neighborhood safe for your children, please let us know."

"Sure, doll face." He tapped the card on the counter. "You'll be the first to know."

They walked out of the store, and Mallory handed Ashley a Mars Bar. "We intimidated the shit outta that guy."

Ashley took the candy bar and lost some of her anger. "We sure did, doll face."

"That's Special Agent Doll Face to you." They both sniggered and chomped their chocolate as they eyed the tobacconist store.

"Think this will go any better?" Mallory asked around a mouthful of chocolate.

"Nope."

"Me, neither. Boy, do I ever love my job." Mallory crumpled the wrapper and tossed it in the garbage can.

"Me, too." Ashley's cell buzzed, and she checked the screen. "Lucas Randall." She felt her face heat a little and hoped Mallory didn't notice. "He found out one of the fugitives was called 'Cho.'" She lifted her head. "I wonder where he got that sliver of information?"

Mallory drew a zip across her lips.

Armed with this new detail Ashley led the way inside the tobacconist's shop with her badge held high. The sweet smell of pipe tobacco rushed over her. The place was full of looming shadows thanks to more boarded up windows. One lone strip of fluorescent lighting was on behind the counter, highlighting a smiling shopkeeper and a carved, life-sized, cigar store Indian, standing sentinel.

The man behind the counter was rail-thin, with hollowed out cheeks that reminded Ashley of her paternal grandmother the week before she'd died of cancer. The glass displays were highly polished and contained super-expensive cigars and intricately carved pipes. She'd never understood this vice. Why waste money on something that had a good chance of killing you?

She introduced herself and Mallory. The owner's name was Victor Drover. Yes, he had surveillance, but it only covered inside the store, and it recorded over itself every twenty-four hours.

"You didn't think to save the tape from the day the bomb went off?" Ashley asked, not bothering to hide her incredulity.

He folded his hands primly in front of him. "I did. And I gave a copy to the police already."

Ashley masked her surprise. "Who'd you give it to?"

"I don't recall his name. He wore a uniform and was bossy and ill-mannered, but that seems to be a common problem with law enforcement." Drover eyed her balefully. "Anyway, there's nothing incriminating on the tape as you've probably seen for yourself. I sold another copy to the television people. They've been playing it on loop over and over."

"You sold it after you figured there was nothing incriminating on it?" Ashley asked.

"That's not what I said." He looked flustered. "You're twisting my words."

He looked less sure of himself now.

She could use that. "What can you tell me about Mr. Cho?"

"What's to tell?"

"Did he come into your shop in the twenty-four hours prior to the explosion?"

He stood straighter. "I don't believe so."

"But you did know him?" Ashley prodded. This was good intel. "Why haven't you come forward with any information?"

Drover looked impatient. "I didn't say I *knew* him—"

"But you knew his name," Ashley pushed. "You saw his face."

"We weren't friends." His voice climbed higher.

"You can identify him. What about the other men who lived there?"

He kept silent, only his eyes moving between her and Mallory like they were trying to outflank him.

"Did you avail yourself of the facilities across the road, is that why you're reluctant to talk?" Mallory asked. "We might be able to figure out a deal—"

He pressed his hands on the shop counter; his fingers were stained with nicotine. "I did not 'avail myself of the facilities.'"

"But you knew what was going on there?" Mallory said.

"I did *not* know what was going on. I sold cigarettes and cigars, and minded my own business."

While women were used and abused every day.

"Did they use cash or credit cards?" Ashley asked.

"Cash." He eyed her like she was stupid.

"So how'd you know his name?"

"I don't know," Drover said in exasperation. "I assume I overheard someone calling him it at some point."

"What are the names of the other men who ran the place?" Ashley demanded.

Victor Drover's Adam's apple bobbed up and down his scrawny throat. "I have no idea."

"But you knew Cho?" she reiterated.

He grimaced and looked like he wanted to flee.

"Describe them."

Even though he was shorter than them both he sneered down his long Roman nose. "No one around here is going to give you any information." His eyes grew hunted. "Everyone is too scared."

"That's not what the guy in the corner shop says."

Weary humor sparked in his eyes. "Gino has friends in low places. We're not all so fortunate."

Ashley jerked up her chin. "At least thirty young women were trafficked, and sold for sex on a daily basis less than a hundred yards from your doorstep—and then they were brutally murdered along with seven law enforcement personnel, and you're too much of a coward to even give us a description?"

"They all looked like you," he snapped.

Mallory rolled her eyes. "Big help."

"Nothing I do will bring those people back, but if I talk…"

Ashley's gaze sharpened. "So you think they're still around here? Or their friends are? Do you know the name of the organization?"

"I didn't say that." His voice lowered. "But I know if I talk to the cops they'll know about it, and they'll kill me."

"We can protect you."

He snorted. "Not from these people."

"You know who their associates are?"

"I don't know anything." His eyes grew frostier than a Boston winter. "I thought we'd already established that."

He came out from behind the counter and walked quickly to the front door and opened it wide. He looked at them expectantly. Mallory took a long hard look at Drover before heading outside. Ashley followed and a motorcycle with a pillion rider raced by so fast Ashley felt her hair lift off her shoulders. She watched the bike zoom through traffic. It wouldn't be long until they were another statistic.

By the time she turned around Victor Drover was closing the door and turning the sign to "closed."

They were getting nowhere fast. She raised her face to the sky. A plane went overhead, its path reflected in the side of an apartment block just south of the blast site.

A figure moved in one of the upper windows. Ashley squinted. Maybe they were going about this all wrong.

"You said you know who called the cops about seeing Mia Stromberg?"

Mallory nodded.

Ashley faced her. "How about we pay them a little visit?"

Mallory stared at the building. "We're not supposed to know who they are."

"Hey, we're canvassing the neighborhood. It would look more suspicious not to question them."

Mallory looked doubtful.

"What harm can it do?" Ashley pushed.

Mallory eyed the glaziers who were giving them the once-over from the front of the pizzeria. Wolf whistles followed.

"No way anyone will tell us anything useful with so many witnesses around," Ashley pointed out.

Mallory tugged her jacket closed. "This whole community is terrified of the people who ran that brothel, and yet they weren't even on the cops' radar." She pursed her lips. "Let's do it."

———————

THEY SLIPPED INTO the apartment building when some kind soul held the door for them. Ashley refrained from rolling her eyes at their naivety. People were hardwired to be polite, and it put them in danger every day.

They knocked on the door of the building manager and flashed their badges. When they told him they wanted to conduct door-to-door interviews he waved them along with an uninterested gesture. Then he started following them, complaining about the cleanup from the explosion, the fact they hadn't caught the guys yet, and that the cops had already questioned everyone in the building. They walked away before he started blaming them for the lousy weather and last week's crushing defeat of the Bruins.

There was nothing unusual with repeat canvassing, especially after an event of this magnitude. Talking to people was an integral part of the job.

She and Mallory started on the seventh floor and worked their way down to six. The walls were painted fern green, and the carpeting was newish but definitely in need of a steam clean. The strong smell of Indian cooking permeated the air and noises could be heard from behind some of the apartment doors—TVs and the occasional voice raised in loud conversation. She and Mallory started at the east side of the floor and began knocking on the doors of apartments that overlooked the brothel. They worked their way along, asking if the occupants had noticed anything unusual about the building below them. Some of them had. Most hadn't. Ashley made notes while Mallory did the talking. By approaching everyone on the two floors they were covering themselves with plausible deniability when they questioned their real target, Susan Thomas. Ashley caught Mallory's gaze as they reached the woman's door. Ashley knocked loudly, but there was no answer from inside.

She swore under her breath and knocked again.

The elevator opened, and a woman in yoga pants and a hoodie walked towards them.

"Hi," she said brightly.

"You live here?" asked Mallory, pulling out her badge.

The woman shook her head and offered a perky smile. "Nope. I'm Trinity Taylor."

Damn.

"But Susan should be in." Trinity lowered her voice. "She never goes out. That's why she hires me to walk her dog."

"You're a dog walker?" Ashley asked in surprise. The woman looked more like a catwalk model.

Trinity smiled. "It's helping me pay my way through college, keeps me fit and lets me hang around puppies." She pulled a lanyard with a handful of keys from around her neck. "Susan's probably in the bathroom, but," she frowned, "Rex usually barks when someone comes to the door. I wonder what's going on?"

Those words made Ashley exchange a surreptitious glance with Mallory, and they both put their hands on their firearms.

Trinity slipped the key in the lock and turned the handle. The door opened ten inches before it got stuck. Something whimpered. A dog.

Ashley elbowed Trinity aside. "Back away from the doorway, please."

She pulled her weapon, poked her head inside and looked down. A golden retriever lay on the carpet, blood seeping from a wound in its flank.

"Stay here," she ordered the civilian. She pushed as gently as she could until she was able to slip into the apartment. The scent of blood was ripe and cloying. Mallory called for backup.

"Get a vet for the dog. Looks like it's been shot," Ashley urged.

The dog walker gave a cry and tried to come inside. Ashley blocked her.

"I'm training to be a veterinarian," Trinity exclaimed angrily.

"Stay where I tell you until we clear the scene or I will arrest you." Ashley gently moved the injured animal farther away from the door so Mallory could join her. She and Mallory were both wearing vests, but Ashley wasn't happy to be teaming up with a pregnant woman. Frazer was probably going to kick her out of the program for this. Alex Parker would smother her in her sleep and no one would ever know.

But they needed to secure the scene and see if anyone was hurt.

The apartment was tidy but crammed full of knickknacks. No one in the bedroom, or bathroom. The bed was made and the bathroom had one of those walk-in showers designed for people with mobility issues.

An even stronger smell of blood hit her when she got to

the open-plan kitchen and living room where a woman sat slumped in a wheelchair, facing the window. Ashley's stomach took a sharp nosedive.

Susan Thomas's wrists and ankles had been bound to her wheelchair. Blood soaked every inch of her front. Both eyes had been removed.

Ashley checked for a pulse but it was obvious the woman was dead. Then she searched every possible hiding spot. The apartment was clear.

She and Mallory holstered their weapons and walked back to the entrance. Ashley bent down and slid her hands beneath the silky fur of the injured animal. It whimpered pitifully but made no move to resist as she picked it up, murmuring comforting words in its ear.

Outside the apartment she laid the dog on the carpet and watched the dog walker try to staunch the bleeding.

Mallory pulled her aside. "How the hell did they know where to find her?" She kept her hand on her weapon and her eyes on the corridor.

"Maybe they tracked her the same way Alex did. Or she trusted the information to someone close to her and they betrayed her."

The elevator dinged and both she and Mallory tensed. She let out a breath of relief as uniforms arrived, and held up her shield.

"Call Alex. Ask him to look for any traces that someone else went snooping wherever he did," she told Mallory. She'd do it herself but she was going to be busy here for the next little while. She strode forward to block the officers' path into the apartment. They needed to call CSU. The last thing this particular investigation needed was more cops trampling the crime scene. They bitched her out, but she held her ground and insisted they call in the detectives first.

"Scene is secure," she insisted. "Get people on all the entries and exits and start taking statements. See if there are any surveillance cameras on site."

The bulky officer looked like he wanted to shove her aside, but she held his stare and dared him to try it. Finally he backed down with a curse and turned away to radio dispatch.

Ashley let out a breath. Good thing she'd never cared much about being popular.

LUCAS RANDALL SNAPPED on latex gloves and stepped inside the small apartment wearing paper booties over his shoes. The smell of blood was thick as an abattoir and drove a nail into the back of his throat.

Jesus.

After he'd left Becca, he'd spent time with Mia and her parents, asking if she recognized the driver of the minivan—she hadn't. Talking with Mia, hearing her laugh at some of his stupid jokes had soothed the rage he felt toward Becca's mother. He couldn't wait to find that poor excuse of humanity. Not only was she a possible lead into the gang's gambling activities, there was another kid at risk.

After seeing Mia, he'd worked with the police sketch artist trying to piece together a semblance of an identikit photo for the tall skinny guy he'd seen by the front door. The results were less than ideal, and looked more like Ashley Chen than he wanted to admit.

He walked over to where the woman in question stood

talking to a tired-looking ME. The morgue was already overrun with bodies. He doubted anyone there had slept since the bombing. "Who's the victim?"

"Susan Thomas. Forty-five-year-old female. Suffered from MS. According to her dog walker she wasn't bedridden, but didn't like to leave her apartment."

Lucas eyed the bindings that held the victim in place. "Why are we here?"

Ashley indicated he follow her into the kitchen as the ME's assistants prepared to move the body onto a gurney.

"Mallory and I drew a blank on surveillance cameras, so we were canvassing the area to see if we could get any additional information on the people who ran the brothel. We started with the stores on the main street but were getting nowhere. I figured we should try the buildings overlooking the entrance, and that's when we found the victim."

He crossed his arms. "Okay. But why are we *still* here?" The FBI didn't investigate single victim homicides without good reason.

She pressed her lips together, and he knew he wasn't going to like whatever she had to say. She walked over to the blinds and held them open for him. From here there was a perfect view of the brothel below. Her voice dropped to a low murmur that he had to lean closer to hear.

"Susan Thomas is the person who called in the tip about Mia Stromberg. She's the one who got the one hundred thousand dollar reward."

Lucas exhaled sharply through his nose. "Do we know for sure that it was the Chinatown brothel people who killed her?"

"Well, her eyes were gouged out and tongue removed, and the woman probably choked to death on her own blood."

Ashley put a gloved fist on her hip. "The ME hasn't decided yet if the eyes were removed pre- or post-mortem, but I think it's safe to say this isn't your average homicide and is a hell of a coincidence under the circumstances."

Lucas's stomach lurched. He'd seen a lot over the years—Edmund Meacher's skanky basement had contained photographs and videos of violent rapes and murders—enough blood and gore and evil to last a lifetime. But this was chilling in its clinical precision. This hadn't been for personal gratification. This was sending a message—*talk to the cops and you're dead.*

"So, it's a warning." He shook his head. "No wonder no one's coming forward with information."

The dead woman was placed in the body bag, and there was a palpable sense of relief as she was rolled away.

He leaned close to Ashley's ear and tried not to notice the graceful line of her neck. It wasn't appropriate for a crime scene, but beat the hell out of thinking about the mutilated human being they'd just taken away. "How'd you know she was the tipster?"

"Alex Parker."

"He told you?" he asked in surprise.

The twist of her lips and narrowing of her gaze told him Alex's mistrust was mutual. "Mallory."

"And how did the bad guys know this was the snitch?"

A fine line formed between her brows. Her skin was smooth and flawless which probably accounted for why she looked so young. According to Bureau records she'd turned thirty on December 26th. Not that much younger than he was.

He hid his thoughts. He was standing at the scene of a gruesome murder, but the subtle scent of oranges on her skin and some weird internal chemistry made his pulse kick up anyway.

Obviously he'd worked too many murders.

"They either used the same methods Parker did, or they have someone on the inside."

"The name of the tipster wasn't released to most of the LEOs working this case. I didn't know it."

"Then it should be easy to narrow down who did know." Ashley shrugged one shoulder.

"What about Susan Thomas? Would she have told anyone?"

Her fingers moved restlessly. "She might, but I get the impression she didn't have many friends. The dog walker said there weren't any relatives. There was a husband, but he left when she was diagnosed."

So much for "in sickness and in health."

The dog walker would be the good looking blonde he'd passed in the hallway who was being comforted by a uniformed officer who looked like he'd won the lottery.

"Where's Mallory?"

"Staying with the evidence."

Lucas raised his brow in question.

"The bastards put a bullet in the woman's Golden Retriever. Rex is being operated on right now. Mallory is making sure the chain of evidence is maintained and we don't lose that bullet."

"The scumbags shot a dog?" He shook his head. Considering what else they'd done it was minor, but it spoke of sociopathy, a virulent disregard for anyone and anything that got in their way.

"I was hoping the woman had taken photographs." Ashley's expression turned pensive. "But we didn't find a computer or tablet. Her cell phone is missing."

"You think they took them?"

"Don't you?"

"Probably."

Ashley clenched her jaw. "Maybe she had a backup somewhere. We didn't find anything in the apartment but maybe she had a cloud service or dropbox. Someone needs to check into that ASAP."

He made a note on his phone. "You gonna tell Sloan why you were here?"

She raised one fine brow. God, she was pretty. "We were canvassing the neighborhood."

"Think she'll buy it?"

"I don't care." She straightened her spine. "Boston PD is in charge of this murder investigation although it's obviously connected to the brothel. They questioned Susan Thomas just after the explosion but she never mentioned seeing the kid or the reward. I've already told the lead detective what I know."

"Everything?"

"Everything I can." She gave another half shrug. Her cell buzzed to life. She answered and her eyes met his. "It's Mallory. She has the slug."

"How's the dog?"

A small smile touched her lips. "In recovery. He lost a lot of blood, but she thinks he's going to make it."

"That's good news." He spotted the detective in charge and went to talk to him to see if the guy had any leads or needed any additional resources. Ashley followed. When her cell buzzed to life again, at the same time as his, he knew it was bad news.

CHAPTER EIGHT

L UCAS FOLLOWED ASHLEY through the bullpen and headed to Sloan's office. He tapped on the door.

"Come in," she shouted.

Diego Fuentes was slouched in one of the chairs wearing the same clothes he'd worn yesterday. Sloan's eyes were bloodshot, her skin pale. Mayfield had a smirk on her face that spelled trouble for someone.

"Anything at the port?" Lucas asked.

"Not yet but containers are stacked three high. The Coast Guard took over searching some of the vessels." Sloan sounded defensive.

Lucas thought it was a wild goose chase, but what if it wasn't? What if the perps were holed up on that last ship left to be searched when the cops gave up and went home?

Giving up wasn't an option.

Sloan turned her attention to Ashley, who stood just behind Lucas. The look Sloan gave her could scorch earth.

"You interviewed the person who came forward with the information about Mia Stromberg? Even though one of the conditions of the reward was the guarantee of strict confidence? And now this person ends up dead?" The questions were clearly rhetorical and Ashley wisely kept her mouth shut. "Give me one good reason not to send you back to Quantico

120

with a letter of censure in your file regarding your inability to follow orders."

Ashley straightened and raised her chin. "We were canvassing locations that had a direct line of sight to the brothel entrance in the hopes someone had video or surveillance footage they hadn't shared with law enforcement." Her face betrayed no emotion.

He wouldn't have known she was lying if she hadn't already told him the truth. That was an eye-opening realization.

Fuentes sneered. "You just destroyed any chance of anyone else coming forward with more information about these thugs."

"In case you failed to notice, Agent Fuentes, *no one* is coming forward with information. No one. Period. That's one of the reasons we can't catch these people. The woman was already dead before I got there. You do comprehend how that makes it impossible for it to be my fault, right?" Ashley didn't back down and Lucas liked that about her. "I had nothing to do with her murder."

"The Strombergs already called me wanting answers," Mayfield interjected.

"As much as I feel for their situation the FBI does not answer to the Strombergs." Sloan gave Mayfield a hard stare. Her phone rang, and she glanced at the number. "Or the mayor, for that matter." She let the call go to voicemail. "Did you find any security footage?" Her implacable tone said she didn't believe the questioning had been random, but she let it drop. Ashley and Mallory had discovered a murder that was less than an hour old. That was good work even if she wasn't prepared to say so.

Ashley shook her head. "And none of the neighbors saw or

heard anything."

"I'm not surprised given the fact Susan Thomas had her tongue and eyes removed for tattling," Lucas commented wryly.

"Maybe they got in and out without attracting any notice? These guys sound like professional hit men." Fuentes shifted forward in his chair.

"And we're professional law enforcement officers," Sloan snapped. She was breathing heavily. "How did *they* discover her identity?"

"Either they traced the initial phone call or someone leaked the information," Lucas suggested.

"One of us?" Sloan frowned at the suggestion.

"Who else knew? Susan Thomas might have told someone close to her, but as she was the one with the most to lose, I doubt it." Lucas pushed away from the door but there was nowhere to go.

Sloan looked thoughtful. "Less than a dozen people between the FBI and the commissioner and the mayor's office actually knew Susan Thomas's name."

"Someone might have blabbed," Lucas insisted.

"Give me the names, I'll check 'em out," Fuentes offered.

Sloan shook her head. "No. I want you back at the port ASAP."

His mouth compressed into a thin line.

"I'll do it," Mayfield volunteered.

Sloan gave her a nod.

"They might have followed the money," Ashley said. "That's what I'd have done in their place. They know the possible sources for the payout—the Strombergs or the PD. They know the amount of money offered. It's possible

122

someone could have tracked it if they really knew what they were doing."

Lucas's eyebrows jacked. "That's some pretty heavy-duty hacking."

Sloan was uncharacteristically quiet.

Ashley shot him a glance. "My theory is they have a high level hacker on their team—someone competent and confident when negotiating the deep web. He's controlling the money and how they attract clients and hide their tracks."

"Is that an official *profile*?" Mayfield asked snidely.

He watched as Ashley clenched one of her fists. "We know they will use extreme violence to keep control. After Agata Maroulis escaped they punished her by public execution— maybe they feared the investigation into her death would lead us to them, so they rigged the brothel with explosives?" *Which it should have done.* "The next person to betray them to the authorities is murdered in the most heinous fashion. Now no one is going to come forward with information—not johns, not witnesses, not whoever supplied these people with pills or medical care." Ashley's expression was fierce. "This gang is much more ruthless, more organized and well established than the feds first thought, but way better at concealing their crimes and their presence than most organizations that size. Hence, on top of being extremely secretive and ruthless, they also have a highly trained hacker on their team. We could use that against them. Did you get into Mae Kwon's cell phone yet?"

Sloan shook her head.

"You need to make *that* a priority and put a team of people on it," Ashley's eyes shifted to Fuentes, "while you guys continue searching the port."

Sloan stared at Ashley like an Army general on a battlefield. After a long pause she finally spoke. "You're the one who turned up the direct connection to the Maroulis case and found the image of the driver, correct?"

Ashley's vertebrae seemed to snap into line. "Yes, ma'am."

"Okay, Chen." Sloan checked her watch. "We already have our cybercrime team looking at the cellphone and they think they're almost there with unlocking it. We heard from a consultant who works with Lincoln Frazer—Alex Parker, whom I believe you know?"

Ashley nodded.

"He identified four more possible brothel locations from Mae Kwon's phone records. The properties were raided. All were empty of girls and clients and wiped down as clean as the inside of an OR."

Dammit. They'd moved too slowly. These people had dismantled the entire organization but he doubted they'd closed it down. They'd probably moved it sideways—new locations, new websites, new cell phones.

"You want to prove yourself?" Sloan leaned over her desk toward the younger agent. "You find out how these people discovered the name and address of Susan Thomas. But if you fail," she warned, "you'll receive that letter of censure for your file. Do you understand?"

Ashley stared straight ahead. "Yes, ma'am."

Lucas couldn't tell if she was pleased or pissed. Maybe both. She'd worked hard and got results, but still had the most to lose.

Sloan's phone rang. "Okay, boys and girls. Time for another awkward meeting with SAC Salinger, telling him we're no further forward than we were twenty-four hours ago. Then I can call my husband back and pretend he wasn't calling me for an update on the case for that moron Everett." She dragged a hand through her gray-blonde hair. "Get out of here and get me some clues as to where these dirtbags are hiding." Before he could take a step she snapped. "Agent Randall, walk me out."

"Yes, ma'am."

Ashley left quickly and he watched her go. Why didn't Alex trust her? Was it the hacking thing? Did he know more than he was letting on? Or was the guy nervous because her skills were similar to his own?

Lucas followed Sloan out of her office. She kept her voice low.

"How's the kid?" she asked.

"Beginning to open up a little. She confirmed the driver of Agata Maroulis's minivan was the same person who took her from her home." He cleared his throat. "She says her mother gave her to him in exchange for canceling a gambling debt." They walked through the bullpen where only a smattering of agents were present, all busy with their heads down. Other advisers and analysts were working on different parts of the case and feeding that information into LEEP—the Law Enforcement Enterprise Portal—which allowed the task force to share and coordinate information at a fast pace.

"I managed to get some information on why she was held in a room alone," he murmured.

Sloan caught his eye. "Select customers?"

He nodded. "I squeezed out a couple tidbits about her family that I'm going to feed into the system. I want permission to ask Agent Chen or Agent Rooney to assist me in running searches to track down the mother. She might be an avenue for more information on the gambling aspect of this organization—especially when she faces charges of child abandonment and child sex trafficking."

"Negative on involving a third party." Sloan's eyes were sharp as she scanned the office before they hit the stairwell. "I don't like the fact the informant turned up dead. I don't like that at all. The information you and I share stays closed down. No one else is to know."

Damn. Lucas wasn't a total klutz around a computer but he knew his limits. He should have spent more time hanging around the freaks and geeks in high school, rather than the jocks.

Sloan looked like she wanted to say something else but wasn't sure how to proceed. Considering how blunt the woman usually was, Lucas didn't know what that signified.

"What?" he prompted.

"I have a bad feeling about this, Lucas." Her mouth twisted. "The idea of them getting hold of that kid again…"

"They aren't going to get their hands on her again."

Sloan paused on the stairs. "What do you think of Agent Chen?"

Uh oh. "She's done great work on this case. She's got a sharp brain, she's dedicated, driven." *Alex Parker doesn't trust her. And she kisses like sin.*

"She's very attractive," Sloan said carefully.

He kept his expression neutral and said nothing.

Her gaze didn't shy away from his. "Remember what I said about the kid."

He forced himself not to react to having his integrity insulted. "Trust no one. Got it."

"Not even pretty agents eager to help."

"Nor people who we've worked with for years," he added.

Sloan's expression pinched. "Nor husbands who're probably going to leave their wives for someone who occasionally turns up to dinner."

Shit. "Like I told you. I've got it."

BY MIDNIGHT ASHLEY'S eyes were gritty from staring at her screen for too long.

Mallory had gone to check on the injured dog before heading back to the hotel under strict orders from the boss to take it easy. Frazer was making noises about pulling them both, but as Ashley had pointed out, not only were the fugitives still at large, they hadn't even been IDed yet.

Frazer had relented for now but Ashley didn't think it would last long. God knew BAU-4 had its own list of monsters to hunt.

She hadn't told him about Sloan's threat of a letter of censure. She wanted to prove herself without her boss making a stink—and he would make a stink. Few people messed with Lincoln Frazer or his unit and came out unscathed.

Ashley was convinced these guys were so criminally sophisticated they had their own computer analyst. And if they did, she wanted to know the caliber of hacker they were dealing with. She dragged her fingers through her hair and sipped on her eightieth coffee of the day.

The advantage of working for the feds meant a warrant had been easily obtained and the bank had been only too eager to cooperate in the event someone had broken into their system. She'd found the transaction easily enough—one hundred thousand dollars had been deposited into Ms. Susan

Thomas's checking account yesterday. The bank's system was double encrypted, so Ashley doubted the perps had been able to access the records directly. If they could, why bother trafficking sex slaves when they could just steal people's money at will?

But any transaction over ten thousand dollars automatically generated a Currency Transaction Record, or CTR, that was sent to the Financial Crimes Enforcement Network "FinCEN." Tax and other customer information was stored within that file and could be used to identify the individuals both sending and receiving the money. She suspected the Asian gang either had an informant at FinCEN, or had intercepted the data as it passed between the bank and FinCEN, or they'd figured out a way to access those files by hacking FinCEN itself.

The implications were huge.

The gray market for zeros—or software vulnerabilities— was still a controversial business. Many argued that governments paying for zeroes had driven up the price of ferreting out software flaws. Others argued that just because "official" organizations and governments bought the vulnerabilities it didn't mean they weren't used for nefarious purposes. The bottom line was if governments didn't buy the software, black hat hackers would. The industry was established now, and it wasn't going away anytime soon.

Ashley had checked various forums and websites for mention of a vulnerability in the operating system FinCEN used but had come up short. Ashley didn't have the time or resources to look for a weakness in the source code itself, but she knew someone who did. She didn't want to call him. She checked her watch and dialed anyway. Parker would be working all hours to plug the holes in his client's security.

"Parker," he answered before the first ring completed.

"It's Agent Ch-Chen." She silently cursed her stumble. He already knew who it was. "I hope you don't mind me calling so late. Agent Rooney said you were working—"

"What can I do for you, Agent Chen?" His tone was cool as liquid Nitrogen.

"A woman was killed today. She's the same person who called in the information about Mia Stromberg being in the Chinatown brothel—"

"Mal told me about it. It appears we're now the proud owners of a Golden Retriever named Rex."

"You're adopting him?" A moment of jealousy slid through her—which was crazy. What would she do with a dog?

"Assuming no family members come forward to claim him," said Parker. "What do you need?"

She heard voices in the background. Someone swearing loudly. "We're trying to figure out how the bad guys tracked down Susan Thomas." She looked around the empty room. It was a very lonely "we."

"The bank security seems solid from the outside," she said, "and it's possible someone inside the investigation leaked the information on purpose or accidentally." The most successful hacks generally involved a degree of social engineering. "But the people directly involved were questioned, and they all swear they didn't give out the information to anyone they didn't know personally."

"People lie." The words were razor sharp. He didn't trust her. She didn't trust him back. But she needed him.

Sweat trickled down her back and made the silk of her

shirt stick to her skin. "There's another potential source for the information."

"The phone company?"

Was that how he'd done it?

"Possible, but there were over ten thousand calls to that hotline so I'm not sure how they'd narrow down the right caller from that data alone." She hated how nervous this man made her. "Look, I don't have any proof but I have this lingering idea they have a hacker on their team. A good one." She cleared her throat. "So I was, er, wondering about FinCEN security."

The silence was so thick that at first she thought she'd lost him. She checked the connection and it was still good. "Have you heard about any zeroes that might pertain to the CRT system? I—"

"I'll get back to you," he said, and hung up.

Ashley stared at her cell. God, the guy was rude, suspicious. Annoying. Secretive. She knew what Parker was thinking. A zero like that would be worth millions on the black market, and as he wasn't convinced she wasn't some mole the communists had planted long ago, he wasn't about to give her that kind of information. Her shoulders slumped as she stared at her screen. She'd hit a wall and she was exhausted. She shoved her laptop into its case and pulled on her jacket. Parker had probably just diverted half his team to work on the FinCEN system. He had contracts with many of the government branches and a flaw in one was a potential flaw in them all.

Fine. Let him work through the night. She needed her sleep anyway.

She slipped into her winter jacket. Purposely relaxed her

jaw and stretched her neck to the side. By morning he'd hopefully tell her if it was possible for a hacker to get a name and address from FinCEN. That's why he got paid the big bucks and she was on a government salary.

She headed out. The overhead lights were turned out in the bullpen and there was no one around. She adjusted her laptop bag over one shoulder and made sure her sidearm was within easy reach of her dominant hand. Outside, the cold air made her breath fog and she shivered. She headed toward the hotel, keeping a sharp eye on her surroundings. Up ahead she noticed a man turn right. The man looked a lot like Lucas Randall.

Her pulse raced a little faster. What was he doing?

She got to the side road where he'd turned off and looked down the narrow street. He glanced backwards as if making sure no one was following him. It *was* Lucas. He didn't see her and she didn't call out to get his attention.

There were viable reasons for an FBI agent to be creeping around the streets of Boston at night, most of them none of her business. A terrible thought entered her brain, something she didn't want to consider, and yet, now the idea had entered her head she couldn't shake it off. What if Lucas was feeding the fugitives information?

Mallory and Alex both trusted the guy—more than they trusted her. But Mallory also said he was hiding something, and she should know given their shared history. He'd miraculously survived an explosion that had brought down an entire block. He'd been privy to SSA Sloan's confidences. He'd denied knowing Susan Thomas's name but that didn't mean he was telling the truth. Had he been threatened? Compromised? Bribed?

Ashley waited for him to dip around the corner, hesitated for a few moments and then reluctantly followed.

Her attraction to him was inconvenient and distracting, and betraying the FBI to these monsters would kill that attraction stone dead. But she didn't want it to be true. She didn't want to be such a lousy judge of character that she'd fallen for a guy who was rotten at the core. She didn't want to be attracted to a man who cashed in on the trafficking of innocents.

Her mouth went dry as she cautiously hugged the shadows. She needed to know for sure that he hadn't sold out; she needed to know for certain that his idea of service was rooted in idealism and duty, not corruption and lies. She needed to know.

LUCAS'S EVASION SKILLS had been honed in the mean streets of Afghanistan, fighting in an arena where friend looked exactly the same as foe. It wasn't even the faint sound of footsteps that triggered the feeling of danger, it was that sixth sense that told him he was being hunted. He darted down the nearest alley, removing his SIG from its holster as he moved. Ever since the explosion he'd been paranoid about inadvertently leading someone to Becca. He moved quickly but silently, cutting through a narrow alley to another street. Sure enough, the muted footsteps tracked his movements.

He headed toward the hotel and then doubled back, sprinting, and coming up behind the lone figure who'd been shadowing him.

A woman. Five ten. One fifty.

He snagged a wrist and twisted it high behind her back and pushed her against the brick wall. She cried out in a voice he immediately recognized and countered with a strong back kick which, had it connected, would have taken out his crown jewels.

He twisted away and she struck a glancing blow off his thigh.

"Ashley?" He loosened his grip and spun her around.

"Lucas! What the hell? You scared the crap out of me." She swallowed loudly, but wouldn't quite meet his gaze. A distant streetlight cast her face in gold. Alex's warning came back to him in a flash.

He pocketed his SIG and held her against the wall with one wrist pinned above her head. He took her other hand and added it to the first, cuffing both her wrists with his much larger hand. He was well aware that as a federal agent she could do him a lot of damage. Defensive tactics training at Quantico was akin to gladiator school, where only the strong and vicious survived.

"What are you doing here?" he asked.

"If this is your idea of how to chat up women, no wonder you don't date much." She tried to joke but he wasn't buying it. The pulse at the base of her throat was beating out a military tattoo. The strain in her voice belonged to fear.

"Why are you following me?" he asked insistently.

Her jaw clenched and her expression turned mutinous. "I left work and saw you acting suspiciously so I decided to see what you were up to."

"Up to?" He frowned at her. He wasn't about to reveal that the ATF agent guarding Becca had called to say the girl was asking for him. He wasn't even going to think about going to the hospital now.

"Why?" He tightened his grip and tried to ignore the feel of her body brushing against his.

"To see where you were going," she bit out. "To see if you met anyone."

"Why is that any of your business?" Then the implications sank in. "You thought I was passing on information about this investigation? Betraying the people I work with, betraying my oath of service?"

She jerked against his grasp, sending waves of lust shimmering through his body. He ignored the lust.

"Fine. Yes," she snapped. "Someone could be passing on vital information, enabling the scumbags to keep one step ahead of us. You survived the explosion, they survived the explosion. You saw their faces but can't identify them. You are in a position to discover the name of the informant who reported seeing Mia taken into the brothel. You keep disappearing—"

He stared in disbelief. "What motive would I have?"

She tried to shrug, which just succeeded in pushing her breasts against his chest and short-circuiting his brain. The fact she was suspicious of him made him rethink his suspicions of her.

"They might have threatened your family."

"My family knows the risks associated with my job and theirs. They take precautions."

"Money?" she stated, but she looked less sure of herself now.

"I have money."

"Lots of money," she reiterated.

He leaned down so he could whisper in her ear without

anyone overhearing. "My grandfather was a West Virginian coal baron. I have more money than I can spend in three lifetimes. But even if I didn't have a dime, I would never sell out my colleagues. Never." He regarded her with disgust.

Uncertainty flashed in her eyes. Then the stubbornness returned. "Then why were you acting so suspiciously?"

"You mean making sure I wasn't followed back to my hotel? The only adult in this whole fiasco who got a good look at the fugitives' faces?"

Her expression faltered, and her eyes went wide. "Shit. You're right. I'm sorry I leapt to conclusions."

She shivered beneath him. Was she cold? She didn't look cold. From the warm skin of her wrists and fast beat of her pulse she didn't feel cold.

"You didn't have to jump me," she whispered.

His blood heated. The feel of her body so close to his meant he very much wanted to jump her despite the fact they were in a dingy alley. "I heard someone following me and decided to see who it was."

"I need to work on my surveillance skills, but I'm not sorry I followed you." That spark of awareness flashed between them. The attraction they'd both been trying hard to ignore. "Part of me hoped you were dirty so I wouldn't keep remembering that kiss."

He looked into those exotically tilted eyes and became aware that he still held Ashley Chen's arms stretched over her head and his body was pressed firmly against hers. The contrast between the hotness of her gaze and the coldness of the brick wall behind her, made him want to press even closer.

Her breath was choppy. Anger and suspicion had morphed into physical awareness and passionate desire.

Yesterday, she'd kissed him. It was only fair to return the favor.

He dipped his head, captured her lips, and she opened her mouth with a groan. It was like diving into sin and temptation. Heat and pleasure flared between them and made the frigidity of the night, the damp dirtiness of the alley, and the grim reality of the case, all disappear.

Her body rose to meet his and he dove deeper, tangling his tongue with hers, feeling the fervor of her response. He didn't let go of her wrists, but his other hand tugged her silky shirt out of her pants so he could reach inside and cup those perfect breasts.

Lace scraped his palm and made him instantly rock hard. He found her nipple through the material, rolled the velvet nub against the scratchy lace and held her up when her knees gave out. He slipped his thigh between hers, then released her mouth and undid the buttons of her shirt with one hand, holding her gaze, still not letting go of her wrists. There was something forbidden about this. Something powerful about having this woman at his mercy.

She shivered as the night air touched her skin, but she didn't protest. Her eyes glittered with want. When the buttons were undone he spread the material wide and his mouth went dry. Black lingerie offered her breasts up to his gaze. He dragged down the lacy edge to expose one cherry tip.

"Not much going on in the chest department, I'm afraid." Her voice held an edge of apology.

How could someone who looked like her have even a sliver of insecurity about her own beauty?

His eyes shot to hers. "You're kidding, right?" He bent down to take her nipple in his mouth and felt her knees buckle again. He let go of her wrists and hitched her up.

She wrapped her long legs around his waist.

"Hold on tight," he ordered.

He feasted on her pretty breasts, showing her exactly what she did to him. Her fingers sank into his hair and tugged him away. Her lips found his, wet and wild. He pinned her against the wall and rubbed his erection against her center. She groaned, the sound a vibration that passed between them like a caress.

This was crazy. They should not be doing this, but after the hell of the last few days he wanted to experience something that had nothing to do with death or depravity.

He lowered her feet to the ground and undid the button on her pants. Eased down her zipper. He watched her eyes the entire time, but saw no objection. They were in a public place and if they got caught they'd both get fired. He slid one finger inside her and she squeezed him, gasping with pleasure. He added another, sliding them in and out, finding the spot that had her eyes closing and her arms shaking as she held on to him.

"I want to be inside you so badly, Ash."

She made a sound that was a cross between a plea and a groan.

"But I don't have a condom."

"I don't either." Frustration strangled her voice.

He'd have given everything he had to slide inside her regardless of good sense, but he wasn't ruled by lust. He took her hand, and held it over her head again, and added the other so she was once again pinned to the wall, shirt unbuttoned, half undressed. She shivered as she looked at him, eyes huge and luminous as he very slowly, very deliberately ran the tip of his finger over her lips, throat, collarbone. Over the turgid peak of one nipple, then down her lean rib cage. He circled her soft navel before following the smooth skin all the way back down to her black lace panties. She gasped as he curled two fingers inside her.

He kissed the side of her mouth, wanting to see her face when she tipped over the edge. He cupped his palm over her mound, used his thigh to press his hand deeper inside her.

"Oh, God. I should w-warn you." Her breath was choppy and her voice shook. "I'm l-loud."

"Loud?" He scraped his teeth over her ear lobe.

"When I come. I'm really lou—"

He swallowed her scream, dragging out her orgasm until she collapsed limply against him. And he had to hold himself very still, controlling his breathing while his heart rate slowed and blood diverted to other parts of his body.

Then he gently put her back together, pulling up her zipper, buttoning her pants, blouse. He gave up trying to tuck in her shirt, but straightened her jacket and coat, pulled them together to help combat the sudden chill in the air. He kept his eyes locked on hers the entire time before backing away a step.

She frowned. "But you didn't—"

"It doesn't matter." The need to come was still pounding through his bloodstream, but his brain was back in control.

She watched him for a long time, trying to read him in the darkness. "We shouldn't have done that. It was a mistake."

"It was what we both needed." He touched her cheek. "I'm not going to tell anyone. I'd actually like to do it again one day. Maybe properly, in a bed with no time limit."

Her eyes were huge and he laughed at her surprise.

"I like you, Ashley, or haven't you figured that out yet?"

Fear entered her gaze and she turned her cheek away from his touch. "Please don't."

"Please don't what?" he asked. "Like you? You think I kiss every woman I come across in the street?"

Ashley sent him a disdainful glare. "If either of us had had a condom you'd have gotten your reward for that kiss, and you know it."

He was so close he could still smell traces of her arousal and it twisted his good sense. "I had my reward, sweetheart. Watching you lose it isn't something I'm going to forget anytime soon."

Her cheeks darkened, but her eyes took on a frosty glare.

"Maybe it's your warm and fuzzy personality that makes me like you so much." He was hoping for a smile but her expression had closed up.

"Don't be naive, Lucas. You don't have to like someone to fuck them," she snapped.

Her attempt to push him away didn't surprise him, but it did make him angry. "You're right. I wouldn't have to like you to fuck you, but God help me, I do." He leaned closer. "And after feeling you come all over my fingers I *really* want to fuck you. So keep that in mind next time you follow me down a back alley at midnight."

She looked a little shell-shocked at his warning and he'd been less than his usual gentlemanly self. She jerked out of his hold and pushed away from the wall as if she'd just become aware of her surroundings.

"I'll walk you back to the hotel."

She shook her head in refusal. "Forget it. I can look after myself." Then she strode off without a backward glance. He tailed her from a discreet distance and wondered why the hell he was attracted to such a difficult woman. He followed her brisk, angry footsteps down the road and smiled grimly. Whatever the reason, he'd put up with a lot more just to taste that mouth again.

CHAPTER NINE

A SHLEY'S MOOD HAD been lousy since last night, when she'd been ready to let Lucas Randall screw her against a brick wall. Despite the embarrassing encounter her attraction to the man was growing rather than diminishing. He'd been so fucking *noble* about the whole thing. The fact they'd both endangered their careers for that fleeting moment of passion, horrified her.

And thrilled her.

Which appalled her.

Her life was so staid. So self-contained. So *boring*.

It had to be.

This unexpected connection to Lucas Randall had side-swiped her and stolen her usually impenetrable good sense. Her life wasn't a game. She'd given into her selfish desires once before and people had died. She couldn't go through that again. She wouldn't survive a second time.

She tapped her pen on her pad of paper and forced herself to take a slow breath. There was no reason to think her enemies were still looking for her. They believed she died years ago. It was just this case that made her antsy.

She stifled a yawn as her sleepless night caught up with her. Alex Parker wasn't returning her calls about the possibility of someone penetrating FinCEN's online security. ASAC

Frazer was making noises about pulling her and Mallory off the case, and time was running out. The last thing she needed after working so hard was a letter of censure in her file. She hadn't even finished her probation with the BAU yet.

Mallory made a noise from across the table.

"What?" Ashley asked, happy to be distracted from her whirling thoughts. As much as she tried not to like the other woman it was proving impossible in close quarters.

Mallory looked up from her laptop. "I asked Alex to look into the tipoff to the hotline about the fugitives being seen near the port."

The authorities had just about completed the search of Conley Terminal. It wasn't looking hopeful. "And…?"

"It came from a burner cell in Chinatown."

Ashley considered the implications. "It's not totally implausible. Someone might have needed privacy to make the call and didn't want their identity known for fear of reprisal—I mean, look what happened to Susan Thomas." The image of the woman's brutalized body flashed through her mind. Ashley had seen more violent death before her seventeenth birthday than most people saw in a hundred lifetimes, but that murder had been particularly grisly. She knew from experience that the only thing that dulled the horror was time.

"True, but the only people I know who carry burners usually have something to hide." Mallory pushed her chair away from the table and climbed to her feet. "The owner of that particular burner just turned it on again. Alex got a hit on the location. The Sun Garden restaurant in Chinatown."

Ashley grabbed her jacket. "You hungry for Chinese food?"

"Starving." Mallory pocketed her cell and checked her

sidearm, her secondary weapon and the Taser she habitually carried.

They headed to the door and opened it, coming to an abrupt halt when they found Lucas Randall on the other side.

Blood rushed to Ashley's cheeks.

"Where are you two going?" He eyed her warily like she was going to bite him. She almost groaned aloud as she remembered she'd told him it was okay to fuck her but he wasn't allowed to like her. She sounded like some sort of morally depraved sex addict, when all she really wanted was to keep him safe.

"Chinatown." Mallory answered when Ashley found herself mute.

"You have a lead?" His gaze sharpened.

"Yup. The cell phone used to make the tipoff about the fugitives being seen in the port area just went live in a local restaurant. We're going to check it out. See if we can eyeball the caller."

Lucas folded his arms across his chest and stared down at Mallory. "And your plan is to what exactly? Walk in and arrest anyone carrying a cell phone? For being a Good Samaritan? Sloan will freak."

Mallory frowned. "I'll get Alex to call the number when we get there. See if anyone answers. At the very least we can photograph the person. If he's genuine he'll never know we checked him out. If he's a bad guy he could lead us straight to the fugitives."

"Does Alex know what you're planning to do? Or Frazer?"

"I need to do my job, Lucas." Mallory put her hands on her hips when Lucas planted his arm solidly against the doorjamb.

"Last time I checked, you were assigned desk duty."

"So...what?" Mallory asked. "I'm supposed to sit here and run ViCAP searches rather than act on time sensitive intel when the Bureau is stretched thin? Send Ashley in alone? That isn't gonna happen."

Lucas looked unmoved by her speech.

Mallory's shoulders slumped. "Do you have a spare emery board so I can file my nails after I finish my typing?"

He smiled at her. "I've known you too long to let you manipulate me with a pity party."

She pulled a face at him. "So what's your idea? Give it to Boston PD?"

"Agent Chen." He turned and addressed her directly. Ashley's mouth felt so dry it was as if she'd swallowed sand. "I hear there's a really good Chinese restaurant in the area and I'm hungry. Would you like to join me for lunch?"

She forced her voice to remain steady. "They'll make you as a fed a mile away."

"We'll stop by the hotel and change."

"You'll still look like a fed," Mallory muttered, but it was the same for her, too. Not many agents could blend into that district. It was an advantage Ashley would happily exploit.

"I'll pretend to be Agent Chen's boyfriend taking her to lunch." The look in Lucas's eyes spelled trouble.

Mallory rolled her eyes. "Then you'd better start acting like a love-struck fool and call her by her first name."

A dimple appeared next to his mouth. Ashley remembered that mouth on her breast and felt a corresponding tingle at the apex of her thighs. Despite the fact they were at work, she wanted him again. From the light in his eyes, he knew it, too.

"I can do that. Ashley." His voice grew husky, sending

shivers of something sensual shooting through her.

This was a terrible idea.

He turned back to Mallory. "We'll call when we get there and Alex can ping the phone."

"Fine." Mallory pulled off her jacket and tossed it on the back of her chair. Clearly she wasn't happy, but Lucas was correct about her officially being on desk duty. Frazer hadn't been pleased they'd only narrowly missed encountering a murderer yesterday. Ashley should have been the one to tell Mallory she couldn't go on the op, but it was hard to hold another woman back, especially on a case as emotionally evocative as this one.

Mallory scrubbed her fingers through her short hair and sat back down at the table. "Do me a favor?"

"Anything." Lucas smiled and Ashley felt a "ping" go off under her ribcage like a pinball having a good time.

"Don't think you're weaseling out of my bad books that easily." Mallory eyed him sternly. "But bring me back something to eat?"

"You got it." He pushed away from the doorframe and let Ashley lead the way.

"Any luck getting an ID on the minivan driver?" he asked, all work.

Her heart raced, but Lucas seemed unperturbed by their midnight encounter. She needed to put it behind her too. She needed to forget they'd almost had sex.

"I ran the image through the DOJ's NGI, DoD's ABIS and DHS's IDENT databases using Interoperability. They all came back with nothing. I'm going to contact Interpol next." She was happy to concentrate on the case. "I'm still looking into how they found out about Susan Thomas but Alex Parker isn't returning my calls. In case you hadn't realized it yet, he's not my biggest fan."

He grunted and changed the subject. "Did anyone find out anything useful about the victims who've been identified so far?"

"Mallory is looking into them, but hasn't found any linkage. I suspect a lot of them were runaways or lured from foreign countries, and the chance of having their DNA in the system is minimal."

His expression was angry. "If you come up with any connections to casinos let me know."

"Okay." She drew the word out. "We started to get some IDs on the johns photographed in the hours leading up to the raid. Agent Mayfield was compiling the list and there's a meeting this afternoon on the best way to approach them and which interview technique to employ. Mallory agreed to sit in on the meeting to help devise tactics." She checked her watch. "What did you get up to this morning?"

"Nothing much."

"You're acting suspicious again," she noted dryly.

"There's nothing to tell." Lucas hit the elevator button and they climbed inside. They stood on opposite sides of the car staring at one another. They both knew what had happened the last time she thought he was acting suspiciously.

She decided to push it. She wanted him to trust her. "Mallory said you had a lousy poker face."

He hiked one brow and indicated she go first when the doors opened on the ground floor.

"She thinks someone else survived that explosion." She spoke so quietly the words barely left her mouth.

"Mallory's wrong." He tilted his head and gave her a cool

stare that made the hair on her nape tingle.

Damn. "Now I wish I hadn't said anything."

He held the door for her and hailed a cab. She got in and crossed her legs, ultra aware of the firm line of his jaw and the flintiness of his gaze. He didn't say anything and within two minutes they were back at their hotel and heading to the eighth floor. For some reason, she couldn't stop thinking that the last time they'd traveled this exact same route, the journey had ended in a red-hot kiss. Now Lucas had become remote and unapproachable.

Which was exactly how she wanted it, she reminded herself.

"If you have a vest, wear it," he tossed over his shoulder as she got to her door. He didn't stop and she watched him walk away with a familiar sense of isolation closing in around her.

Since when did she care?

Irritated with herself, she went inside, unzipped her pants and laid them on the side chair. She pulled on a pair of tight fitting jeans and tucked in her blouse. She eyed her Kevlar vest. It was cumbersome and annoying but she had no idea what she was walking into. Blowing out a breath, she removed her shoulder holster, pulled on the vest and fitted a holster to her belt. Over that she pulled a large white roll-neck sweater that came down to mid-thigh, and grabbed a leather jacket that was long enough to cover the bulge of her weapon. She put her creds in her inside pocket, pulled on tall boots and slung a purse across her shoulders. She was back in the hallway just as Lucas came out of his room, wearing jeans, sneakers, a navy T-shirt and a gray hoodie.

His T-shirt clung to hard pecs and hinted at six-pack abs.

"Where's your vest?" she asked, pretending her voice

hadn't squeaked.

"I don't have anything that'll hide it except my raid jacket. Not sure that's appropriate for undercover reconnaissance."

She hit the elevator call button. She didn't know if he was a sexist ass for telling her to wear hers, or just a good agent looking out for a colleague.

The Kevlar dug into her waist. "Can you tell I'm wearing mine?" she asked nervously.

He ran his gaze slowly down her front. Hot brown eyes rose to meet hers. "Nope."

The memory of last night hung in the air between them. She blanked her face to hide her arousal. She didn't know the last time a man had rattled her this much. Maybe in college? When she'd started to fall in love, and had walked away before anyone else got hurt.

"Where did you do your training?" he asked. The elevator was moving at turtle speed.

His curiosity about her life was a little unnerving. "Denver, Minneapolis and a short stint in New York." The latter had fed her addiction to shopping, but hadn't helped her fear of the ocean.

"Enjoy it?"

Keep it about work and things will be fine. "Good computer people are at a premium within the Bureau so I was always busy. I like busy."

"That's why I keep hounding Alex for help. What's wrong with the Bureau? Why can't we attract more computer geeks?"

They hit the lobby and started moving through crowds of people lined up to check in. Looked like the tractor convention had left town.

She skirted around a group of women with suitcases. "The

really good kids get headhunted in high school. And a lot of the brilliant ones don't even bother attending college or getting a degree, which means they can't apply to the FBI as agents."

His brows lifted in question.

"The brilliant ones already know more than most professors about certain aspects of computing."

"Hacking." Disdain rang through his tone.

"Not just hacking." It was easy to be dismissive when you didn't understand the mindset. "And not all hackers are bad." She shrugged. "It's not that much different from playing with Legos to start with, although 'hackers' are generally more concerned with looking for flaws in a design system than building something from scratch." They walked out the main door and south along the street. "It often starts when they're kids trying to figure something out. It's a game. A puzzle. Even those who do crazy things like try to hack the NSA—they don't usually believe they can get in."

He looked skeptical. "Were you a hacker?"

She held the door for a family. "I played around on the net."

"That's a non-answer."

"Funny," she said sharply. "I thought I passed my background tests and polygraphs during my interview."

Her background was impeccably crafted and she knew it so well it had become more like the truth than her complicated and thorny reality. Hypnosis and hours of practice had enabled her to nail those tests. That and the fact she believed in herself and her reasons for joining the FBI.

The fact she'd lied would only be a problem if she was ever caught.

"You went to college—does that mean you aren't that good at computing?" he asked wryly.

"I guess I left myself open for that one." She gave him a reluctant smile as they hit the sidewalk. The frigid breeze made her hair dance in her face and Ashley wished she'd packed a hat and gloves. "My dad was in the tech industry and always tried to impart the importance of education and qualifications. He taught me code as soon as I could write. Computing became second nature."

"Was? He's not around anymore?"

"My parents died in a car wreck when I was fifteen." Ashley swallowed the lump of grief that always accompanied thoughts of her mom and dad. The more she'd looked into their deaths, the more she was certain it hadn't been an accident.

Lucas's eyes changed, grew somber. "I'm sorry."

She nodded abruptly and turned away. She didn't like lying, which was just one reason she didn't like talking about herself. But the truth was dangerous on so many levels—a good reminder why she couldn't afford to get close to anyone. Being lonely was nothing compared to being responsible for someone's death.

"So you could have made a name for yourself in cybersecurity. Instead you joined the Bureau. Why?"

"Do I get to play twenty questions when you're done?"

His smile was pure male confidence. "My life is an open book. Tell me why you joined the Bureau and you can ask me anything."

"I wanted to make a difference for my country. To fight for justice." She shrugged. "I wanted legitimacy."

He watched her for a moment as if gauging her answer.

Maybe it was too honest. Maybe he thought her reasons were naive, but she wasn't the sort to go to war, and she didn't want to walk the beat. Joining the FBI offered her the best chance of putting her skill set to work in a constructive way.

"How do you want to play this?" she asked as they got closer to Chinatown.

He slung his arm around her shoulders and she froze as he tucked her close against his side. He whispered into her hair. "Just a man taking his girlfriend to lunch. We can sit and eat and scope out the joint. Take some photos and see if Alex can ping the cell. If the signal is nearby we'll try and follow it. If it isn't we can go over the case."

It sounded like a reasonable plan but Lucas's body felt way too good pressed against her side.

"Hey." He squeezed. "Relax and pretend you like me."

She gave him the side-eye because he was openly referring to their encounter last night, which she was trying to pretend never happened. "I like you just fine, Lucas. I just don't *want* to like you."

His lips curled. "I don't even know what to think of that statement. Good thing I have a healthy ego."

"There's definitely nothing wrong with your ego," she muttered.

His grin was the wrong side of dirty. Why she found that so endearing she didn't know. "I should put in a complaint for sexual harassment."

"Hey, you're right." His voice grew serious. "I crossed a line last night. If you're not comfortable doing this—"

"*We*," she emphasized. "*We* crossed a line. I was definitely a willing participant. If I hadn't been, you'd be sporting bruises in some key locations." She already had too much deception in her life to pretend otherwise. She'd already gotten more out of it than he had, especially when she'd been such a bitch afterward.

Determined to play her part, she reached over to stroke his fingers where they rested on her arm. "This isn't a bad plan, though the locals are bound to be suspicious of strangers."

Their eyes met and they both swallowed and looked away. Trying to dispel the tension, she glanced around. "At least there isn't anyone following us."

He hugged her again before letting her go and taking her hand. "I'm being overly cautious. I guess that's what happens when someone tries to blow you up."

"Paranoia can be good," she said carefully. It was how she lived her life.

They kept walking, weaving through people on their lunch break. Holding hands felt strange and unusual. Way too romantic for a woman like her. She'd reduced the romance in her life to occasional sweaty one-night stands and cool *sayonaras*. If she needed dinner and a movie she went alone, if she wanted flowers she bought them.

Maybe hot kisses against cold damp walls weren't so out of character after all.

"So, where'd you grow up, Ash? Mind if I call you Ash?"

No one except her immediate family had ever given her a nickname, but she kept her tone dry. "Well, as we're dating…" She looked up and met his gaze. Those eyes of his were an intense, deep brown. Hers were black as charcoal, but his were a rich, vibrant chestnut. She cleared her throat trying to arrange her thoughts. "After my parents died I lived with my godmother on Long Island. She passed away a couple of years ago."

"I'm sorry." His fingers clasped hers tighter.

There was something so appealing about nice manners and genuine concern, especially when wrapped up in a package of large, sexy alpha male. She hadn't realized she was susceptible to that kind of allure.

"There's no one else? No siblings?" he asked.

"They're all gone." The breeze picked up. A good excuse for the fact her eyes were watering. "What about you?"

"Three older sisters who're all married with kids." His eyes scanned every face they passed. "The good news is that keeps my parents off my back about settling down and starting a family."

"What's the bad news?"

He grinned down at her. "It doesn't stop my sisters."

Her heart fluttered against her ribs. Time to change the subject to something less personal. "There's the restaurant." She pointed to a sign up ahead written in English and Cantonese. The Sun Garden. They stopped outside the window and perused the menu. She used the excuse of calling Mallory to let go of his hand.

"So we're at the restaurant," she said brightly to her BAU-4 colleague. "Want us to pick up anything in particular for you?" She smiled in case anyone *was* watching them. Lucas had made her paranoid, too.

"Alex pinged the burner two minutes ago and they were still there or very close," Mallory said. "And kung pao chicken, please."

Ashley caught Lucas's gaze and nodded.

"No problem." Ashley hung up and followed Lucas inside. The place smelled like heaven and was packed with Asian diners—always a good sign. There was a wait for a table, so they stood near a wall covered in fliers, waiting patiently for a waitress to seat them.

Lucas ran his hand down her arm and took her fingers in his. "I take it that was positive news?" He raised her hand to his lips and she knew her eyes were wide as saucers when he kissed it. He leaned in to brush her cheek with his. "I'm not the only one who needs to work on their poker face."

She blinked out of her daze. He'd succeeded in knocking her off balance, which she didn't appreciate. So she reached up and pulled him toward her, using his hoodie to draw him closer, nipping him hard enough to make him flinch before he opened his mouth for her. Then he surprised her again, his hands moving low, pulling her hips tight against his as he dove deep for a kiss. Raw, basic hunger rushed through her, making her heart thud and her brain pitch. He tilted her chin for better access and demolished what little remained of her defenses.

The sound of a throat clearing with disapproval had them breaking apart like a couple of hormonal teenagers. They stared at each other for a long moment and his eyes told her they weren't finished—not by a long shot.

Her cheeks heated. She'd kissed him to prove she was in control, but he'd wrested it from her again. Her skin was supersensitive, nerves vibrating. She didn't like it. Didn't like it at all. The fastest way to end this attraction would be to fuck his brains out and get the man out of her system. But he'd told her he liked her and she didn't know what to do with that.

He took her hand and tugged to follow the disapproving waitress to the table. The woman pressed her unsmiling lips together and left them with menus and water.

"You hungry?" He took off his hoodie and put it on the seat beside him. He pulled his T-shirt over his sidearm and it clung to his pecs. It turned out the guy didn't need to wear a suit to look completely edible.

"Starving."

His nostrils flared and a muscle worked in his jaw. He nodded his thanks to the waitress as she dropped off tea and chopsticks. "So what did Mal say?"

"He's here."

She didn't see anyone on a cell so she picked up the menu. When the server came back she ordered beef and black bean sauce and Lucas ordered chow mein and kung pao chicken for Mallory. She added fried rice.

When they were alone again, Lucas reached across the table to take her hand.

She eyed him warily. "I think you're enjoying this role way too much."

"Said the woman who just kissed the hell out of me." Dark eyes glittered with what looked like retribution.

She withdrew her hand and poured tea, a ritual she enjoyed, grateful for the excuse it gave her not to touch him. "I was making a point."

"Feel free to reinforce that point any time you want." One side of his mouth curled up in an engaging grin. He was attractive enough to turn heads. Especially here, where he stood out for his sheer size.

She forced a coldness she wasn't feeling into her tone. "You know what happens when you play with fire," she warned.

You get burned.

His eyes told her he got it, but far from looking contrite, he looked interested, and damned if that didn't stir something inside her that spelled trouble. Her cell rang. Mallory. Thank

God.

"Alex is about to call the number with a cold call pretext." Ashley leaned closer to Lucas across the table and quietly repeated what Mallory told her. "It's ringing now."

She kept her head still while her eyes scanned the other customers. Lucas was doing the same in the opposite direction.

"Got him," Lucas said. He played with his cell as if taking a photograph of her, but was obviously taking shots of someone behind her. She mugged and simpered until he put the cell down, then she watched as he sent the photo first to Mallory and then to someone else—probably Parker.

Ashley's stomach started to rumble just as their appetizers arrived. She'd thought she'd be strung too tight to eat, but once she smelled the food she was ravenous. Her cell rang. Mallory again.

"His name is Charlie Lee. He's wanted for skipping bail on assault charges." Ashley relayed the info Mallory gave her to Lucas, who'd already demolished his appetizer.

"Ah, damn," Lucas muttered around a mouthful of spring roll. "He's on the move."

"So much for lunch." She took a quick drink of her tea.

Instead of heading out the front door, Lee turned toward the kitchen. As soon as he was out of sight, Lucas climbed to his feet and they both walked purposefully in that direction. Then the guy reappeared in the kitchen door with a smile on his face, but stopped dead when he saw them approaching. Ashley and Lucas might be in casual clothes, but it was obvious to anyone with half a brain that they were on some sort of official business.

Lee turned and disappeared into the kitchen. Lucas darted around a table and pushed past a couple who were standing to leave. They shouted in protest but Ashley jostled them, too, saying "Sorry" in Cantonese as their voices rose in alarm. She followed Lucas as he sprinted into the kitchen.

Her gaze bounced off the cooks as she chased their mark, who was now heading for the rear exit. The guy slipped out the door with the agility of Wile E. Coyote.

Lucas got to the exit before her, slamming through into the back alley. She was a fraction of a second slower. They both hit the asphalt running, pounding the pavement, desperate to close the distance between them and the perp.

"FBI. Hold it right there!" Lucas shouted.

Ashley's heart hammered and her lungs burned but she didn't ease up. Lucas was gaining on the guy, slowly at first, then faster. Charlie Lee glanced behind him, slipped on a piece of litter and fell to the ground, rolling twice. He stood quickly, but a garbage truck rumbled its way across the alley in front of them, cutting off his escape. Lee tried to dodge but there wasn't enough space between the truck and the Dumpster for him to squeeze through. Lucas tackled him and they both flew through the air, the truck shuddering to a halt as the two men rolled on the ground.

Ashley drew her weapon and showed her badge to the wide-eyed driver. She held eye contact until he put the truck in park.

Lucas had Lee in flexi-cuffs in five seconds flat. Ashley called for a squad car to meet them at the restaurant as he jerked the guy to his feet. They might be able to use the fact he'd skipped bail to get him to tell them everything he knew about the crew running the underground brothel—assuming he knew anything. Maybe someone had paid him to fake the sighting. Maybe he'd done it as a prank because he hated law enforcement.

But right now Charlie Lee was the closest thing they had to a lead.

Was he part of this criminal enterprise? Did they have a solid foothold in the States, or were they just starting out? Everything about these guys screamed extreme sophistication, and Ashley didn't like it.

"I need to pick up my sweatshirt," Lucas told her as she slipped her cell into her pocket. They steered the suspect back toward the restaurant to await the cavalry.

"Why'd you run, Mr. Lee?" Lucas asked, holding the man by the arm.

The guy shrugged and cast her a sideways glance. "Why you work for the feds?"

She exchanged a glance with Lucas but didn't reply.

"You the worst kind of Chinese," Charlie Lee sneered.

She curled her lip. "Forgive me if I'm not overly impressed when insulted by a skip-jumper wearing handcuffs."

Lee started resisting as they approached the restaurant but Lucas gave him a firm shove.

They entered the kitchen through the rear door. The chefs were still cooking, but eyed them nervously as they came back inside. A side door Ashley hadn't noticed before opened and a man walked out carrying a beer. The room behind him was densely packed with card tables and groups of men, all sitting under the heavy pall of smoke. Ashley reached for her weapon and had it in a two-handed grip pointed at the man in the doorway.

"Federal agents! Hands in the air where I can see them." She yelled the instructions again in Cantonese.

Ashley took the guy in the doorway by the shoulder, spun

him, pushed him against the wall and slipped a pair of restraints over his wrists. No way was this one getting away from her.

"What's going on, Chen?" Lucas murmured as the noise in the room turned to intense silence.

The welcome sound of police radios crackled from inside the restaurant. She pulled out her gold shield. "Armed federal agents back here in the kitchen!"

The officers cautiously came through the doorway with their weapons drawn. They eyed her badge. She recognized one from Susan Thomas's murder scene.

"What have we got?" he asked.

"Illegal gambling den—"

And just like that the spell was broken. People scattered like roaches, heading for another exit at the back of the room.

The uniform pushed past her and grabbed the first guy he could reach, holding him against the wall as he called for reinforcements.

Lucas's eyes were full of questions because she could have handled this better. Then she raised the head of the man she'd cuffed and watched Lucas's pupils flare with recognition and hatred.

It was the man who'd driven the minivan the day Mae Kwon had picked up Agata Maroulis. They'd finally scored a hit against the bad guys.

CHAPTER TEN

"THAT'S DAMN GOOD work, Agents Randall and Chen," Sloan said as she came racing back into her office. Icy droplets of sleet spun off her FBI windbreaker as she tossed it on the back of her chair. She ran a hand through wet hair, scooping it back off her face. Her cheeks were ruddy with cold, her expression focused as a laser.

A total of sixteen people had been brought in for questioning, including the staff of the Sun Garden. They hadn't been too thrilled with having to close the restaurant down, but that's what happened when you housed an illegal low-stakes gambling den in the back room. The arrestees were sitting in holding cells, and interview rooms, sweating it out until the FBI decided exactly how to handle them.

"Agent Rooney is the one who tracked the cell phone and Agent Chen recognized the minivan driver from the surveillance footage," Lucas told her, not wanting to take credit for things he hadn't done.

The fact that the man who'd picked up Agata Maroulis from the train station was also the person who'd taken Becca from her mother to pay off a gambling debt was his and Sloan's little secret. They couldn't reveal that information without revealing their source and they weren't ready to do that. Given the violence of these perps they might never be ready to tell the world Becca was alive.

The minivan driver's name was Ray Tan, and only the fact Becca said he'd never touched her had stopped Lucas from plowing his fist through the guy's face.

Ashley had done a hell of a job spotting him, considering the grainy quality of the two-year-old image. She sat in one of the chairs in front of Sloan's desk. Fuentes came to the door, looked around and slumped into the seat next to her. Lucas propped up the wall, too wired to sit. Mayfield came in behind Fuentes. Crossed her arms.

Ashley still wore jeans and the sweater from when they'd made the arrests earlier, although she'd removed the protective vest. Casual clothes softened her hard edges and made her seem less formidable. He wanted to get both versions of her naked and writhing under his tongue.

"Nothing at the port?" he asked Sloan, pretending he wasn't visualizing having hot sex with one of his colleagues.

"Nothing." Sloan huffed out a breath.

He forced himself to stop looking at Ashley. *Dammit.* He'd been attracted to people he worked with before—but he never allowed it to distract his focus. He wasn't a monk, but he wasn't the use them up and spit them out type, either. He liked having genuine relationships with interesting women. The fact none of them lasted beyond six months just meant he hadn't met the right woman yet. He did his best to let them down gently, but his job came first, and when a woman couldn't handle that reality he moved on. No hard feelings. No wasted time on the biological clock that his sisters insisted was always ticking for women over thirty.

But he didn't remember the last time someone had affected him as intensely as Ashley Chen.

"Normal shipping is going to resume at midnight. Considering you picked up the guy who told us he saw the fugitives at the port in the same spot as a known associate of the trafficking ring, there's a good chance the sighting was bogus." Her exhausted features told him exactly what she thought of that idea.

"Or he could genuinely have been wanting them to be caught so he could get rid of the competition," Ashley said quietly.

"Whatever the reason, the fugitives weren't at the port, and we searched every goddamn inch." Sloan blew out a growl of frustration. "The guy lied to law enforcement and wasted thousands of dollars of police resources, and cost the port a fortune. He will pay. Now, what's the best strategy for questioning these people?"

Sloan looked at Ashley.

"Because we initially picked up Charlie Lee for jumping bail, his burner phone is now in evidence. We can flag it as being the phone used to make that anonymous call. See if we can get him to admit to making a false report and obstructing justice," Ashley suggested.

"He's not going to tell us anything," Lucas argued.

Sloan leaned back in her chair. "He's facing a warrant on skipping bail for assault charges. Combined with wasting police time we might be able to build a good enough case against him for him to be looking at real time."

"We could offer him WITSEC," Ashley suggested. "It's the only way he'd go for any sort of deal, but if he has family where the traffickers can get to them, forget it. The guy isn't going to talk."

Sloan pressed her lips together. "I'll talk to the DA about

WITSEC. What about the driver, Ray Tan?"

"He moved here two and a half years ago from Macau. We're waiting for background checks from Interpol. We know he acted as a driver for Mae Kwon but aside from that we don't have anything on him, except for the illegal gambling charges." Ashley smoothed her palms over her thighs in a nervous gesture.

He and Sloan exchanged a quick look and he caught Fuentes watching them speculatively.

"My suggestion would be to question everyone and make them all the same offer to give up any information they have in exchange for dropping the illegal gambling charges," Ashley said.

"Charlie Lee will need to be remanded into custody as that's the reason you gave for being there and going after him," Sloan said pointedly.

"No one's gonna roll for charges that will probably be reduced to a misdemeanor for first time offenders." Fuentes scoffed.

Ashley sat forward on the edge of her chair. "That's my point. But they'll assume we're desperate for information and have nothing to go on. Then we let them go—"

"What? We only just caught the suckers," Fuentes complained, as if he'd been the one to bring them in.

Lucas straightened from the wall. He'd figured out what Ashley was suggesting. "She's right. We don't mention we've got Ray Tan on the surveillance camera with Agata Maroulis—not yet. We let him go. Then follow his every move. Set up surveillance of every place he frequents, put trackers on his phone, car, and anything else we can find."

His eyes connected with Ashley's. It was a good plan. A

really good plan.

"You think he might lead us to the fugitives?" Sloan asked doubtfully.

Lucas nodded. "He's a known associate. He might want to tell them exactly how desperate and clueless we are—if only with a phone call."

Sloan looked down at her desk while she contemplated her alternatives. Finally she nodded. "I'll make arrangements for the surveillance as soon as I clear it with Salinger."

"The commissioner and the mayor called," Mayfield said. "They want to be kept informed."

"You think that's a good idea?" Lucas asked Sloan.

She put her elbows on the desk and pushed both hands through her damp hair. "No." She caught his gaze again. "But it's their city too. Tell Dana to hold them off for as long as possible."

Dana was the media relations officer. Lucas couldn't imagine the pressure Sloan's marriage must be under with her husband working for Mayor Everett.

She caught his eye. It was only a matter of time before others learned about the fact they had a living witness. He nodded as a flash of understanding passed between them. They needed to catch these bastards before that happened.

"So who's questioning the suspects?" Fuentes asked.

"You and Mayfield take Charlie Lee and half of the others. Talk to the DA about Lee before you question him, see how much time he's looking at. Randall and Chen take Ray Tan and the rest. Make sure holding knows none of them are to be released until I personally give them the go ahead, and that won't be until tomorrow morning at the earliest. No more fuck ups." Sloan held his gaze and he nodded.

Becca's life depended on it.

———————

ANDREW STARED AT the screen. The backdoor to FinCEN and various other federal bodies had just been booby-trapped, and any attempt to use it would spring a complex snare that would probably reveal his IPS address and his location. His hands shook.

He'd been lucky to spot the change in the code in time to avoid falling down the worm hole. He was tired and hadn't been paying proper attention. He was getting lazy or arrogant, but it had been a long time since anyone had tested his skills.

Had Rabbit ratted them out?

No. Andrew had monitored the man's communications and activity closely since the explosion. Rabbit had more to lose than anyone and knew exactly what would happen should he talk.

Andrew shut down the pathway that led him to FinCEN and deleted any of the logs in his system. That particular exploit had cost him nearly a quarter of a million US dollars. At least he'd been careful not to leave traces that would allow anyone to follow him back to his other lairs on the web.

He took a sip of coffee. It was actually impressive someone had figured out how he'd tracked down the woman who'd made that phone call to the cops. He regretted she'd died violently but it was better to send a strong message with one victim than to risk any more betrayal. No one informed on their organization and lived.

Controlling his cousin's baser impulses was next to impossible. Instead, Andrew channeled them in a direction that aided their business dealings rather than destroyed them. And while Andrew might not have a taste for violence, he had no intention of spending thirty years in a federal prison, or worse, awaiting execution.

Life was a constant battle and only the strongest survived—he'd learned that lesson more than a decade ago when enduring a disaster that almost destroyed them all. The fact they were still alive was a miracle he didn't intend to disregard.

Family was the only thing that truly mattered. His uncle had taken him in after Andrew had lost everything. He might not understand his cousin, but he loved him like a brother. Loyalty was the only thing they'd asked in return, and Andrew would cut out his own heart before he betrayed them.

The grief from his old life had faded over the years and, rather than the sharp pain it had been for so long, it was now a familiar ache of sadness that welled up at unexpected moments. He forced the memories aside.

He didn't have time to indulge in old regrets. This whole mess had cost their organization millions, and all because some pervert wanted to fuck a kid. The idiot should just get on a plane to Thailand or Indonesia, somewhere life was cheap and there was an excess of young girls. He ignored the part of himself that recoiled at the idea. This was how they made money, and it was better than dealing drugs, which had been his uncle's former specialty.

His email dinged. More bad news. The FBI had raided one of their gambling dens in Boston and arrested several people including Charlie Lee and Ray Tan.

He swore.

Unlike most people in the US, Ray and Charlie knew the real names of the crew who ran the US operation. And the real names could lead the authorities back to the Dragon Devils' clan.

For the last decade the Devils had secretly expanded their operation until it was the largest organization of its kind in the world. Now, thanks to the kidnapping of one little girl, their entire organization had been threatened.

Killing cops and federal agents had been a mistake, and he'd told his cousin that at high volume immediately after the explosion. If the feds ever figured out who was responsible they'd pursue them with the same vigor they'd pursued Colombian narcos, and Bin Laden. He did not want to be on the FBI's Most Wanted list.

Perhaps it was time to temporarily retreat from their activities. The cops were getting too close.

He left his office with its state-of-the-art computers and walked down the hall to his uncle's bedroom. It was early, but the old man rarely slept.

He bowed at the doorway. His uncle's bodyguard straightened.

"Are they out yet?" his uncle asked in his deep, raspy voice.

Andrew raised his head. "No, Uncle, but they are safe. For now." They'd holed up in a duplex they owned that had an attached garage. The police presence and media attention were so intense they'd decided to wait to cross the border. Andrew was working on a way of getting them out without anyone checking biometrics or paperwork.

"But we have another problem." He told him about the fact the feds had found out he was getting into their system, and about the raid on the gambling den. "Two of our people were arrested. The FBI is getting closer to figuring out who is behind this. I think we should move to another location in case they get a break. We need to lie low until they have other things to occupy themselves with."

The old man stared at him with unnervingly intense, black eyes. Andrew knew better than to look away or show weakness. His uncle crushed weakness.

"The other establishments have all been relocated?"

"As soon as we heard about the explosion, Uncle."

The explosives had been Mae Kwon's idea after the Greek girl had escaped. A stroke of ruthless genius that he doubted she'd ever expected to be caught up in. If it had been his decision he'd have left the women alive and made a run for it. Nothing stirred up American fervor as effectively as attacking their military or law enforcement on home ground.

His uncle nodded. "I want this mess cleaned up. I want my son home. Eliminate all the loose ends."

Andrew's eyes widened, but he didn't dare argue with the man.

"And, yes, it is time to move. We've been here too long. Make the arrangements. We should never get too comfortable."

Andrew bowed, hiding his smile.

They owned several islands and many grand estates. They had a virtual army of guards, although he didn't want to test them against Special Forces. Too many people could die in the crossfire and Andrew didn't intend to be one of them. He wasn't a coward, but he was terrified of dying. Stupid really. It wasn't like he could avoid it forever.

"Yes, Uncle."

"You are a very good nephew, Andrew."

"I'm your loyal servant, Uncle." Andrew went to turn

away to begin making preparations when Yu Chang's next words stopped him cold.

"Send me that girl."

Andrew's mouth froze in the act of smiling. "Girl, Uncle?"

The man chuckled; the sound like a rattle in his chest.

"The one who warms your bed. I think she must be good if she comes to you so often." His uncle held his gaze as a test— as if Andrew hadn't proven his loyalty to the man a thousand times over. "Unless she is special and you want to keep her all to yourself?"

Andrew wasn't foolish enough to admit he cared for anything more than he cared for the old man. He hid his distress beneath an even lower bow. He'd been so careful to hide his affection for Lily, but his uncle knew everything that went on in their world. Andrew left the bedroom and strode quickly past his office and through the living quarters until he entered the kitchen. All the women froze when they saw him, except Lily who smiled at him hesitantly, her eyes soft with something that might have been love.

He forced himself to stand in the doorway and say sharply. "Lily. My uncle wants to see you."

"Me?" She had a beautiful voice. Soft and smooth like a whisper over heated skin. Now it crackled with fear.

The other women in the kitchen shot each other wide-eyed looks. No one disobeyed Yu Chang. Not even a beloved nephew. Andrew's eyes raked her small form, and what little was left of his heart shattered. If the man discovered how much she meant to Andrew, he'd kill her.

"Do not keep him waiting," he snapped when the silence went on longer than he could bear.

Ignoring her tear-filled gaze he began giving orders to

relocate their home. Lily lived on the island so she wouldn't be coming with them. The sooner they left the safer she'd be.

Hours later, her sobs reached his ears as she passed outside his door. He pulled on his headphones and turned up the volume of his music. He should have known better than to ever get attached to something as vulnerable as a woman.

BY THE TIME Lucas left the field office with Ashley it was nearly midnight and neither one of them had eaten more than a granola bar in hours. They'd questioned everyone from the gambling den and sent them back to the cells to sweat it out. Lucas had played the hard-ass, but Ashley's presence seemed to unnerve them most. Maybe it was the fact she spoke the language they found off-putting. A few insulted her but she'd snapped back at them and whatever she'd said had made them stop harassing her. Even the interpreter had gone a little pale.

Ashley Chen was her own brand of intimidation and he liked the fact she didn't let anyone push her around.

Ray Tan hadn't said a word. He'd stared at Lucas like Lucas was a dead man. He'd returned the favor but was careful not to treat Mr. Tan any differently from the others even though he knew the guy was a lying piece of garbage.

Lucas's stomach growled as he stepped out onto the sidewalk. The sleet had turned to ice hours ago, making the road treacherous. February was definitely his least favorite month.

"You hungry?" he asked.

Ashley blinked up at him clearly lost in her own world. "Yeah." She sounded surprised.

"There's a diner not far away, unless you just want to grab

room service when you get back to the hotel?" Personally he was sick of hotel food, and he wanted time for his mind to decompress.

"A diner sounds good."

They veered two blocks south. The sidewalks had been sanded but they were still slick. Ashley slipped and he grabbed her arm, trying to keep his distance even though touching her made him want to hold on tighter.

Lights shone brightly from the small mom and pop café. He held the door for her and they found a corner booth. There was a guy at the counter and another couple holding hands on the other side of the room. Lucas asked for water and wished for beer. Ashley ordered a diet coke. The smells coming from the kitchen weren't French cuisine but they made him drool. It had been a long time since they'd been forced to skip lunch.

After they'd both ordered, Ashley inched around the wraparound seat until she was right next to him. She leaned in so no one could overhear. "What happens tomorrow?"

The heat of her thigh so close to his made him wish they weren't working a case.

"Fuentes and I are in a surveillance van for the day and we'll tail Mr. Tan. There are four other surveillance teams taking various positions."

Her lips dropped at the corners. "Why am I not in the van?"

The idea of being in close quarters with Ashley for a prolonged period of time stirred up all sorts of happy thoughts, none of which related to chasing criminals. "Sloan decided you're more useful to the investigation doing some more electronic digging." He wished he could ask her to try to track down Becca's mother, but Sloan had ordered him not to involve anyone else. He hadn't had time to even start looking for the woman.

"Talk to the geeks from HQ and see if they cracked Mae Kwon's cell phone yet." He was convinced that sucker held the mother lode of information if they could just get inside the damn thing.

She nodded tersely. "Will do."

"And if they aren't interested in sharing, see if you have any luck figuring out how the bad guys reach their clientele or how they get paid."

"First rule of any investigation—follow the money. I'll talk to the forensic accountant, see where he's at."

Their food arrived, two full breakfasts worth. Neither of them spoke until they'd cleared their plates.

Finally he wiped his mouth on his napkin. "Did Alex come up with anything new?"

Something in her eyes changed. The antipathy between the two was palpable.

"I haven't spoken to him, but Mal said he isolated another five potential cribs and sent the information to local law enforcement. Early evidence suggests they already scrammed. He's looking at the cell phone data but can't isolate the numbers of the three fugitives because population density in that part of the city is nuts. He's going to generate a list of possible johns, using repeat users of the local cell towers. He said he couldn't exclude people who lived or worked close enough to the brothel to regularly use that tower, nor those who caught public transportation that passed through the area. But he figured their regular schedule might help in eliminating people and giving us a smaller pool to sub-analyze."

Lucas nodded, impressed. "It's better than the entire male population of Boston and the surrounding area, which is our current suspect pool." They had a small but growing list of johns from their surveillance work. They needed someone to start talking. They needed to find these cocksuckers.

The smooth skin of her throat rippled as she swallowed. "I already started digging into the darknet markets trying to find out how they might be advertising their wares," she admitted.

"I thought that was untraceable?" he said in surprise.

She gave him a look. "Nothing's untraceable, especially if they have to pay for it, but it doesn't mean it's easy. VPN and cloaking are becoming more and more common even when not using onion servers."

It was like she was speaking another language. He understood people and social engineering, and the danger of cybercrime, but he didn't understand the mechanics.

He attracted the waitress's attention for the check. "So where did you learn Chinese?"

Ashley wiped her mouth neatly with her napkin. "My mother was Hong Kong Chinese so she spoke Cantonese when I was growing up." She shrugged. "I speak a little but I forgot most of it."

"Enough to scare the shit out of some of the idiots in custody today."

"I just told them not to give me any grief or I'd set their ancestors on them." The look in her eyes was amused but tired. "Why did you become an FBI agent?" she asked him.

He pushed his empty plate away. "When Mallory's sister, Payton, was abducted it turned all of our lives inside out. Everyone was a suspect and everyone was scared to let their kids out of their sights. I remember the FBI coming to our house and talking to my parents about the Rooney family. They asked about her parents and whether or not they could have hurt her. I thought they were stupid to even suggest the parents might be involved." His lips pulled back. "Shows what I knew back then." In the vast majority of cases, murder victims were related to, or in a relationship with, their killer.

"They never found her," Ashley stated.

Old anger reared up inside him and made his voice hard. "But they never gave up looking." He lifted his head. "Did you know the Payton Rooney case was one of the first cases Frazer ever worked?"

Her eyes widened as she shook her head. "Explains why he's so protective of Mallory."

Lucas had wondered about that himself. Frazer, Mallory and Alex hadn't known each other that long but they were thick as thieves. "I think it has something to do with when Mallory confronted her sister's killer."

"She almost died," Ashley stated solemnly.

The fact Mallory had recklessly chased after a serial killer, goading the sick bastard until he'd gone after her had scared the crap out of everyone who knew her. But Lucas understood what it meant to her and how long and how diligently she'd been searching for answers. Sometimes people couldn't move forward until they'd dealt with their pasts. And she'd had Alex and Frazer as backup. He'd put his money on those guys any day over a creep who attacked little girls.

"So, you joined the FBI to find Payton Rooney?"

When she said it like that, it sounded dumb.

"And because FBI agents get to carry a gun without wearing a dorky uniform." He shrugged, uncomfortable with talking about his emotions. "After I left the Army I still wanted to serve my country. This seemed like a good way to do it."

"Thank you for your service." Her charcoal eyes held his for a moment and his throat got tight.

Usually he just nodded and told the person they were welcome, but this seemed deeper. Her words held meaning and sincerity.

"Thank you for yours."

She shrugged. "I'm just a computer geek."

"You're an FBI agent."

She shook her head. "What I've done is nothing like going to war. Much more like personal survival, which is the absolute opposite of service."

She looked away and the moment was broken. He wasn't sure he understood, but she suddenly seemed fragile and he didn't want to push her. Their respite had calmed his mind, allowed his brain to settle. His body was another matter.

"I'm going to head back to the hotel." She pulled her coat on, her movements tired and jerky.

Lucas dug into his pocket for cash but she beat him to it.

She smiled even though she was obviously exhausted. "My treat."

"This the closest you've had to a date in a while, too?" Even as he joked the memory of her crying out in the darkness filled his brain.

"Not quite." Her cheeks reddened.

They walked back to the hotel, careful not to touch one another, and rode the elevator in silence. Neither of them spoke as they walked to her door, but the tension was strung tight as barbed wire.

He stopped when she did, and she looked at him with wary eyes that seemed to draw him in and warn him away at the same time.

They'd finally arrived at an understanding. As much as he wanted to kiss her, as much as he wanted to do much, much, more, he couldn't risk ruining the effective working relationship they'd established. And neither would she.

He ran his knuckle down her cheek. "Goodnight, Ash."

He forced himself to drop his hand when all he really wanted to do was sink his fingers into her hair and pull her closer.

"'Night, Lucas." She opened her door and slipped quickly inside.

He found himself staring at the door, alternately cursing himself for letting her go and at the same time knowing the timing wasn't right. Last night's red-hot encounter had left him wanting more. Despite Alex's warning, Ashley Chen intrigued him on both physical and intellectual levels. It might not be the right time to start thinking about a relationship, but the idea of just walking away without getting to know her better didn't sit right.

And maybe he was just making sexual desire into a bigger deal than it needed to be. He wanted her, and she seemed to want him.

And neither of them was going to do a damn thing about it because the job came first. He turned away and headed back to his suite, knowing a cold shower was in his immediate future.

CHAPTER ELEVEN

A SHLEY STUMBLED OUT of bed at nine AM, cursing like a sailor whose shore leave was revoked two hours into a much-needed bender. The alarm on her cell phone hadn't gone off and Mallory hadn't woken her. Ashley tossed off her nightshirt and hit the shower, gasping as cold water drenched her warm skin. She adjusted the temperature and scrubbed the late night out of her brain.

This was the problem with being a computer geek. Four AM might be perfect for tiptoeing around the dark web looking for clues, but it made getting to work by nine a bit of an issue.

She brushed her teeth and simultaneously hitched up her pants, spitting out into the sink. She hadn't even gotten anywhere last night. Just examined a depressing array of sites that sold sex. There were a staggering number in the US alone.

Ironically, the darknet lived and breathed on the Tor browser. Tor had been developed and funded by the feds as a secure network for government agencies and dissidents from around the world to use. Tor made it possible to mask your identity and the location of your server. All well and good if you were trying to avoid a stalker, or blog about antigovernment sentiment in a country where intellectual freedom got your throat cut. But not so great when the tables were turned and the feds were trying to catch someone who—for example—was selling sex with kids to pedophiles.

She checked her Glock 27 and her backup weapon and pulled on her suit jacket. Sex trafficking was massive with an estimated between six and eight hundred thousand victims moved across international borders *each year*. It was the fastest growing industry in the criminal world with profits estimated at over a billion dollars. But the fact it was so prevalent in society today meant it was even more difficult to track specific organizations. Ashley had used a search engine developed by the DOD's Defense Advanced Research Projects Agency to crawl through hidden sites, so they could be scoured later, but it was going to take time to find these people, especially as they'd removed the original sites.

Lucas and Fuentes and the others on the surveillance team had a better chance of tracking down the fugitives with good old-fashioned police work than she did trawling through cyberspace.

She was glad she wasn't the one doing surveillance. Firstly, Lucas Randall was proving detrimental to her good intentions and she couldn't afford that. Second, the Chinese connection to this case was beginning to seriously bother her. There might be 1.4 billion Chinese people in the world, and there might be hundreds of Tong and Triad groups in existence, but the sophistication of the network, the fear with which the perpetrators were regarded…

No.

It couldn't be.

There'd been no definitive trace of them for the last decade.

For her own peace of mind, she needed to stay in the

shadows and not draw any attention to herself—another reason to avoid Lucas Randall. He hadn't been kidding when he'd said he was loaded. She'd looked him up and the guy was the sort of wealthy that hung out in society pages at the Kentucky Derby. His parents actually owned racehorses for crying out loud. One of his sisters was married to a freaking senator.

Ashley just wanted to do her job. Sex would be nice occasionally, but not essential. It was just scratching a biological itch. A weakness she couldn't afford to indulge in right now. Maybe when she was back in Quantico she'd find some hot stud in HRT and take him for a ride.

She gave her pale reflection a stern nod and ignored the fact she looked miserable.

She was going to end up a lonely old prune, but that was better than being reckless and dead, or worse—getting other people dead. She grabbed her laptop and coat, noticing that though the sun was shining, it looked frigid outside. February in Boston was a bit of a bitch.

She took the stairs down to the hotel lobby, needing the exercise. On the street she scanned her surroundings. It was always smart to be cautious but Lucas had made her overly suspicious.

On the street the smell of coffee had her making a quick detour to grab a latte with an extra shot of espresso, and a banana that had seen better days.

She'd just ditched the peel when she spotted the first sign of trouble. Ray Tan—the driver of Mae Kwon's minivan and general all around sleaze bag—strolling toward her. She kept her head down and watched him through her lashes, but he'd recognized her.

Dammit.

She didn't dare look around for the surveillance teams or call for assistance. It had been her idea to let this guy back on the streets and she wasn't going to ruin it by arresting the idiot again.

The guy walked right up to her and she was forced to stop or crash into him.

"Excuse me." She lifted her chin and used her steeliest voice.

"Why you work for the feds?" He sidestepped when she tried to go around him.

She let a cool smile touch her lips, refusing to show him an ounce of fear. "I see you've been released, Mr. Tan. I suggest if you want to remain out of custody you get out of my way. Otherwise I'll be happy to escort you back to the field office for impeding an FBI agent from conducting her duties."

He inclined his head but his next words froze her marrow. "It's funny, Agent Chen, but you look very much like a friend of mine."

"So you can't tell us apart either?" she sneered even as her heart clenched hard enough to hurt.

"On the contrary." His eyes lingered on each of her features and then moved slowly down her body. *Creep.* "I'm very good with faces."

"And yet you had surprisingly little to tell us during the interview last night. You're a lot more talkative now. Want to come in to make a statement?"

His eyes narrowed and she saw the violence he kept leashed—the lack of empathy for other human beings. He was not a good man. He was a criminal who would quite happily kidnap, rape, sell, or kill her if he thought he could get away with it. She kept her smile in place and her hand on her weapon. His gaze followed the movement and this time, when she took a step around him, he let her go.

"I'll be seeing you again, FBI Agent Ashley Chen," he called after her.

She walked backwards so she didn't have to take her eyes off the guy. "Oh, you can count on it, Mr. Tan." She opened her mouth to make another biting retort but a sporty-looking motorcycle carrying a pillion passenger slowed near the curb and diverted her attention. The bikers wore black helmets with tinted visors. Suddenly, she remembered a similar bike passing her in the street near the bombed-out brothel yesterday.

One of the men pulled a pistol from inside his jacket.

"Gun!" she screamed, drawing her own weapon. The massive plate glass window behind her shattered and large shards of glass crashed to the sidewalk. People started screaming and running. A woman with a stroller stood between her and the motorbike.

"Get down!" Ashley yelled. Ray Tan was on the ground, blood pouring from a hole in his chest.

The bike took off. Ashley swung her weapon toward the motorcycle and lined up her shot. She fired once, clipping the one guy in the arm. The gunman didn't return fire. Instead, he clutched his injured arm and stared over his shoulder at her as the driver snaked between vehicles and sped away. There were so many bystanders in the crossfire she didn't dare shoot again.

Shaken, she pushed herself to her knees and crawled toward the man who lay bleeding out on the sidewalk. There were shouts and screams as people ran around her, panicked, probably thinking it was a terrorist attack, not an assassination.

She pulled off her coat and then her suit jacket, balling up the latter and pressing it hard against the gaping wound in the man's chest. She knew other agents would be scrambling, calling for backup and an ambulance.

Ray Tan opened his mouth and gasped for breath. His eyes had a faraway look in them as they locked on hers. An amused light entered them and he whispered in a voice that was barely audible over the chaos of the street. "You seek the Dragon Devils, and yet you look exactly like one of them," he spoke in Cantonese.

The blood drained from her face. "Who?" Ashley demanded urgently. "What did you say?"

But he didn't answer. Instead, his eyes rolled before his entire body went slack. Someone grabbed her and tugged her away as other agents rushed to give CPR, but most of Ray Tan's blood was already soaking into the Boston concrete and Ashley had seen enough death to recognize its grip. Her insides felt like they'd shriveled up. Her knees buckled, and she found herself swept up into strong arms.

Lucas.

He carried her away from the mayhem of the shooting, propping her against another storefront, searching her for wounds. Pieces of glass clung to her knees and palms and small cuts bled profusely. But she hadn't been shot in the attack.

"Ashley, snap out of it. Were you hit?" Lucas asked fiercely.

She shook herself out of her stupor and realized he'd been talking to her the entire time.

"I'm okay." She blinked away the shock and her training

kicked in. She brushed the glass away from her clothes, and picked a shard from her thumb. "Really, Lucas, I'm fine." She sounded hoarse, breathless, as if she'd been running. "I realized when that bike pulled up that I'd seen it before—near the brothel, just before we headed to the high rise and found Susan Thomas's body."

Lucas's eyes were almost black as he looked down at her. She glanced around and saw paramedics working on Ray Tan. Unless they were in the business of resurrecting the dead, they were wasting their time.

"What did he say to you?"

"Who?" She blinked up at him, fear gripping her insides. The Dragon Devils were one of the most fierce, most ruthless, most elusive Chinese gangs. She'd thought they'd stopped operating more than a decade ago. She'd thought they were all dead.

"Ray Tan. It looked like he was telling you something just before he passed out."

He hadn't passed out. He'd died, but no one was ready to admit that yet. Ashley pulled away from Lucas and forced herself to stand on her own two feet. She couldn't believe her life had just been irrevocably altered and yet everything looked the same. Same sky, same street, same handsome FBI agent making her long for more than she had to give. She needed to get out of here, but running screaming down the road would probably draw too much attention.

"What did he say to you, Ash?"

She snapped out of it. "He called me a bitch for working with the feds and getting him killed." She looked away, unable to hold Lucas's gaze as her eyes filled with tears. She wasn't crying because a man had been killed, and Ashley hated herself for that too. But her empathy for gangsters and criminals had died years ago on a beach in Thailand. Instead, she was crying because, for the first time since she'd joined the Bureau, her background had impeded an investigation. She'd lied to keep her own ruinous secrets.

Now she had to figure out what to do about the fact that her worst nightmare had come true. Her family, who for years she'd thought were dead, was behind this trafficking organization and she faced a choice. Did she do her job, a job she'd trained for and worked hard at and loved with every ounce of her being, and help put these bastards in prison where they belonged? Or did she run and hide like the spineless frightened sixteen-year-old she'd once been?

Her brain screamed *run*, but the warm arm around her waist made her want to stay.

Blood trickled down her hands and knees as she watched the paramedics load Ray Tan onto a gurney and whisk him away. Everything she cared about, everything she'd worked so hard for was about to come crashing down. Another catastrophic explosion. Another devastated life. But she was the only one who could see it. She was the only one who knew.

———

ALL THE PREPARATIONS for moving their headquarters to another island were set. Andrew had packed up the computer system to be shipped on the next flight, although he kept his laptops with him, always. The fact Lily still hadn't come to him stung. Surely she'd known he had no choice? Everything he'd done had been to protect her.

Had she been forced to go to his uncle again? Or had she

enjoyed being with one of the most powerful crime bosses in the world?

His uncle was not an attractive man, but power was a tremendous aphrodisiac. Andrew had seen some of the most beautiful women in the world walk past him and Brandon like they were little boys, to kneel at his uncle's feet.

Bile burned the back of Andrew's throat but he swallowed it down and washed it away with water that sat on his desk. Women weren't trustworthy. They cheated and lied and pretended they loved you and then fucked half the football team.

But Lily wasn't like that.

Sweat gathered on his brow. Lily was quiet. Sweet. Innocent, until he'd come along. She lived with her mother on the island and had avoided his attention for months before even talking to him.

Did she hate him for not standing up for her? For not laying claim to her? Didn't she know that would have meant certain death? He'd had to pretend he was just using her for sex so his uncle wouldn't see her as a threat.

Had he lost her?

Of course he'd lost her.

He held his head in his hands. She'd said she loved him, but he hadn't said it back. He never did. Not anymore.

Once he'd found out exactly who his uncle was, it had been easier to understand some of the man's actions. Yu Chang had to show strength. He had to be the dominant male in the organization, especially now. Andrew understood all that. But how often did Andrew have to prove himself to the man? How many women would the old man claim for himself? And what would happen if Andrew ever wanted to take a wife? Would his uncle insist on bedding her, too? Or would the old man pick Andrew's bride as another way of controlling him?

The thought appalled him. He'd learned long ago his own survival depended on his loyalty to Yu Chang and he'd given it unconditionally, but the notion of marrying someone he didn't care for just because his uncle told him to?

The idea made his stomach clench.

They'd taken him in as an orphan, loved him, and given him tremendous power and responsibility. After losing his parents, and then Jenny, so close together, he'd needed the security of belonging somewhere. He'd needed his extended family, no matter how illegal their business practices had turned out to be. And over the years they'd come to need him, too. They couldn't exist without him. They wouldn't even know where to find the goddamn money. He slammed his fist into the table and relished the streak of pain that ran from his wrist to his elbow.

His cell rang.

Brandon. It didn't matter how many times Andrew told Brandon how rash his actions were, the idiot always did exactly as he pleased. But Andrew would be the first to be blamed if Brandon was caught because the feds had tracked his frickin' cell phone.

"You shouldn't be calling me," he hissed.

"This is important. I think I saw something after we went to…tie up those loose ends." Brandon said it easily, as if they weren't talking about killing real people. People who'd been loyal accomplices until circumstances had made their allegiance questionable.

Andrew had resigned himself years ago to the fact that his

cousin was amoral and depraved. The bigger surprise was the fact Andrew was even halfway normal.

"Are you there, Andy?" Brandon asked.

"Yes," he spat out. What the hell did Brandon want? Andrew was doing everything possible to get Brandon and the others out, but with every cop and federal agent in the land looking for them, it wasn't easy. No one wanted to involve themselves with the Dragon Devils' problems. And the Devils would never reveal how desperately they needed help for fear of other gangs seeing them as weak and trying to take over their operations.

"You need to sit down," his cousin said calmly.

What the hell had he done now? "Just spit it out."

He was probably the only person in the world who could talk to Brandon this way, but they were more like brothers than cousins. He'd saved Brandon's life during one of the worst natural disasters ever to strike. The fact they'd lived through it was a miracle. Thousands hadn't.

"There's an FBI agent working in Boston called Chen. She was one of the people who made the arrest at the gambling den yesterday, and she was on the street with Ray Tan when the shooting went down this morning. She clipped me, but I'm okay."

"Don't tell me you killed another fucking federal agent?" And a woman to boot. The country would be in an uproar.

"That's not it." There was something fearful in Brandon's tone. Not something Andrew usually associated with the brash hothead, not even when on the run.

"I don't have time to play guessing games—"

"The FBI agent looked just like your little sister."

Andrew felt as if someone had punched him in the throat.

Rage spewed inside him, rage that someone would taunt him this way. "Jenny's dead."

"I know, brother, I know. But...she looked so much like *you*. I couldn't grab her because the place was swarming with cops. You should check her out, it's probably just a stupid coincidence, but it saved the bitch's life today."

Andrew would have rolled his eyes or snapped at his cousin about the idiocy of shooting FBI agents if he hadn't been struck mute. His sister was dead. She'd died moments after they'd had a terrible fight and he'd never forgiven himself.

"I have to go. I can't believe I'm still stuck here. Fuck, Andy, get me the hell out of this shithole!"

"I'm working on it," Andrew snarled as if Brandon hadn't just catapulted him back into that nightmare of anger and grief.

"Just look the woman up using your crazy ninja computer skills. I might have been seeing things, or she might just look similar. Whatever. But it was freaky, brother. Really fucking freaky."

Andrew let out a hoarse breath. "Yeah. Fine. Hang up and get rid of this damn phone or the feds *will* track you down."

He picked up his glass to take a drink of water, but could barely hold the cup because his hand was shaking so much.

This was stupid. Jenny was dead. He put down the glass and booted up his laptop, mentally figuring out the best approach to look for this woman called Chen without anyone sensing he was in the system. He needed proof this fed bitch wasn't his beloved sister. She wasn't Jenny. She couldn't be Jenny.

CHAPTER TWELVE

"**W**HAT THE HELL just happened?" Sloan stood in the doorway of the break room looking like an avenging angel.

Lucas shook his head and took a large gulp of coffee. He'd been expecting to spend the whole day squeezed tight into the back of a van with Diego Fuentes, but that was the FBI for you—never a dull moment, as long as you didn't count paperwork.

It was a miracle no one else had been killed. The feelings that had churned inside him when that gunman had pointed his weapon at Ashley were like a tourniquet around his throat. In that moment he'd been completely helpless. He forced the strangled feeling aside. He needed to be professional. He had things to do.

He poured them both another cup of coffee and followed Sloan through to her office.

"They took out any potential threats to their organization before they became a problem," Lucas answered gruffly. "And they made us look like a bunch of fools while doing it."

"These guys are leading us in circles and we're still no closer to IDing the group responsible, let alone the three men who escaped the brothel. They've undercut every plan of action we've made." Sloan rubbed her eyes as she settled in behind her desk.

He placed the coffee at her elbow.

"Thanks." She took a sip and grimaced.

The coffee was thick as tar, but did a good job of kick starting sluggish neurons.

"Funerals start tomorrow." The sadness in her eyes was echoed by the heavy feeling in his chest. And there were still many unidentified bodies at the morgue. The case was a mess of callous death and destruction.

Sloan gritted her jaw. "And I haven't seen my bed, let alone my husband in six days. I think Brian's gonna leave me for someone who doesn't treat him like an enemy spy and who's occasionally home at night. Hell, the cat is better company than I am."

Randall closed the door and sat down, leaned forward with his elbows on his knees. "We have to start working the very real possibility they have someone on the inside. Someone they compromised and blackmailed into working for them."

Sloan's mouth went wide on a yawn, but she looked far from shocked. "I had the office swept for electronic listening devices the day Susan Thomas was murdered," she admitted. "It's clean, so if there's a leak, it's a human one." She picked up the coffee again. "Tastes like someone threw in a handful of dirt." She wiped her mouth on the back of her hand. "So, how do you suggest we go about figuring out who might be the leak?"

"Feed different tidbits of information to different pools of people and see what surfaces in the wrong place?" he suggested.

Her lips twisted. "Easier said than done until we have some real clues about these guys."

"We have clues—that's why they're panicking." And their panic had meant more bloodshed on the streets of Boston.

There was a knock on the door and Ashley poked her head inside. Mallory had fetched her fresh clothing from their hotel room and at some point Ashley had showered and changed. Her hair was wet. Skin pale. Lips pinched. A gunfight would do that to a person. She wore all black, which seemed grimly appropriate given the mood. He wanted to touch her, to take her in his arms and make sure she was okay, but this was work and she was an FBI agent, not a civilian, not his girlfriend.

"Agent Chen. Come in. Take a seat. Glad to see you're still with us," Sloan said with a strained smile.

His stomach clenched at the reminder of how close she'd come to dying today. Bloodstains had covered the knees of her pants, and her palms were crisscrossed with minor lacerations, yet she'd escaped relatively unscathed. The EMTs had cleaned her up on the street, after she'd refused to go to the hospital.

"What happened out there?" Sloan asked.

"I've written up and submitted my reports," Ashley said. The Bureau loved paperwork, especially when an agent fired their weapon in public.

If she thought that let her off the hook, Sloan's patient gaze persuaded her otherwise. "I stayed up late, poking around the Tor server until four this morning, so I overslept. I'm very sorry about that." She stared straight ahead, obviously waiting to be chastised.

Sloan eyed her. "Agent Chen, I'm aware our jobs aren't always nine-to-five. I'm smart enough to appreciate the different skill sets people bring to the table."

Some of the stiffness eased out of Ashley's shoulders but her mouth remained tense. "I was walking to work at about nine-thirty. I grabbed a coffee, but when I came back outside I spotted Ray Tan walking toward me. Obviously, I know he's being tailed, but I didn't want to give that away. He started giving me grief about working for the Bureau. I told him to keep hassling me and I'd take him straight back to the field office for impeding an agent trying to perform her duties." A line formed between her brows. "He finally left me alone and that's when I heard the bike roar to a stop beside us. And I remembered."

"What?" Sloan leaned forward.

"The same bike drove past me and Agent Rooney after we questioned the tobacconist near the brothel. I remember because they were going so fast as they weaved through traffic."

"You think the same guys killed Susan Thomas?" Lucas asked.

She nodded. "I should have connected it to the shooting yesterday."

"Can we put a rush on ballistics to compare the slug we pulled out of the dog and the ones fired this morning?" Lucas suggested.

"I'll request it." Sloan made a note on a pad of paper. She turned to Lucas. "The guys on the bike—could you tell if they were the same ones from the brothel or not?"

Lucas shook his head. "They wore tinted visors and were bent over on the back of a bike. Too hard to tell their height and build, but they could have been."

When Ray Tan had confronted Ashley on the street he'd been torn between running to her aid, arresting the guy on what they had on him, or trusting she could handle herself and staying put. Only concerns for Becca's safety had kept his ass in the van. They needed to get the major players off the streets if that kid was to have any chance of a normal life—but every second watching Ashley on the street without backup had made him silently scream.

Then the bullets had started to fly.

"So what's the next plan?" Ashley's voice wobbled and her hands shook. She wouldn't meet his gaze. She was probably still in shock and should take the day off.

"ASAC Frazer is making loud noises about you and Rooney heading back to Quantico and continuing your assistance from there. He's pissed you were involved in a major shooting incident this morning and found a still warm body before that. He took great pains to explain to me the role of the BAU in an investigation." Sloan's lip curled. "In the meantime, our people are convinced they'll be able to crack the cell phone in the next twenty-four hours and get us whatever information is on it." Her expression turned sour. "But then they said the same thing yesterday."

Sloan stared at the surface of her desk for a few moments. "I hear you figured out how these guys tracked down Susan Thomas."

"I did?" Ashley mumbled wearily.

"Frazer told me you'd given a suggestion to a cybersecurity consultant he worked with. They ran with it and found evidence someone had hacked the FinCEN system and pulled the information attached to the money transfer between the Strombergs and Susan Thomas." *Alex.* "They've set up a trapdoor, fixed the intrusion and patched other federal systems. All thanks to you."

Lucas sat down. Wished he could take Ashley's pale hand in his.

Did Alex still not think they could trust this woman? She'd more than proven her worth.

Ashley sent Sloan a fierce grin. "We just cost these people a lot of money—that's gonna piss them off."

"Not to mention improving the security of the United States federal government," Lucas added.

Finally Ashley met his eyes, but hers were cloudy with internal turmoil. Then they hardened and turned back to Sloan. "I wanted to spend time trying to figure out if they've set up shop again on the darknet. Because they will, it's just a matter of time." Her eyes flicked between them in agitation. "I just need a starting point. If we could nail one of the johns and find out how he paid—"

"Remember that lawyer we picked up before you went in on Wednesday?" Sloan interrupted, addressing Lucas.

"The one who gave us the password to get me in the door?"

Sloan nodded sharply. "Theo Giovanni."

"He's one of the few starting points we do have," Lucas agreed. "But we can't touch him because of the deal he made." Protecting people's privacy and civil liberty was important to him, as was keeping his word, but Theo Giovanni was pure slime.

"I know, but it's a shame we can't get into that slippery bastard's financial or internet or phone records and see if there's anything there that can help us." Sloan sighed dramatically. "Unfortunately, *officially*, we can't use him in any way."

Ashley stared at them both as if they'd lost their minds. Lucas was beginning to think he might have.

"I'm just going to excuse myself and go work on searching

the dark web. You know where to find me if you need me," she said.

"Check in with Agent Randall at the end of the day," Sloan ordered. "And if you need to take time off, do it."

"Yes, ma'am." Ashley didn't look at him as she left, closing the door behind her.

Lucas eyed Sloan with a frown. "I take it that's your first test?"

Sloan smiled grimly. "Most of the squad, including you, knew his name from the initial surveillance and subsequent deal we did with him, but the degenerate is still alive and well. Wouldn't he be dead if the leak was one of us?"

Lucas shrugged. Maybe they just hadn't got to him yet. The gangsters had been pretty damned busy mopping up other loose ends. "Let's hope Theo Giovanni stays alive for Agent Chen's sake."

Sloan's phone dinged and she checked the screen. Her eyebrows rose almost to her hairline. "Well, this is new. The Chinese are sending us one of their people to *assist* in the investigation."

"They have information?"

"I guess we'll have to ask Detective Nelson Shaw of the Hong Kong Police Department tomorrow morning. He works for their Criminal Intelligence Bureau."

A spark of anticipation lit his blood. "What time is he arriving?"

"Nine."

"I'd like to be in on that meeting." The criminals they were dealing with weren't newbies. They were too well organized and disciplined not to have honed their craft somewhere. Maybe that somewhere was Hong Kong.

"Are you going to see our little friend today?" Sloan asked. She meant Becca. He nodded.

"Did you mention her to Agent Chen?" For all she must be exhausted Sloan's gaze was sharp and assessing.

He shook his head, too tired to glare at her. She leaned back in her chair, apparently satisfied.

"We need to think about moving her to a safe house soon." Lucas rubbed the top of his nose to try and ease a growing tension headache.

"You haven't found the mother yet?"

He didn't hold back his snort of incredulity. "I haven't even had time to *start* looking for the woman."

Sloan pursed her lips in consideration. "If Chen passes my test and Theo Giovanni doesn't meet with a tragic end in the next twenty-four hours, bring her on board and get her to trace the girl's family. There's got to be someone somewhere out there who cares about the kid."

"And if there isn't?" he asked the question that bothered him most. What if, after all this, there was nowhere for Becca to go except foster care? It would be almost as bad as the system letting down Agata Maroulis.

"Let's take this one disaster at a time, Agent Randall."

For some reason that reminded him of the contraceptive pills the assholes had forced the little girl to swallow. More than five hundred before she'd given up counting. He got to his feet, nodded to Sloan and headed out into the fresh air of Boston, hoping it would be cold enough to quench the anger that wanted to consume him. There was no way he was letting that kid rot in the system. And no way were these bastards getting hold of her ever again.

CHAPTER THIRTEEN

A SHLEY SAT ALONE in the conference room where she and Mallory had been working. She'd finished the endless reams of paperwork associated with this morning's shooting and spent the rest of the day holed up out of sight. The press was going nuts, stirring up the good citizens of Boston into a terrified frenzy until many were scared to leave their homes. Luckily no one had caught the incident on their cell phone and her face wasn't plastered all over the media.

It didn't matter how much training she'd received, or how experienced she was as an agent, being involved in an exchange of gunfire had shaken her. The temptation to run had been almost overwhelming. Having started her life over, twice now, Ashley was reluctant to throw away a career that gave her the power to fight back, especially on the word of some two-bit gangster.

As a civilian she was no one, but as a government agent she could help nail the bastards to the wall. Working for the BAU meant that with a bit of luck they wouldn't even know she existed.

The Dragon Devils had always been by far the most secretive of all the Asian secret societies, but the Devils of today might bear no resemblance to those of 2004. The current leadership might not even know who she was. Her repulsive uncle hadn't been seen since the Sumatra-Andaman earthquake had ripped a hole in the world. The gigantic wave that had resulted from the quake had stolen more than two hundred and thirty thousand lives in fourteen different countries—why not *his*? The tragedy had traumatized a generation and given her the opportunity to fake her own death.

She refused to wonder if her brother had survived, or her odious cousin, although Ray Tan's comments suggested one of them had.

So she could run, or she could keep a cool head and help put these bastards away.

If the Bureau ever discovered the lies she'd told to get into the FBI Academy she'd be out on her ear, and probably up on fraud charges. It wouldn't matter that her intention had only ever been to serve her country, and seek justice for others. The powers-that-be would take a different view.

Whatever she did, fight or flight, she might still lose her career, but at least this way she had the chance to make up for some of the evil her family had perpetrated.

It was late and Ashley yawned widely. Mallory had been assigned to advise the team who was about to begin rounding up men they'd believed visited the brothel as paying customers. The team was figuring out who to approach first and what angle to take. They didn't want a string of dead potential witnesses—at the same time, they needed to end this thing, and punish those who involved.

The port, border crossings and airports remained on high alert for the fugitives, but Ashley had the feeling they were still right here in Boston. How else could they respond so quickly to perceived threats? And the way that pillion passenger on the motorcycle had stared at her... The lab had his DNA from a blood trail after she'd clipped him. They might get a hit.

The ballistics report landed in her email inbox. It confirmed a match between the gun used to shoot Susan Thomas's dog and the men who'd gunned down Ray Tan in the street that morning. It was the same gun used to execute Agata Maroulis in cold blood when the girl had escaped.

Ashley shuddered. Her family were monsters. They needed to be locked up.

Her laptop dinged with the results of another search she'd run on the lawyer who'd given them the password to get inside the Boston brothel. Theo Giovanni.

What a piece of work. A named partner in a small Boston law firm, Theo was as creepy as a red-kneed tarantula. Married with three small kids, he spent a lot of money entertaining in restaurants and clubs.

That could be legit given his job, but he visited porn sites the way most people checked Facebook. She spoofed an email and sent him a link to an explicit site that specialized in young-looking teens. Once he clicked on the link she'd be able to track his every command and listen in to his microphone.

The FBI wouldn't approve.

Despite bad press and widespread public paranoia, the Bureau tried to respect US citizens' privacy, not to mention they were too damn busy to randomly snoop. Giovanni was different. He'd already gotten what amounted to a free pass on this case and he was definitely guilty. Nothing she discovered was covered by a warrant or admissible in court and no way was she going to admit to doing this to anyone. But if he gave her a clue to follow, a breadcrumb that might lead her to the bad guys...she'd take it.

It was almost eleven by the time Giovanni logged into an online banking account under the name of one of his junior associates.

Gotcha.

Ashley wondered if the poor sap knew anything about it.

Giovanni transferred several thousand dollars to another online facility and bought bitcoins, the virtual online currency. He then made a payment to a website on the Tor server that looked innocuous enough, but she doubted anyone paid a thousand dollars for a pound of actual carrots.

She eyed his transaction history and saw he had items delivered to a mailbox near his workplace. Probably coke. It might be worth alerting the US Postal Service about this supplier.

Giovanni logged off and shut down his computer and everything went silent. She turned off all her monitoring programs and sat back in frustration. She didn't have the resources or the authority to put a tail on the guy. Better to call it quits and head back to the hotel.

Outside, reporters were conspicuous in their absence. The field office had released a brief statement with a description of the men they were looking for and asking anyone with information to come forward. The press knew they wouldn't get anything beyond the party line.

She kept her hand near her weapon, glanced over her shoulder. It was only a fifteen-minute walk back to the hotel, but she'd swear she could feel eyes on her every step of the way. Her cell rang just as she entered the atrium of the hotel.

It was her boss, Lincoln Frazer. "I want you back in the office, ASAP," he said without preamble.

"How come?" It was the first time she'd ever questioned

him on anything.

"Mallory gave me the rundown on the types of evidence you've been following. You can do what they need from here."

"I couldn't have recognized and arrested the man who drove Mae Kwon to pick up Agata Maroulis from Virginia," she argued.

"They have more than enough agents on this, Agent Chen." Frazer sounded like he was losing his patience. "You are not a field agent."

Had someone complained about her abilities?

She straightened her back. "I was a field agent for three years. I know how to conduct surveillance and make an arrest."

The line crackled with displeasure. "If you want to go back to being a field agent, Chen, just say the word."

"No, sir." *Dammit.* Sweat coated her brow. Why was she arguing? She'd be less likely to be exposed in Virginia and she didn't want to get kicked out of BAU-4. Assuming she didn't get fired, this was her last rotation before she could concentrate on her specialty—cybercrime, which had been her dream for years. She was being an idiot. Her resolve crumbled. "I'll fly back first thing in the morning."

She hung up and stared at her cell, furious with herself for folding, even though it was the sensible decision. But no one else in the FBI was as good at getting around the seedier sides of the digital environment as she was. And these animals had killed four of her fellow agents, three cops, more than thirty women, and assassinated Ray Tan when he was in the midst of several federal agents.

The Dragon Devils were bold. They'd be less bold if their names were emblazoned across every news outlet on the globe.

Perhaps she could arrange an anonymous tip off about the organization? The idea had merit, but things hadn't gone well for the last two anonymous tipsters. She needed a plan first.

"Ashley." Lucas Randall's voice close to her ear was deep and resonant and made her skin part company with the rest of her body.

She turned, revealing nothing of the fact that he'd startled her. "I was about to email you my report."

"Talk me through it."

She opened her mouth, but he took her arm. "Not here."

He steered her toward the bank of elevators.

As the steel doors opened, three women jogged to catch up with them and Lucas held the doors. The women looked like they'd had a few drinks. They checked Lucas out with unabashed admiration and he shot them a smile as they got out on the third floor.

Alone in the elevator, he turned to watch her with those coffee-colored eyes. The air grew hot and thick, making it difficult to breathe.

She'd always appreciated a good-looking guy in a nice suit, but Lucas had dressed casually today for his surveillance stint. From the way his T-shirt clung to his body, she was pretty sure she'd appreciate him whatever he was wearing. Or not wearing.

Don't do it.

The words thundered in her ears the whole way up to the eighth floor.

He *liked* her.

The doors swished open and she strode out, trying to not remember all the ways she liked him back. The fact he listened to her ideas, and gave credit for the work she did, the fact he kissed her as if she was the most important thing in the world and had made her come without even getting her naked. He hadn't asked for anything in return. He hadn't pressured her for more than she wanted to give.

He was sinful enough to turn her on, and carnal enough to get her off, and that was in public. Heaven knew what he'd be capable of given a bit of time and privacy.

The throb of desire filled her from the soles of her shoes to the tips of her ears. All the reasons for not grabbing Lucas Randall and kissing him like he was her last meal seemed to have evaporated. She was leaving tomorrow. They were no longer on the same squad and the fact they were working the same case was a technicality. The FBI wouldn't care if they hooked up. In fact, no one would ever know.

This was probably the last time she'd see Lucas Randall. The idea depressed her more than it should have.

Nothing to lose—except the antsy, achy, dissatisfied feeling that was making her edgy and horny and distracted when she needed her focus.

She got to her door and cleared her throat. "Let me drop off my stuff."

He opened his mouth to speak, but his cell rang.

"Sloan. I have to take this." He pointed to the direction of his suite. "Let yourself in."

Ashley entered her room quietly so as not to wake Mallory, but the light from the hallway revealed the room was empty. Mallory must still be working.

She placed her personal laptop in the bottom of her case, which she locked, and picked up her purse. Her anger with Frazer, frustration with the case and with her life in general galvanized her into action. She spun on her heel and left her room, striding to the end of the hallway. Even though he'd told her to let herself in, she rapped lightly on Lucas's door and heard footsteps on the other side. When he opened it he was no longer on his cell. He'd shed his jacket, and his dark hair was ruffled in a way that suggested he'd run his hands through it a few too many times. He closed the door and opened his mouth, but she didn't let him speak.

She slipped her hands around his neck and pulled him down for a kiss. His hair was silky soft against her fingers and she rose up to take the kiss deeper. He didn't hesitate. He hauled her against him until her breasts were pressed flat to his chest and his erection was growing at an impressive rate against her stomach.

He shifted her, kissing her neck, her jawline. The scent of strong, clean male overwhelmed her senses with a mad rush of desire. She scraped her teeth over the tight skin of his lower neck and he groaned. His hand slipped under her layers and jerked her blouse out of her slacks. It found the lacy cup of her bra and honed in on her nipple. Her toes curled, fingers fisting in his hair as her head dropped back.

"You sure about this?" he murmured against her skin.

"Positive."

"Someone shot at you today."

"I'm aware." She gasped as he lightly pinched her nipple. "I'd rather be here with you than thinking about that."

When he looked at her with concern etched around his eyes, she took his hand and tugged him into the bedroom. The lights were off but the lamps from the sitting area shone through the open doorway. She let go of his hand and closed the drapes. When she turned he'd propped one shoulder against the doorjamb and was watching her with hungry eyes.

He was letting her set the pace.

She draped her coat over the nearby chair and put her Glock on the bedside table. Then she pulled off her boots and shrugged out of her suit jacket. He didn't move, just watched her undress. If not for those hot glittery eyes and the bulge in the front of his jeans she'd have wondered if he was really into this. But those eyes burned for her, so she slowed down the undressing into a striptease as soon as she'd toed off her socks.

Slowly she undid the buttons of her black blouse and eased it delicately off her shoulders before draping it on the chair. Memories of her ruined suit from this morning flashed through her mind. Ray Tan's blood had stained her fingers and she'd scrubbed them so hard for so long she'd made her skin raw. She pushed the images out of her mind. Death was nothing new to her, and men like Ray Tan knew the risks of their chosen career.

So did she.

She wasn't going to lose sleep lamenting the death of a gangster, but there was no guarantee of tomorrow. All the more reason to spend one night in Lucas's arms.

Her underwear was silk the color of denim, with enough lift to give her small breasts a much-needed boost. Her hands went to her pants and she undid the button and leisurely peeled the material down her legs. Reduced to her lacy bra and barely there panties, she padded toward him. Without her shoes he'd gained another inch on her 5'10" and she liked it. He skimmed his hands over her hips and pulled her against him.

"You look amazing." His fingers stroked the frilled edge of her panties. "But…"

She froze. "What?"

"Are you sure this is acceptable work attire?"

She laughed and some of the tension eased out of her. She was so nervous, she hadn't even realized it. The way he touched her tied her in knots. "Hoover might not have approved it for the day job, but he might have enjoyed it on the weekends."

He grinned. Then he took her mouth like it was his to possess.

A quiver of lust ran through her. She pulled his T-shirt out of his jeans and ran her hands over the wide planes of his chest. His muscles were hard and well-defined, but his skin was soft and warm. She only did this occasionally and she intended to enjoy every moment.

Her fingers moved lower, cupping him through the denim, making him thrust against her palm as if he couldn't control the need to be closer.

He eased a bra strap down her arm and kissed the top of her shoulder, working his way down to one breast, then the other. He lifted her up and she wrapped her legs around his waist and let out a squeak when he set her down on a cold set of drawers on one side of the room. He moved lower and sucked her nipples through the lace of her bra, the rasp of his tongue over the rough fabric making her nerves sing with arousal. He pushed between her knees, hands on her thighs, thumbs gently resting on the gossamer thin skin where her legs joined her hips. He'd barely touched her and she was ready to explode.

"You okay?" His eyes didn't leave hers.

She couldn't look away. His concern stirred up emotions she wasn't prepared to deal with. She nodded and bit her lip, placing one of her hands over his and moving it toward her center.

The feel of his lips on her nipple and his fingers gliding over her skin and then easing into the tightness of her sheath had her groaning, and writhing. She was so wound up, so ready for him, that she burst into a million pieces of light and shattered around him.

She came back to Earth with a sob, but he didn't give her time to recover.

"I thought you said you were loud?"

She laughed though her heart was racing. "That one caught me by surprise."

He grinned as if it were a challenge. He unclipped the bra at the back and kissed his way down her front, shifting her thighs open with those wide shoulders of his. He put gentle pressure on her chest and she leaned back until she hit the wall. The brush of his day-old beard against her sensitive skin had her jerking upright.

"Easy," he soothed.

He ran his tongue along the seam where her thigh met her torso and the touch was so erotic and sensual she wanted more. She opened her legs wider. And wider again when he still didn't hone in on where she needed him to be. He moved to her other thigh and she was on the verge of begging when she felt hot breath against her panties. She gripped his hair as his tongue ran under the lace edge before circling her clit. She tried to move, but he held her hips down, and she thought she might go insane with need.

He tugged her panties down her legs and tossed them aside. She was now completely naked and exposed to him, and he was so focused on her it was mesmerizing. He leaned down and licked her hard between her legs and she jolted like someone had fired a thousand volts through her system. His rough jaw and probing tongue making her tremble until she melted against the wall.

Desire rode her hard, and she could feel her hunger building to the desperate levels of a few minutes earlier. His hands and mouth worked over her with an expertise she hadn't anticipated. This was a man who knew his way around a woman's body and needed no directions in how to satisfy a woman's cravings.

She didn't want to think about where he'd learned these skills. The idea of him being with other women shouldn't have mattered when this was a one-time deal.

He stroked her, keeping the pressure and rhythm constant and she felt her climax building again but she wanted to touch him.

She must have said it out loud.

"Soon."

His hands were on her breasts again, rolling her nipples between thumb and forefinger. Every erogenous zone she possessed was throbbing and she cried out as she came in a shuddering rush. Holy crap. This sort of sex could be addictive. She opened her eyes and found him looking down at her, fully dressed, grinning like a pirate.

Damn. He was too sexy for his own good.

She drew him against her. Dragged his T-shirt up and over his head and tossed it aside. He was muscled but lean, with a smattering of hair on his chest and two small brown nipples. A line of hair arrowed downwards. She followed the trail with her hand, pushing his jeans aside, cupping him and making his eyes glow.

"How about we take this horizontal?" she said huskily.

He lifted her as if she weighed nothing at all, which was an illusion she could go with. He turned them around and they came down together on top of the bed, his weight reassuringly heavy against her hips.

She caressed the hot smooth skin of his shoulders, the tense lines of his neck, sank her fingers into the silky hair at his nape.

He kissed her, taking control again, holding her steady as he plundered her mouth. He reared back, working his way down her body. He seemed obsessed with her breasts, which was ironic considering she barely even needed a bra.

Pretty soon she was gasping for breath, her pulse careening out of control as if she was teetering on the edge of a sharp precipice. Her nails bit into the muscles of his shoulders, holding on, trying to ground herself in the physical reality of his warm, hard body pressed so close to hers. A feeling of hollowness rose inside her and even though his kisses were amazing, and he was worshipping her body, what she really wanted him to do was fill her up. To obliterate the empty space inside her.

She pushed against his shoulder and he understood what she wanted because he rolled onto his back and lay watching her with a hint of amusement in his eyes.

"You're beautiful," he said quietly.

She blinked at the unexpected compliment.

Not knowing how to feel about the sincerity she heard in his tone, she did what she always did when she was unsure of herself. She ignored it. Distracted him. She rose up onto her knees beside him and slid the zipper all the way down, cupping her palm over the hot length of his erection with a groan of female approval. She climbed off the bed and tugged down his pants. Socks and boxers followed in short order and she tossed them aside. Lucas sat up on his elbows, taking in her nakedness with obvious enjoyment.

Was this his first time with someone Asian? Was that what she was seeing in his gaze? The appreciation for something new, something different, something a little exotic? The thought made her hesitate, but what did it matter? They weren't getting married. They were just fucking each other's brains out. The hollowness of the realization threatened to overwhelm her and then she remembered all the reasons she lived her life this way.

It didn't matter why Lucas found her attractive. He'd already proven himself a better lover than any other man she'd been with in her sad, disjointed life.

She straddled one of his thick thighs and eyed him appreciatively. Then she kissed her way up his body and made him do a little begging of his own. She heard the crinkle of a wrapper, then the muted thump as his wallet landed on the side table.

She lifted her head and watched him cover himself. Her insides tightened in anticipation. She pressed her hands to his chest as she straddled him again, leaned down to kiss him on the mouth. He nibbled her, kissing her gently. Then deep until she was almost dizzy with lust.

Carefully she took him inside, until he filled her entirely. She moved over him, slowly at first, getting used to his size and the feel of him so intimately joined to her. She pushed harder and he slid even deeper and she shuddered in pleasure. His hands bit into the sides of her hips and sweat made the hair on his brow stick to his forehead.

His grip urged her on, harder, faster. And even though

there were no spaces left to fill she still wanted more of him; she wanted to swallow him whole. He sank his fingers into her long hair, rearing up until he could graze her neck with strong white teeth. Still he demanded more, forcing her to keep chasing that edge again, but with him this time. He nudged her knees wider apart and she sank even further down his length and cried out. He lay back on the bed and his fingers found her nipple and clit, pinching them both at exactly the same time and making her shatter. Her cries echoed off the walls.

She didn't have time to recover. Keeping her glued to him he turned them over and thrust even deeper. His skin damp and hot beneath her grasping fingers. He pounded, deliciously rough, satisfyingly hard, finding that perfect rhythm that made her tighten around him and the whole room start to spin as she gasped. He let out a fierce groan and her toes dug into the bed as he climaxed inside her, sweeping her right back over the edge in incoherent frenzy.

The room spun like a carousel before slowly returning to normal.

He lay on top of her, heavy, real. Sexy, sweaty man, who'd wrung her out until she was unable to remember her last name.

Her heart hammered and her breath came too fast. This was why she shouldn't have done this. This was why it was dangerous. As she lay limp and ragged from such an intimate coupling there was no room left for deception. Her heart was laid bare.

He rolled away and disappeared into the bathroom.

Oh, God, she had to get out of here. To leave before she did something stupid like confide in the guy. She forced herself to get up and walk over to gather her clothes.

"Where do you think you're going?" The deep rumble was accompanied by hands snaking around her body, one going high, one diving deep. Her knees buckled and he held her against his deliciously naked body.

"I thought we were done." Her voice sounded strangled. She wasn't sure how much more pleasure she could take.

He scraped his teeth over her shoulder and nudged her feet wider apart. Dear lord, the pleasure she was experiencing was ridiculous. He was hard again and everything about this position was different from what they'd just done.

He lifted her feet off the ground, and she was completely under his control—it scared her, but it also turned her on. She was so used to being in charge, it was both terrifying and exhilarating to let someone else take over.

And it was only for a few hours.

Tomorrow she'd be back in Virginia and the chance of running into the handsome, virile Agent Randall was slim to none.

As his hands moved expertly over her she decided to just go with it. Keep her mouth shut, take the pleasure and damn the consequences. They'd both get what they wanted, and tomorrow they could move on without always wondering what it would have been like between them.

She knew now.

It would have been glorious.

CHAPTER FOURTEEN

A SHLEY SLIPPED OUT when it was still dark. Lucas didn't stir.

She'd dozed briefly, but the unfamiliar feeling of sharing a bed with another person had woken her. The novelty of letting her guard down, if only in the throes of passion, unnerved her. She couldn't sleep. She'd watched Lucas sleep for a few minutes, then forced herself to slide off the bed and out of his life.

Her limbs shook as she tugged on her pants and her blouse, and dragged her fingers through her hair. If anyone saw her they'd know exactly what she'd been doing all night long. Careful to leave nothing behind, she tucked her underwear into the pockets of her suit jacket, pulled out her keycard and crept back to her own room.

Inside she noticed a note from Mallory propped up against the sink. The other agent had gone to see Rex, who was recovering nicely from his GSW. Mallory wasn't sure what time she'd be back.

Had she known Ashley was with Lucas last night? She must have suspected something, not that it mattered. It was a one-time thing, not happily ever after.

Ashley showered quickly, then packed her few belongings and ordered a cab. The sooner she got to the airport the sooner she could forget a certain agent with a smile that had snuck its way inside her heart.

Stupid heart.

Stupid woman.

She dragged her FBI persona from the depths of her boots and slapped it in place. It was time to stop taking foolish chances with a career that meant everything to her. It was time to stop risking people she cared about by letting them in even a little bit. Her life wasn't a game. Her deception wasn't a whim. It was a fight for survival just as surely as if she were staring down the barrel of a gun.

She'd already been given her second chance. She wasn't counting on ever getting a third.

———————

ANDREW STARED AT the photograph of Special Agent Ashley Chen. It had been particularly difficult to track down, as if she hadn't wanted it to be found. Now it felt like there was a centrifuge spinning at full speed in his chest. He couldn't breathe. He couldn't stand. He checked her date of birth. December 26th 1984.

December 26th—the day the world had ended. The day Jenny Britton had died.

It was too big a coincidence not to be true.

He stared at the woman's unsmiling features, starker than when he'd last seen her at sixteen, but so like his mother's the resemblance made him ache with longing for the gentle woman who'd raised him.

What would his mother think of him now?

He shoved the thought aside. His mother would never

know.

Jenny had made herself four years older on paper. A clever ruse that would have thrown him if he'd ever thought to look for her.

That December morning in 2004 had shaped his destiny. He'd been swept inside the villa through the open doorway and had grabbed Brandon by his T-shirt and dragged him onto the stairs. They'd scrambled madly and managed to get to the upper floor, climbing out of a window and up onto the roof where they'd sat and prayed the water didn't rise any further. That time on the roof, watching helplessly as people were swept out to sea, worrying that another wave was coming, this one bigger, had seemed to last forever. As soon as the water had receded, he and Brandon had climbed back down and started looking for their family.

His uncle had been badly injured, the bodyguard killed. They'd called in one of their many helicopters, and the old man had been picked up and flown out for medical treatment. Andrew and Brandon had spent days searching the area for Jenny, examining the injured, the dying and finally the dead who'd stared up at him out of faces barely recognizable as human. Some nights he woke with the stench of rotten corpses still in his nostrils.

For several days there was no sign of her, and he'd resigned himself to the fact his beloved sister had been sucked into the jaws of the ocean, her body lost for eternity. Then he'd been told about a female who'd been brought in wearing the same clothes Jenny had been wearing—a red Mickey Mouse T-shirt and blue jeans. The girl's face had been horribly disfigured and he'd been unable to say for sure if it was her until he'd spotted the diamond studs his uncle had given her on Christmas Day sparkling in her blackened earlobes.

Prior to the tsunami, he'd been so angry at the direction his life had taken that he'd barely noticed what was going on with his sister. The loss of his parents, his high school girlfriend turning out to be a slut who serviced the football team. He'd thought the world bleak and depressing. Preoccupied and selfish, self-pity had blinded him to the truth about the world they'd been thrown into.

He hadn't understood the true nature of his uncle's business until he'd watched the man kill Jenny's boyfriend in cold blood. He hadn't understood the twisted feelings his uncle harbored for his sister until she'd screamed it to him on that fateful morning.

He hadn't believed her then. Not really. And moments later it had been too late.

Jenny had always been the rebel. The crusader. She'd been defiant, and so goddamned obstinate. After growing up in California she hadn't adapted well to living in Asia. She refused to back down from an argument. She refused to be meek. She never *bent*.

She would never have survived in their uncle's world of deviance and vice. Although the grief had nearly destroyed him, Andrew had been glad she was dead—at least she didn't know what he'd become.

But she was alive. He touched her picture. Very much alive.

An FBI agent. Jenny was an FBI agent trying to find the men who ran the Boston brothel.

Part of him wanted to laugh. The other part wanted to scream. *She was alive!* How ironic that his uncle's sex trafficking business had brought her back into their lives. The idea of her knowing that he was complicit in all this, how he'd set things up and was in charge all their cyber operations made shame bubble up inside him. He couldn't claim he didn't know what was going on. He couldn't pretend it was somebody else. If she discovered that the perpetrators were the Dragon Devils she'd know it was him. She'd know and despise him for his weakness.

He called Rabbit.

"Hello." From the polite edge in the man's voice Andrew knew it was a bad time. He didn't care.

"There's an FBI agent called Ashley Chen. I want to know where she's staying."

"I'm not sure—"

"You have twenty minutes to find out." He hung up. Maybe it was a good thing he'd let the man live. Even perverts had their uses.

He steeled himself and climbed to his feet. He didn't want to tell Yu Chang the truth about Jenny, but if he didn't, Brandon would, and then Andrew's loyalty would be questioned.

He didn't want to die.

Preparations for their move were almost complete. Men hauled boxes of possessions to a ship nearby. Andrew couldn't wait to leave. There was a very real possibility that the Americans were actively hunting them now. Maybe Jenny herself was telling them everything she knew about her nerdy brother and dubious relatives.

The next compound wasn't somewhere Jenny had ever seen or heard of. It should be safe enough.

He walked down the corridor, knocked quietly on the door.

"Who is it?" The old man sounded angry.

Andrew walked in. Lily was sitting naked on her knees at the end of the old man's bed. Something inside him withered and died. He hadn't expected her to still be here. Blood squeezed painfully through his veins.

She looked up, then averted her eyes as he walked across the room to where his uncle sat at his desk wearing only a loosely tied silk robe.

"I can see why you like the girl, Andrew. I appreciate you sharing her with me." The old man said it like Lily was a bottle of whiskey or some candy, or just another whore. That's what the old man had done. Reduced something that could have been meaningful to Andrew into an impersonal service to be shared between men.

Andrew bowed. "Everything I have is yours, Uncle."

Lily flinched in his peripheral vision, and his stomach twisted. The old man had purposely kept her with him until Andrew had arrived. That's why she was still here, so there could be no lies regarding this. No whitewashing of the reality of what had happened.

Andrew turned and spoke like she was just a maid. "Get dressed and get back to the kitchen. They need help packing." He and Yu Chang would be gone in a few hours, and she'd never have to see him again. She'd be safe from them both.

Tears formed in her eyes, but her gaze stayed on his uncle. The old man had already taught her who was in charge.

Andrew felt sick. He was trying to protect her, but he couldn't let on. His uncle wasn't completely stable, especially when it came to discussing Andrew's sister, Jenny, or his mother, Jun. There was no knowing what the man might do when he heard about Jenny, especially if he had someone he considered disposable within arm's reach.

His uncle looked at Lily and seemed to be considering Andrew's request. Andrew looked out the window until his uncle relented. "You can go. But wait for my nephew in his bed and do for him everything you did for me. He looks tired—help him relax. He deserves it."

His uncle smiled while inside Andrew recoiled. And yet he knew he'd have to lie there and let her touch him and take him, even if he was as limp as a squid. His uncle knew everything that went on in Andrew's world. Everything.

Except about Jenny. He hadn't known about Jenny.

Once Yu Chang heard the news about his sister, the little power play with Lily was going to be of no consequence. Andrew waited impatiently as the young woman ran to get her clothes that were piled on a chair near the door. She dragged her dress over her head, bowed and left as quickly as she could. Humiliation glowed in her cheeks.

The humiliation was his.

He should have known better than to get attached. Pushing her away was the only way to get her out of this nightmare. He'd been a damned fool to think they could have anything approaching a normal relationship.

When the door closed Andrew raised his chin. "You must prepare yourself, Uncle. I have bad news."

His uncle's expression fell slightly, but Andrew held his silence. The old man thought his son had been captured or killed. Andrew enjoyed Yu Chang's grief for a fraction of a second before he realized how low he'd sunk. To rejoice in someone else's grief made him no better than the man across the room.

Andrew walked closer and held out the photograph.

His uncle stood using the cane he'd needed since his leg had been broken in three places by the tsunami. The man's hands shook, and Andrew was shocked to see tears brimming in his eyes.

"Jun?" he said in a shaky voice. His uncle reared back and appeared to stumble.

Andrew shook his head. "Not Jun." His mother would be so ashamed if she could see him now, especially as he betrayed a little girl who'd once meant everything to him. "Jenny. Jenny is alive."

LUCAS SLUMPED INTO a chair inside Sloan's office and checked his wristwatch for the third time inside a minute. "Where is this guy?"

Detective Nelson Shaw of the Hong Kong Police Department was late.

"Damned if I know." Sloan eyed him narrowly, clearly aware of his less than sunny demeanor.

After a night of great sex Lucas should have felt on top of the world. But waking up to an empty bed at five AM had left him pissed off and dissatisfied. Last night had obviously meant something completely different to him than it had to Ashley. The woman had slipped out of his room without a word. When he'd knocked on her door on the way to work no one had answered. Then when he'd arrived at the field office, Sloan had informed him that as of last night the BAU-4 agents had been ordered back to Virginia—a fact Ashley had failed to mention. He shouldn't feel so furious, but fuck if it didn't incense him to be treated like some meaningless hookup.

It wasn't how he operated. It wasn't who he was. He couldn't remember the last time a woman had ditched him…in fact, he was pretty sure Ashley Chen was the first.

"Did Chen find out anything interesting concerning Theo Giovanni yesterday?" Sloan's words were a sharp stick prodding an open wound.

"No, but I'm sure she'd have mentioned any major developments." Maybe between going down on him in the shower and him bending her over the couch. He was furious with himself for losing focus on the investigation. He wasn't a randy kid, but with her he had been.

"The fact Giovanni is still alive is a good sign," Sloan mumbled.

At least it looked like she'd gotten some sleep last night, but there were rumors she was about to be replaced as team leader. After the effort she'd put into this investigation it wouldn't be fair, but knowing how politics worked in the Bureau it was almost a foregone conclusion.

"After this Hong Kong detective leaves I want you concentrating on finding the kid's mother." They were alone, but even so she still didn't mention Becca by name. "Bring in assistance if you need it—as long as you trust them implicitly." She eyed him meaningfully. "I'm going to need to brief anyone who replaces me."

Shit. "Yes, ma'am."

Time was running out and he was torn. If they stopped keeping Becca's survival a secret they could involve victim support and get the kid some real help. But too many people had died in connection to the Chinatown brothel to feel a hundred percent confident they could keep her alive once the bad guys discovered they had a living witness.

They needed to finish this thing.

They needed to shut these people down.

They needed to figure out who the kid was and whether or not she had a family who gave a damn. Becca's mother might give them information on the gambling part of the operation, but there was no way the woman was getting her kid back. Maybe there were grandparents, or an aunt who'd take Becca.

The idea of someone bartering their child for money angered him down to his marrow. He'd grown up in a good family—not just privileged, but *good*. Hardworking. Dedicated to service. Honorable. They made him proud, and he did his best to return the favor.

He stood up and paced the tiny room. He needed to catch these criminals. He needed to know that little girl would be safe.

Sloan replied to an email as the clock ticked.

As soon as he'd spoken to this detective he'd ask Ashley for her help finding Becca's family. That's what he'd planned to do yesterday and damned if he was allowing his job to be affected by the fact they slept together.

The BAU was still assisting them, just from afar. More importantly, he trusted her. Ashley Chen might not be great with people, but she was a good agent. Hardworking. Dedicated. Hot.

Yeah—*hot* was a bit of an issue.

Theoretically he should inform the Bureau they were involved, except, they weren't. She'd left without a frickin' word.

"At least we have ballistics tying Susan Thomas's murder, Ray Tan's assassination and Agata Maroulis's murder together." It suggested a sophisticated organized crime network. One that was starting to unravel. Lucas could practically hear the panic in their actions, but he didn't want anyone else to die.

"Where the hell is this guy?" Sloan's frustration leaked through in the sharpness of her tone.

There was a knock on the door, and Lucas opened it to see an Asian man in a black suit standing in the doorway with Diego Fuentes.

"This is Detective Nelson Shaw, Hong Kong Police Department, Criminal Intelligence Bureau." Fuentes stated. "He says he may have information about the perpetrators." Fuentes leaned against the doorjamb chewing gum with a laconic twist of his jaw.

Nelson Shaw bowed formally. He had short, ink-black hair and intelligent eyes that suggested he knew he was being weighed as an enemy. He shook them each by the hand with a firm grip. "Thank you for meeting with me. I hope we can be of service to one another." His words were formal, his accent more British than Chinese, making Lucas wonder where the guy had been educated.

They set up in the conference room Mallory and Ashley had just vacated. Lucas swore he could smell the sweetness of Ashley's skin cream. He didn't think he'd ever get the damned scent out of his brain.

She hadn't left a note or sent him a text.

He put his coffee on the table with a loud thunk. *Get over it.* He was acting like a love-sick fool. It was a hookup. She'd made that more than clear, leaving the way she had, and he was fine with that. She wasn't relationship material. She was prickly and temperamental, obstinate, rash, opinionated. Determined to be independent. And she lived in freaking

Virginia.

He wanted someone he could spend time with. Do normal things with like go to dinner, the movies, spend time with his family, go hiking, maybe workout with.

Workout naked with…

He scrubbed his hands over his face and took a big chug of coffee.

Caffeine was his friend.

Nelson Shaw pulled a file out of the leather messenger bag slung across his chest. Laid it on the table and pulled out a series of 8 x 10 poor quality glossies. They showed an array of Asian males ranging in age from twenty to eighty.

Lucas had spent enough time with Alex Parker in cyber-security meetings to be suspicious of anything Chinese, which included the guy himself and anything that might be in that bag. Top of his list was electronic listening devices, followed a close second by flash drives that might accidentally get left behind. It was human nature to plug those suckers into machines to see what was on them, and the leading way of introducing a Trojan into an otherwise secure network.

People were always the weakest link. Man's curiosity and ingenuity battled constantly with safety and security. Hell, just look at the origin of the name "Trojan."

He eyed Nelson Shaw narrowly and nodded toward the photographs. "Who are these guys?"

"I believe these are the people behind the murder of your agents and police officers." The HK police detective arranged the photographs but Lucas didn't recognize any of them.

"How do you know?" He sounded surly even to his own ears.

Sloan glanced at him in surprise.

Nelson Shaw's expression became amused. "Have you heard of the old saying, the enemy of my enemy is my friend?"

"These people are your enemies?" Lucas asked.

Nelson nodded. "The Dragon Devils were the scourge of mainland China for many years before they expanded their horizons."

"Dragon Devils? I've never heard of them," said Lucas.

Nelson inclined his head. "Few people have. Fewer still mention their name to the police."

"You obviously know who they are, but you've never been able to catch them or stop them?" asked Lucas.

Nelson lost his smile. "We've come close on occasion."

"Not close enough," Lucas said coldly.

Nelson's initial good humor frosted over. "An experience I believe you share, Agent Randall."

The guy was right, and Lucas gave a sharp laugh. "You have any names?" So far these offenders had run rings around them, and he wanted some way of rounding them all up and putting them in prison where they belonged. And if the Chinese authorities wanted to help, he was all for it. As long as they didn't want anything in return.

"The Devils ran away from mainland China to Hong Kong in the seventies and set up shop. When Beijing regained the territory in 1997 the Devils moved on to Taiwan, but they operated across Asia, transporting heroin and other drugs. They set up gambling dens, extortion and prostitution rings, and human trafficking." Nelson's features were suitably sober. He pointed to a picture of a middle-aged man. "This is the last picture taken of the man believed to be the leader, Yu Chang. Chang was in Macau in 2003 doing business with some other criminal elements. We had a man on the inside who managed to sneak this picture out. The next day our undercover agent was discovered in six parts, laid out on the beach like he was sunbathing. His eyes and tongue had been removed while he was still alive—it's one of their signatures." Nelson's tone was carefully flat.

Lucas's gaze flashed to Sloan. They hadn't released that detail about the Susan Thomas murder, but it was an unusually barbaric MO for this part of the world.

"Is Yu Chang still in charge?" Lucas stared at the man's image. He'd be in his late sixties by now, maybe his seventies.

"We don't know. We do know the organization is fiercely loyal to its leader but we aren't sure who the leader is. They are notoriously secretive about their operations—more so than most secret societies."

"What makes you think the Dragon Devils is the gang behind the Chinatown brothel bombing?" Lucas asked.

Nelson pursed his lips. "We have no proof, but we do have circumstantial evidence."

Sloan blew out a big breath that deflated her whole body. They'd been hoping for a solid lead.

Nelson pulled out an old photograph of Ray Tan. "This man who died was a known associate of the Dragon Devils in 2003. He was an enforcer for their gambling operations in Macau, but we lost track of him. He came to our attention again when he was assassinated on the street yesterday."

Information clicked into place. "And that's why they killed him," Lucas said. "Because they knew he had valuable information he could use to barter for his freedom."

"Ray Tan would never have betrayed the Devils. No one would. You've seen what happens to those who do." Nelson was unsmiling as he held Lucas's stare.

Lucas looked away. Yeah, he'd seen what happened to those who crossed these people. With a series of brutal murders, the perps successfully created an atmosphere of fear and terrified silence. The longer they remained fugitives the more frightened the community became and the more incompetent the FBI looked.

Sloan's phone buzzed. She checked it and swore. "Mayor Everett is in the SAC's office and wants an update. Fuentes, you're with me. Randall, carry on talking to Detective Shaw. Get as much information as you can about this organization."

"We are happy to offer any assistance we can," the detective said formally.

"Thank you. If we can definitively connect the Dragon Devils to the brothel we can start accumulating more information from other sources. We appreciate your help." She shook Nelson's hand, and she and Fuentes left.

Lucas and Nelson assessed one another as the door closed.

"I'm the leading expert on the Devils," Nelson said quietly.

"Why haven't we heard of them before?" Lucas didn't bother to hide the fact he was unconvinced.

Nelson gave a small laugh that didn't sound amused. "The Chinese leaders do not want people to know that someone has bested their efforts to track them down for nearly fifty years."

Lucas frowned. "How have they eluded capture for so long?"

Nelson shrugged. "They're very rich and very careful. They fly under the radar. The gang members are more terrified of their leadership than they are of the authorities. Whenever we get information on them they shut up shop and move on. Disappear. They're smart. They don't take chances. And they always seem to know more than they should about our activities."

"You think they have someone inside your police force?"

"Yours, too," Nelson said. "They know everything my department does. They probably know my seat number for the flight back home."

"They murdered a bunch of law enforcement officials here. That's not exactly flying under the radar."

Nelson inclined his head. "Maybe I'm wrong about their involvement. I just know I've been searching for this gang for many years now."

Lucas raised his brows. The guy couldn't be over thirty.

Nelson spotted the skepticism. "That man who took the last picture of Yu Chang?"

Lucas nodded.

"My father." Nelson's expression didn't alter, but the timbre of his voice changed. "He was an undercover detective with the HKPD. I was sixteen."

"I'm sorry for your loss," Lucas said carefully.

"It was a difficult time." Nelson's smile was stoic. "I loved him, and I didn't let his death define him, but I want his killers brought to justice."

That convinced him more than anything else the man had said. Lucas leaned over the photographs. "Tell me everything you know."

Nelson's stance slumped. "The problem is that even after many years of hunting these people I know very little," he admitted. He spread out the photographs on the table. "These are people we believe were involved in running the Dragon Devils' operations in Macau in association with Ray Tan in 2003."

Lucas squinted hard at the images, then pointed to one.

"Thirty pounds heavier, and he could be a person I saw at the brothel." The man who'd secretly visited Becca's room.

Nelson nodded excitedly. "Xiang Cho. You saw him?"

"Yep. He's heavier and has a lot less hair than in that photo."

"He's a very dangerous individual. Was in the military for many years. Mean as a snake, but not as smart as one."

"Experienced with explosives?" Lucas asked.

Nelson nodded.

Lucas would give every penny he had to spend ten minutes alone in a room with the scumbag. He stared at the other photos but didn't recognize any of them. "If this guy, Yu Chang, is no longer in charge of the gang, who's his most likely successor?"

"The Devils were started by Yu Chang's grandfather in the fifties. Its leadership has passed strictly within the family ever since."

"Their own little dynasty? So I take it Yu Chang has a son?"

Nelson pulled out another photo from his file. A teenage boy with an arrogant smirk who might have been one of the men Lucas had seen in the brothel. "Yes, but the rumor is the entire family was caught up in the tsunami of 2004. We have no firm sightings of any of them after that event—just whispers. They went even further underground, and became almost mythical in how they operated. But someone survived—the empire appears to have expanded dramatically over the last few years, and it's become even more powerful with the advent of the internet."

So they probably had someone good with computers working for them, just like Ashley hypothesized.

"One interesting thing." Nelson pulled out another photograph. "Yu Chang had a sister, Jun, who died in an airplane crash in late 2003."

Lucas dropped to his seat and tried to pretend it had been intentional. The photograph showed a wedding portrait of a tall Chinese woman and a blond white guy with a California tan and teeth.

"Jun and James Britton. They had two kids, Andrew and Jenny."

Another photograph, and Lucas took a sledgehammer to the chest. The kids smiled out of separate school portraits. The boy looked the older of the two and wore thick glasses. The girl had ebony hair that was almost long enough for her to sit on.

He knew those eyes, the line of that elegant neck, the slope of that nose. If it wasn't Ashley Chen, she had a twin.

"What did Jun's husband do?" Grit invaded his throat.

"James Britton ran a computer company out of Silicon Valley."

He taught me code as soon as I could write.

"The police reports suggested the plane crash wasn't an accident," Nelson told him, but the words echoed down a long tunnel of denial.

Lucas took a moment to absorb the information. "What happened to the children?"

"They went to live with their uncle."

"Their uncle the suspected leader of a Chinese organized crime family? How is that even possible?"

"Yu Chang probably paid off someone in the States to make it happen."

Lucas stared at the man with fury in his heart. "I'm going

to need a name."

Nelson inclined his head slowly. "The rumors were that the girl, Jenny, perished during the tsunami. There were reports her brother and her cousin were searching for her in the aftermath."

Keep an eye on Ashley Chen.

Every detail of her life is accounted for, and it all fits together perfectly. It's like the whole thing has been choreographed.

Lucas felt like a fool. He'd been so quick to dismiss a guy he'd gone to war with—whose instincts were razor sharp and honed by a lifetime of experience.

Was it possible that Special Agent Ashley Chen was Yu Chang's niece? Was she working for the other side? Feeding them information? The realization he'd been within minutes of telling her about Becca made bile rise in his throat. He pictured her talking to Ray Tan on the street yesterday—remembered how the shooter had held fire even though she was standing right in front of him.

He'd been such a goddamned idiot.

Had she seduced him on purpose? To have an inside line to the heart of the investigation? Or maybe because Mallory mentioned she suspected someone had survived that explosion? Had she searched his room? He thought hard, but there was nothing there that she wasn't already privy to.

Lucas wanted to excuse himself, but he couldn't leave the Hong Kong detective alone. He needed to take his suspicions to Sloan. Still he hesitated. Ashley had done a lot to aid this investigation, and if he was wrong he could ruin her career for nothing except the fact she resembled a dead woman.

But what if he was right?

He needed to find out where Ashley was, who she was, and

exactly what she was doing.

He took photographs of several of the images and sent a quick text to the one person in the world who would trust him without asking too many questions. Alex Parker.

Nelson watched him speculatively. Did he already know about Ashley? Had he expected her to be here? Was he thinking of using this photograph to blackmail Lucas or the FBI? Was she actually working for the Chinese government?

"What do you want in exchange for this information?" Lucas asked brusquely, clenching his fist inside his jacket pocket.

"My government wants the Dragon Devils brought to justice and put out of business and will help in any way it can." Nelson lost all trace of affability as he held Lucas's gaze. "I want revenge for my father's death."

Lucas let out a breath he hadn't known he was holding. "Revenge?"

Nelson shrugged. "Retribution."

There wasn't much difference in his book.

"I'll let you know what we come up with."

"I want to be there when you arrest them," Nelson stated firmly.

"I'll take it up with my boss." Lucas wasn't making promises he might not be able to keep. He moved to show the detective out. Lucas had a hell of a lot to do, first tracking down the agent who'd rocked his universe last night.

The detective paused in the doorway, a frown marring his brow. "My mother cried every night for a year when my father was murdered. She cried again when I joined the force, but I promised myself and her I'd find his killer and make sure his sacrifice wasn't for nothing." He held Lucas's gaze. "I know you don't trust me, but remember, I came to you with the first solid lead you have." He offered his business card. "I'm staying in Boston for a few days in case there are any developments. Contact me if I can help."

Lucas took the card and showed the guy all the way out to the street and watched him walk away. Then he called Parker.

CHAPTER FIFTEEN

B RANDON COULDN'T BELIEVE Jenny was alive. And that selfish, annoying bitch was not only alive, she'd faked her own death, changed her identity and joined the goddamned FBI. It was a ballsy move by the pampered princess, but his little cousin had never lacked balls. She made her brother look like a pussy.

Andrew *was* a pussy, but he was also the only person on the planet, besides his father, Brandon gave a damn about. And that made this situation difficult.

Andrew had been devastated by the time he'd finally accepted his sister was dead. Brandon had physically dragged him away once the risk of disease had grown too high in a place where the scent of human decay had filled the air.

He walked through the busy kitchens of the hotel where Ashley was staying as if he belonged there. White shirt and black pants made it easy to blend in. In the corridor beyond the main kitchen, a row of room service carts lined the wall.

"You." A red-faced chef carried a large tray of food through the swinging doors and placed it gently on a cart. "Room 441. Where's your uniform?"

Brandon smiled boyishly. "I'm new. Housekeeping told me to wait here for instructions."

The chef's eye twitched with his opinion of housekeeping.

He went back inside the kitchen and returned a moment later, thrusting a red jacket into Brandon's chest. "Hurry up. Room 441. Before it gets cold."

"Yes, sir." Brandon buttoned the jacket as the man went back to his cooking. The guy would piss himself when he realized who he'd been talking to. Brandon took the cart and pushed it to the service elevator just down the hallway. It was almost too easy. He started whistling as he pressed the button, enjoying the scent of the freshly cooked meal. He'd been living on Ramen noodles for the last week and was sick of it. Being on the run and hiding in a dump of an apartment in Cambridge was not his idea of fun. He watched the numbers climb. Jenny, Jenny, Jenny—he couldn't wait to see the look on her face when she saw him.

They should be using the fact she was alive to their advantage. If it was up to him he'd either blackmail her into working for them, or simply leave her alone, let her think she was safe. That way he could kill her at a more convenient time—maybe when the entire law enforcement community of the United States wasn't looking for him. He'd like to spend his time conveying his anger about the fact she'd lied to them. That she'd disrespected his father, her brother, and him by being a conniving little slut. He wished she'd died in that fucking disaster in Thailand. He still had nightmares about the wave, not that he'd ever tell anyone. Then he'd been forced to sift through bodies like trash. He shuddered.

Yeah, if he was in charge, Jenny would pay for her deception in blood. But he wasn't in charge. Not yet.

His father was obsessed. He'd almost died of grief when they'd lost her.

Now the old man wanted her back. He wanted her punished. But mostly he wanted *her*.

Brandon had heard the stories about how his father had gone insane with fury when Jun had met an American boy in college and quickly married the guy. He'd broken every piece of furniture in his home. Brandon suspected the only reason the old man hadn't killed James Britton was because his father's mother had forbade it.

Honoring parents was everything in Chinese culture, even for men like Yu Chang.

Brandon didn't think it was a coincidence that less than six months after his grandmother passed, so had the American. But Yu Chang's grief at Jun's death had been genuine.

Only the fact Jenny looked so much like her mother stopped his father from unraveling completely. Once he'd seen photographs of the girl, he'd paid huge sums of money to buy off lawyers and officials to get Jun's children under his roof, and he'd seemed genuinely happy when they'd arrived. The fact the old man wanted to fuck Jenny was sick, but Brandon didn't give a shit. It wasn't an affliction he shared. His cousin's headstrong ways and defiant manner were decidedly unattractive. He just wished she'd stayed dead.

Brandon shuddered deliciously as he thought about what Yu Chang would do to Jenny, but was less enthralled with what his father might do to him if he didn't bring her home. His father was seventy-three now, but he still controlled the Devils with a fist of iron.

Brandon pushed the room service cart down the hallway to Room 815 and knocked on the door.

"Who is it?" came a voice from behind the door.

"Room service."

A woman with short, dark hair opened the door. Not

Jenny. The other agent? "I didn't order anything. You've got the wrong room." Her eyes went wide when she saw the barrel of his gun he'd hidden under a napkin on his arm.

"Take a step back, and no one will get hurt," he said quietly. "I'm looking for your friend."

The woman's mouth dropped open, but she quickly moved backwards away from the weapon. He pushed the cart inside and closed the door softly behind him.

"Sit," he ordered.

She collapsed onto the nearest chair, then lunged for the telephone. He grabbed her hand and pulled it off the handset, backhanding her lightly with the side of the pistol.

She flopped sideways in the seat. He took the belt from a robe hanging in the closet and tied her hands behind her back.

"What do you want?" Her eyes were full of fear.

He touched her cheek. "I want to know where Ashley Chen is?"

Fine lines appeared between the woman's brows. "I have no idea who that is. I have money—"

He slapped her across the face again, and she gave a high-pitched squeak as if too frightened to scream out loud.

"I don't need your money," he spat. "I want to know where FBI Agent Ashley Chen is, and when she'll be back."

"F-FBI?" Blood dripped from her nose. His handprint was a stark imprint on her skin. "I don't know any FBI agents. I just arrived today. You must have the wrong room."

Her eyes were huge. Under normal circumstances he'd have found her attractive. He let her talk, let her ramble on with her inane denials. He had a description of Ashley Chen's roommate and this woman fit it. Another fed bitch.

He pulled a roll of duct-tape from his pocket and set it on

the cabinet.

"Please don't hurt me. I'll do anything you say. I won't tell anyone you're here. I'm pregnant." She swallowed, and he heard her throat muscles working against one another as she struggled not to hyperventilate. He ripped off a piece of tape and slapped it over her mouth. Then he taped her legs to the chair. She was proving surprisingly docile for a law enforcement agent, but women were weak. All that feminist bullshit, and yet they were so inferior. He had dogs he respected more. He gripped her nose closed until her eyes started to bulge and even though she was tied, she tried to stand and get away. Five minutes too late.

She lost consciousness, and he released her nose so she'd come around again.

When her eyes opened, he pulled his knife from a sheath that nestled in the small of his back. "I don't want to hurt you, lady. I just want to talk to your friend."

Her eyes bugged nervously as the blade came closer.

She shook her head frantically and started to rock the chair. It tipped over and crashed to the floor. The combined weight of the chair and her body broke a bone in her arm.

Her scream from behind the tape sent a shiver of something thrilling running up his spine.

When she recovered enough to focus on him again, he winced in mock sympathy and removed the ties that bound her to the chair. Then he rolled her on her back and put his foot on her broken arm.

Sweat stuck her hair to her forehead, and tears streamed from her eyes.

He leaned closer. "Do you want me to do this all day?"

She shook her head.

He pulled the tape away from red swollen lips. "Where is she?"

She swallowed convulsively and stared fearfully into his eyes. "I don't know."

He sighed. After putting a fresh piece of tape across her lips, he dragged her across the floor by her broken arm. She passed out from the pain, but she'd recover. He tossed her on the bed. He could do this all day. The smell of food had his stomach rumbling, and he grabbed a plate off the cart and started eating, waiting for the bitch to wake up. The sooner she told him where Jenny was, the sooner her suffering would be over.

It wasn't rocket science. He didn't know why it took people so long to figure this shit out.

———————

ASHLEY HAD GONE straight to the BAU from the airport and spent the day holed up in her cubicle avoiding as many people as possible. Her conscience was telling her to hell with her career—she needed to tell her boss what Ray Tan had said about the culprits being the Dragon Devils. These people needed to be captured and held accountable. If they took her down with them, so be it.

She kept watch over Frazer's door, but he hadn't come in, and this wasn't something she wanted to discuss over the phone. She hadn't met her boss's new girlfriend yet, but she'd heard the woman had just sold her property in the Outer Banks and was packing up her teenage sister and pet dog. She hoped they knew what they were getting into. Frazer was the most remote, difficult, ornery person she'd ever met, which was saying something, considering how ornery, remote and difficult she was.

Her cell had remained sullenly silent all day. Lucas Randall's lack of communication shouldn't have unsettled her, but she couldn't help wondering what he'd thought when he'd discovered she'd left without a word. Was he angry? Or maybe he didn't care and was simply getting on with his day?

It was irrelevant how he felt—it wouldn't change anything—but she couldn't stop thinking about him. She'd ended up turning the cell off and stuffing it in a drawer to get rid of the constant distraction of the blank screen. The desire to call him, to explain, to say just exactly how much last night had meant to her...was dangerous. She didn't want to endanger a man who could mean so much to her if she let him.

Instead, she forced her attention back to her computer screen. She'd split her time today between sleazeball lawyer, Theo Giovanni, who was in court most of the day, and tracking down the contraceptive pills they'd found at the brothel. The lab had come back with a chemical match, and the pills were readily, if illegally, available online. She'd ordered some using a false identity the FBI provided. Now she needed to figure out where they were manufactured and where the pharmaceutical counterfeiters did their banking. Then, with a little help from the federal government and judicial system, she was going to freeze their assets.

The good news was the pills themselves seemed to be generic copies of pharmaceutical brands, rather than poisonous concoctions off the factory floor. She figured this meant they planned to be in business long-term, which worked for her as it gave the feds time to make arrests.

And the manufacturers might still be supplying pills to the

sex traffickers, which was another lead, and another possible way of tracking down where the new brothels had relocated.

She'd put a call in to the US Postal Service for their assistance and was expecting one of their agents to contact her.

A headache was building, pressing against her temples and making her feel a little lightheaded. She took a sip from her water bottle and searched her drawer for pain meds. No dice. She picked up her cell and reflexively checked it. The screen was distressingly blank when she slipped it back into her pocket.

She looked up and realized it was nighttime. She was the last person here. She stretched out a kink in her neck.

There was no way she could wait any longer, and the idea of relating the information anonymously had lost its appeal. She'd go to Frazer's home. He wouldn't be pleased to see her, but he'd understand once she told him everything.

He might have her arrested…

The idea made acid boil in her stomach, but the task force needed to know who they were chasing to have any chance of catching them.

As she stood to leave, Matt Lazlo strode into the room.

His brows stretched. "Hey. How was Boston?"

"Grim," she admitted.

"You okay? You look pale."

"I feel like I'm coming down with something." *A belated dose of guilt.* She took another sip of water to wash away the bilious feeling. "You forget something?"

"Nah," the former Navy SEAL shook his head. "I went to visit my mother"—who was comatose in a nearby facility—"and Frazer called and asked me to pick up a file and drop it off on my way home."

She frowned. Why hadn't Frazer asked her to drop off the file? He knew she was back. Had Alex Parker also confided his suspicions to Frazer? Despite everything she'd sacrificed in order to serve her country?

He knows you're a liar, he just can't prove it.

Reality pricked a hole in her affront. Parker was right. She had lied to get into the FBI. She had faked her background and spent months training to beat the polygraph machine to be accepted into the program. Being angry with Alex Parker was like being angry with a cop who pulled you over for speeding. You had to accept responsibility for your actions. It was part of being a grown up.

"How's Scarlett?" she asked, trying to prolong her time as a team member.

Scarlett Stone was Matt's brilliant, slightly scatty physicist fiancée, and daughter of the most notorious spy in FBI history. That was until she and Matt had proved her father's innocence and exposed the real traitor.

Ashley's spirit sank as she realized that, on paper at least, she'd be the traitor.

"Busy. Between spending time with her dad and us moving into a new house." Matt tossed a file on his desk and headed to Frazer's office. She followed him.

"I never thought I'd end up with a woman who chose appliances based on whether or not they can get hacked and who wants to install solar roof tiles." He grinned, looking like a rugged version of Captain America. "Hey, we're having a housewarming BBQ in a couple of weeks."

"BBQ? In February?"

"It's Scarlett's dad's idea. He wants a BBQ and is a bit worried he might not make it to summer."

God. The thought of going to jail made her want to throw up. What had she been thinking? "How's he doing?"

Matt shrugged. "Getting the best cancer treatment money can buy, but he's very sick. They're all just so frickin' happy to be back together again. It's like an episode of the *Waltons.*" His lips canted into the sort of smile that brought women to their knees. But all Ashley could think of was dark hair and espresso eyes, and the sort of kisses that should come with hazard-to-your-heart warnings.

"You should come."

She snapped back to the moment. "I'd love to." But the chances were she'd be out of here by then. *Persona non grata.* Kicked to the curb. Labeled a traitor. Denied access.

A printout of a photograph lay on the floor beside Frazer's printer. "Need this?" she asked, walking over and picking it up.

Matt glanced at what she was holding while he flicked through files in the stack on the side of Frazer's desk.

"Don't think so."

She looked down at the image she was holding. It was an old grainy photograph of Yu Chang and made all the saliva in her mouth evaporate.

"They got a lead on the suspects in Boston." His lips thinned. "You didn't hear?"

She shook her head. "I turned off my email and phone trying to get some work done."

"Why didn't I think of that?" He smiled, and Ashley wished almost desperately that he was single and she'd fallen for this man, rather than a man she'd never see again.

And Matt had forgiven Scarlett her deception, even though it paled in comparison to Ashley's. Ashley opened her mouth to tell him the truth, quickly, before she lost her nerve.

"An organization called the Dragon Devils," he said as he ducked his head to concentrate on the files, missing her open-mouthed astonishment. "Some detective from Hong Kong came into the Boston Field Office and gave them a few leads. Parker managed to narrow down the area for the probable location of the perps to within a half block radius. Cops are staking out the area. I can't believe no one told you. Parker said it was your idea."

"Alex Parker doesn't like me very much," she said glumly even as her mind spun with the implications.

"Hey." Matt slapped her on the shoulder. "It was a good idea, and he gave you full credit. I expect the messages of congratulations are in your inbox. Apartment is in Cambridge. Won't be long until they catch the fugitives."

She blinked at him in sudden realization. She didn't have to bare her soul to Frazer. She didn't need to confess her sins. Her heart fluttered against her ribs with a renewed sense of hope.

"I'd love to come to your BBQ."

"Gonna bring someone?" His blue eyes teased her.

She drew in a deep breath, and the noose around her throat loosened. "Maybe."

She said goodnight, grabbed her stuff, and headed outside, desperately needing to be alone for a few moments to think. Winter dragged its icy claws over her skin, and the bleak wind dampened her mood. Or maybe it was just easier to blame her depression on the weather, rather than looking at the root cause of her unhappiness. She had no life outside work. Whenever she cared about anyone she needed to stay far away to keep them safe.

How would that change if the Devils were arrested?

She headed into the parking lot and strode toward her car.

A bunch of NATs—New Agents in Training—trailed past on their way to the canteen.

She remembered every minute of that sixteen-week training course. The brutal PT, the intense firearms training, the toughness of Defensive Tactics. But failing the grueling course hadn't been the thing she'd feared most. Every time they'd called her name, every time they'd singled her out for censure or praise, she'd expected them to tell her to grab her stuff and that she was done. But they never had.

Instead, she'd excelled, soaking it up, learning federal statutes and laws, defensive driving, situational awareness. Every class had been another weapon in her arsenal to fight back against the people who'd wanted to hurt her.

A branch cracked in the nearby woods, and she jumped, her heart doing a drumroll in her chest. She forced herself to relax and not rest her hand on her weapon. Last thing she needed was to shoot some prankster or idiot marine.

She got to her car, automatically checking the backseat. She dumped her bag and laptop on the passenger seat. Her luggage from her trip to Boston was still in the trunk.

She drove off base, past the Marine guards. She stopped at a pizzeria where you could order by the slice and headed home to her two-bedroom condo ten miles south, eating as she drove.

As she pulled up outside the home she hadn't seen all week, every thought vanished from her mind.

Lucas Randall stood leaning against a white van parked next to her space.

Adrenaline flooded her bloodstream, and she had to force herself not to throw her arms around him and hang on tight.

"What are you doing here?" she asked as she got out. She hated how breathless she sounded. How hopelessly hooked.

His stare was intense on her face. "I needed to see you."

"About the case?"

Who cared about the case?

"We have unfinished business." His tone warned her that he was angry, as she'd known he would be. She just hadn't expected him to follow her to Virginia.

No matter how desperately she wanted to kiss the guy, she had to force him away. Her uncle would destroy anything she cared about.

"I'm sorry you had a wasted trip, Lucas. I thought you understood that what happened last night was temporary. A way of blowing off steam during a difficult case." She glanced up at him quickly. The look in his eyes was almost feral.

"Well, we certainly blew off steam." His smile had jagged edges. She went as if to slide past, but he pulled her against him. And she hated how willingly she let him.

Had she forgotten what happened to Martel? Was she so eager to sacrifice someone else she cared about for a fleeting moment of pleasure?

Lucas turned them so he was the one leaning against her car door, holding her tight. She gripped him, for balance and because she wasn't ready to let him go. Then he kissed her.

It was a hard kiss, a punishing kiss, and she let him control it because she deserved a little harshness after what she'd done to him. She wanted that slight taste of punishment for lying to him. The van door slid open behind her, and she tried to twist around to see if someone needed to get by.

Lucas raised his head, and she expected him to move them aside, but instead he held her imprisoned in his arms while someone stuffed a gag in her mouth and pulled a hood over her head.

Panic engulfed her. She started fighting, but it was too late.

She couldn't breathe. Someone captured her wrists, which were jerked behind her back and secured tightly with metal handcuffs.

She raised her knee, but it deflected off a less vulnerable part of his body. Then she was lifted and shoved into the vehicle, her legs bound as her arms had been, and she was lying on the hard metal floor, panting through her nose, trying not to hyperventilate. Someone patted her down and removed her cell phone, her weapon, and her backup.

Lucas?

Oh, God.

What was happening? Had she been right in her initial suspicion? Was Lucas working with the Dragon Devils?

Everyone had a price—even rich people.

She tried to cry out for help, but the door slammed shut on her muffled screams. The engine started. Tears filled her eyes, but she refused to let them fall. She hadn't cried since she was a sixteen-year-old girl watching her uncle kill a young man she'd thought she'd fallen in love with.

A heavy hand pushed her onto the floor and held her still. "Easy."

Lucas.

A sob reared up.

She'd been kidnapped, and Lucas Randall had helped do it. Panic rushed through her, and she lashed out with her whole body. She couldn't go back to her uncle. She wouldn't go back to the monster. She jerked away from whoever was holding her and whacked her head on the side of the van.

Goddamn!

Her vision fractured like glass shattering. Stars spun as she allowed herself to slide into unconsciousness, all the time fearing she'd been the one who'd been betrayed.

CHAPTER SIXTEEN

LUCAS RANDALL HAD been born into wealth and privilege. He'd gone to war and worked six years as an FBI agent on some of the roughest, toughest cases in the United States. This was the first time he'd compromised his morals.

They'd driven through the night. Ashley slept most of the way. Lucas had removed her gag because he didn't want her to suffocate, and loosened the binding on her legs. She wasn't going anywhere.

The fact he'd had to hold her down as she fought with every ounce of her strength made him feel sick inside. If he hadn't gotten a firm hold of her before she'd realized she was in trouble they'd never have overpowered her without someone getting seriously hurt—probably her.

It went against every grain of his being.

Alex had offered to pick her up alone, but as much as he trusted the other guy with his life, he didn't trust anyone with Ashley Chen's. She meant too much to him.

Detective Nelson Shaw had blown the lid off the case, but Lucas and Alex were the only ones who knew it. Lucas should have gone to his boss with the photograph of Jenny Britton; he didn't know why he hadn't, except there were too many things that didn't add up. He was jumping all over a fellow agent's civil rights but—what if he was wrong? What if it was a coincidence that Ashley Chen looked exactly like the dead niece of their prime suspect?

Questions burned in his mind, and he needed answers.

Alex turned down a narrow lane and the unpaved road rumbled under the tires. Almost there.

Lucas looked at Ashley's inert form and reminded himself not to fall for any act of innocence or ignorance. She was a liar. She'd probably played him every step of the way. She'd initiated the first kiss. She'd initiated sex. Sure, he'd been the one to pin her against that alley wall and finger fuck her, but she'd let him.

Christ.

He felt sick to his stomach. Maybe she'd faked the whole thing—the intense attraction, the blistering orgasms. It made him feel dirty and angry, but none of that mattered compared to people's lives.

He'd almost told her about Becca. The realization made him want to lash out. So he needed to be on guard against his anger, as well as his hurt.

Alex rolled to a stop and stretched before getting out. Lucas eased open the side door and slid outside, grateful to be hit by the fresh morning air that slapped him awake with its icy chill.

"Let's get her inside before the sun rises." Alex walked away.

Dawn was breaking on the Massachusetts coastline; the dusky shadows and diffused light showing Lucas an isolated outpost with a small cottage surrounded by wild looking shrubs and stunted trees.

He turned back to the van. No point in delaying the inevitable. He eased his hands under Ashley's body and lifted her, for some foolish reason, trying not to wake her. She reared back and head butted him so hard his nose crunched, and he dropped her. *Fuck.* He fell to his knees, clutching his face.

Sonofabitch!

He watched her run blindly, stumbling through the gray dawn in the direction of the beach.

Lucas ignored the blood running down his face and took off after her. He could hear her thrashing through scrub. She couldn't see and couldn't save herself if she fell. The woman was going to break her damn neck. She had no idea where she was. It could have been a cliff she was running toward.

Did she even care if she lived or died?

Maybe she *could* see, because she found her way onto the path that led to the beach. For a few seconds she ran as fast as she could, even with a bag on her head and her arms cuffed behind her back. Then, just as suddenly, she stopped moving, every line in her body going taut.

He reached for her shoulder, but she twisted out of reach.

"What's that? What's that noise?" she demanded angrily.

He frowned. What the hell was she talking about? He cocked his head and listened hard. "It's a seagull."

"And waves? Are those waves? Are we near the sea?" Her voice rose in pitch.

This was a damned strange conversation to be having at this exact moment. He loosened the string on the hood and pulled it off her head. Her makeup had smudged, her hair was mussed and her right eye was swollen shut.

His mouth went dry. That was his fault for not restraining her properly.

But her gaze wasn't on him. It was fixed on the miles and miles of exposed sand, and the surf that crashed down in a rhythm as old as the ocean itself.

She started to tremble. Then she backed up. "No. No. No! Get me out of here."

What the hell? He went to touch her, but she jerked away from him like *he* was the one who'd betrayed *her*. She turned and started sprinting up the path, but as soon as she spotted the isolated cottage on the edge of the beach, she stopped and looked back at him. "I can't stay here. Take me anywhere else." Her face was contorted by grimness. "But not here. Not near the ocean."

"You don't get to dictate terms, *Jenny*."

Her bottom lip wobbled, and she looked away. Then she resumed running, fast, in the direction of the road this time.

Lucas caught up with her in a matter of seconds, scooping her up in his arms. She yelled, but the wind stole the sound and wove it into its haunting narrative.

She sank her teeth into his flesh, and he shook her off him with a curse. He shouldered past Alex who stood in the doorway, watching.

She stiffened in his arms when she saw the other man.

Lucas dumped her on the made up bed. The drapes were closed, and there were locks on the window.

It wouldn't stop her smashing them if she got the chance.

Two sets of handcuffs were attached to the metal frame of the bed.

"I can't stay here," she sobbed. "If a wave comes we're all dead."

The woman had gone from icy cool federal agent to insanity, which pretty much reflected how he was feeling.

"Don't you understand how dangerous this is? Just one wave and everyone who lives along this coast is dead!" She was borderline hysterical.

He wiped at the blood on his face and looked at her incredulously. "Seriously? After everything you've pulled you're worried about a tsunami? Do you know how fucked up that sounds?" His words or his tone seemed to shock her out of her panic. Or maybe she realized he wasn't going to fall for this line of bullshit.

She sobbed but stopped begging. It was probably all an act anyway.

He pushed her toward the bed, but she fought against his grip, every inch of her body pushing against his, striving for freedom and stirring such memories he wanted to walk away. Just ditch Ashley Chen or Jenny Britton or whatever the hell her name was. Walk out the front door and forget she existed. Forget that she'd lied to him and played him like a fucking violin concerto.

"I need the bathroom." She raised her voice, and he knew she was serious. *Great.* He'd known this was going to be part of the setup going in, but he didn't like it.

And he sure as hell wasn't letting Alex interfere in this part of the program.

The fact she hadn't even asked why they'd taken her or why he was calling her "Jenny" spoke volumes about her guilt. She'd lied her way into the FBI. She was either a spy for the people they were hunting or employed by some foreign government. He removed the cuffs from her wrists and stood impassively as she shook them out, grimacing against the rush of blood. He opened the door to the bathroom. "Be quick."

The tang of blood on his lips reminded him not to underestimate her.

She flashed him a look full of loathing as she went to close the bathroom door.

He shook his head. "Not on your life."

Tears brimmed in her eyes, but he forced himself to ignore them and think instead of everything Becca had endured over the years. She was the real victim in this.

"I hate you," she said slowly, but with venom. "You pride yourself on being honorable and noble, but you're nothing but a hypocritical, self-righteous bastard. I thought you were different, Lucas."

He didn't let the accusing tone get to him. "My character isn't the one in question."

"Yeah, well maybe it should be," she said bitterly. "They're out there, searching for me, probably killing anyone who gets in their way. And rather than help catch them, you snatched me off the streets and detained me illegally. You're as bad they are."

The hurt shimmering in her eyes battered his resolve, but he was committed now, and that meant seeing this through to the bitter end. He checked his watch. "You have sixty seconds to use the facilities before I handcuff your lying ass to that bed. I suggest you get on with it."

Her mouth firmed, and her chin lifted. "Yeah, I guess handcuffs are the one thing we didn't try the other night."

He held her gaze. "I'd never have touched you if I'd known the truth."

She flinched, and he told himself not to be conned by the rare show of vulnerability.

She turned her back on him and did what she needed to do. He averted his eyes. When she'd finished and washed her hands he handcuffed her to the bed and tied a gag between those pretty white teeth so she couldn't scream her way to freedom.

And all the while her eyes watched him with betrayal in their depths, as if he was the one who'd lied to the FBI.

———————

"WHERE IS ASHLEY Chen?" Andrew asked in a deceptively quiet voice.

"Fuck. Do you want to get caught?" The words were low and hard over the phone, Rabbit finally finding his nerve. "You can't go after the FBI like this! You killed an innocent woman who was four months pregnant."

Andrew didn't approve of Brandon's actions, but it was done now.

"Why are you even doing this? They should be miles away by now. In fucking Canada," said Rabbit.

"The way you're questioning me makes me think you don't care anymore. Have you given up? Are you thinking of turning on us? Do you think you'll ever be safe if you do?" Andrew let his incredulous amusement leak through. "How do you think your family will react to hearing you raped a child? Will the woman you love stand by you?"

"I didn't rape her." Rabbit spoke through gritted teeth.

"She's thirteen and was being held against her will. Do you know what happens to pedophiles in prison?"

"There's no proof," Rabbit insisted.

Andrew laughed, the nasty, bitter sound expressing how he really felt. "How about a video of you bending the kid over the bed and taking her from behind? Would that be adequate proof? Or you telling her to call you 'Daddy'? You sick fuck. How about the recording of you asking Mae Kwon to add pretty little Mia Stromberg to her stable of underage girls? You think people will believe that?"

Rabbit swallowed thickly. "You recorded that?"

"I recorded everything." He let that sink in for a few moments. They were in a new location, and Andrew was confident no one could trace them here. With the commotion surrounding Jenny he'd managed to avoid Lily before he left yesterday. Thank God. He couldn't bear to see the disgust she must feel for him reflected in her eyes. She was safe now. He was better off alone. "I need to know where Ashley Chen is."

"I don't know how to find out. She left," he insisted.

"Figure it out. Else we'll be visiting you next." He put the phone down, and there was a knock at the door. "Go away."

The knock came again, and he strode over and flung it open, ready to ream out the idiot on the other side who obviously didn't understand English.

Lily stood there with her head bowed, holding a tray with a glass and a bottle of water on it.

"What are you doing here?" he snapped. After everything he'd done to try and keep her safe.

"The *dai lo* gave orders I accompany the household." Her tone was as listless as her expression.

Inside he was screaming. He didn't want her exposed to this world anymore. He didn't want his uncle anywhere near her. It had been a mistake not to fight for her. She kept her head bowed as she placed the tray on a nearby table. Her hands shook. "The *dai lo* said that if you didn't want me in your bed I was to warm his."

The horror of the situation crashed around him.

"Do you want to be with him?" Andrew asked carefully.

Her brown eyes flashed with such outrage that for a moment they were back to the way they'd been before. Before he'd fucked it up. There were dark circles under her eyes, and a haunted fear that hadn't been there before.

"I just follow orders, *sir*." She bowed her head and went to leave, but he snagged her wrist.

"I don't want you to go," he whispered fiercely. Seeing her again. Touching her...even knowing his uncle had also touched her, made something inside his chest crack open and bleed.

Her eyes rose to meet his, but rather than love he saw loathing. He tightened his grip. The safest place would be in his bed. She didn't have to like it. "Wait for me in my bedroom. Don't leave for any reason."

He waited for her eyes to meet his, but she refused. Instead she bowed low and retreated from him. As he shut the door, loneliness closed in around him. He hated everything he'd become.

His phone rang. Rabbit.

"Look, I don't know how to find out where Ashley Chen is." The man kept his voice low, as if nervous of being overheard. "But I know someone who would." He gave Andrew a name and address and hung up.

Andrew stared at the piece of paper for a long time, knowing that if he gave it to Brandon he was signing that person's death warrant. This was the man he'd become. This was who he was now. He picked up the glass of water and threw it against the far wall. It smashed into a thousand pieces and scattered throughout the room in razor-thin shards.

Why couldn't his sister have just stayed dead.

CHAPTER SEVENTEEN

"HERE." ALEX THRUST a steaming mug of coffee into Lucas's hands. "Give her this. It'll keep her out of trouble while I go through her machines this morning."

Lucas recoiled from the steaming brew and put it down on the counter. "I'm not drugging her."

Alex gave him a rueful smile. "There are worse things."

The scar that bisected his eyebrow twitched. He'd gotten it during their Army days in Afghanistan, a souvenir from a brawl with a couple of Air Force pilots who'd been kicking the shit out of a cocky young corporal for playing his music too loud. Alex had dispatched the pilots with their tails between their legs and reamed the kid out for being a noise nuisance. The young soldier had later died in an ambush that had earned Alex the Distinguished Service Cross. Living with the aftermath of that ambush had put shadows in Alex's eyes that were still there today.

Sometimes the dog days of war felt like yesterday. Other times it felt like someone else's life.

Alex was a good man to have in his corner. And from the resigned expression on his face, he wasn't any happier about this situation than Lucas was, even though his suspicions about Ashley had finally been confirmed.

"Lucas, we abducted a federal agent. If anyone finds out,

we're in deep shit. Drugging her to keep her quiet isn't going to make that any worse, but it might buy us enough time to figure out exactly what she's been doing."

Lucas rolled his shoulders and looked away. The cottage belonged to a friend of Alex's. Someone who wouldn't ask questions. But they weren't planning a long-term stay.

The fact he and Alex had broken the law pissed him off. Why was he risking his career for a woman who'd lied to him, and to the organization he'd dedicated his life to? Why was Alex? The repercussions, if their actions were discovered, were career ending. Worse, it could land them in federal prison.

"We need to figure out whether she's working for the Dragon Devils or the Chinese government and decide how that affects the case."

"And if it were that simple, you'd have informed the SSA in Boston and set up a surveillance sting." Alex's expression softened. He'd overheard Lucas's conversation with Ashley. He knew they were involved on a personal level. Bad enough Lucas had slept with the woman, but his emotions had started to be engaged and how he felt about her was affecting his judgment. Unlike some people, he *did* have to like someone to fuck them.

It made things more complicated.

"I can't believe she's a mole working for the opposition. She gave us some great leads," he admitted finally.

"You don't infiltrate the upper echelons of any organization by doing a crappy job," Alex argued.

Lucas blew out a troubled breath. His nose throbbed from where Ashley had head butted him earlier.

She was a good agent, but Alex was right.

"As soon as we confirm some facts, we'll go to Frazer and

Sloan. Plus, there's something more important you need to know..." He told Alex about Becca, speaking in a low murmur that couldn't be overheard. "If Sloan is replaced and Becca's survival revealed to the team, we can't afford for the Devils to have an inside source."

The idea that Ashley might have aided in the murder of a little girl made the fact they'd slept together utterly repulsive.

Alex nodded. "We need to catch these people before they figure out the kid is alive. You're right. We need to know if Chen has been feeding them information."

Lucas reluctantly picked up the coffee mug from the counter. The image of Agata Maroulis bouncing on her tiptoes seconds before she stepped off the curb and into Mae Kwon's minivan flashed through his mind. All those victims force-fed drugs so they would be easier to subdue when the traffickers brought in clients. His stomach turned.

He tipped the laced drink down the sink and watched it drain away.

"Taking away her freedom is one thing. Taking away her mind is something else entirely." He leaned against the sink and looked out at the leaves on the dwarf trees quivering in the stiff breeze. "I need to question her."

But he didn't want to.

Alex shook his head. "Let's see what I get from her laptops before we confront her. I've already been tracking her online activity. What?" he asked, seeing Lucas's surprised expression. "I told you her background was suspect—I could just never figure out why." He checked his watch. "Give me an hour, and if there's anything suspicious on the machines I'll know it. We can make the decision about what to do next."

"Does Mallory know about Ashley?" Lucas asked suddenly.

Alex shoved his hands in his jeans pockets. "Not yet."

Mallory would not approve of what they'd done.

"Rex, the retriever, had a complication with his blood work, and they decided to keep him at the veterinarian's for another night before letting him fly. I tried to call her just now, but she's not answering." A frown dented his brow. "With luck, she won't even know I left DC. I might be home for dinner."

Mallory would be upset when she found out. She liked Ashley. *Fuck*, he more than liked Ashley. But the woman's career was over and once this got out, she'd be a pariah. It was just a matter of determining how badly she'd betrayed the Bureau, her country, and exactly what she'd found out about this case. She'd be lucky to get out of this without serving time.

Alex went over and picked up Ashley's laptops, which they'd retrieved from the trunk of her car last night. He set them both on the kitchen table. Then he took out his laptop, a slim line number that looked like something out of a sci-fi movie.

"You should get some rest while you can," Alex told him.

Lucas was tired and frustrated, but the chances of sleep were right up there with him and Alex winning the Nobel Peace Prize.

Instead he scooped up the keys to the van. "I'll go pick up something for lunch."

He headed outside, but instead of taking the van, he turned toward the beach. The scent of the ocean washed over him in a frigid salty breeze. The sand covered his boots as he stalked all the way down to the surf. The waves crashed just a few short feet away, and he stared out at the silver gray horizon and wished to hell he'd never met Ashley Chen. Becca's blue-eyed gaze entered his mind, heightening the feeling to guilt and failure. Part of him wanted to pretend he'd never recognized Ashley in the photos, and another part wanted to post her betrayal on the national news.

He picked up a pebble and rubbed off the gritty sand with his thumb. He bent and skimmed it over the breakers and watched the rock bounce over the surface of the water in ever decreasing strides until it ran out of steam and sank to the bottom.

A fitting metaphor for his career, but his career was the least important casualty of this goatfuck.

———————

A SHORT TIME later, a shout from up the beach grabbed Lucas's attention. Alex was sprinting toward him. His friend had lost all vestige of color, and sweat slicked his short hair to his forehead. Shit. What had he discovered? Had Ashley escaped?

"The bastards sent a hit squad to the hotel." Alex was panting heavily, but not from the short run. "They found a dead woman in one of the rooms, and I can't reach Mallory." His voice shook. "I heard it on the news. Frazer doesn't know anything."

They scrambled back up the beach.

"What's Sloan's number?" Alex's voice vibrated with emotion.

"It's not her." They wouldn't catch Mallory off guard.

"What if it is!"

"It's not her, Alex." Lucas dialed Mallory's cell as he

marched in the front door. He checked the bedroom to make sure Ashley was still there. The door crashed against the wall, jerking her awake with a start. She stared at him, looking like a kidnap victim. Her eye was swollen as if she'd been beaten; handcuffed to the bed like a hostage.

God.

That he'd been reduced to the level of kidnapper made him feel like he was losing his mind.

Maybe Ashley was right. This wasn't what he did. This wasn't how he behaved. But he didn't know how else to protect Becca, and if he was honest, he needed to hear Ashley's story for himself. He cared for her—otherwise this whole situation wouldn't be tearing out his guts.

But as Mallory's phone went to voicemail, he wasn't feeling very caring.

His pulse skyrocketed.

Alex followed him into the bedroom, but stood by the door as if afraid of what he might do if he came closer to their captive. Lucas's hands were sweaty—if anything happened to Mallory he'd never be able to look Alex, Mallory's parents, or himself in the eye again.

Lucas couldn't even imagine how he'd feel if the woman he loved with all his heart, the woman who was carrying his child, was murdered. It was bad enough worrying about one of his best friends. He dialed Sloan.

"Where the hell are you?" she snapped.

"Following a lead on the mother." Apparently lying was easy.

"I need you back here ASAP. SWAT raided the Cambridge location—they'd scrammed."

His heart gave a painful clench as he forced out the next

words. "I heard there was another murder—"

"They slaughtered her." Sloan's voice quavered. "Her unborn baby died, too. Perps must have found out we had agents staying in the hotel and sent a hit man."

His knees buckled, and he sank to the bed. *Please not Mallory. Please not Mallory. Please not Mallory...*

"She was a beauty consultant named Catriona Malcolm, and the bastards tortured the shit out of her."

The grip on his heart and throat eased even as the awful reality that another woman had died hit home. He covered the mouthpiece. Turned to Alex who looked like animated death. "It's not her."

Alex's head shot up, eyes straining for hope.

Sloan continued. "They must have figured out what room Chen and Rooney were staying in and targeted them—"

"But Rooney's okay? You're sure?"

"She was when I spoke to her this morning. She got lucky. Catriona Malcolm didn't. Mary Kay convention hit town, and the hotel was fully booked last night. Rooney checked out yesterday expecting to fly back to Virginia, but she was delayed. She had to find someplace else to stay last night. I tried to call her again when I found out about this murder, but I couldn't reach her. I'm assuming she's in the air. I called Frazer. Told him to send a protection detail in case she's being specifically targeted."

Was this retaliation for grabbing Ashley? Christ, if his actions had led to a woman's death...

He covered the microphone again. "She switched hotels last night. She's probably flying. That's why you can't reach her."

Alex dropped to his haunches and buried his face in his

hands.

Sloan was still talking. "Frazer was trying to reach Agent Chen. He sounded pretty pissed."

Lucas glanced at where Ashley lay handcuffed on the bed, watching their every move. "Chen's with me."

"Tell her to call him ASAP if she wants to keep her job. I need you back here."

"I found a lead we need to follow." It wasn't a lie.

"Chances are my time as task force leader can be counted in hours if not minutes—unless we catch these perps," Sloan sounded strained. "I don't have time for you to be playing house."

Lucas shook with anger. House? Fucking *house*?

He barely controlled his temper. He was AWOL and shacked up with an agent he'd recently had sex with, but playing house didn't quite fit the situation. He could hardly tell Sloan the truth. All their careers were on the line.

He swallowed back the outrage. "Then let's make sure we catch these assholes."

"Damn right. *She's* asking for you."

Becca. "I'll be there by this evening."

"Make it sooner," she muttered angrily. "Call me as soon as you get in, even if I'm taken off the case, understand? I want more security on our friend, and ATF can't spare any more agents."

"Roger that." He hung up and consumed a breath. "Mallory probably doesn't even know they found a body in the hotel yet." He rubbed his watch as he felt Ashley's eyes on his back. "She'll be landing soon."

Alex lifted his head. "I should never have turned off the tracking device on her laptop. I should never have left her alone." His hands were still visibly shaking.

"Yeah, I'm pretty sure women don't go for the paranoid stalker personalities as husband material—at least not the ones I know."

Alex laughed. "Don't I know it." He looked up. "I need to get home to her."

"We need to finish this first," Lucas said sharply. As much as he loved Mallory, she wasn't the only one in danger. "Frazer is sending agents for extra protection when Mal hits the airport. Arrange for one of your company jets to wait for you at Logan so you can leave as soon as we're done here, but let's not lose focus."

Ashley made a noise behind him. Then kneed him in the back. He grunted and got up, walked around so he could remove her gag without getting a boot in his face.

"What happened?" Her voice was hoarse, and the sound of it sawed across his nerves like a violin bow. So did the sight of her black eye.

"Your buddies butchered the next occupant of your hotel room in Boston. I guess they figured the vic was FBI and tried to beat your location out of her." He didn't bother to hide his disgust. "The woman was also pregnant."

Alex swore.

"You think I had anything to do with that?" Her gaze was unflinching. "They're looking for me."

"Exactly. When they realized we were onto you they sent someone to try and help you escape."

"Help me escape?" She glared at him just fine with one eye. "Dear God, I hadn't realized you were an idiot until this exact moment."

He ignored the insult. "Where are they?"

"If I knew that, we would have arrested them already." Her bitterness sounded genuine, but he wasn't going to be fooled this time.

"I thought you guys had a lead on the secondary location? Why aren't they in jail?"

"You knew about that?" Lucas asked in surprise.

"Matt Lazlo mentioned it before I left work last night."

Alex tilted his head to one side and said flatly, "They raid-ed the address, but there was no one there. The perps were obviously warned."

It was another nail in her coffin, and she knew it, too. "That had nothing to do with me. Check my cell phone—"

"Already did. You could have used an internal phone at the office," Alex argued.

"But I didn't." She blew out a big breath, and her eyes got distant. "I'm so stupid. They must have figured out I'm still alive. You have to let me go. They will stop at nothing to get me back."

"Your threats don't bother me—"

"They aren't *threats*! Can't you see I'm trying to *save* you?" Her expression was filled with righteous indignation and disgust, which mirrored his feelings exactly.

"They won't stop looking until they find me, and they will kill anyone who gets in the way. I don't want you to die." Her voice cracked. Her eyes shimmered. "I don't want anyone else to die."

He'd never been good with tears. For a moment, he want-ed to reach out and pull her into his arms. Comfort her.

Fool me once…

"Save the histrionics." He hardened his heart. "You faked your own death, fabricated your background, and joined the

Bureau under an assumed identity. Those are not the actions of an innocent."

Her gaze slid off his.

He held up the copy of the school portrait Nelson Shaw had so generously provided. "Tell the truth, Jenny. Help us catch these people and put them away. We'll tell the DA you cooperated."

"Pah. You think the DA can protect me from these people?" She sneered at him. "And while you're filling him in, are you going to reveal your little kidnap and interrogation plot to him, too?"

"Of course."

"Well, don't bother," she said with a bite in her tone. "No one is gonna believe what I say anyway."

He ignored that. "The right thing would be helping us catch these people—"

"What the hell do you think I've been trying to do?" she snapped.

Sure.

"So why didn't you tell us you knew Ray Tan?"

Lines formed between her brows. "I didn't know him—"

"Well, you had a hell of a conversation with him just seconds before he was gunned down in the street, and you were left unharmed!" The rafters shook with the force of his words, and she flinched. *Fuck.* He reined in his temper.

"I didn't know him. I'd never seen him before." She turned her head away and stared at the small window. "But, you're right, he recognized me. Said I looked like one of the Dragon Devils the FBI were looking for."

"If he'd never met you how'd he recognize you?"

She squirmed restlessly against her restraints.

Lucas forced his eyes away from her writhing body. Even in the middle of a discussion about betrayal and murder she affected him.

"I'm assuming he either knew my mother or my brother. The family resemblance is strong. Or maybe he saw a photograph of me as a kid like the one you have. My uncle worshipped my mother." There was something sour in her tone. "He had a large portrait of her in most of his homes, and I look just like her, except I'm more 'white.'"

"So by your own admission you knew it was the Dragon Devils who killed Ray Tan, but didn't bother to tell the FBI who they were looking for?" Lucas didn't feel good about interrogating a woman tied up on a bed.

"I was going to tell Frazer yesterday, but he wasn't in. Then I was going to tell Matt, but he informed me Boston FO already knew the name of the criminal organization behind the brothel explosion and said you guys had figured out a secondary location,"—which had been her suggestion, he recalled belatedly—"and I figured I didn't need to give it all up."

"Your cover, you mean?"

"My *life*!" She glared at him, and he kept out of range. His nose still hurt like a bitch.

"Who are you working for?" This came from Alex as he stood in the doorway.

"Uncle Sam, same as you do—"

"The Chinese? Koreans?"

She shook her head and spat the hair out of her mouth. A harsh laugh escaped. "Do you hear how prejudiced you sound?"

"Prejudiced?" Alex's expression said it all. "Me?"

"You've been looking for an excuse to kick me to the curb from the moment we met. What the hell are you anyway? A *consultant*? Bull-fucking-shit."

He opened his mouth to argue, but she cut him off.

"You have it all figured out, don't you? I'm some slanty-eyed bitch using her sexuality and femininity to pry secrets out of susceptible men."

Lucas had never considered himself susceptible, but he'd certainly been susceptible to Ashley Chen's brand of woman.

"You think I'm just biding my time, collecting as much information as possible before I run home to...where, Beijing? Except, I've never been to Beijing, and I consider myself an American, not an Asian, not even an Asian-American although people can't get away from the freaking labels that society needs to pigeonhole us."

There was silence in the room for a long moment before Alex answered very slowly and carefully. "It's not your ethnicity that bothers me, Ashley. It never was. It's your duplicity." His words sliced to the bone.

"So you investigate everyone who works for the BAU—"

"Yes." Alex folded his arms across his chest. "I do."

She blinked, clearly taken aback.

"Do you deny that everything you put on the entry forms to the FBI was a lie?" Lucas asked.

Her gaze shifted between the two of them. Her voice grew small. "Not all of it."

Alex's lip curled.

"So tell us the truth. All of it." Lucas pretended to himself she wasn't someone he'd made love to. She was just another criminal being investigated. "This is your opportunity. Tell us why you—the niece of one of the biggest crime bosses in the world—switched identities and infiltrated the FBI."

"Infiltrated? I didn't infiltrate anything." She drew in a deep breath and then let it go, along with some of her outrage. "Fine. Let me out of these damn cuffs, and I'll tell you everything. But I need to get as far away from people I lo—" She cut herself off and stared at him. "Make sure everyone I work with—neighbors, anyone with any sort of association with me—is protected. I know it isn't going to be easy, but the Devils won't care whom they hurt or kill to get the information they want. Tell Matt to watch out for Scarlett, and Jed to warn Vivi and Michael." Her eyes turned to him. "Make sure your family takes extra precautions. Frazer and Darsh, too."

"Okay." He couldn't help how dubious he sounded.

"I mean it. You have no idea who you're dealing with—"

"And whose fault is that?" he asked quietly.

She looked away.

He reached up and unlocked first one wrist, then the other. Her hands just flopped against the pillows as if too weak to move. Slowly she started clenching and unclenching her fists, trying to get the blood flowing again.

"Start talking," Alex said dispassionately from the doorway.

Ashley glared at him then forced her arms in front of her so she could shake them out. Lucas didn't touch her. Didn't try to help. He was pretty sure if he did he'd reveal everything he felt for her. He couldn't afford to show her that weakness.

She sat up with a grace that belied her recent ordeal. "I need to use the bathroom, and then I'd appreciate a drink of something warm. Tea would be preferable." Despite everything she'd been through, she still managed to pull that icy cloak of hauteur around her.

Alex's brows rose. He'd obviously recovered some of his humor because he gave a small smile before bowing low and leaving. Lucas stood in the bedroom as Ashley used the facilities and washed up. She left the door slightly ajar, and he didn't push it. The situation between them was precarious enough.

She came back into the room, with damp hair from where she'd washed her face. The skin around her right eye was mottled black.

There was that goddamn sick feeling in his stomach again. "Let's get you some ice for that eye."

"Seriously?" Her disdain made him wince.

She'd injured herself when she'd been trying to get away from him, and the shame he felt was very real. But he wasn't the villain here.

"What the hell did you expect?"

Anger seemed to drain out of her, and her bottom lip wobbled. "This. *This* is exactly what I expected." She glanced at the bed. "Minus the embarrassing fact that I'd slept with the person who figured it out." Her chin raised a notch. "How did you, by the way? Figure it out?"

He hadn't figured out a damned thing. "Detective Nelson Shaw from the Hong Kong Police Department came into the Boston Field Office to tell us his suspicions about the Dragon Devils. You got lucky. Fuentes and Sloan left the room before he told me a sad story about Yu Chang's poor dead niece."

She closed her eyes for a moment. "Nelson Shaw lost his father to the Devils."

"You know Shaw?"

"Not personally." She rubbed at the red marks on her

wrists. "I did a lot of research on the organization over the years—"

"To help them stay one step ahead of the law?"

"No." She stared down at the floor, but her tone was anything but meek. "To make sure I stayed one step ahead of them."

CHAPTER EIGHTEEN

T IME WAS UP. Five minutes after returning from the murder scene at the hotel, Sloan had been called to the office of the Special Agent in Charge.

She glanced at the clock above the secretary's desk. High noon. Seemed appropriate considering she was about to get fired. She rapped on her boss's office door, a little harder than necessary, but at least she hadn't kicked it down.

"Come in."

SAC Don Salinger wasn't a bad guy, but he knew results— or lack thereof—reflected poorly on his evaluation. It was a week since the bombing—an eternity in this kind of investigation. The public expected more, and deserved better. They wanted to feel safe.

"Carly, this is Supervisory Special Agent Greg Trainer," Salinger introduced them. "He's going to be taking over the task force."

Trainer was a tall, slender man with stooped shoulders. She'd heard of him. He had a reputation for dogged determination when it came to chasing bad guys, and nitpicky politics in the workplace.

"You've done good work, Sloan," Trainer told her, reaching out to shake her hand.

She tried to tell herself he wasn't being condescending. "I

have a good team, but these perps always seem to be a step ahead of us. I think there's a leak somewhere."

"That's quite an accusation." Trainer's pale blue eyes assessed her steadily.

Maybe her inner crazy was showing. A mass casualty event where you lost three cops and four of your own people, followed by a series of gruesome homicides, would do that to a person.

"Yeah, well, it's been a hell of a week."

Her boss looked upset by her attitude, but she didn't care. This would be a black mark in her record regardless of how much she sucked up right now. Frankly, she didn't have the energy. She was working on maybe eight hours sleep since the day Mia Stromberg had been kidnapped.

"Is that why you insisted on keeping the fact we have a witness who survived the explosion a secret, even from your own team?" Trainer asked casually.

Unease trickled down her spine. "I considered it a need-to-know piece of information." Her eyes flicked to Salinger. She'd only told him after she'd set up the protection detail with the ATF.

Salinger backed her up. "Considering what happened to every other witness or potential witness we've had, it was a sound decision."

"Does your husband know?" Trainer asked.

"No." Her shoulders pulled back, and her eyes narrowed. "He does not."

Trainer settled back against the SAC's desk. Maybe measuring it up for his next promotion. "For such a key witness she's given us very little to go on." He managed to make that sound like that was her fault, too.

"She's a sexually abused thirteen-year-old who was held captive for two years and survived a major bombing incident," Sloan told him bluntly. "She needs time to adjust, and she'll come into her own as a witness when we actually catch someone she can testify against. We have people working to locate the mother."

Trainer's brows rose over those pale eyes. "How many agents do you have tracking down the mother and the gambling angle?"

"Two." She hadn't sought approval from Salinger for Chen to get involved, but they'd needed someone with above average computer skills, and FBI agents always worked with a partner in the field.

The tightening of her boss's lips told her he wasn't happy, but he didn't say anything.

"How far have they got?" Trainer asked.

"They're pursuing an angle, right now." She resisted the urge to check her watch. Why the hell Lucas Randall felt it was appropriate to take off at this exact point in time she had no idea. She'd expected better from the man.

"You should have put more agents on that instead of wasting your time searching the port," Trainer told her.

Considering how many hours she'd spent searching dank shipping containers, he could shove his opinion. "We had viable information placing them at the port."

"That we now know came from one of their associates. It was a decoy, and we fell for it," Trainer said bitingly.

She put hands on her hips. "This has been a fast-moving, dynamic investigation. We couldn't afford to ignore that information. Would you have had every ship sail without being searched?"

Trainer pursed his lips, and Sloan wished she had the energy to really go after him. *Jerk.*

Salinger cut in. "You've been reassigned to the Counterterrorism Unit. There's been a steady increase in underground chatter since the bombing, suggesting certain factions want to exploit our supposed weakness while we're searching for this Asian gang."

It wasn't exactly a demotion, but being replaced because you didn't get results sucked. She held her boss's gaze. "Thank you, sir. Should I stay and update SSA Trainer on the situation here?"

Salinger shook his head. "I've brought him up to speed, and I'm personally assigning Agents Mayfield and Fuentes to his team—I know they've been assisting you closely. Take the rest of the day. Get some rest." He was all benevolence and warmth, and wanted rid of her as fast as possible.

She nodded to Trainer and turned on her heel. The elevator was full of people who couldn't meet her gaze. She gritted her teeth and raised her chin. For the best part of two decades, she'd been either in the military or the FBI. She knew how the system worked. Being kicked when you were down was part of the process.

She grabbed a box from near the photocopier and went into her office. Fuentes and Mayfield both scurried inside after her like a couple of oversized pups.

"What happened?" Fuentes asked.

"Is it true? You're off the case?" Mayfield had a white-knuckle grip on the file she was holding.

Sloan opened her top drawer. "Yep, I'm off the case, but that's not exactly news. You two have been assigned to assist the new task force leader, SSA Greg Trainer. He's out of the

New York Field Office."

She grabbed a few items, but she wasn't one for clutter. She packed up some pens and notebooks off her desk, a couple of textbooks on criminal investigation. The photograph of her husband was last, and she placed it carefully in the box. She hoped he was still talking to her after this. He knew her career was important, but he probably wanted a wife he saw once upon a blue moon.

Mayfield was indignant. "I'm going to send a letter of complaint—"

"Telling the boss he made the wrong decision?" Sloan pulled a face at the young agent. "That's a dumb move." Although pushy women tended to get noticed in this kind of environment, so maybe it wasn't the wrong thing to do. The ones who were quiet and unassuming got walked all over, then sidelined and forgotten. She grinned. No one had ever described her as quiet or unassuming.

Fuentes scratched his head. "We got a bunch of DNA from the apartment in Cambridge that we are running through CODIS. Place was registered to another company in the Caymans. Forensic accountant says it's a shell company."

"I'm off the case." Sloan held up her hand. "Tell it to SSA Trainer."

She slipped her laptop into its case, wound up the power cord, and stuffed it beside the computer. "There is one thing I need to tell you." It would be better coming from her. "And I'd appreciate you not sharing this information, or revealing to Trainer that I told you."

They both watched her expectantly.

"That second kid Randall rescued from the brothel?"

"What about her?" Fuentes asked warily.

"The one who died?" asked Mayfield.

"She didn't die. Randall and I snuck her into a local hospital where she was admitted under a false name. ATF is guarding her."

"ATF?" Fuentes sounded like she'd stuck a blade in his back.

"A personal friend of mine. From my Army days."

"You didn't trust us with this, but you trusted Randall?"

"It wasn't personal, Diego. He was there, and we made the joint decision to keep the kid's survival under wraps." It wouldn't be secret for long, and she needed to update Lucas, which would have been a damn sight easier if he'd been in the office. "Once information gets out it becomes something no one can control. Seeing what happened to Susan Thomas, Ray Tan, and Agata Maroulis, I don't regret it. It was the right decision."

Fuentes and Mayfield both looked a little stunned by the turn of events.

"Is that where Pretty Boy is?" Fuentes asked.

Sloan laughed. "Pretty Boy?"

"He's handsome," Mayfield agreed. "If I wasn't engaged…"

"To an asshole." Fuentes grouched.

"Derek isn't an asshole," Mayfield defended the guy she'd been dating for just over a year, although Sloan had never warmed to him either. He was Kurt Stromberg's PA. That connection was how the FBI got called in on the case so quickly.

"Total asshole," Fuentes muttered under his breath with a grin.

Mayfield punched him in the arm, then seemed to remember this situation wasn't even remotely amusing. She turned to watch Sloan with sad eyes. "Where are you going next?"

"Home." Sloan deliberately misunderstood the question. She pulled on her winter coat, grabbed her umbrella from behind the door, shouldered her purse and laptop case, and folded her tactical vest over her arm. She picked up the box. Fuentes went to help, but she jerked away. She didn't need anyone's help.

They followed her out of the office and trailed her to the door of the stairs. Other team members watched silently. Then the elevator opened, and Salinger and Trainer stepped out.

"Go," Sloan urged them. "Catch those bastards." She gave Mayfield a gentle shoulder push. The case was more important than her ego.

Sloan strode down the stairs to the parking garage and dumped her belongings in the trunk of her car. She waited until she was alone inside her vehicle before calling Brian. The call went to voicemail, and she closed her eyes.

Her hands shook. It was possible the mayor's office already knew she'd been replaced, which was a painful thought.

Maybe he'd given up on her. Maybe he was in freaking Aruba with some leggy blonde, and she didn't even know.

Their marriage had been on the rocks for a while now, but she'd consoled herself that at least she had her work. But her marriage suddenly seemed a lot more important than she'd realized. Something worth fighting for. Tears wanted to form, but she didn't let them. She just hoped this case hadn't sunk their marriage completely. She dialed Randall, and his cell went to voicemail, too. She left him a message telling him she'd been reassigned and to meet her at the hospital. She tossed her phone on the passenger seat. She didn't know why people bothered with phones anymore. No one ever picked up.

Hopefully Randall and Chen would track down Becca's mother. Hopefully they beat Trainer's team to the punch although, as the task force leader, he'd get the credit.

She suspected Randall and Chen were also screwing each other's brains out. Steam had practically poured off them when they'd looked at one another.

It had been months since she and her husband had had sex, and the lack of intimacy was helping to drive a wedge between them.

She caught sight of her reflection in the rearview.

Holy crap. No one in their right mind would want to have sex with her. She'd seen corpses with more color. She dragged her purse across the seat and applied some foundation and lipstick.

Frazer had ripped her a new one in the last message he'd left her. Chen was going to be in deep shit if she hadn't reported in. But Sloan was glad Chen was still working this case. The agent was smart and tenacious—like she'd once prided herself on being.

Sloan smoothed her lips against each other and checked her teeth. Satisfied, she flicked up the sun visor and started the engine.

Her career might be in the shitter, but at least they'd managed to salvage two of the most important things from this operation. They'd retrieved Mia Stromberg from her kidnappers without harm, which was the original reason for forming the task force. And they'd rescued Becca from a life of sexual slavery.

Becca's freedom was better than a letter of commendation

any day of the week. Sloan checked that the way was clear and slid smoothly out of her space. She knew exactly where she needed to be.

———————

"LET'S GET THIS over with." Ashley didn't care that she'd slept in her clothes and that her right eye throbbed like a bitch or that she couldn't see much of anything through it. Everything that had happened was her own fault, her reward for the foolishness of wanting to work for the FBI. For being a liar and a cheat. For trying to make a difference when she should have stayed firmly out of the spotlight.

She'd never seen herself as naive, but looking back at her career decisions, they stank of foolish idealism and blind optimism.

Lucas waved her ahead of him, and she walked down a small hallway in the quaint cottage. It was a sweet place if you discounted the proximity to the ocean. She forced the fear out of her mind. Didn't matter how irrational it was, she'd lived through the worse tsunami in recorded history and wouldn't apologize for being scared of the ocean's power.

She glanced at Lucas. Dark stubble sandpapered his jaw. Tired lines fanned out from the corners of his eyes. Shame washed over his features whenever he looked at her.

The fact he was regretful of what they'd done twisted a knife in her gut. She shouldn't have touched him, but she'd been falling for him since the moment she'd first seen him.

I'm not going to tell anyone.

For his sake, she hoped not. She knew better than to give in to her impulses. It wasn't a lesson she could have forgotten in this lifetime, but somehow, with Lucas, she'd allowed herself to be blinded by the illusion that she was in control. She'd made all the wrong choices.

The small sitting room held overstuffed couches and a hearth already set with kindling. Her footsteps slowed. Her time with this man was coming to an end. As painful as the situation was, she wanted to be able to savor these remaining moments alone.

She touched a photograph of a smiling couple embracing a small child and moved on. What mattered now was persuading these two supposedly intelligent human beings that they needed to let her go. She wasn't the villain. She hadn't betrayed anyone. She'd been trying to help. Maybe she deserved to be arrested, but first the FBI needed to catch the Dragon Devils. Her continued presence in their company put them and everyone they loved at risk. She couldn't bear the thought of being responsible for anyone else's death.

It was a situation that would have been helped if she hadn't seduced Lucas while lying about her identity—except she hadn't been lying. She was FBI Agent Ashley Chen. She just hadn't started out that way. God knew who or what she was going to be when this was all over.

She stopped dead at the threshold of the kitchen, but Lucas gave her a little nudge, and she sank into a chair opposite Alex, who had both her laptops up and running.

The invasion of privacy hurt. Not that she blamed them for thinking she was a traitor. She knew what this looked like. There was no place for pride after the fall.

"I'll give you the password—"

"I don't need it." Parker's attitude made her want to smack him. She'd attempted to run some background checks on him when they'd first met and had set off traps and alarms at every step. That's when he'd started to view her with suspicion.

Parker turned her laptop toward her and sure enough, he'd gotten into her system.

Her laughter was bereft of mirth. "Does Mallory know you planted a key logger on her? Or was she in on the ploy?"

All the layers of herself curled over one another into a ball of self-preservation. This was why she didn't do friendships. It hurt too much when you were betrayed. She glanced at Lucas and knew that behind the blank expression he was thinking the exact same thing.

Parker turned the machine back toward him. "I got lucky."

"Liar. No way you'd have cracked it otherwise. You found out we'd be sharing a room and decided to use the opportunity to do some snooping."

He shrugged one shoulder as if this wasn't her life they were talking about. "If there'd been nothing untoward about your activities you'd never have known, now would you?"

"Glad to know you're looking after my constitutional rights."

He seemed amused, which pissed her off.

"Oh, trust me, I get it. It's all my fault, and I got what I deserved."

Lucas put on coffee. He looked tired. Worn around the edges, more rugged than usual, but handsome as hell. Her heart gave a little roll in her chest. She needed to get him far away from her. She couldn't bear it if anything bad happened to him.

"I take it no one knows I'm here?" she asked carefully.

"Just us," Lucas answered.

"I won't tell anyone." The last time those words had

passed between them they'd been talking about sex. A flicker of acknowledgement sparked in Lucas's dark eyes. "Let me go, and I'll disappear. No one will ever know you kidnapped me."

"You'll forgive us?" The cynical humor in Lucas's voice took her aback.

"I thought you were working for my uncle when you snatched me, and that fear is something I won't forget in a hurry." His brown eyes widened, and a look of remorse crossed his features. *Yeah, too late.* "So, no, I won't forgive you—not for a long time. But I understand it."

Parker ignored her, typing furiously. "No electronic trackers on this system."

She rolled her eyes. "Well, thank goodness for that."

"Rather than sniping at him, why don't you tell us your version of events?" Lucas spoke from the other side of the room in a deceptively soft voice.

She narrowed her good eye at him. "What's the point if you won't believe a word of it?"

"Try me." All the different meanings of the phrase buzzed between them. For a moment, his pupils flared with heat. Then his gaze frosted over like the Arctic in January. He turned away to pour coffee, too disgusted to converse with her any more than necessary. He placed a steaming mug in front of her and moved away again.

Parker picked up her personal laptop and took it to a nearby counter to work on, no doubt to prevent her from tipping her drink and frying the circuit boards. Something she'd definitely do if she had something to hide.

"Why did Jenny Britton fake her own death?" Lucas asked. "Or did the whole crime family see the tsunami as some huge opportunity to leverage?"

The word "tsunami" had her mouth going dry, and she glanced out the window. Her fear was something she'd managed to control with some intensive hypnotherapy and by never staying too close to the edge of the sea. She was embarrassed she'd lost it yesterday, but then, she had been abducted by parties unknown, so maybe she should give herself a break.

Lucas sat in the chair Parker vacated, close enough she could smell the male scent of his skin. "We don't have much time, Ashley," he said impatiently.

The reminder made her shake off her inertia. She might not be part of the fight anymore, but she was part of the problem. And she wanted these animals caught even more than Lucas did.

"When I was sixteen years old, my parents were killed in an airplane crash off the coast of Malibu." His expression registered the fact she'd lied to him when she'd told him her parents had died in a car wreck. Car wrecks were harder to track, but the emotional impact had been the same. She wrapped her hands around the mug for warmth. "We were devastated."

"We?" Lucas asked.

"My brother Andrew and me. He was a year older than me." She was pretty sure he was the one running the computer systems for the Devils. "As if losing our parents wasn't bad enough, two weeks later we were told by the family lawyer that we were being sent to live with an uncle we'd never even heard of in Macau. I freaked out." She stared down at her coffee. She was still protective of the girl she'd been and didn't want them judging her actions. Jenny Britton was the very best part of Ashley Chen. "I complained and rebelled. I even ran away, but the cops caught me and took me back. They shipped us off in October in what should have been Andrew's final year of high school."

The coffee was strong and bitter so she added some sugar. It helped to have something to do with her hands. "My uncle and his son tried to make us feel welcome. At first I thought it was going to be okay. As soon as I was eighteen I'd receive my inheritance from my parents and be able to leave. I was too stupid to realize my uncle was placating us in the short-term. He hired a private tutor, who included all sorts of Chinese cultural shit into our lessons—how women should be demure and feminine. Seen, not heard. Homemakers. How they should learn to please a man in the home and the bedroom." She'd wanted to gag. "That's not how I grew up. My mother was well educated and very much the equal of my father. Needless to say, I continued rebelling and things got real, fast. Yu Chang took us to Thailand for the Christmas break, and I began sneaking out." She looked up and caught Lucas's gaze. "He never imagined I'd be foolish enough to disobey him."

Lucas's smile was tight. He could obviously imagine it all too well.

"I met a boy, a German guy. I lied to him about my age. Yes," she said, seeing his expression, "I've been doing that for a long time. I snuck out on Christmas night, and I let Martel make love to me for the first time on a secluded beach."

The memory of losing her virginity was tainted by blood and violence. Tears still wanted to fall when she thought of it. If only she hadn't met him. "The next day at the villa, when I came downstairs, my uncle and cousin were in the garden beating Martel. My cousin had followed me and seen the two of us having sex."

Rage and horror flowed through her at the memory, and her hands shook so badly she carefully put the coffee down on the table so as not to spill it. "Yu Chang gutted Martel in front of me."

Lucas's expression turned grim.

Martel's murder had never been solved. She was the only witness who wasn't tied to her uncle's organization, and she'd pretended to be dead for more than a decade. He'd never found justice. He'd never been avenged.

"Then the wave came." Her knuckles whitened in her lap, and she forced herself to relax.

"That's why you freaked out about being on the beach yesterday." Understanding dawned in Lucas's eyes.

She glanced at the window and held back a shudder. "If you'd seen what I've seen you'd understand why living on the beach is lunacy."

One side of his mouth quirked. "People pay millions of dollars to live on the beach."

"Idiots. All of them."

"I'll be sure to tell my mother," he said wryly.

The words caused a weird pang in the region of her heart. Sadness at the thought she'd never meet his mother was ridiculous. They'd had sex, nothing more. She'd never have been invited to meet the parents, never have gained approval in a relationship. She might be a fuck buddy for a while, but she sure as hell wasn't wife material.

Then she shook her head at herself. That ingrained need for parental approval never left no matter how old she got. She didn't know if it was because she was an Asian-American female or because she was an insecure orphan. Whatever it was, it sucked.

"What happened after the wave hit?"

Her heart started thumping as she thought of the nightmarish aftermath, of being dragged through the water and flipped like a rag doll. Nature had been cruelly indifferent to her victims. No mercy was shown.

Her therapist had helped rationalize her fear. Hypnotherapy helped control it. Neither method was foolproof.

"I thought I was dead. I mean I literally saw the tunnel of light and heard my parents calling me. I lost consciousness. When I woke I was tangled up in the branches of a tree wondering why Heaven hurt so damn much." At first she'd been joyous to have survived, then horrified.

She'd known the only way to escape her uncle's grasp if he was still alive—and cockroaches always survived—was to disappear and hope he believed she'd succumbed. It was a daunting prospect for a sixteen-year-old girl thousands of miles from home.

"I knew this would be my one and only chance to escape. I didn't recognize the landscape, but I figured out which way was south and headed in that direction." Her pulse pounded a rhythm in her ear. "People were rushing past on mopeds and in jeeps, but there were places that were impassible, and everyone had to get out and start walking. Most were milling around, dazed. Then someone would scream that another wave was coming, and we'd all run for higher ground." She made fists with her hands to stop them from shaking. "As the sun started to set on that first day, I went into the bush to relieve myself and found a dead girl who was about my height and build." It had taken all her courage to swap T-shirts with a fresh corpse. Then she'd put the diamond earrings that her uncle had given her the day before into the small holes in the girl's ears and stolen the shoes off the dead girl's feet. The next thing she'd done was the one thing in her life she was truly ashamed of. The girl had been dead, and it hadn't mattered. It had been a desecration.

Ashley had made sure that young woman would never be visually identified.

The two men watched her carefully. Maybe they'd figured out the awful unsaid things she'd done to escape her uncle. Maybe they didn't care.

"The next day, I carried on walking. I didn't speak to anyone, because I didn't want them to notice my American accent. You could say I acted traumatized, but I wasn't acting." She frowned. It was odd the things that came back to you. The sight of women comforting barefoot children on the side of the road. Of tourists helping locals. Locals aiding strangers even as they faced the total destruction of their homes and livelihoods.

"After a day, I was delirious from lack of food and water and couldn't carry on, but just as it was getting dark a rescue convoy came along and pulled me onboard. When I woke up I was in an overcrowded hospital in Phuket. I borrowed an American tourist's phone and called my great aunt on my dad's side. She was a retired diplomat."

She saw the spark of interest in both men's eyes. Her aunt had immediately understood the importance of getting her out of the country and back to the States without Yu Chang finding out she'd survived. Her aunt had wanted to get Andrew out too, but Ashley hadn't known if he was alive or dead. She still didn't know for sure.

"My aunt had a friend who worked for the Red Cross." Ashley didn't know how she'd managed it, but two excruciatingly tense days later, Jenny Britton had found herself on a cargo plane bound for Australia. "I made it to Canberra and from there my aunt enlisted the help of another friend of hers and secretly got me back to the States using diplomatic channels." There was no record of her arrival or departure from Australia.

"What was her name?" Lucas asked.

"My aunt? Meredith Beauchamp—Merry. She died a couple of years ago." She held Lucas's gaze. "She's the godmother I told you about."

She needed him to know she hadn't lied about everything. He looked away.

"How'd you construct the false identity?" Parker asked.

She'd been trying to pretend Parker wasn't there in the room, judging her.

"My aunt's long-term boyfriend was retired CIA. Frank Pratsky. He died last year." That loss had hit her doubly hard.

Parker's face showed recognition.

"He used his Agency contacts." And her false identity had been so good, it had fooled everyone, including the FBI's screening service.

The only people to ever question it had been Alex Parker and Lucas Randall.

"You changed your age." Lucas's tone was accusatory.

"I'm way past the age of consent if that's what you're worried about," she snapped. She tried to dampen her resentment. "I added four years to deflect anyone who might have been searching for me online."

"So you finished your degree at Cornell at nineteen?" Parker was still typing on her workstation.

"Worked in the tech industry and joined the FBI as soon as I could."

"Except you were actually only twenty-two," Lucas admonished. As if *that* was her biggest sin. "And you're twenty-seven now?"

"Jenny Britton would have been twenty-seven next week." Valentine's Day. "Ashley Chen is thirty."

"And who's next? You have a new identity all mapped out?" Anger lit the depths of Lucas's eyes.

She stared at him, stunned. *That* was all he had to say after she'd told him of her narrow escape from death and epic journey halfway around the world?

"Hmm..." She put a finger on her bottom lip. "Maybe a high class call girl to take care of the needs of middle-aged white guys? Pretty sure I'd make a fortune."

He glared at her.

What the hell did he care? He'd told her he hated liars, but not everyone was as lucky as he was with their relatives. And he'd told some corkers to Sloan today. It was probably another black mark against her. Corrupting his soul.

"How'd you beat the polygraph?" Parker asked.

She stared at the tabletop. It was unfinished wood. She touched her fingers to the raised grain. "I had a lot of nightmares after the tsunami and spent years in therapy. It included a *lot* of hypnotherapy. I started using that for pretty much every aspect in my life that stressed me out. Exams, being near the beach, cocktail parties."

"Maybe I should try it for when I visit Mallory's parents," Parker quipped.

She blinked at him in shock. He had never made a joke with her before. Never. Not once. He seemed to realize it, too, and looked away.

"When I decided I wanted to join the FBI, Frank got hold of a polygraph machine, and the two of us practiced until I could beat it nine times out of ten."

"He approved of what you were doing?"

She didn't like the judgmental tone Lucas was using against one of the few people to have offered her their unstinting support. Ashley hadn't had many people she trusted in her life, but Frank was solid gold.

"He thought I was crazy for applying to the FBI, period. He thought the feebs were a bunch of uptight know-it-alls with sticks up their asses—his words, not mine."

"He had a point," Parker murmured.

"He wanted me to join the CIA, but I knew if I did they'd send me to China or Asia, and I'd have more chance of running across someone who recognized me."

"So instead you join the Bureau and end up investigating your nearest and dearest," Lucas jeered.

Her eyes narrowed. "They are not my nearest and dearest."

"So you say," he bit out.

"They are monsters, and I hate them."

"Why didn't you admit this to the authorities before?" Lucas put his hands on his hips, and she had to force herself to look away. She didn't want basic physical attraction to scramble her thought processes. "They could have protected you."

"Seriously?" Was he really that naive? "I didn't even know if they survived the tsunami. They'd have stuffed me in a room and pumped me for information. Then they'd have kicked me out. They'd never have let me near law enforcement or computers."

"You're the niece of one of the biggest organized gang leaders in Asia. You don't think you'd have something useful to share?"

She noticed he didn't deny the fact she'd never have been

allowed to join the feds.

"So, for a few tidbits of information that were probably outdated, I'm supposed to sacrifice my life? You think Yu Chang wouldn't figure out someone was feeding the FBI information? You think he wouldn't come after me? Did you see what happened to Susan Thomas?"

"You don't think the FBI could have protected you?"

She crossed her arms over her chest. "No, I don't."

"You ever heard of WITSEC?"

"Look, I love and believe in the FBI. But in the old days Yu Chang had people everywhere. He collected blackmail material and was rich enough to buy anyone he wanted. There was no way I was risking him getting wind that I was still alive. I just wanted to fight bad guys and serve my country in a meaningful way."

"And yet, your lies and lack of faith have made a mockery of the organization you claim to love. You know that, right?" It was the disappointment in Lucas's gaze that finally got to her.

She swallowed tightly. "I never made a mockery of it. I dedicated my *life* to it—no husband, no kids, no friends, *nothing* except my job."

And how did it repay her?

By calling her traitor.

She watched them exchange a look that told her they still didn't believe her. Hurt boiled over, and she stood. "Fine. Whatever. I ran away from everything I knew when I was sixteen. I was swept away by that terrifying wave, and I was *glad* that I was going to die. Do you understand how much fear I lived in? My uncle wanted me in his fucking bed." That stunned them both out of their cynicism. "Do you have any clue what it is like to feel a man's eyes on your body, on your breasts, between your legs, and know it's just a matter of time before that deviant rapes you? And no one will come to your rescue no matter how loudly you scream?"

Lucas flinched.

"Sixteen years old," she stared him down, "and I would rather have died than subject myself to all the things he wanted to do to me. So, yeah," she spat out, "lying about my identity to stop that kind of violation didn't feel wrong at the time. It felt *necessary.*"

She was breathing heavily through her nose, striving for calm. "And he isn't going to stop now he knows I'm alive. He's going to keep looking for me, and when he finds me, he isn't going to kill me. He's going to confine me and use me the way he wanted to all those years ago. He's going to find a way to force me to fuck his brains out and suck his dick, probably by threatening someone I love. So I'll pretend I love him, because for some crazy reason—and I do mean *crazy*—he was obsessed with my mother, and now he's obsessed with me." Tears filled her eyes, and now she couldn't see at all. Goddamn it. She'd sworn she wouldn't shed tears over this. "He won't stop until one of us is dead, and you are not safe with me."

"That's why you don't let anyone close." Lucas's soft words drove a spike through her heart.

"I prefer to be alone," she insisted.

"What if he finds out we already slept together?" Lucas had to push it.

A vision of Martel flashed through her mind. The wrenching sound as metal ripped through flesh. Rivers of scarlet blood, vivid against pale, smooth stone. She turned away so he couldn't see the devastation on her face.

"Let's hope we never find out."

CHAPTER NINETEEN

"FIFTEEN. TWO FOR a pair." Becca's eyes lit up, and she moved her peg forward in the cribbage board. Sloan looked at the cards in her hand and knew she was going to get thrashed, but if it put a smile on Becca's face it was worth it.

Agent Curtis had gone to grab some lunch, and also talk to her boss to finalize arrangements on the safe house and protective custody detail for someone who'd been legally declared dead. Tonight if possible. Sloan wanted Becca out of this hospital before the news broke about them having a living witness. She'd tried to call Randall again, but the agent wasn't picking up.

The FBI might use the information to set a trap in the hospital, but that was a risk. Whatever they chose to do, Becca didn't need to be here.

"You might be leaving here soon." Sloan broached the subject and laid down a seven. "Twenty-two."

Becca put down a nine, but her smile had slipped. "Thirty-one."

"You're good at this," Sloan told the kid as she moved her peg again. Sloan would be lucky not to get skunked.

"I used to play with my mom."

The quiet admission was the perfect introduction to another subject Sloan needed to bring up. "Agent Randall is out searching for your mom."

The flare of panic in Becca's eyes suggested the kid wasn't thrilled with the idea of reuniting with her.

"We won't send you back, sweetheart. Your mom committed some serious offenses against you."

"I don't want her to go to jail."

Sloan put her hand over Becca's and squeezed. "That's not your decision to make. She has to face the consequences of her actions. And we need to find your little brother. To make sure he's being looked after properly."

Big blue eyes met hers. "You think I could be with him again?"

"Possibly, but I don't know for sure." Sloan didn't want to get Becca's hopes up.

The door handle turned, and two doctors Sloan didn't recognize walked in. But Becca did. The cards went everywhere as the girl threw herself off the bed and ran to the window.

Sloan went for her weapon, but she was too slow. Fuck. The taller man had a 9-mm pressed against her temple.

"I think you've been looking for us, FBI Agent Sloan. We decided to make it easier for you." His English was very good, barely an accent.

The other guy walked over to where Becca stood trembling by the window. He thrust a plastic bag at her. "Put these on." His English was much more guttural.

Becca didn't move, and the man slapped her on the head. "Do it."

"Leave her alone," Sloan bit out.

The gun pressed harder into her temple as her arm was ruthlessly forced up her back. Even if she managed to disarm this guy, the other was too close to Becca for her to prevent the girl from being hurt.

The kid's eyes were wide as silver dollars as she stumbled and then frantically tore into the bag, pulling out clothes.

Sloan had made a critical error. Early on, she and Randall had decided that too much security would draw attention to the fact Becca was here and put her at higher risk of being spotted. They'd opted for less security and therefore less attention, but somehow the bad guys had figured it out. Had they followed her? The idea was intolerable.

Or had Trainer told the team about Becca without upping security here first?

What did it matter?

Her heart was beating madly as her brain whirled trying to figure out what the hell she should do. There was no doubt they'd kill the thirteen-year-old if Sloan fought back—the teen was the primary witness in the case against them. The bigger question was, why weren't she and Becca already dead?

The guy retrieved her Glock out of her side holster. The loss made her feel physically ill.

"Don't do anything stupid. I just want information."

"Is that what you told the woman in the hotel?"

He actually laughed. "An unfortunate error."

Sloan blinked at his callousness. His lack of feeling suggested she was dealing with a psychopath, but they had their traits and weaknesses too. Namely their huge love of themselves. "If you leave Becca alone I'll help you leave the country without anyone knowing."

He shook his head. "Just do as I say, and she won't get hurt."

Her mouth went dry. What the hell choice did she have?

"Fine. What do you want?"

"We're going to walk out of here, quickly and quietly. My friend Cho over there will put a bullet in little Rosie if you do anything to call attention to us."

"Her name's Becca," Sloan hissed.

He leaned closer. "Her name is whatever the fuck I want it to be. She will die by a bullet to the brain if you give us away. Understand?" He grabbed her hair and twisted her face to look at him.

She'd seen evil before and recognized it now. She nodded, wishing she could risk some move. If it had just been her she'd have gone down fighting, but the idea of them hurting Becca again...

But they'd hurt her at some point.

God, she felt so useless. All her training and still, she'd been caught completely unprepared.

Where were they taking them? Why not shoot them both here? Were they scared of making a scene and drawing security? They hadn't given a damn when they'd shot Ray Tan dead in the street.

He pushed her toward the door, let her arm down, and put his hand in his pocket, clearly with his finger on the trigger. Cho held Becca's hand in a grip that had to hurt.

"No theatrics, or you both die along with anyone else I come across on my way out the door. We go to your car, and we drive away without anyone getting hurt."

She nodded jerkily. It wouldn't be long until ATF realized they were missing and picked up their trail. If she could keep them both alive in the meantime they had a fighting chance.

LUCAS WATCHED ASHLEY lie down on the bed and raise her hands over her head. He tried not to notice the red marks on her wrists. Even though she was being obedient and pliable, the idea of her being weak or submissive was laughable.

If what she was saying about her uncle was true, the guy was a monster, and she'd shown incredible bravery escaping him. But it could be a lie. Intricate and compelling, but a lie nevertheless. She'd already admitted to being good at those.

"Why did you sleep with me?" he asked before he could stop himself.

"I didn't sleep with you. We fucked." The icy expression on her face tried to warn him off, but with a start he realized he knew her better than that. He'd seen her soft underbelly when she'd tracked Agata Maroulis's every move, and when she'd pressed her jacket to the gaping hole in Ray Tan's chest even though he could destroy her. Why would she do that if she was really working for her uncle?

Alex's theory about her working for the Chinese didn't make much sense either when she had no affiliation with anyone there.

"Don't mention it again in case my uncle finds out." Her voice dripped icicles.

His lip curved even though he should know better. "Why? Worried about me?"

Her nostrils flared.

He fastened one metal bracelet around her wrist. Then he leaned over her to secure the other, but he paused, his mouth hovering over hers. He clicked the handcuff shut, but not as tight as it had been. Then he brushed his mouth gently over hers.

"Please. Don't." Her ragged whisper against his lips

brought him back to the reality of their situation.

He pulled back, shocked to see tears brimming in her eyes. He jerked away from the bed and dragged his hand through his hair. "Jesus, I'm sorry. I shouldn't have done that. *Christ.*"

Her hair spilled like black silk on the pillow. "You can't dismiss my warnings about what my uncle will do to you if he finds out we slept together. I know you don't believe me, but I watched a young man die for that. He was viciously murdered right in front of my eyes." Her words were thickened by emotion, but the tears never spilled over. "I'm not joking when I say you need to get far away from me and keep quiet about the fact—"

"About the fact that from the moment we met we were attracted to one another? That working with you was hell because no matter how important the case, I couldn't stop thinking about how good you tasted?"

"It was just sex," she insisted.

"It wasn't just sex, Ash. If it was just sex I wouldn't be fascinated by your beauty or intrigued by how goddamned smart you are."

"It's just an Asian fetish—"

"I don't have an Asian fetish!" He was shouting again, and that sucked when the woman he was arguing with was already vulnerable. Suddenly the idea that she was guilty of anything except secretly changing her identity seemed remote.

Christ.

This had been a huge mistake. He should just have arrested her, but then he'd never have gotten to talk to her in private again. And he'd needed to hear her explanation from her own lips. The trouble was, her story rang horrifyingly true. Alex would be verifying as many details as he could so they could figure out what to do next. Lucas's phone buzzed, and he checked the screen. Sloan had texted him that she'd been removed from the task force, and he'd need to report in to SSA Greg Trainer.

He scrubbed his hands through his hair. More good news. Trainer had been in his office in San Antonio. A rule-bound prick who was gonna go far in the Bureau.

He didn't reply to Sloan. Anything he said would compound the lies he'd already told. He went to the window and looked outside. The overcast sky and freezing wind matched his mood.

After a few moments, he spoke. "I'm not scared of your uncle, Ash. I'm taking that sonofabitch down and dismantling the rest of his empire one brothel and gambling den at a time."

"You *should* be scared of him. He's a monster."

Lucas sat next to her on the bed and moved her hair gently off her forehead. "He's a bully."

"A bully with a private army," she argued.

"I'm not scared of a bully, no matter how many hired guns he has. My job is to capture people like him and put them away so they can't hurt others. It's what we uptight, know-it-all feebs do." He gave a soft laugh that wasn't even close to being amused. "In fact, the only thing I'm scared of is you— that you might be lying and that I'm foolish enough to fall for it. Or worse—that I hurt and terrorized an innocent woman. I'm not sure I could forgive myself if that's the case."

"I'm not sure I can forgive you either." She turned away.

Alex came to the doorway and rapped on it loudly. "We've got a problem."

He led Lucas outside, and they walked down to the beach. When they got to the edge of the surf, Alex finally spoke. "I called an old contact from my Agency days."

Alex didn't often admit to having worked for the CIA, and Lucas was surprised he'd done so now.

"He knew Frank Pratsky, and I asked the guy about his family and home life. Her story checks out from that angle. As far as the world knew, Ashley Chen was his niece via his long-term partner, Merry Beauchamp."

"What about Ashley's laptop and cell? Any hint of communications between her and the Dragon Devils?"

Alex rubbed the back of his neck. "Well, her laptop isn't squeaky clean, and she's really good at covering her tracks. I do see evidence of her doing some computer pen tests of her own."

Lucas blinked. Was that Alex's subtle way of saying she was a hacker?

"But everything I've tracked relates to cases she worked on—a lot of which she helped solve, or old ones she's still investigating. There is a file on the Dragon Devils."

Lucas tensed.

"But she hasn't added to it in several years." Alex paced. "Her cell phone is clean, and I didn't find any burner in her belongings. Financially she's solvent. She sailed through her degree at an accelerated pace and on a full scholarship. She has expensive tastes in clothes, but she's always had a good job and lived within her means. Both her aunt and Pratsky left her everything they owned, so she has a healthy 401K."

"So she doesn't need the money."

Alex looked up at the churning clouds. "I don't doubt she has a backup plan for changing her identity and escaping her uncle, and probably the FBI, too. But if I was in her position, so would I." He stopped pacing. "Lucas, I think she might be telling the truth."

It was one thing for him to believe her, but Alex had been suspicious right from the start. If he was having doubts… "So, you're saying we abducted and confined a woman who's already gone through hell?" His teeth felt like they'd been welded together.

"Pretty much." Alex didn't look happy about it either. "Better us figuring this out than Sloan—"

"Sloan just got replaced," Lucas told Alex. "Task force leader is now a guy named Greg Trainer."

"What do we know about him?"

"Blue flamer. Brown noser. Rule follower. He gets results, but he's an obnoxious prick."

"Great." Alex grinned. "I just spoke to Mal. She's fine." You'd never have known the guy had been unglued by worry just a short time earlier. They stared down the beach toward a woman walking her dog. "I put two of my firm's men on her from the airport, but if she finds that out, she'll kill me. She's already bitching about the detail Frazer put on her." He glanced at Lucas. "I also sent a guy to the hospital to watch out for the little girl."

Emotion swelled in Lucas's throat. He nodded. Sloan said he needed to get back to Boston and help protect Becca until they could get her into a safe house. If Trainer was going to do a big team reveal—like Becca was some show and fucking tell—then he needed to get moving.

"What do you want to do with Ashley?" Alex asked.

"Let her go." And pray she got as far away from the Dragon Devils as possible.

"What about the fact you've fallen in love with her?"

The lump in Lucas's throat kept growing, but he didn't

deny it. Maybe he hadn't known the first moment he'd seen her, but his feelings had grown slowly and only solidified the more time he'd spent in her company—and that was despite the lies she'd told.

"I need her to be safe." Running was the best chance she had of staying alive, even though the thought of never seeing her again was like a punch in the gut.

"The only other person who knows about this dead niece is the Hong Kong detective?"

"Plus the Dragon Devils themselves."

They began walking back up the beach.

"Any chance they'll keep the information to themselves?"

"Sure," Lucas felt his heart turning black. "As long as they're all dead."

The only noise that followed them up the beach was the scream of gulls.

SLOAN HAD A clear view of the front door.

She was tied up to one of the new dining room chairs she and Brian had bought themselves for Christmas. The expensive wormy maple matched the live-edge table they'd also purchased. But no matter how nice the setting was, they still never made it home in time to eat together.

Every late night, every heated argument or stilted conversation screamed inside her head. Why had she neglected him so badly? Why had she always put his needs second to her own?

Please, God, let him be safe. It was a Tuesday, and he usually went to the gym on Tuesday nights, but these guys didn't know that. Had he been told she was missing yet? If he had, there was a good chance he'd stay at the office to be closer to the mayor, and the FBI, if and when they found her. He often slept there anyway.

Don't come home.

Cho was watching Becca with a hungry expression on his ugly face. They'd gagged her because she'd started screaming at one point and wouldn't stop. Sloan had tried to show the girl some strength, but it was hard from a position of weakness. To think that this was what Becca had been enduring for years—this psychological and physical abuse. The FBI had failed to keep her safe. They'd failed to appreciate the danger.

The other guy, Mr. Psychopath, was lounging on an otto-man that had belonged to her parents, drinking Brian's fancy single malt. He had a bandage wrapped around his bicep—from Ashley Chen's bullet when he'd gunned down Ray Tan on the street? Maybe. She didn't know.

He was good-looking and vaguely familiar, but she couldn't place him. Pity he was evil personified.

They'd first made her drive to a warehouse in Southie, but then had taken a different car and driven to her home in the 'burbs.

She trembled. It made a crazy kind of sense. No one was going to look for them at the home of the former task force leader. On the positive side, the longer they delayed here, the more chance the feds had of catching up with them. She knew some pretty talented negotiators who might be able to talk them out of this alive. And if that failed, they had some of the best marksmen in the world. She'd be quite happy to take a bullet if it meant these two asswipes died and Becca lived.

"What are you waiting for?" she asked.

Mr. Psycho smirked at her. "I want to know where Agent Chen is."

Her head jerked up at that. What the hell? And then she realized that was why he looked familiar. He looked like Chen.

Was that a coincidence? Or were they related?

His cell phone rang before she could ask him. She listened hard to this side of the conversation trying to glean clues. He was placating the other person, telling him it had gone down without a hitch and not to worry. He perked up at one point, sitting upright and grinning.

He was making details for their departure, she realized suddenly. She had the horrible feeling she wouldn't live long enough to say goodbye.

Why not just shoot her? Why tie her up? Why wait it out in her fucking house?

I'm going to make it up to you, Brian. Just stay far away.

She thought her prayers were working, right up until she heard his key in the front door.

"Brian. Run!" Mr. Psycho smacked her in the side of the head with her own Glock.

Cho grabbed her husband, dragging him inside and closing the door behind him.

"He doesn't know anything! Leave him alone!" she yelled.

Mr. Psycho smirked and shook his head. Becca's eyes went wide.

Brian looked around wildly. "What the hell are you doing here?"

Cho shoved him into a seat so he was facing her. Then the man bound his wrists behind his back with duct tape.

"I'm so sorry, honey." Tears filled her eyes. She'd never

meant to bring danger into their home.

Brian's eyes bounced off every person in the room, landing on Becca as if he couldn't believe what was happening. "What do you want? Why are you in my fucking *house*?" He started to struggle, but Cho pressed down on his shoulders.

"I want to know where I can find a certain FBI agent," Mr. Psycho said silkily.

Why was Chen so important?

Brian gaped at him. "You think you can torture it out of my wife? She'll never tell you a damned thing."

The smile the psycho sent him gave Sloan chills.

No.

Cho slapped tape over Brian's mouth.

"You're right. I think she's too brave and stoic to save herself, but you? I'm counting she has a soft spot for you." The psycho pulled out a knife and tested the point. "It's a little blunt I'm afraid."

A tear spilled over and slid down Sloan's cheek. Becca's eyes were still wide with horror, but Sloan couldn't save the girl from what she was about to witness.

CHAPTER TWENTY

ASHLEY SHOWERED WHILE she waited for the men to come back. Lucas had restrained her one wrist just loose enough to slip the cuff and, with a free hand, she'd made short work of the other. Had it been a test? New Agents in Training learned to get out of handcuffs at the academy, but it was more likely he'd underestimated the narrowness of her wrist bones.

They'd brought her luggage from her car in Virginia so she had a fresh change of clothes and a full makeup kit. It didn't do much for her black eye, but it did boost her self-esteem.

She resisted the temptation that was Alex Parker's laptop, even though it was right there out in the open, and she'd probably never get another chance to look at it. She doubted she'd be able to crack his password in the time available. She didn't touch her machines because she was trying to prove a point.

She wasn't trying to escape. She wasn't the bad guy.

By the time they'd finished their tête-à-tête on the beach she was once again the consummate professional, dressed in a navy pantsuit, sitting with both hands resting in clear view on the tabletop.

Lucas came to an abrupt halt when he walked in the door. Alex offered a small smile over Lucas's shoulder. She watched him replace his gun in his holster.

Christ, the guy was scary fast.

"I guess you saved us the trouble," Lucas said cryptically.

"Trouble?"

"Of letting you go." He checked his watch. "Where do you want us to drop you?"

"Pardon?" She didn't understand.

"We believe you." Alex spoke up. "We owe you an apology. *I* definitely owe you an apology. I'm sorry that my suspicions put you in danger, but you can't say they weren't warranted."

She frowned.

"We need to get out of here ASAP. I have a meeting to get to…" Lucas eyed her as if she was holding them up.

Her eyes widened at the implication. They were actually letting her go? They believed what she'd told them. Or they were pretending to. "I've changed my mind about running away."

"You don't get to change your mind about that." Lucas walked into the bedroom she'd been held in, and she heard the rattle of handcuffs and the straightening of sheets. He came back thirty seconds later and pointed his finger at her. "You stay, you die. Simple as that."

She shook her head. "I'm the best chance the FBI has of catching these people."

"What?" He huffed out a cynical laugh. "After all these years, you're finally going to sacrifice yourself to that cause?"

She jerked away as if she'd been stung.

"You said it yourself, Ash, you've got one chance of surviving this, and we're giving it to you. Call Frazer, resign from the Bureau for personal reasons with immediate effect, and disappear. You can send in your creds and weapon. Alex and I never saw you. *This*"—he waved his finger between them— "never happened. That keeps you off the FBI's radar and gives you a head-start on the people hunting you."

Something in his voice gave him away, and she remembered what Mallory had said about his poker face. She stood up and placed her hand gently on his arm. "He'll never stop looking for me, Lucas. I will be on the run and looking over my shoulder until the day I die. I do not want to live like that."

"It's the only way you *will* live."

"Use me as a lure."

"No." He wouldn't look at her.

"Tell him, Parker. Tell him the best way of catching these animals is by using me as bait."

Rather than replying, Alex stared at her for a long moment. Then he zipped up her laptops into their respective bags, grabbed her luggage, and headed out the cottage door.

She was stunned by his silence. She'd thought he'd be the first to stake her out as the sacrificial goat.

She crossed her arms over her chest. "You can't stop me from going to Sloan."

"Sloan is no longer in charge of the investigation. A guy named Greg Trainer is. He's one of the stick-up-his-ass agents your godfather warned you about. You tell him who you really are, and he will stick you in jail and wave you like a red flag to prove to the world his team is cracking down on the Dragon Devils and their associates. You'll be vilified as the inside source. The Devils will know exactly where you are and how to get to you."

He crowded her against the kitchen counter. "You need to get out of here before I change my mind about letting you go."

The words were supposed to be a threat but sounded like a wish.

"Do you really believe I am on the FBI's side?" she asked. "Or is this some game you're playing to see what I do next?"

He gripped her elbows and kissed her deep, like he'd never get the chance to kiss her again. She kissed him back, wanting to stretch the moment for as long as possible but knowing it would end far too soon.

Finally, he pulled away and rested his forehead against hers. "I'm sorry I kidnapped you. And I'm sorry that the only way I know to protect you is by letting you go."

Ashley closed her eyes and gripped his shirtfront. She nodded, then pushed away from his chest, breaking them apart. She brushed past him and headed to the van. He had it backward. The only way to protect him was to walk away.

THE SMELL OF blood was so cloying that Sloan tried to breathe through her mouth. The look of agony on Brian's face, the fierce way he fought with his attackers, destroyed her. They'd cut off his ear, and blood soaked his neck and shirt collar. She twisted and struggled against her bonds, but she couldn't get free.

Becca's reaction was the most surreal. It wasn't horror or repulsion—it looked oddly like satisfaction.

Mr. Psycho's cell phone rang, and he answered it with a slight frown. He'd barely drawn a sweat. He hung up and ran the knife down Brian's front and slowly lowered it until it rested on his penis. "Perhaps we need to speed things up a little." He flicked the button off Brian's trousers and lowered the zipper as if opening a surprise. Brian went rigid, eyes popping. "A husband might forgive a wife for getting his ear mangled, but he'd never forgive her for losing his dick. Not that it's much of a dick right now." The psycho's gaze rested on Becca. "Fetch her."

Cho untied Becca and ripped the tape from her lips so viciously she cried out. Then he dragged her over and forced her to kneel at Brian's feet.

The psycho tipped up her chin with the edge of the blade. "Touch him. You know how."

Oh, God, no. No.

This, Sloan could not bear to watch. "I don't know where Chen is!"

"Do better. I just want to talk to her. I don't need to know where she is."

"I don't have her number." Her voice cracked like ice on a pond. The psycho moved the knife closer to Brian's genitals, and she said quickly. "But I have the number for the agent who is with her."

The psycho brought her phone over to her. "Which one is it?"

Sloan cleared her throat. "Randall. Lucas Randall."

The slimeball smiled as he slapped a strip of tape over her mouth.

He took her phone and sat cross-legged on their beautiful dining room table.

"That wasn't so difficult, was it?" His eyes caught Sloan's horrified gaze as he smiled.

Oh God. He was a monster. She shouldn't have told him, but there was no way she'd make Becca endure more torture. She slumped in defeat, tears filling her eyes as he made the phone call.

———————

LUCAS WAS PRETTY sure everyone in the vehicle knew his heart was shattering, but no one mentioned it. Alex had wanted to drive, but Lucas refused to let him, so the guy was now asleep in the back. Lucas needed something to concentrate on or else he'd change his mind and come up with another plan that involved keeping Ashley at his side for as long as physically possible.

But even if they used Ashley as a lure—which he refused to even consider without full FBI backup—there was no guarantee they'd capture the uncle when he was probably holed up in some exotic location far away from US jurisdiction. And there was no telling how extensive a network the Devils had in the US. It was Lucas's job to find out—just as soon as he said goodbye to Ashley and Alex, and made sure Becca was securely installed in a safe house. He'd been ignoring calls from Sloan and Fuentes for the last two hours and at this rate he'd be lucky to have a job to go back to.

Logan International Airport came into view and within minutes he pulled up outside the drop off point for Departures.

The last time he'd been this miserable he'd just found a basement full of dead people.

He focused on saying goodbye to this woman he'd only known for a few days, and yet already liked more than anyone he'd ever met.

She sat beside him in silence. Her face was tense, her knuckles translucent beneath her pale skin. "I'm sorry for everything."

"Everything?"

She huffed out a sad smile. "Not everything."

"I'm sorry for this." He raised his knuckle to her black eye but didn't touch. If he touched her he wouldn't let go. And no way could Ashley Chen stay.

Her hand was on the handle, and she started to open the door, and he forced himself to hold tight to the steering wheel.

She hesitated. "I know it doesn't make any difference, but I didn't lie to you about the things that are really important. I just wanted you to know that."

His cell interrupted. It was Sloan, and he had to take it. "Give me thirty seconds, okay?"

If ever there was a bad time to take a call, this was it. She nodded. Maybe she was as reluctant as he was to say goodbye. Or maybe he was fooling himself.

"Randall," he said.

"I need to speak to Ashley Chen." He didn't recognize the male voice.

"Who is this? Where's SSA Sloan?"

"Sloan can't come to the phone right now. Put Ashley Chen on the line immediately."

He wanted to tell the guy to go fuck himself, but he was already in enough trouble. He put it on speaker and held it out to her.

"Yes?" she said uncertainly.

"Ashley Chen?"

Ashley's eyes widened as the color faded from her skin. "Yes." Her voice was firmer.

"Can anyone else hear this conversation?"

"No," she denied, looking at Lucas and then Alex.

The man laughed. "Long time no speak, cousin. How's life as a ghost?"

"Better than when I was with you."

Lucas glanced into the back of the van, and Alex was on his phone speaking rapidly to someone on the other end. Shit, if they had Sloan's phone where was the SSA?

"What do you want? Where's Sloan?"

"No words of welcome or love? Didn't you miss me?"

"Where is SSA Sloan?" she repeated forcefully.

Alex leaned forward and showed them a text message on his cell. Sloan and Becca had both been abducted from the hospital.

"She's a little busy right now," the man said.

Ashley looked confused. And no wonder, considering she didn't know who Becca was. But she knew what to do.

"Do you have Becca with you?" she asked.

"The girl is fine. Having fun."

His tone made something cold slide down Lucas's spine.

"I need to know she's not dead," Ashley insisted.

Proof of life was important in a kidnapping. It provided a reason to keep people alive.

"And I need you to slip away from your FBI pals and head home for a family reunion. I'll send details in a few hours, and you better be on your way or else you'll miss the fun stuff. But the kid won't."

A photo appeared on the screen, and Lucas wanted to vomit. They had Becca. After everything he'd done to try to protect her...

He'd been so busy worrying about his suspicions regarding Ashley that he'd taken his eyes off the ball. The guilt almost crushed him, but he had a job to do.

Bottling up his rage, he muted the phone. "Tell him you'll come, but if Becca or Sloan are hurt in any way, you're in the wind and no one will ever find you."

She nodded and conveyed the message. The man on the other end laughed. "Sloan sends her apologies. She probably won't make that rendezvous, but the kid will be there. She'll go free if you come alone. If you don't…" He hung up.

"Did you trace it?" Lucas asked Alex.

"Yep. Sloan's home address. Cops are on their way."

SLOAN HAULED HERSELF across the hardwood floor, blood oozing from the knife impaled in her left side. Every inch was torture, the blade sinking into virgin flesh whenever she moved or sucked in a breath. Blood ran in messy streaks down her body, leaving ugly smears across the gleaming boards.

She recognized the pattern from crime scenes. She'd never expected to live it.

The psychopath had stabbed her and then smacked Brian so viciously on the side of the head with her Glock he'd been knocked unconscious. Then the sonofabitch had grabbed Becca's hand and strolled out like nothing had happened.

The psycho had spoken to Chen. Called her "cousin." Sloan didn't know the story, but it hadn't sounded like a happy family reunion. It had sounded like the agent was asking for proof of life, which meant she was still working toward rescuing Becca. Hopefully the cavalry would trace the call to this location and turn up any minute in time to save her and her husband.

Brian hadn't moved.

When she finally reached him, she rolled him on to his back. His semi-naked state reminded her of what had been done to him, and she dragged up his boxers to give him a little dignity. She knew better than to mess with a crime scene, but they weren't dead yet.

"Brian, wake up." His pulse beat steadily beneath her trembling fingers. She was starting to feel dizzy from loss of blood and didn't want to pass out. Not yet. Not if they were dying. His breath was a faint brush of air across the back of her hand.

"Brian." She tapped his cheek gently, and he stirred.

He rolled onto his side and vomited. Not a good sign for a head injury.

"Are you okay?" she asked.

"Yeah. I think so." He rolled onto his back and swore.

"They're gone."

He groaned and held his head. "Did they take Rosie?"

"Rosie?" She frowned in confusion. Then their eyes met and she knew…

She recoiled away from him. "You knew that girl?" It was her turn to feel nauseous.

"No! No." He was indignant. "One of them must have called her that. I wouldn't go to a brothel."

She held her side as she laughed mirthlessly. The head injury had affected his wits. "Then how do you know she was from the brothel?"

She laughed harder as facts clicked into place. All those late nights, their passionless sex life, sleeping at the office, it all started to make a grim sort of sense. Her head pounded as the laughs turned to sobs, and blood continued to seep out of the wound on her side.

She pushed herself away from him, pain secondary to the revulsion of being near him. "I don't believe it. *You're* the leak. You. Everything we told the mayor's office. Tidbits you pried out of me by pretending to be interested in my work. *Fuck*." She'd been so worried about him, so guilt-ridden that she'd brought these criminals into their home, and it was him!

She was so stupid. So goddamn stupid. She held onto her side as a wave of agony crashed through her.

He crawled over to her on all fours. "Carly, I love you. Please don't say anything. I'll be ruined. You'll be ruined! No one will want an FBI agent whose husband…"

She glared up at him. "Fucked children? You're right. But you're a pedophile. You deserve to be ruined."

"Carly," he beseeched.

But he must have seen the stark reality etched between the grimaces of pain. There was no way she'd conceal this.

"You sanctimonious bitch. You think I would have gone seeking it elsewhere if you were any good?"

She swallowed, wishing her vision wasn't going gray. She thought she heard sirens. "I deal with people like you every day, Brian. You can insult me and, sure, it might hurt a little, but I know how deviants like you justify your own twisted appetites. You blame someone else like the cowards you are."

"Bitch." Fingers encircled her throat.

"What are you doing?" She started to scramble away but found no purchase on the blood-slick floors. She reached for her weapon, but she didn't have it anymore. She couldn't breathe.

No.

Her vision started to fade as her lungs screamed for oxygen. She'd survived this nightmare to be murdered by her own husband? And she knew as she stared into his pitiless eyes that he'd find a way to spin this. That he'd probably make himself a fucking hero for trying to save her from the bad guys.

No way.

Her fist circled the hilt of the knife, and she shuddered as she drew it out of her burning flesh. He didn't notice. He was too intent on tightening his grip on her windpipe as he throttled the life out of her.

She plunged the blade as hard as she could in the direction of his kidney. His eyes went wide, then wider still as she twisted the blade.

He was dead before he hit the floor.

CHAPTER TWENTY-ONE

LUCAS PUT THE van in drive. Ashley's door slammed shut as he accelerated away from the curb.

"Lucas," Alex yelled at him.

"What?"

"We can't go to Sloan's place—"

"Why not?"

"'Cause you and Chen will be pulled back into the investigation if you do. We won't be able to go after Becca."

Shit. "But the cops might catch them before they get away." The bastards couldn't be more than a few minutes ahead of the police.

Alex shook his head. "They would never show their hand without a valid escape plan. They're gone, buddy."

Disbelief sideswiped him. A blaring horn brought him back to the moment, and he jerked the wheel to avoid a collision.

"Who is Becca?" Ashley asked in confusion.

Alex answered for him. Lucas wasn't capable of doing anything but concentrating on not crashing the damn car while his heart tried not to explode in his chest.

"A thirteen-year-old girl survived the explosion in Chinatown. Lucas and Sloan kept her survival a secret to protect her."

"So Mallory was right. You were hiding something," she said quietly.

"She's not the only one who figured it out." Alex checked his cell. "One of my close protection guys is texting me from the hospital. Surveillance shows four of them walking out of the place under their own steam. Sloan, Becca, and two Asian guys."

"Probably holding a gun on the kid," Lucas bit out. Sloan wouldn't risk Becca. "What about the ATF agent? She okay?"

Alex waited a moment after he texted. "Reilly says he spoke to the ATF agent. She was taking a break. Sloan was alone with the kid when the gang members waltzed in dressed in white coats and waltzed right out again."

"Why didn't they kill them then and there, like they killed everyone else? Why take them?" Lucas's jaw fused together. The pressure in his brain threatened to blow off the top of his head. Why had they suspected someone survived the blast? Did they have someone inside the FBI? If not Ashley, who?

"Maybe to prove a point? They can get to anyone anywhere, no one is safe?" Ashley suggested. "Or to use as hostages to get themselves out of the country?"

"They could grab anyone as a hostage." Alex nixed that idea. "They took Sloan to get to you. They took the kid to control Sloan and eliminate a witness."

"If they hurt Becca..." But they already had. The photograph was seared into his mind. After he'd promised she was safe. He smashed his fist on the wheel and didn't finish the sentence. "Any news on Sloan?"

Alex called someone as Lucas slammed on the brakes. He'd gone around in a circle and didn't know which way to go next.

"She's alive and being rushed to the ER. She's lost a lot of blood, and they don't think she'll make it. Her husband was found dead at the house. No sign of the perps. No sign of Becca."

So Alex was right. These guys were on the move. "I fucked up."

"We all did, but we don't have time for regret. We need a plan," Alex told them. "Let's go to the jet and figure out our best course of action."

"The best course of action is to do as they say and swap Becca for me," Ashley said.

"Suicide," Alex objected.

"You have a better plan?" she asked.

Alex shook his head. "But if we get to wherever we're going first and set up the meet?" He shrugged. "We might be able to surprise them and get the kid back."

Lucas held Alex's stare in the rearview. "And if it were Mallory?"

Alex's jaw flexed. "I wouldn't let her within a hundred miles of the bastards."

"You seem to forget I'm still officially an FBI agent, and this is my fault." Ashley cut in. "I get a say in what we do, and I want to rescue the kid and catch these offenders. I'm aware of the danger."

Lucas was jolted. Officially nothing had changed. No one else knew about Ashley's fake background, except for the Devils themselves. Whether they said anything would depend on what Ashley did. Rationally, the only possible move the three of them could make was one that looked like she was obeying their instructions.

Lucas's brain was tired from stress and lack of sleep. He

needed time to untangle the web of thoughts whirling through his mind.

A security guard was approaching to shoo them away from the area. Lucas's knuckles tightened on the steering wheel.

"Ashley and I might be able to track them using their cell phones," Parker suggested. "We can work on the plane and maybe narrow down the location of the main headquarters before we even get there."

She swung around in her seat, clearly surprised. "You'd work with me?"

"To save a kid and a federal agent? I'd work with Satan himself."

Ashley laughed, and it sounded honest and real.

Lucas believed her. There was no more doubt in his mind. No more stupid uncertainties.

What a life she must have lived. To always be running. Always be guarded. And she'd been so good at it that the Dragon Devils hadn't even known she was alive until two days ago. And they'd already killed two people and kidnapped another trying to get to her. How many more would be hurt before she confronted them head on?

The security guard knocked on the passenger window, but Lucas had made his decision. He put his foot on the accelerator and sped away.

———————

ASHLEY DRANK COFFEE like the zombie apocalypse was imminent and caffeine the only cure. The last twenty-four hours had been an emotional rollercoaster. People had died because of what she'd done, and now her family had kidnapped a teenage girl in an effort to force Ashley to come to them. She didn't want to think about what Becca would be going through. She was an FBI agent who specialized in cybercrime. She'd seen videos and read enough victim reports to understand the ugly truth. She was also a woman, and every woman lived with the very real fear of sexual assault.

"We should tell Frazer." Lucas was sipping his own coffee, watching her carefully like she might lose it.

"No." Ashley hated the pleading edge that entered her tone.

"He can give us a legitimacy we're lacking right now. Wasn't legitimacy one of the reasons you joined the FBI?"

She wiped a hand over her face. "I'm not sure I'm in a position to pursue that particular goal anymore."

"He's right," Alex said quietly. "Frazer could help, especially when we're abroad."

She sent him a glance. Alex Parker had always been wary and watchful around her. This new friendlier version unnerved her more than the suspicious one had. "If I'm exposed before we catch these guys, I lose all my powers of arrest. Once he finds out the truth, he'll boot me out the BAU so fast—"

"Why did you want to join the BAU so much, anyway?" Alex asked.

She eyed him, trying to figure out whether or not he was being genuine. "I wanted to beef up the cybercrime team. We both know the best people don't work for the feds—I mean look at the idiots trying to crack Mae Kwon's phone."

His brow quirked. "They gave in and sent it to my tech guys yesterday. We cracked it and got some data from the files, but not as much as we'd hoped. She cleaned out the records on a weekly basis."

"So we have a week's worth of johns?" Ashley asked.

He shook his head. "Nope. We have three days' worth of new customers."

She swore.

Lucas sat quietly watching them. She couldn't read him, but she was hyperaware of his every move.

"You're checking the deleted sections?" she asked.

"Of course. There's some minor traces but whoever they have doing their tech—"

"My brother," Ashley interrupted. "I think it's my brother." She finished her coffee and got up to pace. "My career at the BAU is over."

"There are other ways to fight the good fight," Alex said softly. "They generally pay better, too."

Ashley smiled brightly, as if her dreams hadn't been crushed. "I guess that's what I'll do then. Assuming I get through the next few days alive and without being arrested or killed."

Lucas flinched.

"For what it's worth," Alex said, "I think it's 50/50 as to whether or not Frazer fires you."

She'd put it at an odds-on certainty.

"But if he does, you should give me a call." Alex slipped her his business card. "My firm can always use people with your skill set."

"Seriously?"

He nodded, but she wasn't sure she believed him. She stared at the card, wondering if it contained a tracking device. "Thanks."

She pocketed the card and turned to Lucas. "Fine. Tell Frazer everything. Make sure he knows how important it is that everyone takes extra safety precautions. We don't know for sure that they left the country. I couldn't stand it if someone else was hurt because of me."

Lucas nodded.

His cell buzzed from where it rested on the table. He leaned forward. A picture of an old cathedral appeared on the screen. The message below said, "Ashley Chen. Come alone, or the girl dies."

"Where is that?" Lucas turned the phone toward Ashley.

"Macau," she and Parker answered in unison. She looked at him in surprise before continuing. "Yu Chang had a house there. It's where Andrew and I went to live when we first left the States."

"Write back and demand proof of life." Lucas spoke with a calm that belied the tension in his jaw.

She texted back and, a moment later, a photograph appeared—a blonde-haired girl, bound and gagged in what looked like an aircraft cargo hold. Ashley leaned back in her chair, wishing like hell she'd stayed far away from Boston, and that her relatives weren't a bunch of ruthless gangsters.

Lucas stared at the screen. "We need an alternate location where the Dragon Devils don't hold all the power," he told her. "Somewhere it's going to take them time to get to. Somewhere that puts us on more equal footing."

"No home field advantage," Alex agreed.

"Hong Kong?" she suggested. "We could get Nelson Shaw and the HKPD involved."

Lucas shook his head. "No. If Nelson Shaw sees you, your secret is out."

Ashley looked up in surprise. She'd assumed her secret was already out. She swallowed the lump in her throat.

"Can you think of anywhere?" Lucas pushed.

She knew a place. It was a fitting location for a family reunion. She did a quick Google search for a picture and then sent it back to the sender. Was it her brother? Was he helping her uncle and cousin hunt her down?

"Where's that?" Lucas asked, looking at her screen.

"Thailand." Ashley forced herself to relax. "It's the beach where we were staying when the wave hit. It'll freak them out as much as it does me."

She texted a quick message. "When I get there, she goes free. Hurt her in any way, and you'll never see me again. I want your word, Andrew."

She held her breath, waiting for the reply to come through.

"You have my word, Jen-Jen."

Her heart stopped for a beat at the use of the old nickname. It really was Andrew. Her brother was involved in trafficking and sexual slavery.

Alex picked up the phone and removed the SIM card. He was making sure there was no way for the kidnappers to call and arrange a different location at the last minute. If they wanted her—and she knew they wanted her—they'd have to do it on her terms at this location. It wasn't much of an advantage, but it was better than nothing.

"I need to go talk to the pilot." Alex stood. "It's a long way to Thailand. We might be better off getting on a commercial flight. Easier to blend in with the tourists, but not as easy to plot our next move."

"You should go home to Mallory. This isn't your fight," she argued.

Alex gave her a look that made the hair on her nape rise. "They made it my fight when they tortured and murdered a woman they thought was my fiancée. Mallory has the protection she needs for now. I'm going to make sure they don't repeat their mistake." He excused himself.

She and Lucas were completely alone, and she was achingly aware of the fact. She closed her eyes and felt herself sway. She was exhausted. She'd been too scared to do more than doze during her abduction and too busy jumping Lucas's bones the night before.

"You need to lie down." He took her arm and pulled her gently toward the bedroom at the back of the cabin. She let him lead her, wanting to keep him near her until the time came to push him away forever. Inside, he closed the small shutters and drew back the coverlet. She sat on the mattress and pulled off her boots, lying down on the pillow, wondering what would happen next. Her uncle had friends in many places. How would she handle being at his mercy again? She didn't know if she'd be able to.

Lucas leaned down to kiss her cheek.

She grabbed his sleeve. "Stay. For a little while."

She didn't like the needy vibe to her voice, but she held on until he relented and kicked off his own shoes and lay down beside her, spooning her body and wrapping his arm around her waist, hugging her to him.

"Go to sleep, Ash."

She thought she felt his lips brush her hair, but she wasn't sure.

Emotions threatened, the growing feeling of love for this man swamped her fear, even though she knew she couldn't have him for more than a few short hours.

But, for the first time in her adult life, she was sleeping with a man who knew everything there was to know about her—and still he cradled her gently.

The weight of the lies she'd been telling all these years released from her shoulders. She hadn't realized what a burden they'd been until the weight was gone.

She snuggled into his arms and felt herself being pulled into sleep.

Despite everything, she was clinging to the side of law and order. It was a heady realization to know she didn't need to do everything alone. But it was her fault they'd gone after her fellow agents. She had a plan to get Becca away from her captors. She just didn't know if she'd survive the aftermath.

ANDREW SAT REELING in his darkened office. He'd just heard from his sister—a sister he'd believed was dead until a short while ago. On a cerebral level, he'd known she was still alive and pretending to be FBI Agent Ashley Chen. But seeing that message directed at him had made the abstract thought real. Everything inside him had frozen.

"Hurt her in any way, and you'll never see me again. I want your word, Andrew."

She now knew without a doubt that he was involved in their uncle's business. She knew he was trying to track her down and bring her home. And when Yu Chang caught up with her, he would hurt and humiliate her for tricking him and running away.

Andrew had betrayed her in the worst possible way.

He shoved his laptop away. He'd done what he had to to

survive. She'd gotten away. He'd been stuck with their uncle and forced to join his organization or get crushed. He hadn't had a choice.

He pulled out a different cell phone and called Brandon, who'd finally found a ride in a private jet that belonged to a Libyan arms dealer they occasionally did business with. Andrew didn't like dealing with people like the Libyan. The man brokered death in a way that made their people trafficking operation look positively warm and fuzzy. Now they owed him a favor.

"Did it work?" Brandon asked.

They'd discovered that one of the girls from the brothel had survived the explosion courtesy of Rabbit who'd called them as soon as he'd found out. Cho had already been following Sloan, so when the ex-task force leader had driven straight to the hospital after getting fired, Andrew had known the survivor was probably there, too. The plan to take them both had been Andrew's idea. Sloan would know how to contact Special Agent Chen, and taking the child hostage would be enough of a reason for his bleeding heart sister to do his bidding.

Rabbit had paid for the mess he'd created. Andrew had heard on the news that Brian Templeton was dead.

"She's coming," Andrew said. "But says if you hurt the kid, she'll disappear."

His cousin swore.

"I gave her my word, Brandon."

"What does it matter? She'll never know."

"I gave her my *word*, Brandon. And she'll know. You want to be the one to tell Yu Chang she ran again?"

"Bitch." Brandon heaved out a frustrated sigh. "Once she

sets foot in Macau she's ours."

"She's not going to Macau." This was the part he didn't want to tell his uncle.

"What?" Brandon growled.

"She said to meet her at the villa in Thailand."

"Thailand?" There was fear in Brandon's voice, fear none of them ever admitted. It was a nightmare they shared, an unspoken terror. She'd made a clever choice. "You told the old man yet?"

"No." Andrew wished he could give the job to his cousin.

"He'll never go for it."

"She disconnected and disabled her SIM card. I have no way of contacting her. If he wants to wait while we send someone to Thailand to pick her up—"

"He won't do that, either," said Brandon.

The old man was too proud to back down from a challenge, especially from a woman. He'd be there.

"Talk to him," Andrew urged. Brandon was good at handling his father. "This could be a trap set up by the FBI. It would be a lot smarter to regroup and watch from a distance. Try and pick her up when she's alone."

"I'll talk to him, but he won't change his mind. See you in a few hours."

Andrew hung up and once again did his best to ignore the fact that Yu Chang wanted to have sex with his sister. The idea was abhorrent. Maybe the old man had just been scaring her all those years ago, trying to get her to toe the line the only way he knew how.

Except, he'd seen how the man had looked at her during those few months. He'd seen the way Yu Chang had pressed her against the wall after he'd killed the German boy. With heat, with lust.

Lily was still in his bedchamber. He swallowed the knot of tension. He'd been too busy to go to her, too ashamed.

He should have made it clear to his uncle that she was important to him, not some whore they could take turns with. In many ways, what had happened was Andrew's fault, and he'd make sure it never happened again. Not that it would be an issue. The old man was so obsessed with Jenny, he'd probably already forgotten Lily.

That would change if Andrew didn't bring his sister back into the family fold.

He rubbed his hand over his face. He needed to make travel plans. But for the first time since coming to stay with Yu Chang, he knew he didn't want to live this way anymore. But what was the alternative? Running away and hiding, the way Jenny had? Look at how well that was turning out for her.

He went back to his computer and tried to remember who they knew in Thailand, and who they could buy.

CHAPTER TWENTY-TWO

L UCAS KNEW THAT getting into bed with Ashley was a mistake, yet he could no more have refused her plea than stop breathing. He'd fucked up. The least he could do was hold her.

He hadn't expected to fall asleep.

He hadn't expected to wake up with the woman in question pressing a soft kiss against his cheek, as if quietly saying goodbye. He reached out, cupped her jaw, and turned his head, capturing her lips with his.

She moaned but, for a moment, he thought she was going to pull away. He took the kiss deeper, tasting the real her for the very first time. There were no lies between them now. No barriers. He started working the buttons on her shirt.

"We can't," she said, but pressed closer to his raging hard-on.

"We are." He had her shirt open and bra pulled down, diving in for a taste of one cherry tip, making her groan again.

"What about Parker?" she whispered breathily.

"Parker's got his own woman." He sucked hard, and her heels pressed against the bed, thrusting her breast against his mouth. He pulled back to admire his glistening handiwork—she was so beautiful. Then he went back for more.

Frantically he undressed her, and she pulled at his clothing until they were naked, limbs entangled, mouths exploring, fingers touching. He rested his palm over her heart and felt the fierce thud of her life force, reminding him how strong she was, how strong she'd had to be. A fine shudder ran through her bones and matched the trembling in his. Everything slowed down into a sensuous dance.

"You kill me, Ash." He brushed the hair off her forehead and stared deep into her pretty eyes. He pressed a kiss to the corner of her bruise, wishing he could take the injury back. "Would you rather be called Jenny now?" he asked.

Her pupils flared, and she shook her head. "Jenny died that day on the beach."

He nibbled her bottom lip. "I think there's still a lot of Jenny Britton buried deep inside where she can't get hurt again."

Her expression turned sad, so he concentrated on making this woman feel so good she couldn't remember the bad times, or consider the uncertain future. By the time he was done, her eyes were unfocused, and her skin was damp. Last time had been all passion and fire. This time…he wasn't ready to put a name on it. Not yet. Maybe never.

He found a condom in his wallet and moved on top of her, loving the way she parted her thighs to welcome him. He slid inside, and they both held their breath in wonder.

He started moving, holding her hands above her head and staring deep into her eyes, thrusting slow and deep, then harder, faster until she bit her lip and wrapped those long strong legs of hers tight around his hips.

She closed her eyes and tipped her head back, tension rife in the lines of her neck. He wanted to run his tongue over her and taste the salt on her skin, but she was too close to coming, and he didn't want to deny her, not when she'd been denied so much. She cried out even though she tried not to, and he didn't care if Alex heard, or the crew, or the entire goddamned country. He pushed her harder, prolonging the orgasm that throbbed and pulsed around him until it finally tipped him over the edge, his own climax tearing through him.

After a few dangerous heartbeats, his mind came back to the room. It was his first time making love in an aircraft. And, judging by the clamor of emotions clanging in his head, the first time making love.

She lay there quietly contemplating him, and he avoided her gaze because the last thing they needed was him getting carried away. There was too much going on to deal with that right now. Too much at stake to get distracted.

He pulled away and got rid of the condom, then leaned down to kiss her temple. She flinched when he caught her bruise.

"I really am sorry," he said, climbing back in beside her.

She touched his jaw. "It was an accident. I'm the one who head butted the side of the van."

"And me." He rubbed his nose. "Where'd you learn that move?"

"One of the instructors at the academy. He told me I'd never pass training. One day he had me pinned against a wall with all the other NATs looking on. He started laughing, saying I fought like a girl, and he was sure all the bad guys would go easy on me. I was so angry. My head was the only part of my body I could move, so I used it. He wasn't expecting anything and got a busted nose for his troubles. I thought he was a total prick until he came up to me at graduation and personally congratulated me. Told me I'd done a good job, and he was proud of me." From her expression that had meant a lot to her.

"Are you saying he was actually a nice guy under the bullish bravado?"

She laughed as she traced her thumb over his bottom lip. "I suppose you breezed through that part of the training."

"I loved sparring in defensive tactics. I especially loved going up against the instructors." They'd driven everyone hard, and he knew what the guy had been trying to do with Ashley—make her forget social conventions and use as much force as necessary to get the job done and stay alive. "It was trying to memorize all the federal laws that kicked my ass."

She laughed, a sparkle entering her gaze, but then it extinguished as she frowned. "I fought you so hard because I thought you might be working for my uncle."

Fuck. "I really am sorry."

"I know." She ran her thumb over his lip, and the touch was like fire igniting his blood, stirring his desire.

She pushed him onto his back and eyed his growing erection. "Looks like you can make it up to me in the very near future, especially if you have another condom."

He gave a jerk of his head because she'd taken hold of him and was stroking him with those slender fingers, stoking his need. They needed to work. They needed to rest. They needed to figure out a plan. But there were endless hours before they reached their destination, and this might be the last time they were ever together like this.

Her tongue trailed down his body, and suddenly he didn't think he was going to survive Ashley Chen. But if anything happened to her, he wouldn't want to.

ASHLEY SHOWERED, DRESSED and slipped out of the cabin. Alex Parker sat in a soft white leather armchair working at a table. She tried to calm the blush in her cheeks. Apparently stripping her lies away had also torn away some of her armor.

"Any word on Sloan?" she asked.

He shook his head. "Still in surgery."

She looked at the window. They were still flying over land.

"You better not hurt him," he said unexpectedly.

She paused. "You seem like an unlikely protector."

He eyed her under his brows as she slumped into the seat opposite. "Do I?"

"Yeah, you do."

"I've never seen him smitten before."

"Smitten?" The old-fashioned word both thrilled and depressed her. She was going up against one of the biggest criminal godfathers in Asia, if not the world. The only thing that would stop his vengeance was death. Now was not the time to be thinking about having a man in her life.

"How long have you two known each other, anyway?" She was curious about Lucas Randall.

"We served together in the Army."

"Huh. I thought you met through Mallory."

"Other way around. Lucas introduced us." The look in his eyes told her exactly what that meant to him.

It was humbling to see how much the guy loved her fellow agent. She wanted that. She wanted it with the man sleeping in the next room. Chances of getting it were infinitesimal.

"I'm sorry I dragged everyone into this mess." She worried at the skin on her cuticles. "Considering all the people who've been hurt, I guess it would have been better if I'd never joined the FBI."

She met his gaze and was surprised by the empathy she saw there.

"They would just be hurting someone else." His lips pulled back in a wry smile. "I understand the need to fight evil, just as I get that justice isn't always about following the rules." Those silver eyes looked straight into her soul. "But not everyone thinks the way we do. Most people play by the rules."

She looked away at the reminder. "What did Frazer say?"

Alex grinned. "It was more colorful than I'd expected, but could have been worse. He didn't send the military after us."

Crap. She crossed her arms over her chest and braced herself. "Is he going to keep it to himself or am I going to be arrested the moment I go home?"

"I don't think he's decided yet."

She processed that. "What are you doing?"

"Searching for any activity I can trace to the Devils."

"Can we bring our weapons into Thailand?" she asked.

"I doubt it. Frazer's reaching out to people to try to get some assistance on the ground. And I'm trying to figure out alternatives." He leaned back in his chair. "Greg Trainer has been calling for Lucas's head. He's made noises about Lucas's dereliction of duty being the reason Sloan and the girl were taken."

Anger and guilt warred inside her. Her actions had badly affected Lucas's career. "How do I fix that?"

He grimaced. "Might be hard without coming clean."

"Then I'll come clean."

"Frazer said to leave it with him for now."

Nothing could jeopardize Lucas's job. She wouldn't allow

it.

"We found the source of the leak at the hotel—someone hacked their system the night before."

Ashley grimaced. *Her brother.* "How'd they find Becca?"

"They followed Sloan from her office."

"She didn't notice them?"

"They put a tracker on her car."

Damn. "How did they know she'd lead them to the girl?" Ashley wondered.

"Good question." Alex frowned then raised his brow at her. "Wanna help me search through a few phone records and see if we can't figure out if someone on the inside was feeding them information?"

She looked at her watch. Only another ten hours to Bangkok. "Let's do it."

CHAPTER TWENTY-THREE

A NDREW STOOD OVER the cowering form of the young blonde girl. One of Brandon's henchmen, Cho, went to kick the girl, but Andrew held up his hand.

"Leave her," he said sharply in Cantonese. Cho looked to Brandon before bowing to him and walking away.

"I promised she'd be unharmed." He shot his cousin a look.

Brandon shrugged.

Andrew cleared his throat. "How old is she?"

"Thirteen. She worked for us for a couple of years. She says she didn't tell them anything, and I believe her." His smile told Andrew he hadn't just *asked* her. Torture was one of Brandon's specialties. "But we aren't in the States anymore so it doesn't matter what they know."

There was a good chance the feds knew their identities now. His uncle had sacrificed their anonymity in order to get Jenny back. They'd have to burrow so deep they'd barely see daylight. The only advantages they had were lots of money, a fiercely loyal crew, and they owned land all over Southeast Asia under various guises.

Lily entered the room and placed a tray of food on the coffee table. He watched his cousin's eyes slide over her, and the light bulb went off. Brandon had known he'd had a thing for the young woman. Had Brandon told his father Andrew had managed to get her into bed?

He hadn't wanted Lily to accompany them on this journey. He'd wanted her sent home. But his uncle had insisted.

"Where did we get the girl from?" He spoke in Cantonese, and the words rasped in his throat. Being confronted by the grim human reality of their criminal enterprise was different than posting pictures of smiling nubile young women on the internet and funneling the money into safe hiding places. Suddenly his heart pounded, and his skin burned. If his parents were alive, they'd be so ashamed of him.

"We didn't steal the brat if that's what you're thinking." Brandon spoke with his mouth full of apple. "Her mother gave her to us to pay off a gambling debt."

Andrew tried not to be aware of Lily leaving the room, but he was. He could feel her presence like a ghost in his mind. Or maybe that was his conscience.

He looked out the porthole. They were on a large boat in the middle of the Andaman Sea. Jenny was winging her way to them as they spoke.

The door opened, and his uncle appeared. He and Brandon both bowed low. The old man hobbled into the room using a cane, clasped his son to his chest, and closed his eyes. Andrew had never seen him more grateful.

Yu Chang looked toward Andrew. "You have done well, Nephew." Then he stepped away from Brandon and pulled out his knife. Andrew stood frozen as Yu Chang grabbed the terrified girl by the hair and pulled her head back, exposing her throat. Andrew watched the old man's hand tighten on the hilt.

"Stop!" Andrew cried out.

The old man turned as if startled.

"Jenny said that if the girl wasn't released safely she'd disappear forever. I gave her my word the girl would be unharmed, Uncle." He bowed low, knowing the man could easily turn the knife on him instead.

Yu Chang paused and breathed deeply in and out through his nose. Then his expression calmed.

Andrew hoped it was safe to go on. "Jenny wants us to release the girl as soon as she gets to the villa."

His uncle's gaze drifted to the shoreline. They'd all almost died here. Yu Chang's manservant had drowned, and Yu Chang had been gravely injured.

I wish he'd died...

Andrew banished the thought and glanced away. He'd never imagined he'd want to betray the only family he had left.

What about Jenny?

She'd abandoned him to this life. What the hell had she expected?

"I will honor your promise, Andrew." Yu Chang's lips curved, but there was no smile in his eyes. "But if she escapes or Jenny doesn't come, I will take payment from your pretty little whore."

Andrew froze. *That's* why he'd brought Lily with them. His uncle didn't trust him—not when it came to choosing between Yu Chang and his sister. Andrew wanted to scream that Lily wasn't a whore and to leave her the hell alone, but if he did that, they were both dead. Instead he did what he always did. He bowed. "Yes, Uncle."

"THIS CAN'T BE good." Lucas stared out the window as a group of Army vehicles surrounded the private jet on the small airfield just outside Phuket. "They friends of yours?"

Alex shook his head. "Nope. Give me your weapons."

Lucas and Ashley both handed over their government issued pistols and watched Alex place them in the safe along with his own firearm, a M1911. He placed his and Ashley's personal laptops inside too.

"Combination is clockwise seven, three, two, counter-clockwise six, four, clockwise one. Let's not make it easy for anyone to find a reason to arrest us."

"What can I do?" Ashley asked.

She'd dressed in tactical gear and looked sexy and capable. Considering her life and her career were on the line, he didn't know how she did it. "Put your vest on. Make sure your creds are visible." His were on his belt, the gold shield gleaming in the hot Thai sun.

Lucas called Frazer, but carried on talking while waiting for the other man to pick up.

"Grab your work laptop, put on your sternest FBI face. Any government official getting paid off by a criminal gang might think twice before taking us on in our official capacities."

"Do we? Have official clearance?" she asked.

But he didn't answer. Frazer was on the line. The man had called in favors from just about everyone he knew, and he knew a lot of people. He repeated the facts to the others. "Frazer says the FBI Director authorized this mission just before we entered Thai airspace, but they're waiting for the Thai government to green light our stay."

The Thai army was pushing steps toward the aircraft door.

Thirty seconds later they were hammering on it, demanding entry.

"I have to let them in before they start battering down the door and destroy our exit strategy." Alex eyed them both critically. "Stay calm. Say nothing except we are here on official business, following a viable lead looking for a kidnapped US citizen. It might take time for the green light to filter down the ranks. Don't mention anything else. Either they let us go immediately or we'll wait for someone from the embassy to turn up. We'll regroup here as soon as we're released."

He opened the main door before they could reply and men in green Army uniforms stormed into the plane, pointing their weapons at them and the crew, yelling at them to get down on the ground, before placing them in handcuffs.

"We're here on behalf of the US government—" Lucas began to argue.

"Be quiet!" The hard-faced lunatic who screamed at him wasn't kidding around.

Fuck. Lucas did not like where this was going.

They were jerked to their feet and marched down the steps, the subtropical heat making his T-shirt immediately cling to his body like a wet cloth. Ashley hadn't said anything, but she had to be worried her uncle had set this up.

They pushed him and the others toward a bus. This did *not* look good. Suddenly one of the soldiers cut Ashley from the pack and started herding her toward a different vehicle. Anger and fear boiled over, and he shouldered a guard out of the way and got between the man and the woman he'd gone and stupidly fallen in love with. Staring down the barrel of a rifle was not the best place to have this epiphany, but timing had never been his strong point. He opened his mouth to tell Ashley exactly what she meant to him when a rifle butt smashed into the side of his head, and the world flooded into darkness.

―――――――――

"DON'T TOUCH HIM!" Ashley screamed. But the soldier hit Lucas again. "You're going to kill him, you idiot." She fought to reach him, but another man came and helped the first, and they dragged her away and shoved her into a jeep. Alex was shouting at the individual who seemed to be in charge, and didn't notice she was being kidnapped. She'd rather he concentrate on saving Lucas. The driver gunned it. The second soldier sat in the passenger seat and held his pistol at her. She turned around and looked out the rear window. Lucas was lying immobile on the tarmac; Alex was struggling against his captors.

Please be okay.

As she watched, Lucas finally rolled over. Two soldiers lifted him onto his feet, and he stood staring after her.

Ashley was going to have to get herself out of this mess. "I'm an agent of the United States Federal Bureau of Investigation. I demand to know, what is the meaning of this outrage?"

"We have orders. Be quiet, and no one will harm you."

She was getting a little tired of being abducted, but at least they'd cuffed her wrists in front of her.

"I demand to be returned to my colleagues, immediately."

"Your colleagues are being detained while we search the plane for the victim of a kidnapping. There was a tip off."

Huh.

"Why am I being separated? I demand to stay with them." She was only saying it to have an excuse to lean closer.

The man in the passenger side gestured wildly with his pistol. She grabbed the weapon, turning it in her grip so deftly he sat there, dumbfounded.

"Pull over," she demanded to the driver, sitting far enough back that passenger-guy couldn't grab his weapon back. The driver started scrambling for his sidearm. "Hands off your weapon, or I put a bullet in you both. Pull. Over. Now."

When he complied, she told him, "Toss the key to the cuffs into my lap." She raised her eyes to his and knew he wanted to do something foolish. "Try anything, and your friend dies. Hands on the dash. You," she yelled at passenger-guy as it seemed to be the only volume he responded to. "Key, now."

He seemed to realize she was serious, and the key landed between her thighs. She picked it up and kept it in her grip, never taking her gaze from the two men in front of her. No doubt her uncle had paid someone handsomely to get her away from her teammates.

"Out."

Passenger-guy got out of the car and stood in the middle of the road clearly not knowing what to do. She locked his door and held the gun to the driver's head. "Take out your gun slowly and toss it in the passenger foot well. Leave the keys in the ignition and get out of the car." He obviously understood English and carefully did as she told him. As soon as he was out, she locked his door. She slid into the driver's seat and drove just far enough away to safely stop and remove the cuffs. The two men had pulled out their phones and were calling reinforcements. From her uncle, or from the Army?

They'd done what she was sure they were supposed to do—get her alone without backup.

She recognized this part of the coast. The lush tropical vegetation. The craggy limestone bluffs. She toyed with the idea of sneaking back to the aircraft, but the likelihood was it would be well guarded, and the chances of finding Lucas and Alex there were slim. She had no idea where they'd been taken, and she'd only be detained if she tried to find them.

It was better this way. Seeing Lucas injured had ripped aside any blinders as to how she felt about the man. The idea of him being murdered in front of her the way Martel had been was unacceptable. She'd never survive that. Never. She'd rather rot in jail or submit to her uncle's warped desire than see Lucas harmed.

She was approaching a small village filled with tourist shops, small hotels, and dive centers. The area had revitalized and rebuilt since the tsunami and everything looked fancier, more expensive. Blue and white tsunami warning signs pointed to an evacuation route. A newly installed public-address system gleamed in the setting sun—an early warning alarm that gave locals and tourists a fighting chance should the unthinkable happen again. She could see the blue sparkling sea on her left, and her hands shook at the memory of that wall of water crashing over her. She pulled over beside a dive shop, panting and sweaty from heat and fear. It didn't matter how much time passed, she would never trust the ocean again. But the ocean wasn't the enemy today. She stripped off her flak jacket, pulling her damp T-shirt away from her skin. A bus already packed with people sat idling a few yards away outside a small convenience store. She stuck one handgun into the back of her pants, and the other in her boot.

347

Moving swiftly, she gestured to the bus driver that she was just getting a drink and then jumped on board. Thankfully the shopkeeper and bus driver were happy to take her US dollars.

She'd also purchased a sun hat. Now she pulled the brim low over her eyes and sank into her seat, patiently trundling onwards to her obligatory family reunion.

LUCAS FELT LIKE he'd been run over by a Mack truck. Alex was shouting and gesticulating at their captors, but all Lucas could think about was the sight of Ashley in the back of that goddamned jeep.

He spat blood near the boots of the soldier who'd bashed his fucking brains in with a fucking rifle. The look on his face must have promised retribution, because the little fucker backed up another step.

A limousine rolled up, and he blinked when Detective Nelson Shaw of the Hong Kong Police Department and another man jumped out and hurried over to the upstart who seemed to be in charge. The letters "FBI" were being repeated over and over at increasing volumes.

Lucas's head throbbed like a bitch as Alex sidled up to him.

"Know him?" Alex asked.

Lucas was saved from speaking by Nelson Shaw himself.

"Agent Randall." His mouth was a grim line. "I'm sorry this happened."

"I'd heard the Thai people were friendly. Apparently not." Lucas could barely force the words past his aching jaw.

"This is my fault. I asked them to detain you for a few

minutes so we could get here. I didn't ask them to beat you up."

The man who'd arrived with Nelson came over and shouted at the nearest soldier to unlock their handcuffs before he introduced himself. "I'm Detective Benny Shinwari. Royal Thai police, Crime Suppression Division." He offered his hand, and Lucas shook it reluctantly. "They say you resisted arrest. I apologize. They thought you were kidnappers and that Agent Chen was in fact a victim." He was carrying a SIG Sauer P320 in a side holster.

"Where is Agent Chen?" Lucas asked, wishing the double vision would stop.

The soldiers had climbed back into their trucks. The upstart major strode over and barked something to the Thai detective in their own language.

The Bangkok detective blanched. "There was some miscommunication. He says he received orders to take Agent Chen to a different location."

"Tell him he better figure out where those orders came from because that's got to be someone in league with the Dragon Devils," Nelson said quickly. "And tell his soldiers to bring her back ASAP."

Detective Shinwari went to pass on the message. Lucas watched as one of the major's soldiers handed him a phone. The man's eyes widened, and he started barking instructions at his troops, who all ran to board the convoy. The drivers started the engines, and the trucks rumbled away.

"What just happened?" Lucas asked.

"Get in the car," Detective Shinwari said urgently, "I'll explain while we drive."

But Alex instead ran back to the plane and up the steps.

Lucas watched him speak quickly to the crew, who were standing around not sure what was going on. Alex dipped inside, and Lucas knew exactly what he was doing. Two minutes later, he reappeared carrying a black bag, two bulletproof vests, and their weapons.

Neither cop mentioned the SIG Alex handed him. Lucas checked the chamber as the detective took off after the Army truck. They caught up with them after a couple of miles, pulled up on the side of the road. The truck had stopped to pick up the two soldiers who'd driven Ashley away. No sign of her or the jeep.

The detective jumped out, and Lucas rolled down the window, wishing he understood the language.

The detective came back and climbed inside. "Seems Agent Chen got away with the jeep and took both their weapons. They don't know where she went."

Lucas exchanged a look with Alex. They knew. He rolled up the window.

"Why are you here, Nelson?" Lucas asked. Last time they'd spoken, the guy said he was staying in Boston for a few days.

"My boss ordered me back to Hong Kong." He didn't sound happy about that. "Then the news of the attack on the FBI agent in charge of the task force hit the wire, along with the kidnapping of your only witness, and I knew the shit was well and truly stirred. I received a tipoff that Yu Chang had been spotted climbing onboard a boat off the coast of Thailand. I headed straight here. I tried to call your office to coordinate an operation, but I was redirected to a man called ASAC Lincoln Frazer. He did not sound very happy."

Lucas grimaced.

"He told me he had agents en route to Thailand, and if I

wanted in on the arrest to get my ass to the Phuket airport as soon as possible and assist you." Nelson glanced at Detective Shinwari. "Benny and I have worked together many times in the past. We knew we weren't going to make it in time for your arrival, so we asked the military to detain you long enough for us to get here."

Lucas glared at him.

Benny interrupted. "We said it involved a kidnapping. We didn't say you were the kidnappers." His hands flexed around the steering wheel. "Do we stay here and help search for Agent Chen, or do we head for the exchange Frazer mentioned?"

A thousand thoughts zapped through Lucas's head, and none of them were good. "The exchange is to be at Khao Lak. Drive."

"You brought cash?" Benny eyed the black bag via the rearview mirror with interest.

"They didn't want money."

"Immunity? They have to know that won't legally hold up with Thai authorities," Benny argued.

"They didn't ask for immunity."

"So what did they want?" Benny lost his patience.

Lucas looked out the window. "Ashley. They want Agent Chen."

"Why the hell would they want—"

"Her real name is Jenny Britton. The dead niece from the tsunami? That's Agent Chen."

Nelson's bottom jaw dropped. "Holy fuck. And Yu Chang found out? Does he want to punish her for her betrayal?" His expression twisted into anger, and Lucas read his mind. "Or is she running back to the safety of her family? Is she the reason we've been unable to catch these bastards all these years?"

"No," Lucas gritted out.

"Are you sure you haven't been blinded by a pretty face?" Nelson asked.

The detective had no idea how close he came to permanent injury in that moment.

Lucas stared the man down. "She said her uncle had an unhealthy sexual obsession with her mother and then with her. She told me that, just moments before the wave hit, he killed a boyfriend of hers, a Martel Gunter?" The local detective's eyes widened. "She used the natural disaster to disappear and escape from Yu Chang, until someone recognized her, and the Dragon Devils discovered she was still alive."

"I remember Martel Gunter. His father was a high ranking German diplomat, and he was never happy with the cause of death being declared as natural."

"He was right to question it." Lucas blinked away the blurry vision and tried to pretend it was from the blow to the head instead of from a blow to his heart. He'd never hurt so damn much in his life.

"Where's the backup?" Alex asked, checking his weapon. They'd passed through town and were driving past rubber and palm-oil plantations.

The two detectives exchanged a look. "We're it."

"Seriously?" Alex shook his head.

Benny shrugged. "The commander in Phuket has a reputation for taking bribes. If that's true then Yu Chang probably already got to him. We could call in the military—"

"No," Alex interrupted. "We've seen the military in action."

"How many men do you think Chang has with him?" asked Lucas.

Nelson grimaced. "A man that paranoid with a world full of enemies...I would expect him to travel with at least twenty well-armed guards. Where exactly is the meet? Perhaps I can arrange some kind of assistance."

"The villa where they were staying when the tsunami hit."

Benny nodded sagely. "It's gonna be nightfall before we get there."

Nelson checked his watch. "Then drive faster. I'm not wasting this opportunity to catch Yu Chang."

"Let me drive," Alex demanded.

The Thai detective laughed. "You don't know the roads—"

Alex pressed his gun to the man's temple. "It wasn't a request."

They swapped drivers at the side of the highway with the Thai detective loudly complaining about Alex's manners. Nelson shifted seats so Benny could sit in the front and direct him. Lucas zoned out as he stared at the sparkling ocean, sprinkled with stunningly beautiful islands. It was impossible to imagine the devastation the wave had caused to this region. The fact Ashley had survived that disaster was a miracle.

How was she holding up? She was terrified of the ocean, but going after Yu Chang anyway.

She really was an incredible woman: smart, brave, determined. The FBI was lucky to have her.

His mouth went dry. He was lucky to know her, the real her, not the aloof persona she showed the world. No one else saw that. No one else knew her the way he did.

All the lost opportunities were screaming at him that he'd made another massive mistake. He hadn't told her he loved her. And now he might never get the chance.

CHAPTER TWENTY-FOUR

A SHLEY GOT OFF the bus and walked past a coconut plantation and a wild, sprawling tropical forest, to the spit of land where the villa once stood. Now it was a crumbling ruin, one of the few locations not to have been bulldozed and rebuilt. Sapphire blue water stretched out to the horizon, calm and deadly.

She'd fought the impulse to run with every step she took. Her fear wasn't abstract. It was as solid as titanium and resided inside her mind like a living, breathing monster. And right now that monster was trying to escape.

That, and the memory of Lucas being driven to his knees by that soldier's rifle made her glad she hadn't eaten anything for hours.

How could he ever forgive her lies and stupidity? She'd gotten some people hurt, and others killed. Even if by some miracle she survived this thing, the chance of them being together was zero. No one in their right mind would love someone like her. Someone whose relatives had caused suffering for multitudes of innocents in order to line their own pockets.

They repulsed her. She repulsed herself.

None of it mattered, anyway. They'd connected during a period of intense stress. The attraction between them was real enough, but the rest probably wouldn't last beyond a couple of dates. They had no common interests—hell, she didn't even know what his interests were outside the bedroom and work.

So why did the thought of never seeing him again hurt almost as much as the thought of dying?

She had no idea, and couldn't afford to deal with those feelings right now. She needed clarity. She needed revenge, and God help her, she needed redemption.

The only thing that mattered was finding a way to rescue this teenager and end this nightmare for good. Then she'd figure out the rest—her job, the fact she might be going to jail, Lucas. First, she needed to see her family's criminal empire destroyed.

Agitatedly, the beast inside her mind started to pace its cage as the scent of the ocean grew stronger. She concentrated on the hypnotherapy techniques she'd mastered over the years. The fact she kept putting one foot in front of the other meant they must be working.

The black tactical pants and long-sleeved shirt were not the usual tourist garb and earned her a few odd glances. At least her hat kept the fierce rays of the setting sun out of her eyes.

Fishing boats bobbed on the water. A large boat was anchored out to sea. It had been the same the day the wave came, and many boats had been swept far inland. She fought the icy surge of dread that tried to drag her under just as surely as that wave.

Khao Lak was a paradise. Only an hour's drive north of Phuket, it was a mecca for tourists. On that fateful day, the 9.3 magnitude quake that occurred 160 km off the coast of Sumatra was the second largest recorded. The fault line affected extended twelve hundred kilometers and left a scar in the ocean floor that was still there today.

Islands or currents off the coast of Thailand had funneled the displaced water until the resultant wave was more than ten meters high when it finally hit Khao Lak. Nearly four thousand people had lost their lives that day in this region alone.

Emotions swelled inside her as she forced her feet toward the beach. The trauma was still there, etched on her mind as vivid today as when it had happened. The scent of the salt water, the sound of the surf, the feel of sand between her toes, were all tied to the feeling of horror.

All the therapy in the world didn't matter if you couldn't face your fear.

She made herself walk through the remains of the villa's front door, then through the crumbling ruins that were being steadily reclaimed by the forest. Her limbs trembled when she reached the patio where poor Martel had died. All because he'd been seduced by a girl who'd turned out to be poisonous.

She could see the ship more clearly now. A massive cruiser with its own helipad. It had to be her uncle. She smiled grimly.

Shivers set in, so she set about building a fire from driftwood scattered around the margins of the beach. The scent of paraffin lamps drifted on the air, pitching her back to memories of lying in a hammock pressed close to Martel, his fingers slowly stroking her arm.

She shook off the reminders of the past. Martel would get justice. She'd make sure of it.

She begged a matchbook off workmen who delivered a pile of lumber to a hotel under construction next-door. Thankfully they left soon after and all was quiet. Less people to get caught in the crossfire.

She wasn't hiding. She'd realized in the last few hours that until she faced up to her past, she'd never be free to live her life. She stood with a wide stance, arms crossed and chin held high. She was issuing the devil a challenge, one she knew he wouldn't be able to resist.

"Come and get me, asshole."

"WHAT THE HELL is she doing?"

Lucas didn't know what Ashley was doing, except sitting on the beach in front of a blazing fire, waiting for the Dragon Devils to come get her. If that was her "plan," it sucked.

Thanks to Alex's driving, the four of them had reached the area before Ashley, but had kept out of sight and waited until dusk to move into position, spanning the perimeter.

For all the good they'd do. They needed rifles, night vision optics, and a special ops team to take out these bastards. All they had was limited range side arms, PTT headsets, two pairs of binoculars, and plenty of motivation.

Lucas was closest to the sea on the northern side of this small bay, hidden by the night and a small stand of palm trees. Alex and Nelson were secreted in the ruins of the villa, and his new pal, Benny, was on the second floor of a hotel under construction just south of the villa. The latter position wasn't great in terms of being able to assist in a fight, but it gave them a good vantage point to see what was going on. Assuming the guy could be trusted.

Benny said his boss in Bangkok was making some phone calls about getting them backup. After the military intervention Lucas had recently experienced, he sure as hell hoped they knew which side they were on.

"You sure she hasn't gone over to the dark side?" Nelson asked over the headset.

"I'm sure," Lucas replied.

But was he?

The woman had beaten polygraphs. How did he really know whether or not she was telling the truth? Should he bet Becca's life on her veracity when his emotions made this difficult situation a virtual quagmire?

The question remained, if Ashley was working for the family business, why would the bad guys kidnap Becca? Why not just kill the kid in the hospital or at Sloan's house?

But Ashley had been MIA when Becca and Sloan had been taken, he realized suddenly.

Maybe the Dragon Devils had figured someone was holding Ashley against her will and devised a plan to get her back. Now she, and they, were all safely out of the US, and she sat casually waiting a few hundred feet from her uncle's army of mercenaries.

The fact he loved this woman even though he wasn't sure he one hundred percent trusted her made him seriously question not only his sanity, but his abilities as an agent. But he'd taken an oath of faith and allegiance to the United States of America. He might be conflicted about his feelings, but he wasn't conflicted about where his loyalty lay. And that's when he realized he *did* trust her. One hundred percent. Because she'd taken that oath too, and she'd lived that devotion. You didn't fake a decade of dedication—not when your relatives were billionaires in control of the biggest criminal organization in Asia, and possibly the world.

It was easy to be self-righteous when you'd never faced a

life-or-death moral dilemma. The realization crashed over him. How could she ever forgive him for what he'd done? Acting morally superior, questioning her motives and values, when he'd kidnapped her off the streets of Virginia, held her against her will, questioned her honor and integrity every step of the way.

Hell, he wouldn't blame her if she never spoke to him again, but it wasn't going to stop him trying to do everything he could to get them all out of this situation alive.

He believed in her. He wasn't about to let anything happen to her. Not tonight. Not tomorrow. Not next year.

For the next hour there was no movement except for tourists going in and out of the water about a half-mile down the beach. The scent of meat grilling on a barbecue made his stomach growl. At least they'd grabbed water and food from one of the small bustling towns on the way here.

He was beginning to wonder if they were mistaken about the occupants of the boat. Maybe it was some film star, or royalty trying to get some alone time. Then two launches appeared from the other side of the vessel, moving at high speed toward the beach.

Show time.

"What have we got?" he murmured to Alex and Benny who had the binos.

"Ten adult males, seven of whom are carrying assault rifles. I see Yu Chang and his son. Also the nephew, Andrew Britton." Benny sounded gleeful. To all intents and purposes this was the entire leadership of the Dragon Devils. "I should have trusted you, Nelson. We should have had this place surrounded. My boss is going to have a heart attack. Backup is on the way."

But who knew if it would arrive in time?

Capturing these dirtbags would be a massive coup for the Thai authorities, and Lucas was sure the Americans would move Heaven and Earth to extradite these criminals back to the US to face federal charges. But, as long as they were securely locked up, he didn't care where they were incarcerated.

"Any sign of the hostage?" Lucas asked. Christ, he hoped Becca was alive. He'd never forgive himself for not keeping his promise to the kid.

"Negative."

"I see a bound figure in the bottom of the second boat," Alex corrected. How the hell he could see that in the dark, Lucas didn't know, but he didn't question the guy.

As the boats sped toward the sand, Ashley stood. In the light of the fire, he watched her pull out a handgun she must have stolen off one of the soldiers earlier. She checked the chamber, then held it loosely at her side.

"What good does she think that will do against all those AKs?" Nelson asked tightly.

Lucas couldn't reply. His mouth tasted like he'd consumed a cupful of sand. His heart revved like a single combustion engine struggling to power a V8. He had never felt so helpless before. Never had to watch someone he loved barter herself for a child who deserved better.

The boats reached the edge of the surf, and he was about to move a little closer when a noise behind him and a swift slide of air told him he had company.

Ah, fuck.

CHAPTER TWENTY-FIVE

A FULL MOON shone over the Andaman Sea as Ashley watched the man she'd spent more than a decade hiding from clamber with difficulty from a small boat into a few inches of water.

Fear made the whites of his eyes stand out as he struggled up onto the sand. She was glad she'd chosen this spot for her last stand.

His fear turned to hunger as his gaze found her standing next to the fire that crackled and spat just like her mood. A shiver crawled up her spine as she recognized that hunger for what it was—twisted obsession. Not just the desire to claim her body, but the need to bind her to him, to possess her soul. No wonder her mother had cut him out of her life and never mentioned him. Had he abused her? Was that why she'd run to the States and never gone home again?

Ashley was glad her mother had escaped and found happiness with her dad, even if their lives together had been cut brutally short.

She looked away from Yu Chang to her cousin, who greeted her with his usual insouciant grin. Sick freak. Then her brother arrived.

He watched her with hooded eyes, but the angle of his chin gave him away—even after all these years she knew that, although he looked calm on the outside, inside he was freaking out.

Good.

Her uncle stepped closer, and the fire danced in his eyes like some demon come to life.

She raised the gun, and two of his men immediately placed themselves in front of him, aiming their rifles squarely at her head—as if the thought of a bullet could scare her. She almost laughed out loud.

She lifted her gun farther and pressed the muzzle to her skull. "One more step, and I pull the trigger."

Her uncle shoved his guards aside and jabbered at them in Cantonese. They moved away, even though they clearly didn't want to. Yu Chang took a hesitant half-step forward, and another, until there was only fifteen feet separating them.

"That's enough." Her knees wobbled. Her finger tightened slightly on the trigger. "One more step, Chang," she warned, "and you'll have lost me forever."

His eyes narrowed. Brandon went to move around to her right. "Stay where I can see you, Brandon." She didn't trust her cousin as far as she could teleport. "Where's Becca?"

"Fetch the girl," Andrew snapped.

And now Ashley had to face the reality that he really was one of them. The brother she'd once loved was just as evil and debauched as they were.

A young girl stumbled up the beach away from the boats, her hands tied behind her slight frame. The light of the fire showed she was filthy. Blood smeared her chin, running beneath the wide strip of duct tape covering her mouth. She had wide terrified eyes and tangled hair, but moved quickly, without any obvious signs of injury. Becca had learned the art of survival in a hostile world. *Do whatever it takes.*

Her uncle grabbed the girl, shoved her onto her knees, took out his knife, and held it to her throat.

The grip on Ashley's intestines doubled. Did he plan to recreate the scene of Martel's murder just to prove he was in control? God, how she hated this man. The intervening years had not dulled her revulsion.

"Kill yourself, and I will kill her—slowly." Yu Chang's tone turned gleeful. He thought he had her now. Thought he could predict her behavior.

He didn't know shit.

"Show the child mercy, and you get what you really want. Me. Otherwise, she and I both die here tonight." She sent Becca a small apologetic smile. Then she met her uncle's gaze. "And with the FBI on your trail, your death won't be far behind."

Her finger started pulling back on the trigger. Her heart punched her ribcage in a quick one-two. So be it. She didn't want to die, but she wouldn't back down. Backing down would gain her nothing but the knowledge she'd failed to do the one thing she'd come here to do. Save Becca.

Was Lucas nearby?

The thought terrified her on one level, and on another, she wanted to prove herself worthy of him, worthy of the Bureau they both believed in. She wished she'd told him that she loved him. For a woman who'd been too scared to even go on a second date for years, it was a heady admission.

Yu Chang narrowed his eyes at her, trying to figure out whether or not she was bluffing. She wasn't bluffing. She wanted to close her eyes as the slack on the trigger was fully absorbed, but didn't dare. Another fraction of a millimeter, and she'd be dead.

"Enough! I will let her go," Yu Chang said sharply. "But how do I know you will keep your word and won't kill yourself once she is released?"

She held his gaze and let her intensity convince him. "I swear on my honor." She'd rather kill him.

He turned to one of the men. "Let her go."

Becca was dragged to her feet, and someone cut away whatever bound her wrists together. Brandon gave her a shove forward, and she stumbled toward the fire. Ashley was ready for his sadistic games, and the gun never wavered from her skull. She leaned down, hauled the kid to her feet, and hissed into her ear, "Go. Get out of here. Run. Hide. Lucas will find you."

Becca squeezed her arm, and that small measure of support made tears flood Ashley's eyes. "Quickly," she said.

Becca stumbled away, but Ashley didn't watch her go. At least now Becca had a fighting chance. Hopefully, Lucas was on his way, or Frazer had used his contacts to leverage help.

She needed to give the kid time to get away. She turned to her brother, and her gun didn't waver from the position next to her brain. "You look well, Andrew." It was a lie. He looked like shit. Pale and gaunt. "Do you have a wife? A girlfriend? Just wondering how she feels about you being in the skin trade."

His lips tightened.

"When I joined the FBI I did a little research. I looked up your high school sweetheart, Monica—you remember Monica, don't you?"

"I remember she cheated on me." The bite in the words said he was still angry about that.

Brat.

Yu Chang and Brandon exchanged a look. Ashley suspected she knew why.

"Monica filed charges for being drugged and gang raped not long after we left California. They never caught the guys who did it." Ashley straightened her spine and thought of the horrors so many women had endured at her uncle's and cousin's hands. "But I discovered something else before I left the US." On the flight to Thailand. "There was a hit in CODIS that linked two DNA profiles lifted from the duplex in Cambridge to semen found in Monica's rape kit."

She sneered at her cousin. "No guesses as to who orchestrated that or the photos Andrew received. Nice work, Brandon. But then hurting women and manipulating people is what you do best, isn't it?"

"You're lying." Andrew's hands curled into fists.

"Then you really won't believe what I found out about our parents' plane crash." She held her uncle's gaze this time, and he blinked and looked away. "How it wasn't an accident at all. A bomb took out the engine. Yu Chang killed his own sister, a woman he claims to have loved—no wonder the guilt addled his mind." Her uncle's mouth tightened. "I have TEDAC looking for any similarities with the Boston bombing." The latter was a lie, but definitely something she'd suggest to Frazer if she ever saw him again.

Andrew shook his head and took a step away from their uncle and Brandon. "That's a lie."

"Bullshit. You *know* it's true. You've known it for years, but you've always been too weak to confront them about any of it."

Andrew turned to Yu Chang. "Is it true?" he demanded.

"Don't raise your voice to—"

"Is it true?" Andrew roared.

Her uncle looked taken aback by Andrew's vehemence. Brandon glanced nervously between her brother and his father.

Yu Chang swallowed. "It was an accident."

"You mean you only meant to kill our father," Ashley stated bitterly.

"Shut up, bitch," Brandon snapped.

Andrew looked devastated. For a smart guy, he was remarkably dense at times. Or maybe he'd also just been doing whatever it took to survive.

A shadow moved in her peripheral vision off to her right. A man was walking toward them with his hands clasped over his head. She immediately recognized the tall, wide-shouldered frame. Clawing fingers ripped at her heart.

Lucas.

No.

A force came out of nowhere and slammed her to the ground. She lost her grip on the gun, and it landed out of reach, near her brother's feet.

The smile on Yu Chang's face was slick and oily.

A boot connected with her stomach and drove bile into her throat. Before she could draw breath, Brandon kicked her again.

"Stop!" Andrew cried out.

She looked up at him through tears of pain and managed a laugh. "What did you think would happen?"

Her mouth went dry when she realized she'd gambled and lost. She'd rather die than let anything happen to Lucas, but because she'd chosen to go it alone, she was going to watch him die, too.

Brandon kicked her in the back, and she screamed in agony. "That's for the lies she just told you, and that's for being a fed bitch." He kicked her again, and her vision grayed. Maybe he'd beat her to death, and she wouldn't have to watch them hurt Lucas, or endure whatever her uncle had planned.

"Leave her," Yu Chang ordered.

Brandon stopped and walked away, glaring like a petulant child.

Ashley rolled in the sand, her body flailing in agony. But she'd take any amount of physical pain over the emotional trauma of what might come next.

As Lucas walked closer to the firelight, she saw his beloved face. The sharp angles of his cheekbones, the stubborn chin, those beautiful eyes. Dried blood encrusted the side of his head from where the soldier had hit him with the rifle earlier.

Christ.

But his expression was completely blank, and she couldn't read him. She wished she could tell him that she loved him, but that would only make Yu Chang hurt him more. Chang was already monstrous.

She pulled herself to her knees. One of her ribs was probably cracked, and it was difficult to breathe. Remorse hurt more.

"I'm sorry for getting you involved in this, Agent Randall," she said breathlessly.

He grinned at her and winked. "It's my job, Agent Chen."

———

LUCAS WANTED TO jump over the armed guards and rip

Brandon Chang's head off. It took every measure of discipline he learned in battle not to immediately leap to Ashley's rescue. They had one chance of making this work, and the odds of any of them getting out of this alive were shitty at best.

One of Chang's bodyguards had surprised him, but Alex had gotten the drop on the fucker and returned the favor. Between the four of them they'd hunted down another three of Chang's goons and stripped them of their clothes and weapons.

Alex shoved Lucas ahead, keeping him between Alex and Chang's henchmen. Benny and Nelson were ambling along the beach from the other side. Feigning confidence and walking right up to the group in the darkness as if they belonged. It was a gamble, but what choice did they have?

No way was he letting the Devils take Ashley. No fucking way.

As soon as Benny and Nelson got within ten yards of the firelight, Lucas dropped to his knees and aimed the weapon he'd clasped behind his head. Someone was firing before the words "FBI" left his lips.

He stayed low, rolled, and used one of Yu Chang's men as a shield while he took out the guards closest to the old man. Alex was picking off the ones farther away with the AKs, dropping them with unerring accuracy.

Didn't take long for the Devils to start retreating.

Brandon tried to drag his father to the boat, but the old man wasn't leaving Ashley. The old bastard grabbed onto her wrist where she lay curled up in the sand as bullets flew overhead.

One whistled past Lucas's cheek, and he ate sand as he rolled into a new firing position. He shot the man who'd fired at him—the asshole *Cho* from the brothel—and the remaining guards scattered and started to run away.

Ashley's brother had dropped to the sand when the shooting started and suddenly appeared to come out of his daze. He clambered to his feet and picked up the gun Ashley had held to her head.

Watching her do that had just about given Lucas a coronary. Andrew raised the weapon, and Lucas was about to nail the guy when Andrew raised it higher and pointed it at his cousin's chest.

"You told your father about Lily, didn't you? You told him I cared for her, and that's why he raped her."

Andrew fired the weapon, and Brandon Chang went down with a flash of surprise in his eyes. He dropped his father's hand.

Ashley kicked at the old man hard enough to break his grip and scrambled backwards in the sand toward where Lucas crouched.

Brandon started laughing in the sudden silence, and the sound sent something disturbing crawling through Lucas's veins. The guy sounded insane.

"*Now* you've decided to grow a pair of balls?"

"You raped Monica so you could send me those photographs and get us to break up."

Brandon leered. "She was seeing other guys, Andy. I just gave you proof. She drank too much, fucked us all, and then cried rape."

"I don't believe you!" Andrew shot him again, and this time blood bloomed around Brandon's chest. Lucas was pretty sure Brandon Chang was dead. The guy had been shot through the heart.

Yu Chang gaped as he looked about him, suddenly appearing like a frail old man rather than a vicious criminal mastermind. His men had fled. His son was dead. His gaze shifted first to his nephew, then to his niece. His eyes stayed on Ashley.

Chang sank to his knees. "I love you, Jun," he pleaded. "Everything I've ever done has been because I love you. Don't leave me again. Please don't leave."

"I'm not Jun, you sick creep. You killed Jun." Ashley's voice shook. "And you don't get to have sex with your sister or niece just because you want to."

Lucas placed Ashley firmly behind him, denying the old man the pleasure of looking at her.

Andrew's gaze swung toward his sister. "God, Jenny, I'm so sorry. I should have protected you."

He turned back to Yu Chang and put a bullet into the man's chest. "That's for Lily, you bastard." He fired again. "For my parents, for Jenny, for me!"

Benny and Nelson sprinted toward him, but Andrew raised the gun to his own head and blew his brains all over this small slice of paradise.

"Jesus." Lucas pulled Ashley to him and buried her face in his shirt. Her entire family had just been wiped out, and she didn't need to see any more than she already had.

Benny went to check Andrew to make sure he was dead while Nelson went to the old man.

Yu Chang was miraculously still alive. Nelson spat in his face. "That's for Detective David Shaw HKPD, asshole. You're under arrest."

No one argued as Nelson cuffed the dying man. He'd been working toward this moment even longer than Ashley had been running. Yu Chang's eyes turned away from Nelson and once again sought out his niece. Lucas wasn't giving him that satisfaction. He hid her with his big body, wishing the bastard would just die already.

"I've got you, baby." He wrapped his arms tight around her. He wasn't letting her go.

ASHLEY'S FINGERS WERE trembling, but she held on tight to Lucas. She couldn't believe they'd come through the firefight unscathed and that Yu Chang, Brandon, and her brother were dead.

"The Thai soldiers let you go?" she asked.

"Let's just say there was a minor misunderstanding as to why we were detained." His pained expression suggested there was more to it than that. "I'm sorry, Ash."

"What for?" She leaned her head back, confused.

"For doubting you, for kidnapping you, for suggesting even for a moment you were in league with those psychos."

"Lucas, you didn't do anything wrong. You were being a good agent. I'd never hold that against you." She reached up to touch the side of his head "That's all I've ever wanted to be." She took a breath. "I'm sorry for everything, too. For lying, for taking off and trying to do this alone. I just needed to get Becca to safety and didn't think you and Alex would be released in time. Thank God you were." She forced herself to push out of his embrace. She needed to put some distance between them, starting now. "So what happens next? Am I arrested, or can I turn myself in?"

He put his hands on his hips and angled his head. "No one

here is arresting you. You just put your life on the line—"

"Good. I'd rather do it stateside." She glanced at the local detective who was walking around making sure all the bad guys were either dead or disarmed. She assumed backup and emergency services were on their way, but it was a good thing none of them had been injured. They'd have bled to death by now—like her uncle.

The sea breeze suddenly felt cold, and the fire was dying. She wrapped her arms around herself and wished her teeth would stop chattering.

"It's not that I don't trust the Thais, it's just that I'd rather be in a prison where I understand the process—"

His jaw clenched. "You're not going to prison."

She raised a brow. "You don't know that."

"Wanna bet on it? One of my brothers-in-law is a top criminal defense attorney in DC. He'll figure it out."

"I'm not involving your family in my mess."

He frowned. "Why not?"

"They're already going to hate me, Lucas." Her voice reached the others who glanced their way and then went back to studiously ignoring them.

"They won't hate you."

She scoffed. "I'm going to be a national pariah when this gets out. My family did terrible things, and yours are practically American royalty."

"I don't give a shit about misperceptions."

"But I do." Her eyes narrowed. "I won't have you tainted—"

"Tainted?" Now he sounded angry.

"Look, my relatives were scum, Lucas. And I'm just as bad. I lied to get into the FBI and may have jeopardized an untold number of cases that I was involved in." Her stomach churned when she thought about the possible consequences of her actions.

He held his hands wide in exasperation. "You faked your own death at sixteen years of age to escape an evil despot. Then fooled polygraphists in order to join the FBI and help bring down one of the biggest criminal organizations in the world. If that gets out, you'll be a frickin' hero."

She turned away from him, but he swung her around to face him again. "Do you know what it was like to watch you put that gun to your head and know you were willing to pull the trigger? To watch the woman I love gamble with her life, but have to sit silently, praying the fucking gun didn't go off, and the pervert who wanted to rape and kidnap her backed down?" The pain in his eyes destroyed her. She'd never meant to hurt him. "It felt as if someone was ripping out my throat, and I couldn't breathe." His voice broke.

"How can you love someone like me?"

He took a step toward her. "How can I not, Ashley?"

Her vision blurred, and she swallowed thickly. "I'm disgusting."

His eyes glinted with fierce determination. "You are amazing. You are brave, dedicated, smart, tenacious, proud, and great in bed." He grinned to tell her he was joking. Then his expression grew serious again. "You did what you had to do to survive."

Like Becca. Like Andrew.

"And then you came back swinging." His stare drilled into hers. "How could I not love you?"

Maybe he was right. Fighting to survive wasn't a crime—it was what you did afterwards that mattered. And she'd fought for justice and against evil. Maybe that was worth something.

"I don't understand you." Emotion clogged her throat, and she was sobbing. "But I love you, Lucas." Tears finally spilled over and dripped off her chin. "I've never let myself love anyone before. I never realized it wasn't a choice."

He pulled her against his chest, and she buried her nose, inhaling the familiar masculine scent, the reassuring heat of him through his T-shirt.

"It's a choice I'd make over and over."

Ashley didn't know how she'd been so lucky as to find this man. She didn't know if she'd ever be able to fully forgive herself, but maybe she could try. She'd always relished a challenge, though this might be the biggest one of all.

———————

SHE LOVED HIM. Knowing that made Lucas believe they'd be able to get through this mess. "I love you, too, sweetheart." He hugged her closer, kissed her hair. "And nothing's going to happen. It's over."

Ashley wiped her eyes. "Stop saying that. You don't know for sure."

He smiled into her worried face. "Neither do you."

Her mouth thinned. "Well, I'm pretty sure the truth is about to come out."

Lucas looked from Benny to Nelson. "Maybe. Maybe not." They'd talked in the car earlier about the possibility of keeping Ashley's identity to themselves. If he could convince Sloan and Frazer, they might be able to keep a lid on this thing.

She looked over at her brother's body. "Is he definitely dead?"

He nodded.

Her expression grew pensive. "I let him down."

"He was a grown man. He made his own choices."

She nodded, but the sadness remained in her eyes. It was going to take time for her to recover from this, but he wasn't going to fail her again. He had her back. And he was going to prove how much he loved her, every single day.

Suddenly the whole area was lit up by the lights of a battle-ship. A spotlight rested firmly on Yu Chang's boat and showed people running around the deck.

"Now *that's* a boat." Beside him, Alex grinned.

"Typical Navy," Lucas said, one side of his mouth quirking. "Always show up late to the party. Any idea who it belongs to?" His vision was still double. Something he should probably get checked out.

"It's ours."

He nodded with satisfaction. Frazer's idea of backup. "Let's go find Becca and make sure she's safe," Lucas said. They nodded to Nelson and Benny and started walking up the beach.

"Don't go far," Benny told them.

They found the teen on the road with a tourist she'd flagged down. Becca threw herself into Lucas's arms, and he squeezed her tight.

"Think you can fit us into your jeep and get us to Phuket airport ASAP?" Alex asked the tourist after Lucas ponied up his official credentials. "I can guarantee a substantial reward and the eternal thanks of the US government."

"Can you throw in a good word with the IRS?" the guy joked.

"I don't do miracles, sorry."

There wasn't much space, and Ashley had to sit on Lucas's

lap the whole ride back. He didn't mind. He liked holding her in his arms. The warm night air rushed over them as they drove past towering forests and massive plantations. The towns were bustling with tourists and travelers, and it seemed surreal that life went on as normal even when people were dying just a few miles away.

Becca's fingers crept into his as she sat next to him, and more regrets washed through him. "I'm sorry I didn't keep my promise, Becs."

Her smile was sweetly innocent. "You came for me. I knew you would. And now they're all dead, and I'll be safe." Her eyes were huge. "I'm going to become an FBI agent, too. I want to carry a badge and a gun and make people do what I say."

He smiled. *If only.* "I think you'd make an excellent federal agent, but how about you spend some time being a kid first?" He pressed her fingers with his. "I still owe you a trip to the mall."

She smiled, and then asked, "Is Agent Sloan alive?" Her voice grew very small.

He nodded. "She's in intensive care, but the doctors think she's going to make it."

A frown worried her brows. "You know I told you about the man who made me call him 'Daddy'?"

Ashley tensed in his arms. Lucas nodded. Like he'd ever forget.

"He was there."

It was his turn to frown. "What do you mean?"

"At Sloan's house."

Realization was blinding. "Her husband? Brian Templeton?"

She caught her bottom lip in her teeth. "I didn't know his

real name, but I don't want him to hurt me again."

She didn't know. Christ.

"He's dead. Sloan killed him." And now he knew why. It was a damn shame. Lucas would have loved to punish the motherfucker himself.

So Brian Templeton was the reason the Devils were always one step ahead of them. One mystery solved.

"What about the others? What if they find me?" Becca whispered.

Ashley raised her head and answered. "You see Mr. Parker sitting there in the front seat, Becca?"

Becca nodded.

"He and I are going to work together and identify every last one of these people, and you are going to help us put them away in prison. You up for that?"

"Promise?"

Alex turned in his seat, and he and Ashley spoke together. "Promise."

A rush of emotion threatened to choke Lucas. He turned his face to the window, not wanting to reveal weakness in front of the teen, but Ashley knew. She laid her cheek against his. "Thanks for saving me, Lucas," she whispered. Her fingers tightened on his arm.

"Pretty sure you saved yourself," he said gruffly.

He felt her smiling. "You gave me the strength to stand up to my past. Without you I'd still be running."

And he'd be alone. The thought was an unsettling one.

"Time to stop running. Time to start building a future with me." He kissed her, keeping it soft and gentle with Becca sitting beside them, but needing to tell Ashley that his feelings for her hadn't changed. They'd only grown stronger until the idea of her not being with him felt like a hacksaw working its way through his chest.

Truth was, he didn't know what was going to happen next. He could only hope for the best and be there for Ashley and Becca, and Sloan too.

That was all anyone could do.

EPILOGUE

Five months later...

ASHLEY SMOOTHED DOWN her favorite Calvin Klein skirt as she sat in a Boston courtroom and waited for the judge to announce the verdict. She'd been here every day for the last week and had listened to the witness provide heart-wrenching testimony that the accused had repeatedly visited her in a brothel to have sex.

SSA Carly Sloan sat at the back of the room along with the SAC from the Boston Field Office. Sloan had never revealed the family connection between Ashley and Brandon. Ashley didn't know if she'd not known or simply chosen to keep quiet about the fact once the perpetrators were dead and Becca had been saved. Sloan's face was gaunt with dark circles under her eyes. She'd taken several months to physically recover from the knife wound but still didn't look ready to be back at work. The woman had taken full responsibility for her husband's actions even though it hadn't been her fault. She'd tried to resign. The director hadn't let her.

As the shootout had occurred in Thailand, and most of the bad guys were dead, the full extent of Ashley's involvement with the Dragon Devils had never come to light. Benny and Nelson had been given the major credit for taking down the notorious crime family and rescuing Becca, with the FBI's role being played down to minor. Everyone was fine with that, and Sloan and Frazer had insisted she and Lucas were following orders.

Greg Trainer had gotten credit for finding and closing down many other establishments run by the Devils, and the FBI had cracked down sharply on sex trafficking—although the problem was still huge.

DNA from thirty-four women and four men had been found in the bombed out brothel, not counting Mae Kwon. The lab had also isolated DNA from used condoms in the garbage. They were using that physical evidence, combined with the cell phone and financial information she and Alex Parker had painstakingly obtained, to try to convict as many johns as possible.

Becca had identified six men from the photographs so far.

The accused today was an anemic-looking accountant with two daughters about the same age as Becca. His wife sat on the other side of the courtroom, her face stark with suffering as the verdict was read.

Guilty of Child Rape.

Ashley let out a satisfied breath, even as the man's wife crumpled. Ashley ignored the wave of sympathy she felt for the woman. His family wasn't responsible for his actions, but they'd carry the stigma of his shame for the rest of their lives. It was a phenomenon she was more than familiar with, and sometimes she still struggled to get past her own secret shame.

The accused was looking at his wife, aghast. The woman turned away from him with a look of disgust on her face. Halfway through the trial, the degenerate had admitted to having sex with Becca, but tried to suggest he hadn't realized she was underage, and that she'd seduced him, in a brothel—

where she was locked up as a sex slave.

Ashley and Alex had unearthed enough evidence to prove the guy regularly trawled the internet for underage girls. She hoped that worked against him when the judge sentenced him tomorrow. Theoretically, someone convicted of child rape could get life, but she doubted the judge would be that harsh. But they might get lucky. Especially in a city still mourning its dead.

She waited for the room to clear before she stood and headed down the hallway in the opposite direction of everyone else. She knocked on a heavy wooden door and let herself in. Lucas and Becca were playing cribbage.

Lucas's gaze was piercing. Becca's was worried.

"Guilty," said Ashley.

Lucas grinned. Becca's face lit up.

This was the first trial of many, but Ashley hoped this verdict would persuade the other accused to accept plea bargains.

Theo Giovanni, the lawyer who'd cut a plea in exchange for the password that had gotten Lucas into the brothel had been pulled over for erratic driving with a thousand dollars' worth of crack cocaine in his glove box. He'd lost his high-rolling career and his wife. Ashley wasn't sorry even a little bit.

Lucas looked especially handsome in a dark gray suit with a red tie. Every day, she didn't think she could love him or want him more than she had the day before, but she did. He'd been promoted to SSA and was running his own team down in Charlotte. Ashley had left the BAU.

"Ready?" she asked.

They both nodded, but she knew Lucas was lying. After these last few months together she'd learned to read him well.

"Let's go," he said.

It was a short walk to a different judge's private chambers. Ashley braced herself before they went inside.

The lawyer Lucas had hired stood in front of the judge's desk. But when the men turned to face them, they wore matching expressions of unhappiness.

"Where is she?" Lucas looked around.

Neither man spoke.

"She's not coming, is she?" Becca said quietly.

Lucas muttered what was probably an obscenity under his breath.

It had taken a month to track down Becca's mother. It turned out the woman was already serving time for armed robbery, trying to steal enough money to pay off her latest gambling debt. She had more charges pending.

But they'd discovered a grandmother who'd taken Becca's brother, Jackson, into her care.

She and Becca had met up on several occasions, and Ashley had thought Lucas had persuaded the woman to take Becca, too. Apparently, she'd changed her mind at the last minute.

Ashley looked at Lucas's devastated expression. He still hadn't forgiven himself for everything Becca had been through. And, after spending a lot of time working with the kid, he loved her like a daughter. They both did.

"We'll take her," Ashley said firmly.

Becca gasped.

Lucas's eyes widened. His stare was intense, as if he were trying to gauge whether or not she was serious. She was. Deadly.

"You both work full-time." The judge looked at them from

under his considerable brows.

"As do hundreds of thousands, if not millions, of other American parents."

"But we've already established that Becca's situation is not ordinary."

She needed counseling and special tutoring to catch up with schoolwork. Lucas stood flexing his fists. "Foster care is not an option for a child in her situation," he said.

"Please let me live with them." The words rushed out of Becca in a heartfelt plea.

Lucas squeezed her shoulder.

At Lucas's request, Becca had been placed in a safe house in North Carolina, and they'd spent as much of their free time together as possible. But time was up. The Department of Justice had suggested WITSEC, but Becca was only thirteen. The program wasn't designed for children.

"I'm in a financial position to provide everything Becca needs. We live in a house with enough bedrooms and space to give Becca a good upbringing."

"You and Agent Chen aren't married," the judge argued.

"I'm wearing her down, Judge. It's just a matter of time."

Ashley burst out laughing. She really didn't know how her love continued to grow and grow, but it did.

"Did we just get engaged?" he asked with a manly smirk that made her want to hit him and kiss him all at the same time.

She inclined her head. Just enough to tell him yes.

"We both have training in the psychology of abuse, and we know what happened to Becca. We can help her deal with it, and we have access to child psychologists should problems arise," Ashley told the judge.

"You'd adopt her?"

"Yes," Lucas said.

Ashley nodded, but she was a little unsure about how her fake identity might affect that if the truth ever came to light. Frazer had blistered her ears and given her hell when she'd gotten back to Quantico. Then he'd made her teach him how to beat the polygraph. The guy was beyond scary, but he'd let her finish her training, after which she'd transferred to Charlotte to be with Lucas, working on cybercrimes just like she'd always wanted.

Becca was practically vibrating on her toes.

"How do you feel about being part of a mixed-race family, Becca?" the judge asked.

Lucas bristled, and Ashley shook her head. He never seemed to realize she wasn't pearly white, but it was something she had to deal with every single day. And it was a potential difficulty for a kid who'd already suffered at the hands of other Asians. Ashley's relatives, no less.

Damn. Maybe this was a bad idea. Except—who better to try to help Becca through this? She owed it to both Becca and Lucas to try to atone for her family's sins, even if they didn't see it that way.

"I love Ashley." Becca bit her lip. "I just don't want to get in the way."

Lucas looked as stricken as Ashley felt.

She wasn't a crier by nature, but holy crap, the tears were flowing now. She wiped her eyes, knowing her makeup was toast. "You won't ever be in the way, honey. You'd be part of our family." A family she'd never thought she'd have. She pulled the girl into her embrace and felt Lucas's arms wrap around them both, sheltering them and giving them strength.

The judge huffed out a gruff laugh. "Fine. I'm going to assign you temporary custody, SSA Randall. We'll reconvene in six months and start the formal adoption process if that's what you all still want."

They thanked him, said goodbye to their lawyer, and stood looking at one another in the wide hallway of the courthouse.

One side of Lucas's mouth curved. "Did you just say you'd marry me?"

Ashley pointedly wiggled her naked left hand. "I said I *might*."

Lucas and Becca shared a grin. He leaned closer to the teen and said in a stage whisper, "Looks like we better go find a jeweler's quick before she changes her mind."

"It's gonna cost you," Becca stage-whispered back. "She has expensive tastes."

Ashley leaned over and pressed a kiss to Lucas's lips. He picked her up and twirled her around. Then he picked Becca up at the same time and spun them until they were laughing and dizzy.

"This might be the happiest day of my life," Lucas told them as he put them down.

Ashley's head was spinning, and she gripped him by the arm. "It keeps getting better and better."

He kissed her quickly, then grabbed both their hands. "Then I can't wait until tomorrow."

"Can I have a dog?" Becca asked and then caught her bottom lip with her teeth.

"You'll have to look after it," Lucas said firmly.

Becca nodded like crazy.

And Ashley knew he was going to make a great dad.

"We'll go visit the pound and see who else needs a new

home."

Becca looked like she might physically burst with happiness.

Ashley felt a huge well of emotion swelling up inside her. Lucas squeezed her fingers, reading her mind.

"Let's go pick up your things, Becs, and go home. I, for one, am eager to get started."

Ashley walked beside them both and knew without a doubt she was the luckiest woman on the planet.

USEFUL ACRONYM DEFINITIONS FOR TONI'S BOOKS

ADA: Assistant District Attorney
AG: Attorney General
ASAC: Assistant Special Agent in Charge
ASC: Assistant Section Chief
ATF: Alcohol, Tobacco, and Firearms
BAU: Behavioral Analysis Unit
BOLO: Be on the Lookout
BORTAC: US Border Patrol Tactical Unit
BUCAR: Bureau Car
CBP: US Customs and Border Patrol
CBT: Cognitive Behavioral Therapy
CIRG: Critical Incident Response Group
CMU: Crisis Management Unit
CN: Crisis Negotiator
CNU: Crisis Negotiation Unit
CO: Commanding Officer
CODIS: Combined DNA Index System
CP: Command Post
CQB: Close-Quarters Battle
DA: District Attorney
DEA: Drug Enforcement Administration
DEVGRU: Naval Special Warfare Development Group
DIA: Defense Intelligence Agency

DHS: Department of Homeland Security
DOB: Date of Birth
DOD: Department of Defense
DOJ: Department of Justice
DS: Diplomatic Security
DSS: US Diplomatic Security Service
DVI: Disaster Victim Identification
EMDR: Eye Movement Desensitization & Reprocessing
EMT: Emergency Medical Technician
ERT: Evidence Response Team
FOA: First-Office Assignment
FBI: Federal Bureau of Investigation
FNG: Fucking New Guy
FO: Field Office
FWO: Federal Wildlife Officer
IC: Incident Commander
IC: Intelligence Community
ICE: US Immigration and Customs Enforcement
HAHO: High Altitude High Opening (parachute jump)
HRT: Hostage Rescue Team
HT: Hostage-Taker
JEH: J. Edgar Hoover Building (FBI Headquarters)
K&R: Kidnap and Ransom
LAPD: Los Angeles Police Department
LEO: Law Enforcement Officer
LZ: Landing Zone
ME: Medical Examiner
MO: Modus Operandi
NAT: New Agent Trainee
NCAVC: National Center for Analysis of Violent Crime
NCIC: National Crime Information Center
NFT: Non-Fungible Token
NOTS: New Operator Training School

NPS: National Park Service
NYFO: New York Field Office
OC: Organized Crime
OCU: Organized Crime Unit
OPR: Office of Professional Responsibility
POTUS: President of the United States
PT: Physiology Technician
PTSD: Post-Traumatic Stress Disorder
RA: Resident Agency
RCMP: Royal Canadian Mounted Police
RSO: Senior Regional Security Officer from the US
Diplomatic Service
SA: Special Agent
SAC: Special Agent-in-Charge
SANE: Sexual Assault Nurse Examiners
SAS: Special Air Squadron (British Special Forces unit)
SD: Secure Digital
SIOC: Strategic Information & Operations
SF: Special Forces
SSA: Supervisory Special Agent
SWAT: Special Weapons and Tactics
TC: Tactical Commander
TDY: Temporary Duty Yonder
TEDAC: Terrorist Explosive Device Analytical Center
TOD: Time of Death
UAF: University of Alaska, Fairbanks
UBC: Undocumented Border Crosser
UNSUB: Unknown Subject
USSS: United States Secret Service
ViCAP: Violent Criminal Apprehension Program
VIN: Vehicle Identification Number
WFO: Washington Field Office

COLD JUSTICE WORLD OVERVIEW
All books can be read as standalones

COLD JUSTICE® SERIES
A Cold Dark Place (Book #1)
Cold Pursuit (Book #2)
Cold Light of Day (Book #3)
Cold Fear (Book #4)
Cold in The Shadows (Book #5)
Cold Hearted (Book #6)
Cold Secrets (Book #7)
Cold Malice (Book #8)
A Cold Dark Promise (Book #9~A Wedding Novella)
Cold Blooded (Book #10)

COLD JUSTICE® – THE NEGOTIATORS
Cold & Deadly (Book #1)
Colder Than Sin (Book #2)
Cold Wicked Lies (Book #3)
Cold Cruel Kiss (Book #4)
Cold as Ice (Book #5)

COLD JUSTICE® – MOST WANTED
Cold Silence (Book #1)
Cold Deceit (Book #2)
Cold Snap (Book #3) – Coming soon
Cold Fury (Book #4) – Coming soon

The Cold Justice® series books are also available as **audiobooks** narrated by Eric Dove, and in various box set compilations.

Check out all Toni's books on her website
(www.toniandersonauthor.com/books-2)

ACKNOWLEDGMENTS

Some books are harder than others to write. This one was made particularly difficult due to many upheavals in my personal life throughout 2016, including major renovations, and my husband's work taking us to Japan for three months. There were some constants though—my wonderful critique partner Kathy Altman, my editors, Alicia Dean, and Joan Turner at JRT Editing. My cover artist, Syd Gill, who did a great job capturing the essence of this book. And Paul Salvette (BB eBooks) who formats my ebooks with such care.

Thanks for informative conversations with Sunny Lee-Goodman, Rachel Grant, and Carolyn Crane, regarding issues of diversity in America today. A special thanks goes to Angela Bell of the FBI for answering my questions about what agents can and can't do, and for arranging a tour of FBI Headquarters in Washington, D.C. Any mistakes in this book are down to me, and the ever-forgiving concept of artistic license.

Mostly, I want to thank my husband and kids just for being them. We do manage to have some grand adventures as we navigate this thing called life!

ABOUT THE AUTHOR

Toni Anderson writes gritty, sexy, FBI Romantic Thrillers, and is a *New York Times* and a *USA Today* bestselling author. Her books have won the Daphne du Maurier Award for Excellence in Mystery and Suspense, Readers' Choice, Aspen Gold, Book Buyers' Best, Golden Quill, National Excellence in Story Telling Contest, and National Excellence in Romance Fiction awards. She's been a finalist in both the Vivian Contest and the RITA Award from the Romance Writers of America. Toni's books have been translated into five different languages and over three million copies of her books have been downloaded.

Best known for her Cold Justice® books perhaps it's not surprising to discover Toni lives in one of the most extreme climates on earth—Manitoba, Canada. Formerly a Marine Biologist, Toni still misses the ocean, but is lucky enough to travel for research purposes. In late 2015, she visited FBI Headquarters in Washington DC, including a tour of the Strategic Information and Operations Center. She hopes not to get arrested for her Google searches.

Sign up for Toni Anderson's newsletter:
www.toniandersonauthor.com/newsletter-signup

Like Toni Anderson on Facebook:
facebook.com/toniandersonauthor

Follow on Instagram:
instagram.com/toni_anderson_author

Made in the USA
Middletown, DE
15 July 2024